"Once again Kate Breslin has crafted a story with grappling hooks—it'll catch you from page one and reel you in! With spies, romance, and characters with mountains to overcome, *Far Side of the Sea* is a complex and riveting tale that you won't be able to set aside. Bravo!"

—Roseanna M. White, bestselling author of the LADIES OF THE MANOR and SHADOWS OVER ENGLAND series

"With writing rich in historical detail, Kate Breslin weaves a tale of intrigue, suspense, and romance against the turbulent backdrop of WWI. From the shores of England to Paris and Barcelona, this action-filled story will delight history buffs and romance lovers alike."

—Susan Anne Mason, award-winning author of *Irish Meadows* and the COURAGE TO DREAM series

"Kate Breslin continues her tradition of writing sweeping historical romances that pair the adventurous spirit of Kate Quinn with the historical detail of Susan Meissner and Hazel Gaynor. A universe in itself, *Far Side of the Sea* sweeps the reader to dashing European locales seen through the eyes of two unforgettable characters whose greatest daring lies in finding restoration and wholeness against the broken backdrop of a world at war. The thinking person's adventure story—Breslin evokes classic literary tropes to create a robust and beautifully written yarn capturing the heart while engaging the mind."

—Rachel McMillan, author of the VAN BUREN AND DELUCA series

"Not everyone can write a good war story. Still fewer can bring love, faith, and romance into the mix and make it work. Kate Breslin can do all this with strength and style. She is a remarkable writer, and this book is a remarkable story."

—Murray Pura, author of *The Wings of Morning, Majestic and Wild,* and *My Heart Belongs in Gettysburg, Pennsylvania*

Far Side of the Sea

Books by Kate Breslin

Far Side of the Sea

KATE BRESLIN

BETHANYHOUSE
a division of Baker Publishing Group
Minneapolis, Minnesota

© 2019 by Kathryn Breslin

Published by Bethany House Publishers
a division of Baker Publishing Group
11400 Hampshire Avenue South
Bloomington, Minnesota 55438
www.bethanyhouse.com

Printed in the United States of America

Library of Congress Cataloging-in-Publication Data
Names: Breslin, Kate, author.
Title: Far side of the sea / Kate Breslin.
Description: Minneapolis, Minnesota: Bethany House, a division of Baker Publishing Group, [2019]
Identifiers: LCCN 2018034298 | ISBN 9780764217821 (trade paper) | ISBN 9781493417261 (e-book) | ISBN 9780764233111 (cloth)
Subjects: | GSAFD: Christian fiction. | Love stories.
Classification: LCC PS3602.R4575 F37 2019 | DDC 813/.6—dc23
LC record available at https://lccn.loc.gov/2018034298

Scripture quotations are from the Holy Bible, New International Version®. NIV®. Copyright © 1973, 1978, 1984, 2011 by Biblica, Inc.™ Used by permission of Zondervan. All rights reserved worldwide. www.zondervan.com

This is a work of historical reconstruction; the appearances of certain historical figures are therefore inevitable. All other characters, however, are products of the author's imagination, and any resemblance to actual persons, living or dead, is coincidental.

Cover design by Kathleen Lynch/Black Kat Design and Paul Higdon
Cover photography by Richard Jenkins, London, England

Author is represented by Hartline Literary Agency

19   20   21   22   23   24   25   7   6   5   4   3   2   1

In loving memory of Kenneth Swinney:
gray eyes, strong hands, soft-spoken, and wise—
my dad.

For Cher Ami, G.I. Joe, and all trained
carrier pigeons of the two world wars:
may these unsung heroes that saved countless lives
in the face of injury and death never be forgotten.

If I rise on the wings of the dawn,
if I settle on the far side of the sea,
even there your hand will guide me,
your right hand will hold me fast.

Psalm 139:9–10

CHAPTER

1

HASTINGS, BRITAIN, APRIL 9, 1918

*H*e was suffocating.

Trapped beneath several feet of earth, he tried to claw his way through the dirt and rubble to reach the blue sky above. His starving lungs screamed for air, the torn flesh beneath his broken fingernails bleeding into the soil as he scrabbled toward the surface. The agony in his chest grew unbearable, yet darkness continued to swallow him, the heavens overhead always beyond his grasp. Futility settled over him. He would die here, in this place. Buried alive . . .

Colin awoke with a start. Chest heaving, his sweat-soaked body gave an involuntary shudder. The nightmare was always the same; even using both of his hands, he could never reach the precious blue sky.

A sharp rap echoed at the door. Dawn's gray light filtered through his bedroom window in the cramped seaside flat as he rolled toward his nightstand to turn on the lamp. Blinking against the sudden brightness, he stared at the clock. *0530 . . .*

The next knock accompanied a hesitant male voice. "Lieutenant Mabry?"

His protégé, Corporal Albert Goodfellow. "A moment, if you please." Colin rose to sit on the edge of the bed, planting his bare feet against the rag rug covering the hardwood floor. He used the bedsheet to wipe at his clammy skin, then leaned to snag the pair of suspendered britches from his clothes valet near the foot of the bed. After donning the khaki riding pants, he started to call out, then paused, grabbing the woolen sock from his nightstand. He fitted it over the stump of his left wrist. "Enter."

A tall, painfully thin young soldier in uniform stopped at the threshold to his room. Corporal Goodfellow removed his cap, revealing a short crop of thick red hair. He flashed a sheepish grin. "Good morning, Lieutenant. Did I wake you, sir?"

Colin shot him a sour look. "Corporal, why are you here at this unholy hour?" He walked to the wardrobe across the room and withdrew a clean undershirt. When his visitor said nothing, he turned. "Well?"

Albert Goodfellow's gaze was transfixed on the clothes valet near the bed—and the prosthetic harness that hung there. He jerked his attention to Colin. "Dovecote's got a heap of messages needing attention, sir. They're marked priority, so the colonel sent me down the hill to request your presence in the office as soon as possible. It's going to be a bear of a day."

Colin's jaw set as he imagined the ensuing hours decoding encrypted messages from the Front. Both the British Army and Secret Service deemed everything a "priority," including daily reports, supply requisitions, and weather conditions in France.

He maneuvered his arms through the sleeveless undershirt, pulling the fabric over his chest. "Tell the colonel I'll be there presently."

More silence. Colin reached for a pressed uniform shirt from the wardrobe. Shrugging into the olive khaki top, he turned again to glance at the corporal. Goodfellow hadn't moved. "Was there something else, man?"

"I was ordered to wait, sir." The corporal shifted. "May I assist in any way?"

"You mean to hurry me along?" Colin scowled. Had the colonel sent Goodfellow to be his nursemaid as well? "I've been dressing myself since I was three years of age, Corporal. I think I can still manage on my own, thank you."

"Sorry, sir, I just meant . . ." The corporal's cheeks flushed. "Yes, Lieutenant, I'll just wait beside the pier with the truck."

His protégé sketched a quick salute and made a hasty departure. Colin stared at the door, anger and shame coursing through him. His gaze dropped to his open shirt and the task before him. Infernal buttons! Almost a year ago, they had become a curse on his life.

He decided to postpone the chore long enough to scrape a razor across his face and tame his hair with a wetted comb. Afterward, he drew together the edges of his shirt with his right hand and began the painstaking task of tucking each button into its corresponding hole, working his way down the shirtfront. The cloth fit snugly against his chest, and he was reminded again to purchase new shirts. Months of recuperation working on his uncle's Dublin farm had produced more muscle than what he'd started out with after leaving the hospital.

The button chore complete, he slipped a brown silk tie around his upturned collar and single-handedly knotted and fitted the popular four-in-hand up between the points of his collar.

Shirt tucked in, he slid his cotton suspenders into place and strode toward the prosthetic harness dangling from the clothes valet. The apparatus seemed to mock him as he fitted the terminal sleeve close against his left wrist before he buckled the arm brace. Securing the shoulder harness in place, he swung the long strap across his back and brought it forward to fasten at his chest.

By the time Colin had donned his tunic and leather riding boots, his brow was damp with sweat. Wiping his face with his sleeve before donning his cap, he then strapped on his leather holstered

Colt .455 revolver and turned his attention to the canvas satchel still hanging on the valet.

Shaking out the bag's contents onto the bed, he stared at the choice of accoutrements: two steel hooks, a steel pick, a glove-encased wooden hand, and one eating fork, each with a metal stub that fastened to the terminal sleeve at his wrist.

Out of habit, Colin chose the gloved hand, fitting the prosthetic into place. Once he'd repacked the satchel and slung the strap across his shoulder, he went to give himself a quick once-over in the cheval glass.

A smartly attired British officer stared back at him, although the hazel eyes beneath his uniform cap looked haunted and world-weary, not those of a young man twenty-one years of age. He thought about the nightmares he'd struggled with during the nine months since his return from the Front. The war had aged him tenfold.

Lord, please renew my spirit. He let his critical gaze linger another moment before dismissing his reflection. Heading toward his tiny kitchen, he grabbed a few biscuits from the tin in the cupboard and exited his flat.

April's coastal breezes nipped at his freshly shaved skin as Colin walked briskly along the shoreline road toward Hastings Pier, where Goodfellow was waiting. He took a moment to breathe in the tang of salt air, reveling in the sense of relief at again being outdoors.

The sun's reflection was already beginning to crest the watery horizon. Dawn was breaking, and while the seaside town slept, he savored the relative quiet, broken by the cries of hungry gulls and waves lapping against the sandy shore.

A peace that would disintegrate once the sun rose into the sky.

Colin soon spotted his corporal with the truck, and a few minutes later, they were driving up the hillside toward the nondescript building that served as the offices of MI8 secret communications in Hastings. The two-story wooden structure sat just fifty yards away from the Home Defense Pigeon Service, a stationary dovecote that housed a few hundred carrier pigeons.

"I'll put the kettle on, shall I?" Goodfellow said, parking the truck.

"Capital idea." Colin's spirits lifted. The nightmares always managed to rob him of sleep, and tea would be just the thing.

Goodfellow quickly disappeared inside the building while Colin followed at a slower pace. At the entrance steps, he raised his head and caught sight of a grayish-white pigeon heading for the traps built into the dovecote's angled roofline.

Colin knew little about the birds, though he'd seen them at the Front, taking off from the trenches to deliver messages to headquarters. His job with MI8 was to decipher those messages—most arriving from MI6 and British Army General Headquarters at Montreuil, in northern France's Pas-de-Calais—and to send them on by courier to his supervisor at the Admiralty in London.

As he watched the bird, the sun chose that moment to rise fully above the horizon, illuminating the pigeon's fluttering descent and bathing its feathers in golden-white light.

For some reason, the story of Noah rose in his mind, and he envisioned the biblical white bird returning to the ark with an olive branch in its beak. The signal to the end of the flood. A symbol of peace . . .

The mental imagery faded. These birds brought only words of war and unrest, the threat of German invasion, or perhaps a casualty roster from the Front. He glanced at his lifeless gloved hand. Despite his prayers, a year of fighting had taught him that peace was someone's naïve ideal, a vague optimism offered to comfort the suffering.

A distant dream beyond reach.

Colin continued inside the building to the second floor and entered his cramped office. On the wall beside his equally compact desk hung a glass-framed picture taken two years before, when he was shiny and new in his full cavalry regalia and mounted on his sorrel steed, Wyatt. Along the opposite wall, a high, barred window allowed morning light to brighten the room's drab green walls.

"The colonel brought over these messages from General HQ in France." The corporal stood just inside his office and removed from a leather pouch at least a dozen tiny rolls of thin paper, each an inch long and the diameter of a cigarette. A roll might contain up to fifty messages needing decryption.

Colin's mouth hardened as he stared at the mound. The corporal seemed to read his mood. "I'll get that tea, sir."

When he was gone, Colin sat down and withdrew from his desk drawer the decorative pincushion his twin sister, Grace, had made for him when he first took the post in Hastings. A smile touched his lips as he read the crooked stitching and the amateurish needlepoint lettering: *Those Who Sew with Tears Will Reap with Songs of Joy.*

He knew the words, taken from Psalm 126. They were a means to give hope to those in despair, a promise of better days ahead.

Colin's smile wavered. Would he ever reclaim that sense of elation and hope that had always come so easily before the war? Battle had changed him, and not just on the outside; he prayed daily for the return of himself, to be able to continue the course upon which he'd once set his life. . . .

He glanced to the gloved hand lying inert against the desktop. And if not the old path, at least to know the new one God intended for him—His reasons for keeping Colin Mabry alive.

He set the pincushion gently on the desk. His twin would never make a good seamstress, but Colin loved her for her efforts. And with Grace's upcoming marriage to a peer of the realm less than a month away, he was genuinely happy for her. Somehow, knowing love and hope still existed in the world, at least for his sister, gave him a measure of comfort.

His hand reached for the first tiny roll of paper, and using his thumb and forefinger, Colin spread the curled message flat against the cardboard sheet he'd installed on the desktop. Holding the paper in place with his prosthetic, he took pins from the cushion and secured the note to the board.

Once he'd retrieved his codebook and paper, he was about to settle into his task when Goodfellow returned with the tea. "Ah, thank you, Albert." Colin breathed in the welcoming scent of Darjeeling. "Any dispatches from London?"

"Yes, sir, from the Admiralty. I've coded a dozen messages so far, and after you've checked my work, I'll take them next door to be sent to France."

Colin pushed out a sigh, reaching for his tea. It *was* going to be a long day. "I've no doubt your work is impeccable—"

A sudden boom echoed from across the channel, startling them both. With a clatter, Colin's cup dropped against the saucer.

"Sounds like they're bombing Paris again, sir."

"So it would seem." He tried to mask his discomfort and again lifted the cup. The next blast erupted before he'd raised the rim to his lips. He clutched the teacup's handle to keep from sloshing the hot liquid. "You may get back to your work, Corporal."

Colin barely acknowledged the soldier's departure as he set down the cup again and regarded his shaking hand, making a fist. "God, please help me."

He closed his eyes and tried to quash his fear. Another boom followed, and he ground his teeth. How much of Paris had the Germans destroyed? Only weeks ago, they had launched their Spring Offensive and begun firing a new type of long-range siege guns at the French capital. The daily explosions, while distant, reminded him that only fifty miles of water separated him from the war.

Titan's teeth! Why had he agreed to accept this post in Hastings?

As if taunting him, the guns stopped. The air grew quiet again, and Colin managed to drink his tea. After several minutes, he was steady enough to get back to his work.

He'd memorized much of the codebook, so it didn't take long to recognize the monotony of supply requisitions and troop reports he would forward to London's War Office. There were also orders for more carrier pigeons, as the supply at Montreuil was getting low. Colin had learned the birds flew only one way—back to their lofts—so it was necessary to send Hastings pigeons to France to bring messages into Britain.

Head bent to the task, Colin worked through his lunch. By the time his shift was about to end, he was hungry and his shoulders ached.

He was decrypting his last message of the day marked *FOR-WARD TO LONDON* when the telephone rang in his office. Relieved at the diversion, he reached for the receiver. "Lieutenant Mabry here."

"Colin, how are things in Hastings?"

He straightened at the sound of the tinny male voice. "Lord Walenford."

"Enough of that. Either Jack or Benningham will do. We're going to be brothers, after all." Jack Benningham's voice warmed. "Speaking of which . . . I thought you might join me for dinner this evening. My man can meet you at Victoria Station and bring you around to the house."

The town house? Colin still hadn't gotten used to the idea his sister was about to marry a viscount and the future Earl of Stonebrooke. A man who also happened to be Colin's boss.

Which meant, despite his reluctance to travel into London tonight, he could hardly refuse his employer and brother-to-be. "I can take the train from Hastings if that is acceptable."

"Splendid. I'll expect you at eight. Mrs. Riley is making her ration stew."

Colin stared blindly at the unfinished work on his desk, still surprised at the invitation. "Very well, Lord . . . uh, Jack. I look forward to it."

"Excellent. I'll see you tonight. We'll have dinner in my study, and you can bring any dispatches for the Admiralty directly here."

"Of course . . ." Colin's hand groped to replace the receiver as his gaze fell to the last message he'd been working on, noting for the first time the letters he'd already deciphered. *LT. C . . . O . . . L . . . I . . .*

He continued breaking down the other cryptic numbers, his pulse hammering as more words began to form:

> *Lt. Colin Mabry, British Army, c/o Swan's Tea Room, London:*
> *Urgent you remember your promise of love. Meet me Café de la Paix, Paris. 10 April, 1500 hours. You're my last hope.—J. R.*

J. R. . . . Colin's shock overrode his rapid pulse. Jewel Reyer . . . *alive.*

He'd thought of her often over the past year: her beautiful face, her laughter. Like her namesake, Jewel had glowing skin, lustrous golden hair, and soft blue eyes that sparkled when she sang. She'd also kissed him. . . .

Another explosion rumbled across the channel, and Colin flinched, staring at the note. Jewel was alive. In Paris.

Sweat broke out along his forehead while his heart stirred with emotions from the past, including another memory.

He had given her his promise to return.

CHAPTER

2

KENSINGTON, LONDON

How was the trip from Hastings?"

Lord Walenford's dark blue gaze studied him from across the small, linen-covered table.

"Well enough . . . Jack." Colin sat in the chair facing his blond employer after being escorted into the study by Knowles, the elderly butler. He quickly scanned his surroundings, noting the paneled room in the elegant, Victorian-styled brick residence on Holland Street was larger than his entire flat in Hastings.

Grabbing up his white linen napkin before Knowles could reach for it, Colin snapped the cloth open and draped it across his lap. When he looked up again, he noticed for the first time Jack's tan linen business suit and the red tie slightly loosened at his neck.

Jack caught his look and smiled. "It's rare that I get to take the liberty of casual dining."

Colin was grateful to be excused from wearing formal dinner dress; the military had withdrawn the use of colored uniforms during the war. And though his white tie and black dinner jacket remained at his family's London home in Knightsbridge, by the time he made himself presentable with all of those buttons and cuff links, Jack might starve. "Casual dining suits me fine, and my uniform takes the guesswork out of dressing."

"Another benefit of being in the military." Grinning, Jack reached for his wineglass. "Anyway, with the new rationing laws in Britain, food these days suits a more casual palate." His eyes gleamed as he leaned back in his chair. "Though if you tell Mrs. Riley I said so, I'll deny it. At least she makes the meager fare edible."

He took a sip of red wine before returning his attention to Colin. "So, how are you getting on in that picturesque little town by the sea?"

"Hastings is certainly better than being here in the city." Colin recalled his anxiety upon arriving in London two months ago, after leaving his uncle's farm. "Not so many people. I thank you for offering me the post."

"My pleasure." Jack's smile caused the scarred flesh around his eyes to pucker. He'd suffered his own casualties of war. "Yet I would imagine that since Kaiser Wilhelm began his Spring Offensive last month, you are plagued by noise from across the water. We sometimes hear the guns in London as well."

Colin reached for his crystal goblet of water and stared at the glass a moment before setting it back down. "The sound is . . . distracting but not unmanageable." He glanced up to see compassion in Jack's handsome features.

"Every so often a German plane will get through our home defense and drop a bomb or two here in town. I nearly jump out of my skin." Toying with the stem of his glass, Jack paused. "Grace asked me to tell you that your father still wishes you to come and work with him at Swan's. Once your sister and I marry, she will resign her position as the tea room's floor manager. Patrick wants you to take the reins and learn the tea business from the ground up."

Colin's mouth compressed at the sudden stab of guilt. With their mother gone from tuberculosis these two years, he and his sister had become closer than ever, and Grace occasionally traveled to Hastings to visit him.

Yet he rarely returned to the Mabry family's London home in Knightsbridge. It was difficult to endure the doleful looks Grace tried to hide as she watched him eat his meals or button his coat, and Father, always looking away from the prosthetic while trying too hard to provide accommodation for what his only son lacked. Even worse were his father's continued attempts to recruit Colin into the family tea enterprise.

"You know I cannot work the floor at Swan's. Being in the public eye . . ." He slid his arm with the wooden hand farther out of view beneath the table.

Jack sighed. "I told her as much. I spent months hiding away from society after the explosion, knowing I frightened the locals." He touched his scarred brow. "Blinded, I wanted nothing more than to remain invisible."

Colin merely nodded.

A knock sounded before an aged footman with a slight limp entered the study with a tray bearing a white soup tureen. Under the watchful eye of Knowles, he began serving up steaming bowlfuls of Mrs. Riley's ration stew.

Colin had been relieved to know stew was on the menu. Reaching for his spoon, he breathed in the fragrance of beef broth and thyme and realized the fresh vegetables had likely come from Jack's farm estate in Kent, where Colin's sister had met the heir to Stonebrooke while baling hay with the Women's Forage Corps.

The two men tucked into their supper, and Colin tasted bits of beef much like those from the rationed tins of bully beef sent to the soldiers overseas.

"Now that you're here, I have a favor to ask." Jack glanced up from his stew. "I need your help with the wedding."

Colin paused, his spoon halfway to his lips. Curiosity battled his wariness. "How so?"

"I want you to be my best man."

"Me?" Colin's stomach lurched as his spoon fell back into the stew. "But . . . I assumed you had a best man. Captain Weatherford?"

Jack's expression sobered. "I can see this comes as a surprise. And yes, Marcus was to do the honors. However, he left London on Crown business a few weeks ago, and no one has heard from him." His frown deepened. "Not even his department chief can give me information."

Colin had met Captain Weatherford on two occasions after returning to London. He knew the man worked for MI6 at the Admiralty and that he and Jack Benningham were close friends. With the day of the nuptials drawing near, why hadn't he contacted Jack?

Colin didn't want to consider the possibility the captain had met with foul play.

Moisture broke out along his upper lip as he imagined himself standing beside Jack in a church filled with hundreds of society's nobility. Every one of them would be staring forward to the bride and groom . . . and Colin's prosthetic.

"Captain Weatherford could still return in time for the wedding." Desperation edged his tone while his neck heated against his too-tight collar.

"I assure you, if Marcus returns, you'll be relieved of the duty." Jack leaned forward, spoon in hand. "Colin, I know how you feel about being on public display, but I won't risk ruining Grace's wedding day by coming up short a best man." He smiled. "And who else aside from Marcus would I ask to stand up with me, but my future brother-in-law?"

Colin eyed him across the table. Despite his reservations, he owed Jack a great debt. His host had done far more than grant him a post where he could still be useful to the war effort yet live away from London, where people gawked or eyed him with pity.

Jack Benningham had saved his life.

21

He glanced at the prosthetic hand in his lap and was reminded that, while his life would never be the same, by God's grace, at least he had one.

Jack had traveled across the channel to the Front and used his uncanny sense of direction to locate the collapsed tunnel where Colin and several other soldiers lay buried. He'd done it for Grace, of course, but Colin was nonetheless grateful to be the recipient of the gesture.

Acting as best man was little enough to ask in return. He swallowed and met the gaze of his brother-to-be. "It will be my honor to stand with you at the wedding."

"Excellent!" Jack's smile held relief as he took up another spoonful of stew.

Colin stared down at his food, hesitating. During the train ride from Hastings into London, he'd wondered how to broach the subject of Jewel's message.

Yet Colin himself was living proof that his future brother-in-law was a brave and honorable man. Surely Jack would understand his reasons for wanting to aid the woman to whom he owed so much. "I have something I wish to discuss as well."

Jack raised his head. "What's that?"

Colin's pulse quickened as he thought again of the daily bombing across the channel. "Before the wedding, I need to go to Paris."

"When?"

"Tomorrow."

Jack rested his spoon in the bowl and picked up his napkin. "Care to explain?"

"I . . . need to meet someone."

"I see." Jack glanced toward the elderly butler near the door. "That will be all, Knowles. I'll ring if I need you."

Once the butler exited, Jack's attention returned to Colin. "That *someone* must be very important if you're willing to go to a city currently being bombarded by the enemy."

"I made a promise I need to keep." Colin laid his palm against the table. "A year ago, I was fighting in the British Expeditionary Force's Second Cavalry Division at Arras. A few of us rode east during maneuvers and somehow went off course. Mortars rained down, and a shell landed in our path. When I awoke, I saw the others, or what was left of them, lying dead. I also lost my sorrel, Wyatt." He clenched the white cloth in his fist. "I managed to get up and start walking. I was completely lost, and it was dark when I finally reached an isolated farm outside the French village of Havrincourt."

"Havrincourt?" Jack's gaze narrowed. "That place would have been crawling with Germans about then."

Colin nodded. "I believe God was on my side, because I saw a young woman coming out of the barn carrying something in her apron—potatoes, I think. I greeted her in French, telling her what had happened. She took me inside and hid me away in a cellar beneath the barn floor."

Jack whistled softly. "I'd certainly call it Providence."

"I'd caught a bit of shrapnel in my right leg, and Jewel and her aunt took care of me. They practically starved under the occupation, yet they fed me from the few enemy rations they received. Jewel also had a remarkable voice. She learned a few Boche songs to sing for the *kommandant* and his officers at Havrincourt's town hall, and shared the spoils they gave her as tribute." He relaxed his fist. "I was there a month, and we spent much time together. . . ."

"Ah, so that's it."

Seeing Jack's knowing grin, Colin's face flooded with heat. He wasn't about to add that Jewel had been the first woman to ever kiss him.

He cleared his throat. "My chance to escape finally came." Colin stared at the paneled wall beyond Jack's shoulder, remembering those last poignant moments. "She begged to go with me. Even her aunt tried to convince me to take her only niece away from the Boche."

Colin turned to his host. "Jewel's father was off fighting in the French Army, so it was just the two women. Still, I refused. I couldn't risk taking her through no-man's-land in order to return to my regiment. She could have been killed, or worse."

"Of course." Jack's humor ebbed. "I was there for just a brief time, but I saw it was no place for civilians, especially not a woman alone."

"I told Jewel she would be safer remaining in the village, so long as she had a patron in the *kommandant* and she kept singing. I promised her I'd come back after the war."

His chest tightened with the old regret. "I returned to my regiment, and for weeks, the fighting was intense. I never received word from her—not that I expected to, with the town occupied by the enemy. Shortly after that, I was sent to Passchendaele to help with the tunnels." He shot Jack a grateful look. "You know what happened after that."

Jack nodded.

"This past December, when I was still in Dublin seeing the head doctor at Richmond, I overheard talk that our tanks in France had pushed past the Hindenburg Line at Cambrai, near Jewel's village. The Boche began a retreat, and their artillery fire left Havrincourt all but destroyed. Most of the townspeople are dead or missing." Colin's gaze fell to the table. "I wrote to the Red Cross, hoping to get word about Jewel and her aunt, but there was no information. I thought they had both been killed."

"That's why you stayed away at Christmas."

"It was one of the reasons." Colin's sister and father had been crushed over his absence, but he'd been in no condition to come home and spread holiday cheer. "I thought it best."

"And this Miss . . . ?"

"Reyer. Her name is Jewel Bernadette Reyer."

"Reyer, you say?" A slight frown touched Jack's lips. "I take it, then, your Miss Reyer is alive?"

Colin explained the encrypted message he'd received that afternoon. "The meeting at the café in Paris is set for tomorrow, the tenth. Her request sounds urgent."

"Reyer . . ." Jack rose from his place at the table. "Excuse me a moment."

Colin watched him stride across the room to the oak desk situated near the hearth. After shuffling through a stack of papers, Jack withdrew a file and returned.

"I know that name. . . ." Once again taking his seat, he opened the file and began flipping pages, his features intent. "Here it is. J. Reyer."

"What are you looking at?"

"It's the Allies' enemy watch list from France."

"Enemy list?" Colin fell back against his seat, eyes wide. "You think Jewel is working for the Boche?"

He almost laughed until Jack's grave look ignited his anger. "That's ludicrous! With all she has suffered living in enemy territory, Jewel would never betray France."

"Are you so certain?" Jack spoke quietly. "Perhaps she had no choice. You did mention she'd found favor with the *kommandant—*"

"Not like that!" Colin tossed down his napkin and rose to his feet while memories rushed him: Jewel singing softly as she rebandaged his wound, then sharing with him her last crust of bread; amusing him by mimicking the Boche *kommandant* as she strutted about the cellar floor, talking German nonsense and twirling the end of an imaginary moustache before falling into gales of laughter at Colin's feet.

"It's not her." He stared at Jack, his mouth hard. "Reyer is a common enough name in France, and the initial J could stand for Jean or Joseph or a hundred names other than Jewel."

When Jack merely gazed at him, Colin blew out a breath. "I just told you all that she did for me, what she sacrificed for my safety. You cannot know what it was like for her, having to hide me those weeks from the enemy, taking risks to feed and care for me." *Kissing me . . .*

Colin still remembered the warm press of her lips and the love shining in her soft blue eyes. "Please, Jack, I have to go to her." *Especially if the Allies think she's an enemy spy!*

A long moment passed before Jack finally spoke. "I'll grant you, there are thousands of names on this list, and it is possible J. Reyer is someone else entirely." He tipped his head. "That corporal in Hastings you've been working with . . . Goodfellow? Would he be able to hold the fort during your absence?"

"Absolutely." Colin suppressed his nervous excitement as he returned to his seat.

Jack hesitated, then set the file off to one side. "All right. I'll approve your flight out of Kenley in the morning. When will you return?"

"Two or three days at the most." The thought of seeing Jewel again after nearly a year made his pulse race.

Jack eyed him sternly. "It probably goes without saying, but with the enemy knocking at the back door to Paris and spies all over the capital, vigilance is key. You're a seasoned soldier, Colin, and you've trained with the secret service, so I know you can take care of yourself. But until you learn more about Miss Reyer's situation, please be on guard."

"Of course." Colin's heart sped up. By this time tomorrow, he'd be in Paris. *The siege guns . . .*

"Will you see Grace before you go?"

He focused on the question and frowned. His sister would not take the news of his leaving well at all.

Jack read his thoughts. "Since you'll only be away a short time, I can tell her once you've gone. Do me a favor, though, and check in with the British MI6 office in Paris when you arrive, so they know you're there." An edge of his mouth lifted. "I'll sleep better." Colin smiled his gratitude. "I will, and thanks, Jack."

"Good enough. Now let's eat."

The two men resumed their repast, yet as Colin ate, he mulled over Jack's words. What if Jewel was the J. *Reyer* on the Allies' watch list? It might explain her urgent message. And while he would never believe her culpable of such a heinous crime as treason, Jack had suggested she might not have had a choice. If that were the case, it could mean she was in real trouble.

Colin's thoughts drifted throughout the rest of dinner, and later, as Lord Walenford's chauffeur drove him toward the Mabrys' Knightsbridge home, Colin tried to convince himself that it was all in his imagination, that Jewel was simply anxious to see him again after all this time.

Or was it more than that?

CHAPTER

3

*P*erhaps he had been lured into a trap.

Seated at a window table inside the café, Colin checked his watch a third time.

This morning, he'd crossed the English Channel, risking death as the Bristol F.2B Fighter carrying him and his pilot were easy prey for any German Jasta squadrons flying along the French coast. After his arrival, he had checked in with the Paris MI6 office as Jack had requested before taking a room in Le Grand Hotel on Place de l'Opéra.

Now Colin awaited his coffee in the Café de la Paix downstairs while his anticipation at seeing Jewel turned to uneasiness as the minutes ticked by without a sign of her.

In the light of day, Jack's warning about Jewel seemed almost benign. Colin again imagined her inviting smile and the heart-shaped mouth pressed softly against his own. She'd certainly surprised him with the kiss, but he'd been glad of it. He remembered too the sacrifices she and her aunt had made to keep him safe, and his cool reasoning returned, siding with his first impression—that the name *Reyer* on the enemy watch list was a coincidence.

So why isn't she here, Mabry? Unwillingly, his thoughts returned to Jack's other warning, about spies lurking all over the city. The MI6 desk chief in Paris had elaborated even further, telling him the enemy often recruited pretty young Frenchwomen to charm information from any green soldier they came across. Colin was to trust no one.

He might be young, but he took exception to being thought "green." He'd changed much in two years and was no longer the idealistic recruit clamoring to march off and defeat the Hun. Not that he had regrets about serving his country; he'd been proud to fight alongside his cavalry regiment. But war was nothing like he had imagined. And despite an increase in rank and a couple of medals to compensate for his loss of limb and peace of mind, it was a daily struggle not to be bitter.

Shouts of male laughter erupted behind him, and Colin jerked his head toward the boisterous Allied soldiers at the bar, each dressed in their varying pleated uniforms. He'd also observed dozens of soldiers and French seated outside on the café terrace. Jewel's assigned meeting place seemed a popular watering hole in the city.

Had it been Jewel who contacted him . . . or some Boche spy intent on luring him to Paris? Though kidnapping in the spy trade was rare, Colin had been educated on the possibility. His father was extremely wealthy, and Grace would soon become a future countess and member of the British peerage.

Colin also considered the fact no one had heard from Captain Weatherford since his departure weeks ago. Both Colin and the captain were connected to Jack Benningham. Was his thinking mere folly . . . or was something sinister going on?

Resisting another urge to glance at his watch, he returned his gaze to the window. Beyond the busy terrace, several older men wearing professional linen suits and straw boaters or derby hats passed each other on the street. Some carried walking sticks while others gripped leather satchels, each striding with purpose as if attending a meeting somewhere or rushing back to the office after a late lunch.

Others, mostly younger men, looked to be uniformed soldiers on furlough. During his cab ride to the hotel, Colin had noticed a number of demobilized soldiers in patched army uniforms begging for change on the street. So different from the starched and polished tunics on the men seated at the bar.

A small cluster of soldiers stood in front of the opera house, Americans by their appearance. Pausing to admire the ornately majestic Palais Garnier, they finally moved on, doffing their hats to a pair of matrons who waved them to come over and view their carts full of pink roses, white lilies, and yellow daffodils. Adjacent to the flower sellers, an outdoor market pulsed with activity as women, most clad in mourning black, carried wicker hampers and made their selections from the remains of the morning's produce.

Having already surveyed the ladies along the café's busy terrace, Colin scrutinized the women at the market, trying to see the faces. A year had passed since his time with Jewel. Had she changed so much that he might not recognize her?

His gaze swept back along the opposite end of the street, colliding with the gutted shell of what remained of a multistoried stone building. He'd seen the structure upon his arrival at the hotel, one wall still poised drunkenly beside an enormous pile of rubble while shredded curtains billowed through blown-out windows in the light spring breeze. With such normal activity only yards away, the evidence of war seemed bizarre . . . and a glaring reminder of the shells that regularly hammered the city.

Colin's pulse thumped at his throat. He'd been in Paris only an hour when he dove for cover on the cab floor as a deafening blast erupted across town. He had yet to experience a direct attack, and the anticipation was as unnerving as the explosion itself.

"A gift from the dirty Boche and their cannon, Lieutenant."

His attention snapped around to the waiter, who set a steaming *café au lait* in front of him. The wiry, dark-haired man in a black bow tie and starched white shirt nodded toward the building.

"When did it happen?"

"Two weeks ago, when the shelling started." His brows veed downward. "Those big guns and the Gotha bombs have pocked the face of my beautiful city."

He turned his eyes on Colin. "Your *amour*, she is not coming?"

Colin blinked. "Who said anything about—"

"Ah, but why else would a handsome young soldier sit here all alone and stare out the window when he is not checking his watch every ten minutes?" He flashed a row of crooked teeth beneath his pencil moustache. "I am French, Lieutenant. I know these things."

Without awaiting a response, the waiter turned with his empty tray and headed back toward the noisy crowd at the bar.

Colin glanced at the man's retreating form before he gave in to the impulse to recheck the time. 1530. Thirty minutes past the appointed meeting . . .

The growl of an engine directly outside the café drew his attention. A motorcycle with sidecar had backed up to the curb out front. The driver, clad in a leather trench coat and matching motor cap, swung a booted foot over the side to dismount. Gloved hands reached to pull away the riding goggles and then the cap, and Colin stared at the long shank of dark blond hair that escaped to tumble against the upturned collar of the coat. *Her* coat.

Heart pounding, his eyes darted to the disarrayed knot of golden hair pinned at the top of her head. *Jewel!*

She spun around and faced the window. Except where she'd worn the goggles, a layer of dust and streaks of mud covered her face. Yet unlike Jewel's soft blue gaze, a pair of deep-set eyes the color of lapis ensnared him through the glass.

Not Jewel. His disappointment mingled with curiosity as she abruptly turned from him, and it was a moment before he roused himself to see her walking away. He nearly pressed his face against the pane, trying to find her on the café's busy terrace.

She had disappeared.

His attention returned to the motorcycle. Colin couldn't imagine the very feminine Jewel ever driving such a machine. Nor had he experienced one himself, preferring a good horse to get him around instead of a petrol-guzzling conveyance.

The loud bell above the café door chimed over the animated voices of customers, and Colin turned to see the mysterious woman enter the establishment. As she strode through the café her muddied leather coat parted slightly, and he was jarred to see she wore dark britches and a tunic along with the boots.

Was she a courier? Since his return to London, he'd learned there were women who wore men's clothes and worked as dispatch riders for the Royal Navy and the RAF, though he'd never seen one up close.

This woman seemed intent as she scanned the face of each soldier at the bar, then threaded her way through the wall of bodies, dodging a couple of the more inebriated louts who tried to grab at her. She drew her coat tightly together as their whistles and jibes followed, and unexpected anger surged through him. Drunken fools!

Slipping past them, she removed her gloves and surveyed the rest of the café's patrons. When her gaze eventually came to rest upon him, she briskly closed the distance. *"Êtes-vous Lieutenant Colin Mabry?"*

Her French accent was slightly off. Colin rose from his seat and answered in French. "I am Lieutenant Mabry. And you are?"

Instead of answering, she tilted her head, and for an instant, her straight nose and high cheekbones stirred in him a memory. She flashed a tentative smile. "I am the woman you came to see."

"Pardon?" He eyed her with suspicion. "You must be mistaken."

She shifted on her booted feet. "But . . . you received my message, *oui*? To remember your promise of love?"

Hair rose along his nape. This woman had sent him the message. Did she seriously believe she could pretend to be Jewel? His lip curled as he stared at her, the warning from the Paris desk still fresh in his mind. He wasn't about to be taken in by any French Mata Hari. "You're a liar."

She blinked and took a step backward before the blue orbs shot sparks. "And you're a rude clod of a man, sir! 'Tis obvious you've not been taught any manners."

Her French accent might be lacking, but her Irish brogue was perfect. He leaned forward and gave her his most intimidating look. "I know what Jewel Reyer looks like, Miss . . . whoever you are. And you are not her. Perhaps you're one of those women who spy for the Germans?"

"Did I say I was her?" Both hands knuckled against her hips. Her chin jutted outward. "And what makes you think I'd crawl on my belly to work for the Boche?"

Of course she would deny being a spy. His pulse leapt as he considered another, more dreadful scenario. "Where is Jewel?" He took a step closer, every muscle tense. "What have you done with her? She asked me here, signed that message with her initials—"

"J and R." She cut him off. "Yes, I know. Those happen to be mine as well. My name is Johanna Reyer, Lieutenant. I am Jewel's sister."

He could only gape at her. Jewel never mentioned having a sister.

At his astonishment, her smile returned, and she gave him a sympathetic nod that sent her topknot listing sideways. "I understand your surprise, thinking Jewel contacted you." She leaned forward and lowered her voice. "My sister is in terrible trouble, Lieutenant Mabry. She needs our help."

Jo gazed up at the towering man, barely breathing as she waited for his reaction. Thrilled to discover he was indeed Colin Mabry, the man she'd waited months to meet, she tried to ignore his hostility and remember the importance of her plan. Would he help her . . . or decide to turn around and walk out of the café?

Her conscience pricked her as she recalled her remark over his lack of manners. That was no way to coax him to stay, and she hadn't even apologized for being late.

"Let me see your identification."

She flinched at the bark in his tone, yet in truth, she could hardly blame his suspicions. Jo at least had been provided with a description of him, but the lieutenant had no clue as to her identity or if she spoke the truth.

Retrieving her passport from her tunic pocket, she was glad she had decided to take her father's name. Jo offered him the document and noticed for the first time the gloved hand at his left side, slightly larger than his right hand and stiff, unlike real flesh. Was that the reason he'd been sent home?

She observed him while he scrutinized her passport. He wasn't what she had expected. The lieutenant seemed far more imposing in real life than the written account Jewel had penned into her diary. His broad shoulders, coal-black hair, and clear hazel eyes matched her sister's impressions of him, of course, yet he seemed older than Jo had imagined, or perhaps it was just that he appeared world-worn. According to Jewel's notes from a year ago, Colin would now be about twenty-one years of age—a few months older than her sister, and two years older than herself.

His animosity seemed to ebb as he returned the document. "What kind of trouble?"

"Not here, it's too public." Instinctively she glanced about the café . . . and met with her reflection in the large mirror mounted along the opposite wall.

Good grief, she looked like a badger! Seeing the twin streaks of mud on her face, she remembered the puddle on her way into town, the size of a lake and one she'd failed to avoid before it was too late.

Her hair looked just as frightful. The once neatly pinned top-knot had tilted to one side, and errant wisps of hair draped all around her coat collar. She tried to straighten the crooked bun and turned to him. "The Boche have ears all over the city. . . ."

She paused. Was that a smirk on his face? Her spine stiffened. "We should discuss this in a more private place."

The light in his hazel eyes dimmed. "Where?"

"My office isn't too far, and it's very safe."

Again his lower lip curled as he stared at her. Was he weighing her sincerity?

Anxiety nipped at Jo's patience. By some miracle she didn't deserve, she'd found her sister's savior. She could now flee Paris, and with the lieutenant's help, reach Jewel—and their father— before it was too late.

"I assure you, Lieutenant, I am no spy. My sister *is* in dire need, and every minute we stand here puts her life in greater danger."

CHAPTER

4

op in and we'll be on our way."

Colin assessed the leather-upholstered sidecar and didn't move.

"I wonder, is it the motorbike you object to, Lieutenant . . . or the woman driver?"

Sitting astride the Triumph motorcycle with her cap and goggles back in place, she called to him over the chugging noise of the engine. Her smile suggested mockery as she offered him an extra pair of goggles.

His hackles rose. This Miss *Johanna* Reyer claimed to be Jewel's sister. While he'd glimpsed possible similarities in her features, she was a person Jewel had never spoken of during their time together.

How had this woman discovered his whereabouts? It seemed she'd purposely misled him into coming to Paris. She also claimed Jewel was alive and in serious trouble but so far refused to tell him more.

Her passport seemed authentic, but the document could have been forged. She had a distinctive Irish accent, making her place of birth—listed on the passport as Paris—seem suspect. In any case, Colin knew nothing else about Miss Reyer, if that was her real identity.

His jaw clenched as he glanced back at the sidecar. Only a fool would let her cart him off without further explanation—

A sudden explosion vibrated the air, shaking the ground around them. Colin dove for the sidewalk, his heart thundering in his chest, his ringing ears deaf to the shouts and cries of the patrons along the terrace. *Dirt filled his mouth, pushing into his nostrils . . . lungs convulsing . . . no air . . . trapped . . .*

His chest heaved with coughs before he opened his eyes and saw where he was. *Not the tunnel . . .*

Thick black smoke snaked upward into the sky from the next block. He sat up slowly, scanning the sea of frightened faces for Miss Reyer.

She was still on the motorcycle, crouched low against the handlebars. Dark blue eyes turned to him, wide behind the goggles, and her chest rose and fell rapidly.

"Where is your office?" His words came out harsh.

She straightened, her mouth still slightly ajar. "The . . . town of Vernon. An hour's drive to the west."

Away from the shelling. He clambered up from the sidewalk, snatching the goggles from her grasp. Stepping into the rattling sidecar, he packed his tall frame down into the seat. "Drive."

She wasted no time. Shifting gears, she released the clutch and adjusted the throttle to propel them forward. Colin glanced at the gutted building as they passed, his breath easing once they distanced themselves from the wreckage.

Regardless of her motives, anywhere she might take him right now seemed better than staying to become a target for the Boche guns.

She drove west along the busy avenue de Friedland, and Colin noticed many tree stumps amid the leafy chestnuts lining the thoroughfare. Likely cut down for firewood, since the war had made coal scarce in Europe. He realized the Parisians must be as desperate for fuel as his own people in Britain.

At the Arc de Triomphe de l'Étoile, sandbags reinforced the arch against attack. He'd noticed other Paris monuments being protected in the same way.

Beyond the arch, they continued on toward Nanterre and Poissy, leaving behind Paris and her damaged extremities for the more rural farmlands of France. Verdant fields rolled out before them, punctuated with white daisies and red poppies, while cottages with orange terra-cotta roofs sprouted among the green. The occasional château could be seen rising among gentle rolling hills, the manors accessible by narrow dirt drives and, unlike Paris, lined with flourishing oaks, maples, and blooming yellow mimosas.

The sun beat down on Colin's shoulders, and his head grew hot beneath the wool officer's cap worn backward and held in place with the goggles. Sweat itched his brow, yet the spring air was blessedly cool against his face. He had to admit the drive was pleasant, albeit bumpy. Like riding a horse, only faster and involving a lot more noise.

Miss Reyer was a fair driver too, dodging rough patches in the road and slowing to almost a halt when they traversed a rather deep puddle, no doubt left by a recent rain. From time to time he glanced at her, and once or twice, their eyes met. She offered an encouraging smile before returning her attention to the road.

His suspicions began fading with the miles that took them away from the city. If she were an enemy spy, she was putting on quite the elaborate act to convince him otherwise. Perhaps Miss Reyer was who she claimed to be.

After they crossed a branch of the Seine, she slowed the motorcycle and wheeled onto a long dirt drive. Soon a château came into view, cast in a pink brick and white marbled framework and accommodating three tall peaks along its roof line. Eventually the dirt turned to concrete as they pulled into the semicircular drive and stopped in front of an elaborate portico.

She killed the motorcycle's engine and faced him, a smile on her lips. "Welcome to Château de Gall. We call it La Maison des Oiseaux. The birdhouse."

She swung off the motorcycle and removed her headgear while Colin levered his prosthetic against an edge of the sidecar and used his good hand to pry himself from the cramped space. Once he stood on solid ground, he took off his goggles and saw her watching him. "Are you entertained, Miss Reyer?"

She averted her gaze, then looked back at him as if to say something. Only a sigh emerged, however, before she turned and mounted the steps leading to the massive front door.

He remained next to the sidecar. "Who is this *we* you speak of?"

She glanced at him over her shoulder. "Me . . . and the French Army. Here at the birdhouse, we work with pigeons that bring messages from the Front."

"Obviously you send those messages as well."

Again she avoided his gaze. Yes, she *had* purposely misled him.

"We send intelligence on to your British Army headquarters at Montreuil."

Which was how he came by Miss Reyer's dire note.

"Please, come inside and meet my friends."

He followed her up the curved entry steps into the château's cool interior. Parquet wood tiles formed V-shaped patterns along the polished floors of the grand entryway. At the far end of the spacious hall stood an arched opening that led into what appeared to be a larger room.

"If you'll wait a moment, I'll go and . . . freshen up."

He caught the proud tilt of her chin beneath the grime and nodded.

Once she disappeared, he moved deeper into the château. To his right, beyond the faded silk-and-wood-paneled wall, rose a white stone staircase, the ornate ironwork bannister winding upward to the next landing.

He looked higher, to an expansive mural decorating the vaulted ceiling: a depiction of the heavens, the deep pink and azure colors marred in places where the paint had peeled. Edged along the blue skies were seven rosy-cheeked cherubs, their plump bodies clothed in gauze as they looked toward a large white dove haloed by streaks of gold. Its wings spread in flight, the bird seemed an image of the Holy Ghost.

"She's not here."

Miss Reyer reappeared, her voice agitated. Colin was again jarred to see her in men's britches, as she had abandoned the muddy trench coat altogether.

She'd managed to wash her face, though a streak of the dirt remained along her hairline. The grime had semiconcealed the dark blue eyes, high cheekbones, and small, straight nose that complemented her blond hair and pale features. Jewel had not such fair skin, but her hair was the same golden color.

Miss Reyer's pursed lips were as pink as the flower cart roses he'd seen in Paris. "Isabelle was supposed to wait for us."

"Who is Isabelle?"

She ignored his question and strode purposefully past the marble staircase toward the larger room at the far end.

Colin stifled his annoyance and quickly caught up with her. They passed the dining room with its long oak table and chairs set against a colorful Turkish rug, then reached another hall to their left.

He paused at the low murmur of male voices.

"Those are the two agents from the Deuxième Bureau, the French Secret Service. They keep an office here in Vernon." She'd halted with him and nodded in the direction of the voices. "The men decode messages from the Front, and a secretary types the reports. The documents are then sent on to the Bureau in Paris."

Much the same as his job with MI8. "Where is the dovecote?"

"At the back of the estate. My friend André—Sergeant Moreau—should be there now."

"Do you work with the pigeons as well?"

She nodded. "I help the sergeant raise and train them. Before my grandfather died, he loved racing pigeons, so I grew up in Ireland with the birds. Now come, we must hurry."

She took him through the great room, with its ancient, elaborate furnishings, and pulled open a set of tall French doors leading onto a veranda.

Outside, the air held the heady scent of lilac. Leaving the covered porch, they strode across a manicured lawn surrounded by a perimeter of tall, leafy poplars and red-flowering horse chestnut trees. Beyond the row of trees, he had to shield his eyes against the afternoon sun as they paused to admire a circular brick tower standing at the far end of the grounds.

"The dovecote was built in the seventeenth century by a French nobleman." She indicated the turret, its roof resembling a pointed hat. "When his descendants handed over the estate for the war effort two years ago, the army replaced some of the timbers and filled in the missing bricks, but inside the stone *boulins*, or pigeon-holes, are still in fine condition."

"How many birds?" Colin knew approximately a hundred pigeons were kept at the dovecote in Hastings.

"We have up to two hundred and fifty pigeons here at any given time."

He gave her a sidelong glance. "You send and receive that much information?"

She nodded. "Now let's be quick; we're wasting time."

She continued on toward the dovecote, and as he followed, Colin couldn't help noticing her graceful movements despite the mannish dress. She opened the entrance door slowly and crossed the threshold before she motioned to him to follow. "I should tell you—"

A flurry of flapping wings rose at Colin as he stepped inside, and he instinctively raised a protective arm toward his face as scores of birds suddenly took flight. Amid a cacophony of cooing noises, the air in front of him clouded with feathers and dust so that he could hardly see.

"The birds become alarmed with strangers!" Miss Reyer called to him as she reached into a bin near the door and scooped out a handful of dried corn. Once she flung the kernels out into the dovecote's center, many of the pigeons resettled and began feeding while others ascended toward the rafters.

"Thanks for the warning." Colin growled the words as he lowered his arm, his nostrils flaring as the pungent, fecal odor of birds assailed him. When the debris in the air finally began to clear, he brushed off his uniform and surveyed the dovecote's shadowy confines. Every inch of space in the circular structure held a series of concrete holes, most of them filled with birds. Above them near the roofline were four large openings fitted with traps.

"Who has entered my *pigeonnier*, and why are you upsetting my birds?"

At the sound of the indignant shout, Colin looked across to the opposite side of the dovecote, where a lean figure stood atop a high ladder. The ladder was attached to a crossbeam and fastened to a vertical wooden pole that ran the center length of the building.

"André, it's me." Miss Reyer's voice held humor. "I have brought someone for you to meet."

The man was looking their direction. "Jo, *ma chère*! He is here? *C'est formidable!*" His booming voice caused another massive fluttering of wings before the feeding birds resettled. "I will be down in a moment."

He reached to grab at the concrete ledge and slowly pulled himself around the circular wall toward them. The center pole easily turned with the ladder. When he was directly overhead, he descended the rungs.

His middle-aged face creased with relief and gladness, and in the dim light Colin saw that his rich brown hair and moustache held traces of gray. He wore the blue uniform of the French army, and strapped across his chest was a small wooden cage housing a white bird.

He wiped his hands on his trousers before offering one to Colin. "It is good to finally meet you . . . Lieutenant Mabry, eh? I am Sergeant Moreau and in charge of the *pigeonnier*. And this is Little Corporal." He glanced down at the white bird. "We welcome you."

"Thank you, Sergeant." Accepting the man's hearty handshake, Colin sent an arched look at Miss Reyer. "It was a welcome I will not soon forget."

"*Certainement.*" The sergeant chuckled. "We are the birdhouse, after all."

Colin sensed Miss Reyer shift beside him. "Well, André, now that he's come, we can go and find my sister. Where did Isabelle run off to?"

"Patience, *ma petite.*" The sergeant turned to wink at Colin. "Jo, she is headstrong, no? Since having learned her sister is found, she is like a wild bird ready to flee the cage."

It seemed Miss Reyer had been telling the truth. Jewel *was* alive. Colin's pulse quickened as he turned to her. "Who is this . . . Isabelle?"

"Miss Isabelle Moreau is my daughter, Lieutenant," the sergeant spoke up. "She works for the Deuxième Bureau. She wished to be here in case you arrived, but an errand sent her to Rouen. I expect her back soon." He glanced at Miss Reyer. "She will be glad to know that Jo now has a protector to accompany her."

"*In case you arrived . . .*" Did they not think he would come to France to save Jewel? He frowned, staring at the sergeant. "Why does Miss Reyer need protection?"

"*Ma fille* will answer your questions once she returns."

Colin's mouth thinned. More stalling. Was this Isabelle Moreau the only person who had information about Jewel?

He considered interrogating the sergeant further, but the older man's untroubled smile made him hold his tongue. If his daughter worked for the French Secret Service, it was possible she'd withheld certain information from him *and* Miss Reyer.

"Jo, you have offered our lieutenant some refreshment, *oui*?"

She ducked her head before turning her attention to Colin. "Would you care for tea, Lieutenant?"

Patience, man. He drew a deep breath, letting it out slowly. "A cup of tea would be appreciated."

"*Très bien!*" The sergeant laughed and gave him a hearty slap on the back. Inside the small cage, the white bird's wings fluttered.

Miss Reyer reached for the cage. "André, please don't distress him." She directed a look of displeasure at the sergeant, but he shrugged and continued to grin.

She opened the cage and gently gathered up the bird, holding it close with one hand while she smoothed its white feathers with the other. "*Tout va bien*, my little corporal. All is well."

Her soothing voice seemed to calm the bird, and after a few moments, she carefully returned the pigeon to its cage. "We'll go inside until Isabelle returns. Ready, Lieutenant?"

Colin exchanged a salute with the Frenchman before following Miss Reyer back toward the château. Both had brushed the remaining feathers from their clothes by the time they reached the veranda, and she indicated he should take a seat. "We'll have our tea out here. I won't be long."

After the shadowy confines of the dovecote, Colin was relieved to be outside. He refused to sit, however, and remained standing beside a pair of high-backed wicker peacock chairs. He wasn't about to get comfortable while they awaited Isabelle's return. He'd left off questioning the sergeant, but Miss Reyer wasn't getting off so easily. She still had much to answer for.

"I hope you like Pekoe."

She stepped back through the French doors with a tray, setting the white porcelain tea service on the small table between the chairs. There was also a plate of biscuits dusted with real sugar.

"I see the French Secret Service eats well."

She sat and began pouring the tea. "Believe me, the biscuits are a rare treat. Miss Moreau went to school with the owner of the *pâtisserie* near her office in Paris. She works here at the Vernon branch on Wednesdays and brought them to the château this morning."

She shrugged. "Otherwise, like most of the French, especially those in Paris, we've had to ration."

Colin hadn't sampled a sugared biscuit in a long while, and his stomach growled. She smiled. "Please help yourself, Lieutenant. Do not let them go to waste."

She set the saucer with its cup of steaming tea on the table beside his chair and then began to serve herself. "Won't you take a seat?"

He waited until she glanced up at him. "I'm tired of games, Miss Reyer. What do you know about Jewel? Where is she, and why is she in trouble?"

———

Jo poured a dollop of milk into her tea as she weighed her response. The lieutenant had been more than patient, and she owed him an explanation.

How much to tell him was the real question. "We . . . that is, Miss Moreau and I—believe Jewel was taken away from her village a few months ago by a German officer."

"Is she behind enemy lines?"

His gravelly voice drew her attention. Seeing his pale features, her pulse accelerated. Surely he wouldn't change his mind and leave! She'd waited years for this chance. *Papa* . . .

A familiar ache pierced her, and she instinctively sought the ring on her right finger, twisting the silver band round and round.

"I don't believe Jewel is in occupied France anymore, Lieutenant. We would not be able to get to her otherwise."

The blood returned to his face. "I suppose you're right."

His relief was contagious, and her heart resumed a normal beat. "I am sorry I cannot give you more information on her whereabouts. My friend Isabelle will explain when she arrives."

When he made no move to sit, she sighed. "And if I have to keep looking up at you, my neck is certain to get spasms."

After a tense moment, he removed his cap and dropped into the adjacent wicker chair. Ignoring the tea, he stared at her. "Explain to me, Miss Reyer, how you and Jewel can be sisters, since it is obvious you are not French." He leaned forward in the seat. "She never mentioned you. *Not once.*"

His demand shattered her hope of any respite from his interrogation. "To address your second statement, I don't believe she knows about me." She busied herself stirring her tea. "As to the first, Jewel and I share the same father, but not the same mother."

"Half sisters, then."

She nodded. "She is two years older, and I know that her mother died giving birth to her. Sometime afterward, our father came to Paris, where he met my mother, who was studying art." Again her pulse quickened, the old defiance raising her chin. "I am the *illegitimate* daughter, Lieutenant."

Surprise touched his features, but his gaze held none of the condemnation she'd expected. "Who is your mother?"

"Was. She died two years ago in Dublin. That is when I came to France to find my father. I met him once when I was a child." The hazy images she'd clung to for years suddenly rose: *Blue eyes, strong hands. His smile kissing her palm. The smell of tobacco mingled with an ineffable scent imprinted on her before remembrance . . . the knowledge she was a part of him. Her papa . . .*

"Did your mother tell you about Jewel? Or was it your father? He's still with the French Army, isn't he?"

Jo turned to him. "Neither of my parents ever spoke of my having a sister, at least that I remember. And Papa . . ." She fought off a wave of anguish. "When I first arrived in Paris two years ago, I contacted his regiment through the Red Cross." She glanced at her lap. "I learned he was reported missing."

"I'm sorry." The edge in his tone eased. "When I was with Jewel last year, she never said . . . well, I suppose being cut off from the outside world in occupied France, she had no way of knowing about his situation." He paused. "So, how is it you found out about Jewel?"

She looked up to see him reaching for the creamer on the tray, and her glance flitted to the gloved hand resting motionless against his thigh. Jo tried to imagine life without the use of both hands and realized she wouldn't be able to drive the Triumph, a part of her duties for the Bureau she cherished. How did the lieutenant get dressed each morning? She'd had enough experience with buttoning her uniform britches to know it would be impossible—

"Miss Reyer?"

Reeling in her thoughts, she picked up her cup. "I found her diary at Havrincourt."

He went still. "Havrincourt? You were there?"

"Two months ago." She took a sip of her tea. "Before the Boche retook the village in their latest spring attack. News arrived in early December that the enemy had been pushed back from my father's village after a tank battle at Cambrai. I begged Sergeant Moreau to take me there, but he insisted we wait. Several weeks passed before the weather changed and the Allies had reasonably secured the area. We drove in by truck and found much of the town destroyed. A villager who remained told me where to find my father's farm. I walked among the ruins of the farmhouse and outbuildings, looking for some sign Papa had been there."

She glanced at the band on her finger. The tiny silver bird's sapphire eye seemed to wink in the light. A dove's eye. Her papa had given her the ring when she was a child, but at Havrincourt she'd wanted something more—his photograph, perhaps the pipe she remembered. Some scrap of his life that would tell her where the army had sent him.

"I found the diary instead." Her gaze lifted to the lieutenant. "So I brought the book back to Paris and began reading about my sister."

Jo recalled how she'd devoured every word of the diary, reassuring proof that she was no longer alone in the world. Because of Jewel, she still had a family. "My sister began making entries not long after the war began and recorded the events of her village while they lived among the enemy." She eyed him over the rim of the cup. "Jewel also wrote about you, Lieutenant."

Her sister had grieved at his departure, the writing on the pages alternating between anger at being abandoned by him and joy in the hope he would come back for her and make her his wife. "She spoke of her love for you and your promise to return."

Jo saw how her words cut him, and a part of her felt justified, especially after reading Jewel's description of the deprivation and filth, the horrors so many endured while living at the mercy of the enemy. And still he had left her there.

Another part of her sympathized to see the way regret marred his handsome face. She knew firsthand what that kind of sorrow tasted like: the inability to recall one's actions, like murder and rebellion. Treason against the Crown . . .

Her attention returned to the lieutenant as he cleared his throat. "What makes you think Jewel was taken from the village by this Boche officer?"

"She wrote about him in her diary." Jo stared into her teacup, thinking about all the words her sister had penned. "There was an attack on the village. Jewel knew he was coming for her. He said he'd managed to locate our father and promised to take her to him." She looked up. "Perhaps some prison camp."

"It sounds more like an enticement to get her cooperation."

Jo endured his tone, as she too had considered the possibility. Still, she refused to give up hope. "Jewel believes Papa is alive. I must believe it, too." *It is all I have left.*

"Does this Boche officer have a name?"

"Werner Kepler. My sister wrote that he was a captain in the German Army and had been recently posted to the *kommandant*'s office in Havrincourt."

"What about Jewel's aunt?"

"Madame Rochette, her mother's sister." Jo nodded. "Jewel wrote that her aunt died from typhus. It would have been several months after you left the village."

His head sank toward his chest as though in defeat. More guilt pierced her for having reawakened his demons. "I'm sorry, Lieutenant."

He gazed up at her, eyes blazing. "You have had that diary for months. Why did you wait so long to contact me? Heaven only knows what has happened to her by now."

"I had no idea where to start." Jo slowly set down her cup. Was he angry with her . . . or with himself? "In her diary, Jewel always referred to you simply as 'Colin,' so I had no last name. She mentioned you were a cavalry soldier in the British Army, and that you had lost your best friend, a man by the name of Wyatt, but she didn't give his last name, either. She also wrote that you had a swan that drank tea or some such nonsense. Her sentences were so jumbled in places I could not make them out. Nor did I know if you were still in France, or even alive."

Jo recalled her frustration in those weeks and months after reading the journal, knowing "Colin" was her only link to finding her family, yet at a loss to do anything about it.

"So how *did* you locate me?"

He appeared more curious now than angry, and she relaxed. "It was blind luck—or a miracle, if you believe in that sort of thing."

Even she had to admit the lead to finding Colin Mabry was more than simple good fortune.

"As you so clearly pointed out, I did have my sister's diary for quite some time, but no information on you. Then a couple of weeks ago, I took my lunch in the gardens at Versailles. 'Tis a beautiful place and quite the attraction for soldiers on furlough. A British captain was seated on a park bench not far from me, reading a copy of the *Times*. When he'd finished with the newspaper, he left it behind."

Always hungry for news, especially about any new arrests stemming from the Irish rebellion two years ago, Jo had seized the abandoned paper and scanned every inch of newsprint. "I found the name *Colin* in the society section, along with the mention of Swan's Tea Room, an establishment owned by Patrick Mabry, your father. I felt it had to be more than coincidence. Your sister is soon to marry a viscount?"

"Lord Walenford." Leaning back against the wicker seat, he crossed his arms. Again she observed the left hand that wasn't a hand. "And so you made the decision to misrepresent yourself in order to lure me to Paris, is that it?"

His choice of words stung. "I did not think you would believe me, Lieutenant, so it was necessary to use the slight deception. You could hardly refuse a direct plea from my sister, unless of course you were a dishonorable man who intended to break your promise to her."

Now it was his turn to look affronted. "This *slight* deception of yours included the misuse of our secret military communications channel during wartime." He nodded toward the dovecote some distance away. "I cannot imagine the sergeant approved of your methods."

Jo sat up in her seat, meeting his gaze. "Actually, André helped me to plan the ruse."

Satisfied at his look of surprise, she reached for a sugared biscuit. "You said it yourself. Too much time had already passed, and it was imperative I contact you as soon as possible. Ordinarily the Deuxième Bureau would not sanction such a request, but the French are incurable romantics. I wrote the message in a way that any who read it would believe I was a woman desperate to see her *amour*. It really was surprising how easily André convinced an agent here at the château to apply the code before he sent it by pigeon to your British headquarters in Montreuil. I hoped from there it would make its way across the channel to London and the tea shop your family owned." She paused. "And that you would recognize the initials of the sender."

One of his dark brows lifted, his lower lip curling into a frown—an expression she was becoming quite familiar with in his company. "I did recognize *Jewel's* initials, Miss Reyer. Most honorable indeed."

Her gaze wavered, his words piercing her conscience. She would suffer his censure, however, because in truth, she needed Colin Mabry more than he could know. She would use the same ploy again if it meant getting him here.

She, Johanna Dougherty Reyer, had nothing left: no family or country to call her own. She had buried the dead and her troubled past in Ireland, and in this new war-ravaged country of France, she was a stranger.

Yet she clung to her vaguest, happiest memory of home. *Blue eyes and strong hands, a gentle voice . . .*

Maybe she wasn't deserving of a miracle, but she would find Papa and her sister using any means necessary.

CHAPTER

5

*J*ewel's champion has arrived? *C'est un miracle!*"

Colin's head shot up at the sound of a female voice near the open French doors. A slender woman stepped out onto the veranda, and he rose from his seat.

Her height was close to Miss Reyer's, though she appeared to be a few years older. She wore her dark hair swept up beneath a feathered brown felt cap, and her beige suit and sturdy shoes gave her a professional look.

Dark eyes gleamed at him as she approached and extended a hand. "Lieutenant Mabry? I am Miss Reyer's friend, Isabelle Moreau."

He gently grasped her fingers. "*Enchanté*, Miss Moreau. I have already met your father."

She smiled. "It is wonderful to meet you. We have been eager to see if Jo's message would induce you to come to Paris and help us find Jewel."

He glanced at the dark blonde seated in the wicker chair. "Yes, we've just been discussing the loftier principles of truth and honor."

Twin spots of pink appeared in Miss Reyer's cheeks, giving him some gratification. Despite her skewed logic, it irked him knowing she'd tricked him into coming to France.

Colin didn't like to be manipulated. Whether she and her friends knew it or not, he was a man of his word, and aside from his fondness for Jewel, he owed her much.

Did they really take him for some sort of cad?

"I still don't understand why the elaborate deception to get me here." He held Miss Reyer's gaze. "You could have contacted me through the British Army and simply *told the truth*."

"We did ask them, Lieutenant." She rose from the wicker chair. "Isabelle and I made our request to your local army office, but because of mobilization against the new German offensive, we were told it could take weeks to receive information."

"We didn't want to wait," Miss Moreau spoke up. "I work in the typing pool at the Deuxième Bureau and have . . . a friend, Agent Henri Lacourt. I asked him to get word to you in London, but he refused." She darted an apologetic glance at Miss Reyer. "You see, Lieutenant, we were not completely certain you were the man we were looking for, and Henri—Agent Lacourt—could not justify using the Bureau's resources on a hunch."

"So now you can understand why I had to improvise." Miss Reyer held her head high, as though she'd been vindicated of her crime.

Colin's patience was at an end. He turned his attention to the woman who had just arrived. "Fine. I believe we have the business of Jewel's whereabouts to discuss?"

She searched his face, her dark eyes intent. "We do."

As her friend sized up the lieutenant, Jo's insides quaked with anticipation. Two long years she had waited, and now it seemed her family was within reach. "*I want nothing more in the world than to be your papa . . .*"

She tossed the sugared biscuit back onto the plate and brushed off her fingers. "We need to get started, Isabelle."

Her friend's fine dark brows drew together. "I still worry for you, *mon amie*. He is not a man to be trusted."

"*I* am not to be trusted?"

The lieutenant stepped back, clearly insulted. "What do you call the fraud used in getting me to come to Paris? Not to mention the subterfuge you exercised on at least one French agent and a *gross* breach of military protocol in both French and British armies!"

He glared at Jo's friend. "Your distrust is clearly misplaced, Miss Moreau, and I weary of this cloak-and-dagger charade. Tell me where Jewel Reyer is now, or I'm taking the next RAF flight back to Britain."

Panic seized Jo's chest. She flashed a desperate look at her friend.

"*Pardon,* Lieutenant, I was not speaking against you." Isabelle offered a slight bow of apology. "I meant the German officer."

"Kepler? The Boche captain alleged to have taken Jewel from Havrincourt?"

"I see Jo has told you that much. Though now it is almost certain Captain Werner Kepler is more than he appears to be."

Isabelle glanced at her. "When Jo told me about her sister's diary and about Kepler, I asked Henri—Agent Lacourt—to make inquiries. He discovered Kepler's name on the Allies' enemy watch list. Jewel had described the captain with brown hair and a moustache, which is common enough, but also Kepler's scar—a piece of his right earlobe is missing. Agent Lacourt sent out a wire to our branch offices throughout free France, hoping to find out if the man was still in the country."

She paused, and the lieutenant's features stilled. "And is he?"

Isabelle nodded. "Before Jo contacted you, our office received a report that a dark-haired man with a similar scar was seen wearing civilian clothes in a town south of Paris. Agent Lacourt believes it is Kepler—which means our Boche captain could be a spy."

"An enemy agent?" He turned to Jo. "I suppose you forgot to mention that."

"I thought . . . Isabelle should tell you."

His gaze flew back to her friend. "What about Jewel?"

"The report said Kepler was accompanied by a woman. We believe it might be her."

"Might be? You are not certain?"

Isabelle shrugged. "The telegram only stated she was slender and had golden hair."

He frowned. "Those features could describe thousands of women."

"I agree, Lieutenant." Jo moved to his side. "But given all that we know, it seems very likely 'tis Jewel with Kepler. Still, we have no idea what she looks like. I have only the diary, which I found quite by accident in the remains of a root cellar."

She noted his look of surprise; she knew from the diary that the cellar had once been his hiding place. "Everything else at the farm was destroyed, including any photographs."

"So, you need me for more than protection."

He watched her with an unreadable expression. Jo met his gaze with honesty. "You are the only one who can tell me for certain if the woman is my sister."

"What would you have done if I hadn't come to Paris, Miss Reyer?"

She absently twisted the ring on her finger. "I would have taken my chances in trying to identify Jewel. I would have gone on my own."

"Ha! Henri would never tell you where she is, not unless he felt you would be safe."

Isabelle's stubborn expression matched her own. Jo's temper simmered as she regarded the one woman she'd come to trust since arriving in France. "Then I would start from Paris and work my way south." Ignoring the rashness of her words, she added, "Like the lieutenant, I am tired of waiting."

"You should know the rest, Lieutenant." Isabelle's smooth

features creased as she looked at him. "Since we suspect this man is Kepler and working as an agent, any direct confrontation might be dangerous."

She glanced at his gloved hand. "For Jo's safety as well as your own, Agent Lacourt will insist on an interview with you before he decides to reveal more. I will also need to make a photostat of your passport before you leave today. Where are you staying?"

"The Grand Hotel . . . on Place de l'Opéra."

Taut lines bracketed his mouth. Evidently Jo's friend noticed, too. "The noise of the guns, they are *très gênant, oui*? If you would prefer, Lieutenant, you may stay here at the château with my father. I can drive out again tomorrow evening."

"I will return to the hotel tonight." A muscle in his jaw flexed as he removed his passport and handed it over. He turned to Jo. "Where is this diary?"

Her heart stilled. "I have it in Paris."

"I want to see it."

Jo took a step back. If he read all of her sister's words, he might never agree to accompany her. "You don't believe me?"

"Should I? So far all I've heard is hearsay—a woman who *might* be Jewel in the company of a man who *might* be a German officer or an enemy spy or both—and I have yet to learn their whereabouts."

He leaned toward her. "I refuse to listen to any more of your stories, Miss Reyer. You'll show me that diary." He turned and shot Isabelle a look. "Before I *decide* to stay."

At the ultimatum in his words, Jo returned to sit in her chair. So much for trying to bluff.

Isabelle flashed her a look of sympathy before she excused herself to go inside with his passport, leaving Jo to endure his scrutiny and the frown she was coming to know so well.

The lieutenant thought she was lying. Jo's mood alternated between worry and indignation. Perhaps she *could* let him read

Jewel's words—especially the part her sister had penned about their romance.

She wondered for a moment how Jewel might react to having the lieutenant read her most intimate thoughts. However, if he intended to carry out his threat and return to Britain, reminding him of his romantic time with her sister might be the only incentive to convince him to remain and help Jo in her search.

"When we go back tonight, I'll collect the diary and meet you at the hotel for dinner." Jo pressed her shoulders back. "You will see her words for yourself and understand I am not 'fabricating' anything."

He seemed content with the plan and resumed his seat to take up his tea. Jo eased out a breath as she reached for her own cup. She would mark for him the diary pages she had in mind, making certain to ink out a few of the entries Jewel had written near the end.

Entries about her sister's growing affection for Captain Werner Kepler.

Was the woman never on time?

Colin ground his teeth and prayed for patience as he straightened the tableware lying next to his plate. Miss Reyer had left him two hours ago, after dropping him off at the hotel. It had taken him nearly all of that time to perform his ablutions, including brushing the road dust from his uniform and dealing with the blasted buttons on the clean shirt he'd packed for the trip. What was her excuse?

A waiter had begun to close the draperies along the expansive window front of the elegant Café de la Paix. Colin tensed. While the Boche's big guns had quieted for the evening, the approaching dusk brought the new threat of air raids by German Gotha bombers.

He quickly scanned the scene outside the glass but saw no sign of her. A few brave patrons chose to remain outdoors on the terrace while several couples hurried past the restaurant, most of the men in blue or khaki uniforms and walking arm in arm with their ladies. Likely off to dine at some other eatery or to attend the cinema.

Thoughts of Jewel rose in his mind, as well as the events of the afternoon. His trip to the château had raised more questions than answers. If what he'd been told earlier was the truth and Jewel was the woman with Kepler . . . where were they?

His gut tightened at the thought of her in danger, and in the company of a man almost assuredly an enemy agent. What must she be going through right now?

Miss Moreau had said Captain Kepler was spotted south of Paris, in free France. If so, why hadn't Jewel fled? Was she being held against her will, or did Kepler exert some threat over her to keep her chained to him? Her father's life? *"Perhaps she had no choice . . ."*

Colin closed his eyes as Jack's words came back to haunt him.

He reopened them to look across the restaurant. The woman might not be Jewel at all. It seemed Colin was the only one who could identify her. What if she turned out to be another enemy spy working in league with the Boche?

He and Miss Reyer could be walking into a trap.

The unsettling thought clung to him. Between his soldiering and his secret service training, Colin could handle himself. But what of Miss Reyer?

He gazed at the useless appendage he kept hidden from view. Was he up to the task of being her protector? And against what, exactly?

He pressed back against the seat and scowled. Titan's teeth! This Agent Henri Lacourt—likely Miss Moreau's sweetheart—held the key to the puzzle, yet he made them cool their heels while checking to see if Colin would qualify as Miss Reyer's escort to heaven-knows-where to rescue her sister. If in fact it was Jewel at all.

Colin wanted to see the diary. Jewel's own words had to shed more light on her present situation than the cryptic answers he'd received so far.

Again he glanced toward the restaurant's foyer. Miss Reyer agreed to meet him over twenty minutes ago. He had no idea where she lived in Paris, but surely it couldn't take this long to retrieve the diary, give her face another good washing, and return for dinner.

He waited another five minutes before he plucked the linen napkin from his lap and rose from the chair. This was a complete waste of time. Already he was tired of being on the receiving end of her scheme. He would go to the Deuxième Bureau himself in the morning to see Agent Lacourt and demand answers.

Or he would go home.

Tossing his napkin onto the empty plate, he started toward the desk of the headwaiter. He had work to do, responsibilities back in Hastings. Family obligations too, like his sister's wedding and his promise to Jack to stand in as best man.

"Monsieur?"

Colin lifted his gaze. "I'll need to order room serv—"

His words halted as he met the wide blue eyes of the striking woman standing beside the headwaiter.

Colin almost didn't recognize her. Gone were the muddy trousers and boots, and in their place, a fitted skirt and matching jacket in a blue shade that accentuated the color of her eyes.

Beneath the jacket, the open collar of her linen blouse revealed just a glimpse of fair skin at the base of her throat, and as his gaze traveled downward, he saw the skirt's length stop short of a pair of slender ankles encased in ladies' blue-and-white button-up shoes.

He raised his attention to the white-gloved hands clutching a leather-bound book.

"Surely you're not leaving, Lieutenant?"

She seemed unfazed as she innocently looked up at him. He noticed she'd fixed her hair, the dark blond wisps now corralled and pinned beneath her netted blue hat.

The headwaiter retrieved a pair of menus from the desk before he eyed them both questioningly. Colin gave a slight nod and followed Miss Reyer as the man led them back to the table.

She set the book and her purse against the fine white linen, then shrugged out of her blue jacket. Her movement caused a lock of hair to loosen from the pins and fall against her shoulder. Colin smothered a laugh as she glanced at him and quickly tucked the lock behind her ear.

The headwaiter held her chair, then took her jacket and bowed before he disappeared. Colin remained standing as he watched her remove her gloves, noting the silver ring she'd worn at Vernon. The jeweled eye glinted in the lamplight.

He sighed and resumed his seat as she reached for the linen napkin beside her plate and arranged it on her lap. "I do tire of having to wait on you, Miss Reyer."

She busied herself inspecting the silverware, as though she hadn't heard him.

"That color suits you, by the way."

Colin wasn't certain why he'd made the remark, and it irritated him. *She* irritated him.

Her head shot up, the color tingeing her cheeks doing wonders to further brighten her eyes. "Thank you, Lieutenant. And you look quite smart in . . . khaki."

He almost snorted laughter as he glanced at his uniform, the only set of clothes he knew by rote. Still, he acknowledged her compliment with a slight bow before returning his napkin to his lap. He glanced at the book on the table. "Is that the diary?"

She nodded. "I thought we would order our drinks and dinner first."

He curbed his impatience and instead seized on her tardiness. "Where is your flat, by the way? I assumed it was in Paris, but obviously you must live in another country."

She visibly stiffened at his remark, then chose to ignore it as she smiled calmly. "I happen to live with Miss Moreau on rue Boissière, a few kilometers from here, near Place Victor Hugo. And you know, we don't say *flat* in Paris, Lieutenant. 'Tis *appartement*."

He disregarded her words. "You work in Vernon, an hour's drive from here. Why not live there?"

"And miss the excitement?" Her grimace caught him off guard. "I have lived in Paris for two years, Lieutenant. When I arrived from Ireland and couldn't find my father, I had to find work. That's how I met Isabelle, and we became friends. When she asked if I would be willing to share expenses on a place, I agreed, so here I remain." She raised her menu. "When I am not helping the sergeant to train the pigeons, I am a paid courier for the Bureau, so I must deliver daily dispatches to Paris anyway."

Her reasons for living in the city made sense. Still, he'd rather put distance between himself and the German superguns dropping shells on the city with diabolical regularity.

"*Bonsoir*, Lieutenant, mademoiselle. May I bring you an *apéritif* before dinner?"

They looked up to see an elderly waiter had approached. He bowed to Miss Reyer. "Perhaps a glass of *vin* for you, mademoiselle?"

"I'll just have water. Perrier, if you please. *Avec du citron*."

When their server eyed him next, Colin hesitated before he finally nodded. "Make that two with lemon, *s'il vous plaît*."

As the man departed, Colin met with Miss Reyer's speculative gaze across the table.

"Please feel free to order whatever you'd like to drink, Lieutenant. I'll not be offended if you get something from the bar."

She tilted her head. "Or are you usually in the reckless habit of imbibing lemon water?"

He arched a brow. "I could ask the same of you, Miss Reyer. You live in Paris, yet do not drink wine?"

She gave a slight shrug. "I have been known to sip on a glass of sherry once in a while, but honestly, I have no taste for wine or other spirits."

He bent his head. "And for my part, I find alcohol a hindrance to a good night's sleep." In truth, it made his nightmares worse. As for the water . . .

Colin closed off the memory before it began. Concentrating instead on the menu, he perused the restaurant's fare. "Have you eaten here before?"

"Isabelle and I come here often. In good weather, we sit outside on the terrace. Would you like my suggestion for dinner? I saw *filet de boeuf* on the menu board as I walked in. 'Tis quite expensive, of course, with all of the rationing, but well worth the price."

Keeping his attention fixed on the menu, Colin's chest tightened. He flexed the muscles in his left arm, as though willing the gloved hand to work on its own. He hadn't come prepared to cut into a steak.

The words *soupe à l'oignon gratinée* suddenly leapt out at him from the top of the page. *Thank you, Lord.* "I've decided on the onion soup tonight. It advertises to be one of the restaurant's signature dishes."

"Yes, I'm certain you will enjoy it. But that is hardly a meal. Will you have something else with it?"

He placed the menu on the table and met her inquisitive gaze. "I've not much of an appetite this evening."

"Why is that?" A slight crease formed between her brows. "Are you unwell?"

He managed a smile. "Too much traveling today, I think."

"Ah." Her mouth relaxed, and the crease disappeared as she returned to peruse the menu. "I shall have the sole fillet."

Once the waiter brought their drinks and took the order, Colin's attention returned to the diary lying on the table beside her. He held out his hand. "May I?"

She picked up the book and hesitated. "Please, tell me first, what does my sister look like?"

Was she trying to bargain with him? Colin remembered her earlier threat to Miss Moreau: that if all else failed, she would try to seek out Jewel on her own.

"I am simply curious, Lieutenant." Her half smile indicated she'd read his thoughts. "I would like to know."

He finally relented. "She's a bit taller but has your same hair color and high cheekbones. Her chin is more rounded and her eyes a softer shade of blue."

"What about her nose? Her mouth? How does she speak?"

He studied the straight nose and pale pink mouth of the woman across from him. "You share the same nose, but her lips aren't as full. Jewel also has a beautiful, high singing voice."

Miss Reyer seemed appeased and offered him the book. "You are welcome to read the entire diary, but I've marked with a ribbon the page beginning with your arrival in Havrincourt."

His heart thumped in his chest as he opened the cover. A faint musty smell reached his nostrils, along with the scent of violets, conjuring the memory of Jewel's kiss.

He glanced up to see Miss Reyer watching him. Unbidden heat singed his cheeks, and he quickly bent his head and began reading, again grateful to his father for insisting that he and Grace learn to speak and write French.

le 13 avril, 1917

He appeared out of the dark tonight like a wraith, only to collapse at my feet. Startled, I let go of my apron and watched with regret as the contents I had gathered scattered into the shadows. Those potatoes had come from the abandoned pigsty, where at some point they had taken root. Aunt and I haven't eaten since yesterday morning, and that is surely the reason I hesitated for just a moment before helping the poor soldier into the barn. . . .

Jo's pulse quickened as she reached for her glass of lemon water, never taking her eyes off him. With head bent low, his dark, thick lashes shifted slightly as he read her sister's words. The angled lines of his face held an intent look, and she knew the passage he must be reading.

His first encounter with Jewel.

She had used her pen to ink out a few sentences near the end of the diary—her sister's effusive words of admiration and praise for Captain Kepler. Jo hoped Colin Mabry wouldn't take her handiwork amiss, or ask her more questions. It was important he be as eager as she to begin their search.

After dropping him off at the hotel earlier, she stopped at the Paris Bureau. Isabelle had arrived first and was speaking to Henri in his office as she handed over the copy of Lieutenant Mabry's passport.

When her friend reemerged, Jo learned that it would take another day or two before an interview could be arranged. She chafed at having to wait. She also worried.

Would Henri Lacourt trust the lieutenant to watch out for her?

Jo's anxiety continued to mount. Despite her threat to Isabelle earlier, she knew trying to find her half sister and Werner Kepler on her own would be next to impossible. Though the Boche's scar might be distinguishing, France was a vast country, and she still had only the barest description of him and now a hazy sketch of Jewel. At least Lieutenant Mabry could identify her sister, possibly without Kepler's knowledge.

And then what? Would Jewel open her arms in welcome to a sister she'd never met? What about the lieutenant, to whom she'd once sworn undying love?

It was possible Jewel had become an enemy spy, like the man she so admired. Henri Lacourt seemed to think this "mystery woman" with Kepler was indeed an accomplice.

Earlier at the château, Lieutenant Mabry had asked about Papa. Jo told him that, according to the diary, Captain Kepler had promised to take Jewel to their father. Yet if her sister *had* become a spy or even an enemy sympathizer, would she accept Jo as part of her family? Would she allow Jo to accompany her?

A sigh escaped her. Such questions could only be answered once they found her sister.

"Lieutenant, mademoiselle, bread for your meal."

She ended her musing as the old waiter returned and set a plate of sliced bread on the table. Turning to the lieutenant, he offered a stiff bow before placing a small pot of butter alongside the bread. "For you, Lieutenant. I am sorry to say it is *pain national*, but hopefully the butter will hide the taste."

As the waiter retreated, the lieutenant glanced at her questioningly.

"It's what Parisians call 'national bread,' made with flour containing fillers. 'Tis part of the rationing laws." She nodded toward the food. "And the French never serve butter with bread at dinner, but for Allied soldiers, they make allowances . . . for which I'm grateful."

He gave an absent nod and went back to reading the diary. Jo fidgeted in her seat, trying to ease the tight whalebone stays squeezing her ribs. She longed for her trousers and tunic. The loose garments allowed more breathing room than the tailored suit, and they didn't require her to be constrained in a corset!

Of course, with the old Paris law still in effect, she didn't dare wear trousers beyond her duties as a paid courier. Even for that, it had been necessary to receive special permission from the police. Not too difficult, since her work was for the Deuxième Bureau.

Tonight Isabelle had tried to convince her to wear one of her friend's favorite dinner dresses, the pink crepe with capped sleeves and matching *Técla* pearls. A lovely ensemble certainly, but Jo had no need to impress the lieutenant. She was recruiting him to be her guide to find Jewel. Beyond that . . .

She went completely still, noting the change in his expression. The rugged angles of his face had softened.

An unexpected pang shot through her, and she realized he must be reading the more intimate details between himself and Jewel: laughing as they toasted France with a bottle of wine and the raisin cakes Jewel had received from the enemy for her night's singing performance; then later, Jewel repeating the final song she'd sung from her set *in French* rather than the mandated German. Afterward, she had tended his wound.

"Mon noble chevalier." Her noble knight—Jewel had bestowed the name on him in those quiet moments. And before she left him that particular evening, she had leaned in to kiss him. . . .

Jo shut her eyes, and then quickly reopened them to gaze at the lieutenant. His expression held the same look of yearning she'd often experienced herself. She had been alone for so long, and despite her mother Moira's unconventional ways of bringing up a daughter, Jo longed for a home and a family of her own. To fall in love, something her independent mother had often lectured her against.

He glanced up at her then, and for an instant, Jo felt as though he'd read her thoughts. She quickly reached for the bread.

"Pardon me, Miss Reyer. May I borrow the diary? I can read it later this evening and return it to you tomorrow."

"Yes . . . of course. By the way, did you notice the fore-edge artwork along the book's leaf edges? You can only see it when the pages are fanned slightly apart. It's a painting of a redbird and a bluebird with a nested white egg between them."

He feathered the pages with his fingers. "Very clever. And beautifully done."

She nodded. "Jewel wrote that our father painted the design. He asked her to write down her songs and to record her life in Havrincourt while he was away, so she could read the diary to him the next time they were together." Jo didn't add that her sister would undoubtedly omit reading any parts involving her romantic interlude with the lieutenant.

He glanced at the book. "I knew she sang but didn't realize she wrote songs as well."

"'Tis another reason I treasure the book."

He gazed at her. "I promise I will keep the diary safe."

Jo smiled. "I'm certain you will. I spoke with Isabelle this evening. She told me Agent Lacourt has your passport copy and will contact you once he's made his inquiries."

A scowl settled against his rugged features. "Yes, I suppose it will take him some time to see if I come up to scratch as a worthy escort."

She looked away, dipping her knife into the pot of butter. "I feel certain your rank and experience with the British Army will impress him." She slathered butter onto a slice of bread and replaced the knife on the tray. "Care for some?"

When he didn't answer, she looked up at his rigid posture. She opened her mouth to repeat the question, before recalling his food order—a mere bowl of soup, a meal requiring only a single utensil.

Jo, you are such a dolt! How could he butter his own bread? Without missing a beat, she set her serving on a small plate and handed it to him. "'Tis coarse fare, as the waiter said, but hardly a surprise to you after being at the Front."

He hesitated before accepting her offering. "Thank you, Miss Reyer."

She smiled and was preparing another slice for him when the siren wailed outside. Jo's heart thundered as a whistling sound preceded a bomb's explosion near the hotel.

The ground shook, and cries rose among the other dinner

guests. The lieutenant launched from his seat, knocking the table. "Get down!"

She could hear the waiter shouting to everyone to go to the cellar when the lieutenant suddenly pulled her off her chair and onto the carpet, landing on top of her. "Don't move!"

Jo still held the butter knife as another blast rocked the building, followed by another, and another, and she shut her eyes, her mouth pursed tight to keep from crying out as she trembled beneath his weight. After all this time in Paris, the sound of the Gotha bombs still frightened her.

A few moments passed before a stretch of silence ensued. Jo opened her eyes, mere inches from the lieutenant's, and saw his face was the color of ash, his hazel eyes dark with fear.

She glanced around and realized they were the only ones left in the café. The cellar had become a standard haven during bombings for most Paris establishments. Likely it held the other dinner guests.

Awareness shot through her as she felt the lieutenant's chest rise and fall against hers before eventually slowing to a calmer rate. His breath warmed her face, and the scent of spicy cologne filled her senses.

With her initial fear passed, she found herself struggling to pull air into her lungs, the tight corset compounding his heavy weight on top of her. "I believe it's over now, Lieutenant."

She whispered the words, bringing him around as he finally seemed to focus on her. The color returned to his features, yet he continued to lie there a moment, staring at her. Jo's pulse leapt as his gaze searched hers. His voice sounded ragged. "Are you all right, Miss Reyer?"

"Yes, I just need . . . some air."

He immediately rolled off her and rose to his feet. Reaching for her hand, he helped her up, and Jo noticed the other guests returning from downstairs, chatting with one another as though nothing had happened.

It was the French way to be stoic under such conditions. What else could they do but continue on?

She sat back down at the table, and the lieutenant did the same. Neither spoke for a long moment, and Jo took the time to consider her revelation: he'd been terrified, yet protected her with his body. If necessary, he was ready to sacrifice his life for her.

Her pulse thrummed. "I have no doubt whatsoever, Lieutenant, that you will be a most suitable escort on this quest." Her voice was soft. "Thank you."

His hand gripped the table, and though his breathing had slowed, he still seemed a bit rattled. He nodded and offered a weak smile. "Let's hope Agent Lacourt feels the same way."

Jo's hope faltered as she realized that, despite his exhibition of bravery moments ago, there was still a chance he would "scratch out" with Henri Lacourt. If so, her quest was doomed before it started.

She would never find her family.

CHAPTER

6

The sole reason he'd been summoned to Paris was to be kept waiting.

Colin was convinced of the fact as he paused in his pacing beside Agent Henri Lacourt's cluttered desk and frowned up at the wall clock in the small, dingy office.

Two o'clock had come and gone by several minutes. Perhaps France circled the sun in a different orbit than the rest of Europe.

Miss Reyer had collected him fifteen minutes late as well— no surprise there—and he'd endured another bumpy ride in the sidecar, flinching at the occasional blasts from siege guns as she raced them through the dirty, crowded streets of Paris. One of the shells had struck a park, and Colin stared at the giant crater surrounded by green grass as she'd veered them around a snarl of traffic to reach the avenue de Tourville. He'd relaxed once they passed the École Militaire and Les Invalides, finally pulling up at the gray stone buildings that housed the French Secret Service.

A faint echo of footsteps sounded outside the closed office door, and he wondered if Monsieur Lacourt was going to make an appearance at last. The soft murmur of female voices accompanied the sound, and he assumed Miss Reyer and her friend Miss Moreau were both hovering near the door.

In the two interminable days since his arrival, his frustration had turned to sufferance; only the thought of Jewel and the danger she was in kept him waiting here instead of flying back to the relative safety of Hastings. There, at least, the people he worked with were much as they seemed, and punctual, and the siege guns a mere echo compared to the ground-shaking blasts slamming Paris at regular intervals.

He thought again of the other night at the restaurant, when the siren was followed by Gotha bombs. His first thought had been to get Miss Reyer to safety. Only later did he learn everyone else had moved to the cellar, while he fell on top of her beside their table, squeezing the breath from her lungs.

She'd been afraid but hadn't panicked, and Colin had sensed her trying to calm him with her voice after the bombs ceased. He had noticed her eyes were a darker shade of blue than he'd first imagined, and her scent of flowers had eased his breathing.

He was still irritated over her manipulating him, and her tardiness was a point of contention, but he admired her grit. Much like her sister's . . .

The office door suddenly burst open. A tall, lean man with cropped brown hair and an elaborately waxed moustache entered the room.

He wore a harried expression as he rushed forward with a large envelope and began speaking in heavily accented English. "Lieutenant, I must apologize for the delay. Your Paris office sent over the information I requested by special courier, but the gun blast on rue de Rivoli—a taxi crashed into a bread cart, and it took some time to clear the street. I am Agent Henri Lacourt, by the way."

Lacourt extended his hand, and as Colin reached for it, he saw the Frenchman glance at his prosthetic. His gut tightened as he tried to gauge the man's reaction. "Shall we get down to it, Agent Lacourt?"

The agent smiled, indicating Colin take the chair adjacent to the desk while he moved around to sit on the other side. "I will need a few moments. Would you care for tea?" He didn't wait for a response before shouting the order at the closed door. "Mademoiselle Moreau! Can we have tea brought in, *s'il vous plaît!*"

Colin raised a brow at Lacourt's lack of etiquette before settling into the chair, studying the Frenchman as he opened the packet and examined what must be Colin's personal dossier.

Colin shifted in his seat, uncomfortable at having to witness a stranger perusing the events of his life like a novel. His gloved hand rested on his thigh. Lacourt's eyes had gone unerringly to the prosthetic. Had Miss Moreau informed him of the injury?

Anxiety further knotted his insides. Doubtless this interview was to be a mere formality before the Frenchman flat-out refused his candidacy to accompany Miss Reyer.

Colin thought back to the diary and the images Jewel's words had conjured: her taking him in as he stumbled into her life, bloody and wounded, devastated by loss; her feeding him from her scant stores and nursing him back to health. Her risk in keeping him hidden from the Boche.

The tearstained pages he'd read held her grief at his leave-taking, and later, the loss of her aunt. Near the end, her passages had become inked out and choppy as the battle overran the village and began spreading its chaos. She'd been all alone in enemy territory. It was hardly surprising she felt compelled to leave with the Boche captain or spy, whatever he was.

Jewel had written down her dreams as well: Colin, sweeping her off her feet and taking her back to Britain as his wife to live in a small country cottage with enough room for their children to play.

Despite his affection, he'd never thought that far ahead to a future with her. Their time together had been a whirlwind of emotion. He'd been captivated by her kiss and her laughter and tender care of him. Yet as the months passed and the war intruded, he'd come to realize that perhaps it was more his own fancy than any kind of serious love.

But Jewel *was* counting on him. After reading her dreams and knowing what she'd sacrificed, he had begun to consider how his being in Paris might be God's plan for him, after all.

Since returning from Ireland, he'd been at loose ends, without any set course to his life. What if Miss Reyer's note to him had been more than coincidence? Colin's chance to make right some of the past and create a future for himself with Jewel.

His pulse sped up as he thought about the plan he'd worked out yesterday. He would remain in France and search her out, and if the woman with Kepler turned out to be Jewel and her feelings for Colin remained unchanged, he would offer to marry her here in Paris and take her home with him to Britain.

Knowing the situation and being a man of honor and duty, Colin knew Jack Benningham would support the match. He just hoped Grace and their father would be as agreeable to his suddenly taking a wife. Especially since he'd never mentioned Jewel to either of them.

Miss Moreau entered the office just then, carrying a small tea service. She hesitated, eyeing the clutter before she gave Colin a quick look and used her elbow to shove aside Lacourt's books and paperwork, making room for the tray of tea and biscuits.

The Frenchman seemed oblivious as he continued reading the documents. Miss Moreau poured the first cup of tea, adding a bit of cream before holding up the sugar bowl to Colin with a questioning look. He shook his head, and she passed him the steaming cup, along with the plate of biscuits.

Plucking the cup from the saucer, he glanced at the plain flour squares with little enthusiasm. Unlike the sugary edibles he'd been served at the château, these looked like the hardtack in his rations kit at the Front. Even so . . .

He raised the cup in his good hand and gave her an apologetic smile. She glanced down as she obviously realized her error and returned the saucer and plate to the tray.

Pouring Lacourt's tea next, she took her time, occasionally glancing at the agent, who immersed himself in reading Colin's personal and military history.

Miss Moreau finally finished her task. "Shall I bring anything else, Agent Lacourt?"

Seconds passed before the Frenchman lifted his gaze. "*Non*, that will be all, mademoiselle. For now." A smile formed beneath the elaborate moustache. "*Merci*."

A rosy color touched her cheeks, and she nodded to them both before moving back toward the door.

"Lieutenant, I am impressed." Lacourt set down the papers and picked up his tea. "At the Somme, you fought alongside my countrymen." He glanced back at the documents on his desk. "In fact, you were awarded the *Croix de Guerre*. You fought at Courcelette, and then at Combles beside the French Sixth, yes?"

"Our cavalry was assigned to the British Fourth." Colin set his cup on the edge of the cluttered desk. After the failed push through at Courcelette, General Haig had sent them south.

"My good friend fought at Combles." Lacourt looked up at him. "You saved many French lives that day, despite heavy gunfire."

Colin flexed his jaw. He didn't like discussing the details, like the fact it was raining shells at the time he and another cavalryman used their horses to drag a pair of *mitrailleuses* from the back line. They fired on the enemy, aiding seven French *poilus* trapped in the open. In the end, everyone managed to get back to his own unit, and shortly afterward, Colin received the French cross. "I did what any British soldier would do, Agent Lacourt. My duty."

He sensed Miss Moreau's astonished presence behind him before he heard the click of the door closing.

"I would say you did far more than that. France owes you a debt." The agent set down his cup and leaned back in his seat. "I will be blunt, Lieutenant. I have read your file, and I realize you are no stranger to battle or valor. You have also had training with the British Secret Service. Yet it has not escaped my notice that you have . . . a substantial injury, which you received last year at Passchendaele. So I wonder if, as an officer and a man of honor . . ." He sat forward, tilting his head. "Can you honestly provide adequate protection to Mademoiselle Reyer on this journey to find her sister?"

Despite having asked himself that same question repeatedly during his time in Paris, Colin ground his teeth in disappointment. Still, he gave his most candid response. "I will protect her or die trying, monsieur."

The Frenchman looked back at the documents for a long moment. Finally he shook his head. "*Non*, there is too much risk." Compassion mingled with the resolve in his expression. "Lieutenant, I am sorry that you have come all this way—"

"Not as sorry as I am, monsieur." Their interview was at an end. Colin rose from the chair, his good hand clenched at his side. Regardless of his heroics at the Somme, he'd been found wanting. Had the Frenchman read all of the details in his dossier? Colin was still a top marksman with the Colt, and he could handle a rifle, though it now took him longer to reload. He'd also proven his ability to wield a sword in battle.

The polite refusal ate at his tattered pride like acid. He would send a message to Jack through Goodfellow in Hastings, relaying the situation with Lacourt. Colin's future brother-in-law was an esteemed member of the peerage. If he wished, he could exert sufficient influence on this Frenchman.

"You must understand, it has nothing to do with your bravery. . . ."

But Colin had already turned toward the door, his fury mingled with shame, not only at Lacourt's rejection, but for the moment's relief he had experienced at hearing the verdict.

The French agent was right: it had nothing to do with Colin's bravery. Lacourt couldn't know the struggle just to face the day each morning, knowing he would never be whole again. He glared at the offensive gloved hand at his side. *God, what is your plan for me?*

Colin barely broke his stride as he threw open the door and left the office. He shot a fierce look at Miss Reyer, hovering outside the threshold with her friend, just as he'd suspected. "We're leaving."

She blinked at him before rushing to keep up as he stormed toward the building's exit. When he reached the door, she grabbed his sleeve. "What happened back there? What did Agent Lacourt say?"

"I wonder that you would ask, Miss Reyer, since you and Miss Moreau doubtless overheard every word of the conversation."

Her mouth fell open, the blue eyes narrowing at him. "We did not eavesdrop, Lieutenant."

"No? Then I'll translate for you. Lacourt said, 'Sorry old chap, but you're unfit for duty.'"

Her anger seemed to vanish, which only increased his annoyance. She felt sorry for him, did she? He continued past the open doors to the street, breathing in the fresh air as though he'd been suffocating inside. She followed and soon passed him on the steps leading down to the sidewalk. He had expected her to reclaim her seat on the motorcycle parked along the building's front. Instead she made a hard right onto the avenue de Tourville.

"Where are you going?"

She looked back at him. "I want to show you something."

Colin refused to budge. He had to contact Goodfellow, not sight-see.

When she realized he wasn't following, she stopped and turned with hands on hips. "Well, are you just going to stand there all day? You've no time to wallow in your misery; there are plans to make."

Of all the impertinent . . . He blew air through his nostrils. He certainly wasn't wallowing, and *she* was obviously addled. What kind of plans could they make? He had no idea where Jewel and the Boche agent were . . . or did Miss Reyer have more secrets she'd neglected to share?

She stood waiting, one boot tapping the sidewalk with obvious impatience. He had half a mind to call a taxi and leave her there, but his curiosity overrode common sense.

He frowned and joined her.

Together they walked in silence. A short distance later, she led him into the mammoth stone complex of Les Invalides. As they neared the church standing at its core, she ascended the steps. "'Tis inside the Dôme des Invalides."

They entered the cool, quiet interior of what was once King Louis XIV's royal chapel, and Colin noted the large altar and crucifix at the far end of the spacious building. High above his head, the domed ceiling was painted in colorful mural panels, interspersed with beams of gilt gold.

They moved toward the middle of the great open rotunda and reached the marble railing to gaze down. In the room below, surrounded by Greek marble statues and mounted on a pedestal, was a large red quartzite sarcophagus.

Colin recognized the shrine from his history books. "Napoleon's tomb?"

She nodded. "After I arrived here in Paris and learned I could not go to my father, I took long walks through the city and visited the historical monuments. I find that I come back to this place most often when I am in need of . . ." She glanced at him and smiled. "Inspiration."

Again he scanned the interior of what was once a royal church—the art, the crucifix, the altar. "So you come here to seek God."

Following his gaze, she shrugged. "I'm afraid I don't know how. We never went to church. Moira—my mother—was not much for religion." She averted her eyes. "I'm sure you understand, Lieutenant, that a woman who bears a child out of wedlock is treated much like a leper."

Her voice was the barest whisper. Despite his own confused anger, Colin was moved to compassion, knowing she was right. Illegitimacy remained a stigma even in London.

An uncomfortable silence stretched between them before she pointed at the tomb. "Did you know Napoleon was only twenty-four when he became a general? Not much older than you or me." She paused. "It was more than a hundred years ago that he saw an advantage during the chaos of the revolution and used it to quickly rise in the ranks."

"Napoleon inspires you?" Colin eyed her incredulously. "In case you've forgotten the rest of your history, Miss Reyer, he was Britain's enemy."

"I am aware of the facts, Lieutenant. Still, for good or ill, he became one of the greatest conquerors of all time. To Napoleon, nothing seemed impossible." She turned to face him, her blue eyes ablaze. "And you cannot let the opinion of one Frenchman stop you in our mission to find Jewel."

He leaned in and frowned at her. "I happen to have some ideas which I was about to explore before you dragged me to this place." He angled his head. "Or do you have another plan in mind? Is there some small detail you forgot to tell me that would aid our situation?"

"You've read my sister's diary. And Isabelle and I have told you everything else that might pertain to finding my sister."

Her chin nudged upward. She was hiding something. Colin remembered the last diary entry. As the mortars blasted the village, Jewel had been sick with fear, awaiting the moment the Boche captain would come for her.

A sudden sense of dread filled him. "Jewel is still all right, isn't she? Nothing has happened to her beyond what you've told me?"

"No!" she was quick to answer. "I mean, you read the pages, Lieutenant. She did not indicate she had been harmed in any way."

"I need to get back to the hotel."

She searched his face, her expression tight. "So, you're leaving without a fight?"

He released a heavy breath. "Would you rather I return to the Bureau and let my fist knock some sense into Agent Lacourt?"

"Not that it would do any good, but . . ."

She lifted her slim shoulders, and a smile hovered at her lips. Colin's mood lightened. "I daresay I agree with you."

Her expression sobered. "What are these ideas you want to explore?"

"I intend to contact Lord Walenford in London to see about getting better cooperation from Lacourt."

Hope lit her expression. "Oh yes, he's the man your sister will marry!"

He nodded. "Are you ready to leave this place?"

In answer, she covered his hand where it rested against the marble railing. Surprised, he felt her warmth penetrate his skin, and for a moment his mind flashed to her softness beneath him as he'd sheltered her during the bombings the other night.

"I knew you would not give up on my sister, Lieutenant."

She smiled at him before retracing their steps, and as Colin walked beside her to the exit, he refocused on the task at hand, praying Jack would agree to handle the situation with the Deuxième Bureau using the utmost diplomacy. From all accounts, Jewel was being held hostage in a part of France Colin knew little about, and while he'd joked with Miss Reyer about getting in the last round with Lacourt, the worst thing he could do was alienate the Frenchman.

Isabelle stood out in front of the café's busy terrace, waving a bright handkerchief as Jo drew up with the Triumph and parked alongside the curb.

As Jo and the lieutenant disembarked, Isabelle's dark eyes narrowed and she smiled, glancing between the two of them. "I saw your motorcycle outside the Bureau when I left, but you were nowhere to be found. Where did you slip off to?"

The feline smile broadened, and Jo's cheeks burned with unexpected heat. She removed her goggles. "We . . . did a bit of sightseeing. Why?"

Hearing her own defensive tone made her glare at her French friend. Why did Isabelle imagine an attraction when she knew the real reason the lieutenant had come to Paris?

Yet the details of the air raid two nights ago had been constantly in Jo's thoughts: the way the lieutenant had shielded her, his body pressing her against the floor. His intimate gaze in those few seconds after the bombs had stopped, as she breathed in the spicy scent of his cologne.

You're a fool, Jo. She forced herself to recall the minutes before that, when he'd been reading her sister's diary. It was obvious from his reactions that he was still in love with Jewel.

Jo felt another prick of guilt, thinking back to their conversation at the Dôme. While she'd told him the truth—she and Isabelle had shared all they knew pertaining to *finding* her sister—Jo hadn't been forthcoming about Jewel's increasing regard for Kepler.

Still, her sister's last diary entry was dated months ago, and from what little Henri had relayed to her and Isabelle, there was no indication a marriage had taken place. As far as Jo was concerned, Lieutenant Mabry still had every chance to win back her sister's affections.

Her conscience appeased, she tugged off her gloves. "Isabelle, why are you here?"

Her friend tucked the handkerchief into her leather purse and withdrew tickets from a local theater. "Do you enjoy the cinema, Lieutenant? They are showing *L'Enfant de Paris* at the Gaumont tonight at seven."

He frowned and glanced at his watch. "I thank you for the invitation, Miss Moreau, but I have other business to take care of."

Isabelle waved the tickets at him. "I urge you to attend, Lieutenant. You will find the experience very enlightening."

Jo gripped her gloves. She'd seen the film months ago and found the story of an orphaned girl whose father was missing in the war too painfully close to her own predicament. What was Isabelle thinking? She knew Jo had been uncomfortable watching the film before, so why did she insist now? Unless . . .

She stared at her friend's hand. *Four tickets.*

Jo reached to pluck two from Isabelle's grasp. "We'll meet you in the lobby of the Gaumont at six forty-five, won't we, Lieutenant?" She gave him a meaningful look. "It's several blocks from here. I can drive us."

He looked about to object, but Jo shook her head, and he hesitated. His dark brows drew together as he darted a look from Isabelle back to her. "Fine. Now, ladies, if you will excuse me, I have matters to attend to."

The women watched him stride quickly toward the hotel's entrance. When he disappeared behind the glass doors, Jo glanced at Isabelle. "Henri is coming tonight, isn't he? He's going to give us the location?"

Her friend's catlike smile returned as she held up the two remaining tickets.

"How did you convince him?"

"He likes me." Isabelle shrugged before her humor vanished. "You understand he takes a great risk, Jo. Can you imagine what would happen to my dear Henri if it was discovered he sent two *innocents* after a suspected Boche spy? What if something happens to you?"

"Isabelle, Lieutenant Mabry is hardly a fledgling. You told me yourself he is a war hero." It was true, Jo hadn't eavesdropped—the solid wood door to Agent Lacourt's office prevented her from hearing any clear conversation. But her friend had relayed the exchange she overheard while serving their tea. "I'm sure he will take the utmost care."

Worry deepened the lines in Isabelle's face. "I know how much it means to you to find your father and now your sister. But this is no game. Captain Kepler could be a dangerous man."

Jo's anger flared at the stark reminder. "Why doesn't the Bureau simply arrest him? That way my sister could be back in Paris by now."

"I am not supposed to know that kind of information, *mon amie*. However, I believe the Allies have Kepler under surveillance and do not wish our office to interfere, at least for now. Perhaps they wait to trap him." She offered a sympathetic smile. "And it is possible your sister does not yet know your father's location, so you must have patience as well as prudence."

Jo hadn't considered the possibility. Her shoulders eased. "You are right, my friend."

Isabelle placed the remaining tickets in her purse. "How did the lieutenant react to Jewel's . . . impression of Captain Kepler?"

Jo stared at her gloves. She'd shared the diary with Isabelle shortly after reading it herself. Only her friend knew *everything* her sister had written down. "He does not know."

"But the diary . . . ?"

She met her friend's curious gaze. "I blotted out a few . . . er, particulars near the end."

Isabelle gave her a severe look. "I think you do him a disservice, Jo."

Jo raised her chin. "What if I had shown him all that she wrote? Do you think he would still be willing to go with me?" She compressed her lips. "I did what was necessary."

So why did she feel guilty?

"And just what do you plan to do once you find her . . . with Kepler?"

Jo let out a sigh. "I haven't thought that far ahead."

"Well, *mon amie*, you had better start." She reached to touch Jo on the shoulder. "I must return to the office. Will you give me a ride?"

Jo nodded, and as her friend climbed into the sidecar, she started the engine and dismissed Isabelle's disturbing question, thinking instead to the coming evening.

Where in France would Henri Lacourt send them? She would need to pack the proper clothing, of course, and drive out to speak with André and say good-bye to her Little Corporal.

Excitement fluttered in her chest as she drove toward the Bureau.

Their quest was about to begin.

CHAPTER

7

PARIS, FRANCE, APRIL 13

ontact George Petit, Hôtel Blanc, Toulouse.

Colin stared again at the cryptic note on the back of the photograph before flipping it over to gaze at the face of a dark-haired stranger with deep-set eyes and a thick moustache.

Late last night at the café, he and Miss Reyer mulled over the picture Lacourt had passed to him at the cinema earlier, before the Frenchman slipped out with Isabelle.

Was this the face of George Petit . . . or Werner Kepler? With the head turned slightly to one side in the portrait, Colin couldn't see the right ear to determine a scar.

Whoever he was, the man was apparently in Toulouse—a bit more than "south of Paris." Hours in fact, by train. Colin would have preferred more substantial information, but he had no reason to doubt Lacourt's reliability. Monsieur Petit must know how to contact Kepler and Jewel.

He looked up from the photograph and out the café window. The breakfast crowd had thinned, leaving the outside terrace looking nearly deserted in the wake of the usual throng patronizing the place.

Miss Reyer agreed to meet him here at 1100 hours this morning, but already she was late. Instead of irritation, however, Colin's pulse quickened, wondering if she was all right. Despite her habitual tardiness, he'd come to realize after three nights of air raids by Gotha bombers that she could at any time fall victim to a deadly barrage falling from the sky.

He tried to reassure himself she was merely late; twenty to thirty minutes past any given hour seemed to be her magic number. Soon the two of them would be bound for Toulouse, leaving Paris and its destruction far behind.

He returned the photograph to the inside pocket of his tunic, alongside the other document he'd acquired earlier that morning. He had stopped in at the MI6 office in Paris to update his message to Goodfellow, requesting his corporal notify Lord Walenford of his forthcoming travel plans and extended stay in France.

While he was there, the desk chief asked if Colin would courier a dispatch to an aeronautics engineer in Toulouse, a Monsieur Gambette. The Frenchman was aiding in a secret project underway just outside of Paris—a fake City of Light.

Colin still marveled at how a decoy city was being built a few miles to the west, intended to draw the German Gotha bombers away from the real capital.

It was a brilliant plan. As workers secretly constructed a replica of Paris, including a Champs-Élysées and a Gare du Nord railway station, no detail was overlooked. Mock railroad tracks, factory buildings, even phony trees were added to make it seem more authentic. Imitation cannons and camouflaged tanks added to the ruse, and once Monsieur Gambette received the document with dimensions from chief designer Fernand Jacopozzi, he would supply the materials to build a replica plane hangar and planes.

Because the project's completion was critical, MI6 had agreed to aid the French. With Colin's clearance through MI8 and his imminent departure for Toulouse, he'd been asked to assist. He had readily agreed to receive such an important assignment.

The MI6 desk chief had also warned him to be aware of potential spies as they traveled through France. Colin debated whether or not to share his real reasons for going south, but Lacourt had taken a risk by giving him the tip, and Colin certainly didn't want to betray the agent. He also knew that if MI6 forbade him to go, he would not disobey an order.

Better he should ascertain the situation first. If the woman with Kepler *wasn't* Jewel, he need not interfere and could simply accomplish his task with Monsieur Gambette.

A taxi pulled up to the curb outside, next to the café's terrace. Colin held his cup of Darjeeling halfway to his lips as he watched a woman step from the cab, her rather large gray hat with ostrich plumes complementing a tailored gray-green striped traveling suit and gray gloves. Signaling the driver to wait, she approached the café's window glass. Yet it wasn't until she tilted her head upward that he recognized her dark blue eyes and fair features beneath the hat.

She waved a gloved hand at him.

Once again he was startled by her transformation. Colin even forgot his annoyance. Slowly he rose from his seat, reaching for the leather portmanteau at his feet. As he'd already checked out of the hotel, he started toward the exit.

She reached it first and held the door for him.

He had to admit the hat was quite fetching. "Miss Reyer."

"Lieutenant." She glanced at the portmanteau. "Oh good, you are ready to leave." She turned and beckoned the driver standing beside the cab. The short, stooped man with bargeman's cap and a cigarette dangling from the edge of his mouth ambled over to take Colin's luggage.

"Shall we?" Her eyes sparkled, cheeks blooming with color as she took his arm. He could sense her excitement at the prospect of finally meeting her sister. And he would see Jewel.

His heart drummed with anticipation—or was it uncertainty? God, it seemed, had put him back on a course of action, and already Colin was trying to become accustomed to the idea of having a wife. Yet as his glance darted to his prosthetic, he wondered what Jewel would now make of him as husband material.

He recalled her words in the diary: *her* dreams and memories of their time together; her pleasure in being able to do things for him, like caring for his wounds and making certain he received the treats she brought back from the Boche after singing; even the warmth of his lips when she'd kissed him, and the subsequent pages describing her love.

Would Jewel's feelings for him be the same as those she'd penned onto the page . . . or would she find him wanting?

It seemed likely he would know the answer in a matter of hours.

Colin opened the cab door for Miss Reyer, then followed her inside. Once his bag was stowed, the driver slid back behind the wheel. "Where to?"

Miss Reyer issued the instructions. "Take us to Gare d'Austerlitz, if you please."

The cabby grunted his assent, and the taxi lurched forward.

"We can still catch the noon train and arrive in Toulouse in time for dinner." She wore a hopeful look, and Colin noted her small gloved hands twisting in her lap. Without thinking, he reached to steady them, and she gave him a surprised glance before he could pull his hand back.

Her expression softened. "Truly, I've waited so long for this moment, Lieutenant."

"I know." His smile was hesitant, as common sense warned him they could still reach a dead end. The woman with Kepler might not be Jewel.

Leaning back against the seat, Colin gazed out the window as the taxi drove south along the avenue de l'Opéra. Passing the majestic Palais Royal, they eventually traveled along the banks of the

Seine and the site of the impressive Musée du Louvre. Farther along rue de Rivoli, he saw the cratered remains of Saint-Gervais Church, which, mere weeks before on Good Friday, had been the first direct hit from the Boche's big Paris gun. The explosion killed almost ninety and injured hundreds more.

The morning had been quiet so far, but seeing the church reminded him once again that the city would soon feel another daily assault from the superguns, and at night the air raids would resume. He'd lain under his hotel bed each night curled in a ball while sirens blared with the coming explosions, preferring the bombs to being trapped in a cramped, dark cellar with other guests. Colin prayed the fake city of Paris would work for the big guns as well as the Gothas, bringing peace to other soldiers affected by the constant shriek of mortars and artillery blasts.

The railway station proved to be a hive of activity. While Colin paid the driver, Miss Reyer retrieved a large embroidered kit bag from the seat beside her and went inside to arrange their tickets.

As soon as he entered the terminal, Colin spotted her striking figure beside the ticket window, where she was speaking with a female conductor. Scores of Allied soldiers on furlough and crowds of Parisians leaving on holiday or escaping the city packed the space.

Colin wondered how many of them were spies.

Large groups of children were being herded toward the platform by white-capped nuns and Red Cross workers, obviously being sent away for their own protection. Seeing the many nervous, tear-streaked little faces struck a pang of sympathy. He'd been told earlier by the desk chief that, since the bombings began in March, thousands of Paris refugees had already fled to Orléans.

Miss Reyer returned with tickets. "We can board now. The train is filling up, so we'll likely need to sit in coach."

The driver had brought their luggage—Colin's portmanteau and Miss Reyer's two hatboxes and small steamer trunk. Colin hailed a porter, and they started toward the platform.

"We're on our way." Exuberance radiated from Miss Reyer's features. "Soon we'll be in Toulouse and can seek out George—"

He reached to press a finger to her lips. "Let's just call him *our friend*, shall we?"

She blinked at him in surprise, and Colin paused over the soft contours of her mouth before dropping his hand. He took a breath. "There are spies all over France, and I imagine they also ride the train. We must take care in discussing anything involving our journey south."

She lowered her gaze and smiled. "Of course, how thoughtless of me."

"It's all right." His attention drifted back to the pretty mouth he'd silenced only moments ago. *Watch yourself, man.* Clearing his throat, he offered his arm. "Shall we?"

They stepped inside the crowded car, and Colin was amazed to spot two seats at the very back. At least they wouldn't need to worry about eavesdroppers sitting behind them.

He ushered her down the aisle, and once they were both ensconced in the plush velvet seats, he watched her take the utmost care fitting the kit bag down beside her feet next to the window. "Have you got eggs in there?"

He intended the remark to induce another smile, but her startled glance told him he'd failed. "I . . . no, of course not. Why would I have eggs?"

"I was only jesting, Miss Reyer." Why was she nervous? His gaze narrowed. "What have you got in that bag?"

"I . . . I carry my cosmetics and perfumes with me. The glass atomizers are fragile."

He could tell when she was lying . . . or at least, not giving him the whole truth. "And . . . ?"

She waved a gloved hand through the air. "Oh, this and that. A woman's personal items." She reached to crack open the bag. "Would you like to take a look for yourself?"

He recoiled at the idea. "That won't be necessary."

She smiled and sat back against the seat. "I've asked Isabelle to call ahead and secure our rooms at the hotel. Connecting rooms, of course."

He'd barely digested the statement when she leaned over to whisper, "I should also mention that you and I are a married couple on this trip."

At that moment, their conductor—the same female from inside the train terminal—moved along the aisle to their seats. "Tickets, *s'il vous plaît*." She smiled. "Is your seating *confortable*, Madame Mabry?"

Miss Reyer nodded, and the woman stamped and returned her ticket.

The conductor eyed Colin next. "Lieutenant Mabry?"

Colin realized his mouth hung open and quickly closed it, handing over his ticket. When she went through to the next car, he leaned close to Miss Reyer and growled, "Thanks for the warning."

She calmly met his gaze and spoke in a hushed tone. "There wasn't sufficient privacy to tell you earlier. Besides, I knew you would handle it. Henri suggested the idea, so I had Isabelle arrange my new passport this morning. For the duration of our quest, I will be Mrs. Johanna Mabry. After all, 'tis only proper we should appear married if we are to travel together with luggage *and* stay in the same hotel." She gave him a sharp look. "Or would you have me risk my reputation?"

He could only stare at the woman whose customary dress consisted of men's trousers and boots. "I trust these connecting rooms will have locks?" When her eyes widened, he added, "I have my honor to protect as well."

She dipped her head as if in assent, and the hat slid to one side. As she hurried to re-pin the grand chapeau into place, Colin suppressed a grin. Miss Reyer seemed to have trouble keeping herself together.

It suddenly struck him—he was traveling with a pretend wife to observe an alleged enemy spy likely posing under a phony name, and while there, he was to deliver plans to a man helping the Parisians to build a fake city. Was nothing real any longer?

He glanced again at the unusual woman seated beside him. It was pointless to get angry. He'd been in Paris just three days and already knew his moods didn't faze her in the least. He chose a different tactic. "Tell me, *Madame Mabry*, about your life in Ireland. Where did you grow up? Go to school? Any other family?"

She stared at him, her mouth slightly open.

"We've got plenty of time before we reach Toulouse, so we may as well get to know one another better." He did smile then. "After all, we *are* man and wife."

Then he leaned close and whispered, "With spies lurking about, it wouldn't do to have anyone catch us in a lie, now, would it?"

She seemed starstruck. Had her face gone pale?

Colin took pity on her. "Fine, I'll begin. My uncle Brian lives on a farm outside of Dublin, with three cows, a henhouse full of chickens, and a few acres to call his own. It's quite beautiful there."

As he spoke, Colin imagined the green hills and quiet fields. Only birdsong, the jingle of the harness, and the snuffle of the old mare used for plowing had interrupted the blessed silence as he turned the soil with his uncle under a winter sun. "The labor was hard, but it was peaceful."

Jo had shied away from the notion of sharing her past with him, yet as he spoke, she relaxed, watching wistful emotion play across his features as clearly as she'd viewed the film scenes at the cinema last night. It was obvious he missed Ireland and the farm.

A sense of kinship felt only by another *Éireannach* settled over her. She'd lived with Moira south of Dublin and knew the sweet smell of hay and the verdant hills of which the lieutenant spoke. It seemed he too had found comfort in those tranquil surroundings.

Jo couldn't forget the way he'd thrown himself onto the ground his first day in Paris, when the siege guns set off an explosion a few blocks away. Nor that evening at the restaurant, when he'd sought to protect her.

She'd been frightened too, but the sight of his chalky face, the terror in his dark eyes—as if demons chased him—had touched a chord of emotion deep inside of her. Each time they traveled through Paris, he wore a tense look, his body lurching forward in the sidecar when the guns found their mark in some part of the city. And last night, she could almost smell his panic as the Gotha bombers resumed their night raids. Afterward, outside the theater, his paleness had lingered, along with a slight tremor in his hand.

Other soldiers who came to the city had similar reactions, especially those fresh from the Front. It always broke her heart to see men startle at the sound of fireworks on Bastille Day, or at the sudden, sharp rap of drums as the band struck up its music. Even the loud clatter of dishes dropped by a clumsy waiter had the power to affect them.

Jo couldn't imagine how the lieutenant had coped through the all-night air raids of the previous two days. She cleared her throat. "How long were you in Dublin with your uncle . . . before you returned to London?"

"Seven months. I stayed long enough to ready the fields for spring planting."

She glanced over at the hand that wasn't a hand, lying on the armrest nearest the aisle. "How did you . . . ?"

"Manage?" He'd followed her gaze and lifted the gloved appendage. "It doesn't take much to strap this to a plow and walk behind a horse breaking up ground. And a hook is just the thing for manning a pitchfork or carrying feed bags for the animals." He dropped the prosthetic onto the armrest. "Needless to say, I was determined to recover as soon as possible."

Had he recovered? She thought again of his reaction to the bombs. "How do you manage to eat . . . I mean, other than soup?"

"I come with fittings for every occasion." His smile seemed bitter, and she was sorry she'd asked. He leaned back and arched a brow. "Now your turn, Madame Mabry."

She took a deep breath and began. "Shortly after I was born, my mother took me back to live in Kilcoole, along the coast. My grandfather had married into my grandmother's wealth, and after she died, he spent much of the money on vices, like the horses and the pigeon racing I told you about. The rest of the time, he usually raged at my mother . . . about my circumstances."

As a young girl, Jo often hid away listening to heated arguments between Moira and Grandfather Dougherty. Many times she'd overheard him use words for her like *baseborn* and *misbegotten*, and for his daughter, *harlot* and *slut*.

Jo had heard other terrible names, too. The Gaelic *leanbh tabhartha* was often whispered behind the mocking hands and scornful gazes of the villagers. So often, in fact, that after Grandfather's death, Moira used what remained of her mother's inheritance to send Jo off to a boarding school in England.

She shut out the memory. "Grandfather had a dovecote built into the attic at the manor house and secured about twenty pigeons. I was allowed to help him raise and train the birds."

"Much like your work at Vernon."

She nodded. "The birds are my passion. . . ."

A slight stirring against her foot made Jo pause. Reaching toward the kit bag, she pretended to fuss with the floral scarf lying inside the opening. *Rest easy, Little Corporal. All is well.*

She straightened then and turned to him, pulse racing. Had he noticed anything?

The lieutenant wore the same look of mild curiosity, and Jo let out a sigh. Her secret was safe. "I was lucky to get the job with

André." She smoothed her skirt. "I actually started out as a dress-maker's assistant here in Paris. Isabelle was a client."

He smiled. "For some reason, I'm not surprised you would pre-fer working with birds to sewing."

She sighed. "In truth, I loathed having to mend uniforms in Madame Clément's shop."

"I think my sister, Grace, would agree with you. She dislikes needlework intensely."

"Tell me about her."

"She is actually my twin, though we don't look anything alike. Her locks are as red as hot coals, and at times she has a temper to match."

Hearing the affection in his tone, Jo thought Miss Mabry fortu-nate to have such a doting brother. "What about the rest of your family? I read in the *Times* that your father owns a tea shop. What about your mother? The newspaper didn't mention her."

His smiled dimmed. "Mother has been gone these two years. Tuberculosis. And yes, my father is 'steeped' in his tea business. His temperament is much like my sister's. I know he loves us, but as a father, he can occasionally be overbearing."

She nodded. "Moira's nature was like your father's, I think. Seemingly harsh at moments, but I know deep down, her love for me was fierce." She ached as the last memories of her mother swarmed her.

"I notice you call her by her Christian name. Was she not 'Mother' to you?"

Jo shrugged. "My mother did not wish to be confined to a role and preferred the freedom to simply be 'Moira.' I was her small soldier. . . ."

She pursed her lips and glanced away. *Leave the past be, Jo.*

"'Small soldier'? Pardon me, but that seems an odd nickname for a daughter."

She met his gaze. A partial truth would be better than lying.

"My mother was quite energetic in the fight to gain the vote for women in Ireland."

He nodded. "And you carry the same torch?"

Was he making fun of her? Jo bristled. "All women should have equality in deciding the laws of our country."

He laughed. "Yes, I believe you and Grace would get along just fine."

His outburst both pleased and surprised her. When he didn't scowl, he was quite charming. "Your sister is a suffragette, too?"

"She is, and so was my mother." His humor subsided. "I support Grace's efforts wholeheartedly."

It warmed her to learn he didn't fear the notion of a woman having her own ideas and occasionally having better ones than men. "I wish my grandfather had shared your views."

"So he didn't approve of your mother's . . . activities?"

Jo flashed a sardonic look. "That is an understatement. If Moira said a thing was blue, my grandfather would argue it was white. They fought about everything." *Including allegiances.* Before his death, Grandfather had been a stalwart Unionist for Britain, while Jo's mother pledged her support for Irish freedom.

More memories tore through her, and she stared at her lap. A pledge costing dearly . . .

"It must have been difficult for you growing up."

She lifted her face to him, forcing a smile. "At least Moira fought to keep us at home and not incarcerated in one of those institutions for unwed mothers. And I spent much time in the attic with Grandfather's pigeons. I also forgot to mention boarding school in Britain. I was twelve when Moira sent me to Uplands at Poole, near Weymouth, to continue my education."

He seemed surprised. "When did you return?"

Jo toyed with the finger of her glove. "She sent for me just before Christmas in 1915. I was barely seventeen."

Jo would never forget that winter: Moira, driving them through the bitter cold to attend clandestine meetings near Dublin, where they had seen the open caches of German-bought guns and ammunition while Countess Markievicz and other rebel leaders planned a spring uprising. Jo's mother, recruiting women from the *Cumann na mBan* into the more militant Irish Citizen Army even as rebels trained ragtag troops of men into Irish Volunteers.

Nor could she rid herself of the memory of that Wednesday in April, two days after the Easter Rising began. Gunfire raging, Moira, clad in military dress and clutching her rifle, hunkered down in a shoe shop on Sackville Street near Dublin's General Post Office.

The shop had caught fire, and her mother moved outside, taking aim with her rifle at the armed British troops positioned across the street. Jo stood next to the open shop window, too terrified to notice the flames as she watched a stocky soldier move forward with his rifle, shouting for their surrender. Moira responded by firing off a shot, and suddenly the world erupted in a barrage of bullets, her mother disappearing in the haze of smoke. . . .

"What was your grandfather's view about the Rising of '16?"

Jo's head shot up at the lieutenant's question, her throat dry. "He . . . passed away long before the rebellion." She tried to school her thoughts. "What about your uncle?" She dropped her voice. "Is he a Nationalist?"

He nodded. "Uncle Brian supports a free Ireland, but he disagrees with the rashness of taking up arms against British soldiers."

If only Moira had chosen a different path. Anguished, Jo still felt the need to defend her mother's decision. "Some thought it was necessary." She looked away. "They were tired of waiting."

He leaned close to her. "That is no excuse. As a British officer in His Majesty's service, I could never condone rebellion against the king."

She turned to see his face inches from hers and noted the flecks of green in his eyes. "You grew up a Londoner. How can you possibly know what it feels like to be crushed beneath the heel of the British boot?"

His features tightened, yet he guarded his tone. "That, madame, is still no cause for insurrection. While it's true I grew up in London, my mother being English, my father is full-blooded Irish. He worked hard to raise himself from the poverty of Dublin's slums and become the successful businessman he is today." He paused. "I've no doubt Patrick Mabry felt that heel you speak of, but he paid his dues and in the end was victorious . . . without violence."

"How fortunate for him and for your family." She looked past him, working to restrain her temper. "But for every one like your father, there are countless others who continue to struggle in Ireland. They long for the independence to create their own commerce and establish their own laws. Laws to benefit the Irish first."

His expression eased. "I'll grant you, those ideals seem fair enough. In truth, with the exception of the months I spent with my uncle, I'm unfamiliar with Irish life."

He tipped his head. "So you were seventeen when you arrived in France? It must have been a fearful time for you. How did your . . . how did Moira die?"

Seeing his compassion, Jo swallowed her anger. "It was a very difficult death, and I'd rather not talk about it, if you don't mind."

"Of course." Again he reached to comfort her, his hand on her gloves. "Forgive me. I should not have pried."

He gave her hands a gentle squeeze, then leaned in to whisper, "I hope *our friend* is at the hotel when we arrive."

His warm breath tickled her ear, while the scent of his musky, spiced cologne surrounded her. She whispered back, "Isabelle was not able to tell me much. Except she thinks him a friend to Henri."

"Well, good old Henri certainly had a change of heart in our favor."

She nodded, relieved to be back on safe ground. "Doubtless Isabelle had something to do with his decision to help."

"I am certain she had everything to do with it." He smiled at her then, and Jo was struck anew by how handsome he looked when he wasn't scowling. "As my future brother-in-law would tell you, there is nothing a man wouldn't do for the woman he loves."

Her heart gave an unexpected leap. "Such as?"

He leaned back in the seat and lowered his head. "Lord Walenford saved my life at the Front, and it was all for my sister's sake."

"Truly?" Jo's gaze returned to the wooden hand on the armrest. "Will you . . . tell me what happened?"

"Not much to tell. I was buried for days inside a collapsed tunnel at Passchendaele in Belgium."

She drew in a gulp of air and reached for her throat. Even imagining his circumstances made breathing difficult. "How did you get out? Were you alone?"

"It was quite miraculous. His lordship had flown across the channel and arrived at the battlefield. Before that, I was listed as missing, until someone figured out I'd been assigned to help the tunnelers plant explosives. I'm still not certain about all of the details, but I remember lying there in the dark, praying to God to deliver me, and suddenly I thought He'd answered."

"God . . . answered you?"

"He did." A faint smile touched his lips. "Though it was Jack's voice I heard. My sister's fiancé had somehow managed to figure out our approximate location." He hesitated. "And no, I wasn't alone. There were three others down there in the collapse."

He turned and stared straight ahead. "They didn't make it."

The last few days had been hellish: four lives whittled down to just himself and Richards. The meager stores of Boche food they'd discovered in the underground cache were gone, and his water bottle lay empty.

He leaned back against the dirt wall of the cramped space, agonizing thirst threatening to overpower him. In the dim light of an electric torch, Colin watched Richards across from him, breathing noisily as he raised his own water bottle to drink.

Another bottle lay beside the older man—Cleese's. He'd died in the initial collapse, so his jug must still be almost full. Colin swallowed against his parched throat, his pulse slow and heavy in his chest.

Richards lowered the water bottle from his lips and held it toward Colin. "Drink, boy. That hand . . . you need your strength."

Colin gazed dully at his left wrist and the belt Richards had helped to tighten. The gangrenous hand was swollen with pus, aching with a pain he could barely manage.

Still, he hesitated, though he stared at the jug Richards held. He glanced back to Cleese's water bottle lying beside the old man.

"Take this before I change my mind." Richards rasped the words, his features twisted in pain as he thrust the bottle at him. His other hand reached for Cleese's bottle. "I have a full one . . . here."

Colin needed no further coaxing. Snatching the jug from the older man's grasp, he took a long pull of cool, sweet water. "Thanks," he muttered afterward, and Richards offered a weak smile as he leaned against the tunnel wall and stared into space.

Sipping sparingly at the water over the next two days, Colin watched Richards begin to rave and thought starvation drove his madness. On the last day before their rescue, the older man finally succumbed, collapsing at his feet. Believing him dead, and with his own borrowed bottle empty, Colin reached for the one Richards kept. It too was empty.

He realized he'd never seen Richards take a drink. He checked the inside of the rim with his finger. Bone dry. It seemed clear that Cleese had never filled the jug before the tunnel collapsed. That meant Richards had knowingly given him his own share. . . .

At the time of their rescue, Colin discovered Richards *was* alive, just barely. A few days later, he perished at the field hospital. Doctors claimed extensive internal injuries were the cause, but Colin wasn't convinced. It took weeks into his rehabilitation at Dublin's hospital before he would accept a glass of water from the nurses without a struggle. Even now he forced himself to drink, something that had sparked Miss Reyer's curiosity the other night at the café.

"I'm very sorry, Lieutenant. Now it is I who should apologize for prying."

He blinked at her light touch against his arm.

Her blue eyes held compassion. "It must have been awful for you."

"It was worse for the others." His jaw tightened. "I still wonder why I survived. And at times I . . . struggle with it."

The train slowed, and both looked out the window as they reached Orléans, their first stop. Colin recognized some of the refugees and clusters of frightened children he'd seen on the platform at Paris. The war followed him wherever he went. Taking a deep breath, he checked his watch. "What time did the conductor say we would arrive in Toulouse?"

When she didn't answer, he turned to see Miss Reyer still watching him intently. It was another moment before she roused herself. "Oh yes . . . seven-thirty this evening." She scanned the nearby seats before lowering her voice. "We can ask after our friend at the desk when we check into the hotel."

He nodded, nervous expectancy warring with his impatience. Only hours remained before they spoke with Petit and learned the location of Kepler and Jewel. Perhaps Colin might catch a glimpse of her before the night was done.

He cast a quick glance at the gloved hand. Would she accept him now as he was . . . or run away from him?

Perhaps he wasn't so impatient after all.

CHAPTER

8

BARCELONA, SPAIN

he afternoon sun shone bright as Captain Marcus Weatherford stood beside the quay at Barcelona's coast, watching an old fisherman in a rickety boat toss his nets across the water. East of the quay lay the small coastline community of La Barceloneta, where crowds of tourists sat beneath the awnings of open beach cafés, sipping *horchatas* or sparkling *cava*, and sampling an assortment of *tapas*. He wondered how many spies, German and Allied alike, were seated among the throng, watching for U-boats or some unmarked Allied vessel straying too close to Spain's neutral shores.

Despite the cool breezes coming off the Mediterranean, the sun's warmth made Marcus glad for the lightweight linen suit he wore instead of his woolen naval uniform. He adjusted the brim of his felt hat to shade his eyes and turned back to gaze at the busy port behind him, then toward the city as he scanned the seaside street of Ronda Litoral, and the Plaça del Portal de la Pau, with its monument to Columbus. Beyond the statue lay the busy promenade of La Rambla—and with it, the hope that today would be the day the German master spy, Zero, approached him to discuss the deal he had entered into with the Allies.

Marcus withdrew his chain watch from his vest coat pocket and rechecked the time. He wasn't surprised to discover that two o'clock had come and gone. For weeks he'd been in Barcelona, each day coming to the agreed-upon meeting place at 1400 hours, yet once again he saw nothing of the man he was supposed to meet.

His eyes drifted to the tiny photograph opposite the face of the watch, and his heart constricted at the familiar image of his sweetheart, Clare Danner. Her dark hair and gray eyes made him realize just how long he'd been away from Britain and all he held dear. Clare, his family, even his close friend Jack Benningham, who must be wondering why his best man had disappeared.

Snapping the watch closed, Marcus quelled another urge to return home. While each day of the past few weeks had tested his patience, he knew surveillance was often a waiting game. And the stakes had never been higher. Stealing the infamous Black Book from the Germans was a coup for which the Allies would have paid a king's ransom. And if Zero ever did decide to make an appearance, the tell-all book would be within their grasp.

Again Marcus surveyed the crowd at the beach café. He'd been told his contact wore many disguises, and he wondered if Zero was already in the area, watching him.

They had met once in Paris, a year ago, during the trial of the Dutch spy Mata Hari. Marcus sat next to a French journalist, Philippe Tremont, who was there covering the trial. Both men shared mixed feelings about the fairness of the courtroom procedure, and as Tremont was registered at his hotel, they later discussed their similar opinions over dinner, then again at breakfast the following morning. Marcus found he liked the man, sensing compassion and a brilliant mind behind Tremont's quiet speech and piercing blue eyes.

At the time, Marcus had no idea the Frenchman was one of the most notorious German agents in Europe. Then a month ago, he received an urgent summons from "C"—Captain Sir Mansfield George Smith-Cumming, head of the British Secret Service, who told him "Philippe Tremont" had requested a rendezvous in Spain with his old friend.

For MI6, the purpose of the meeting was crucial, not only to aid in the defection of a German master spy to the Allies, but to obtain the "book of forty thousand names" that Zero promised to provide. The kaiser's secret weapon, the book contained the scandalous secrets of Europe's most prominent and powerful persons, which if used to Germany's advantage, could change the entire outcome of the war.

Marcus rubbed the back of his neck. It seemed Zero wasn't planning to show up today, either. He wondered how long C would keep him in Spain and decided he might be forced to remain until the war ended, which could be another year. The thought made him groan.

Pocketing his watch, he considered returning to his temporary office at the British consulate in Barcelona. Instead, he struck out along the quay toward La Barceloneta, absently watching the gulls wheel above the old boat at sea, its hull now laden with fish. The notion of *tapas* and a glass of *sangria* sounded much more appealing.

He hadn't gone far along the shoreline when he spotted an elderly gentleman seated on a bench behind a canvas and easel. The grassy spot where the artist had taken up residence was set back from the quay and hidden in the shade of leafy green plane trees.

The hair on his nape rose. Marcus had been coming to the quay for weeks, yet this was the first time he'd noticed the man. Increasing his stride, he approached the old painter. "*Bona tarda, senyor.* A beautiful day, isn't it?"

The man paused, one gnarled hand gripping the brush. Beneath his brown cap, the wrinkled face was dark and contrasted sharply with his snowy white beard and moustache.

"*Sí, senyor*, and plenty of fish to be had in the sea."

Marcus darted a glance toward the old man in the boat. "He is your subject?"

The aged artist nodded, and Marcus took a step closer. "May I please see your work?"

In response, the old man leaned back with his brush, allowing him a closer look.

Marcus stepped around to study the scene, admiring how well the artist had captured the essence of the old fisherman at sea with his boat, gulls swooping down in an effort to steal his fish. "You have remarkable talent, *senyor*."

The elderly man looked up and smiled. "Thank you, Marcus."

Hearing the quiet statement, Marcus froze. He searched the wizened face and finally recognized the eyes, brilliant blue and full of intelligence.

"Philippe Tremont." Heart hammering, he fought for calm. "Or should I call you Zero?"

The artist shrugged and shot him a sideways glance. "Today I prefer Monet."

"How long have you been in Barcelona?"

He turned back to his work. "A few days."

Marcus stifled his anger. "I hope you've enjoyed playing your games."

"Just hiding in plain sight." He flashed Marcus another smile. "The sign of a good spy."

Zero removed the painting from the easel and reached for a fresh canvas. As he began mixing paints together on a small hand-held board, he met Marcus's stare. "A year ago in Paris, I decided you were a man with a sharp mind. I knew you would find me eventually."

He indicated the bench adjacent to his own. "Now you sit there.

I'll paint your portrait while we speak. That way, we can watch each other's back."

Marcus did as he asked, and a moment later, Zero made the first brush stroke against the canvas. "When last we met, you were still a lieutenant, but I have seen you at the consulate in your uniform. Congratulations on the promotion, Captain." Zero filled his brush. "I also know about your work at Cambrai. For such a young man—thirty, perhaps?—you are very clever."

Marcus clasped his hands together and leaned forward. "I didn't realize you invited me here to discuss my accomplishments. Suppose you tell me about the Black Book instead."

Zero ignored the question and reached for more paint. "I thought as my friend, Marcus, you would be interested to know why I have decided to defect."

Admittedly it was one of the first questions Marcus had asked C. "I'm listening."

"I should really start at the beginning. I was born to German parents sent to France as 'fixed posts' back in seventy-one, shortly after the Franco-Prussian War—part of a colonization plan by Wilhelm Stieber, the German Empire's head of espionage at the time. My parents and others were instructed to infiltrate French life while keeping surveillance. They reported any new fortifications and advancements, military or social, and people's prevailing political sentiment, which of course was ever changing."

Again Zero paused to wet his brush. "My father lived modestly, working as a grocer. He was well liked by our neighbors and involved in the community. His secret job, however, was to act as a collection point for information from other German plants in France—waiters, hotel maids, barbers, clerks, brothel owners—working in embassy cities like Paris and Tours, or playgrounds of the rich, like Biarritz and Monte Carlo. For years, they gave my father secrets about the most powerful and influential men in Europe, to be used one day to further the German cause."

Marcus leaned back and crossed his arms. "The Black Book."

Zero nodded and kept painting. "When I was still a child, I showed an aptitude for art, so my father encouraged my painting. My skill increased as I grew older, and once I became a young man and discovered the truth about my roots, I was captivated with the idea of becoming a spy alongside my father. I was sent throughout France to paint, but of course I first had to learn a particular method taught to me by another German artist." He paused with the brush in hand. "Do you know about steganography?"

"I know it's an ancient art. The ability to hide images or information within other images."

"Very good." Zero smiled. "Steganography enabled me to paint critical intelligence into my scenes, and only the trained eye could detect my forested mountain was in truth a new factory or armory. A scenic outcropping near the shore or a rocky island at sea was in reality a new ship or port building."

"Impressive." Marcus frowned as he wondered how much intelligence the Boche spies in Britain had already gathered in the same way, and what the Admiralty knew about it.

"When the war broke out, I was conscripted into the French Army." Zero grimaced. "A contingency I was not prepared for. I arranged to be taken prisoner by the German Army at the Battle of Champagne. Once I spoke with the camp *kommandant*, he made inquiries, and I was fortunate to be sent on to the German spy school at Antwerp."

"*Fräulein Doktor?*" Marcus had heard rumors about the mysterious German woman who ran the espionage school in occupied Belgium.

Zero nodded, dipping his brush into a cleaning jar. "Eventually I emerged as Zero, taking on any assignment that might hasten a German victory."

"I've read the reports. You've wreaked your share of havoc on the Allies over the past three years. With your talent for evading arrest, you continue to frustrate the French. And now it seems the Americans cannot find you."

Zero's blue eyes gleamed. "Their G-2 agents have been trying to keep up with me."

"Which brings us back to the start of our conversation." Marcus straightened, relaxing his arms. "Why *have* you decided to defect?"

The older man reached for a rag to wipe his hands. "When you saw me last year in Paris, I was already becoming disillusioned with the kaiser's campaign for power. A regime that chooses to blind itself to the hardship and needs of its own people is doomed to failure. Like your countrymen, mine are also exhausted and impoverished by the war. The numbers who wish for an end to it and to form a new republic grow steadily. Also . . ."

He paused, and Marcus eyed him sharply. "What?"

Zero sighed. "Despite all I have done, with the passing of years, I realize I am more French than German. Painting a landscape is one thing, but providing intelligence that leads to the sabotage of a ship full of men or the deaths of French soldiers is quite another."

His aged features hardened. "I have made this arrangement for amnesty with the Americans because I believe they are my best chance among the Allies. I am certain the French still wish me dead."

Marcus couldn't argue the point. "And?"

Zero dropped the rag back onto the bench. "In return, I will hand over the Black Book, after all of my conditions are met."

"Exactly when will that happen?" Marcus was tired of waiting.

Zero's expression eased. "I apologize for keeping you here so long, Marcus. I had to take care of an important errand once I received word a precious package I had been waiting for was delivered by another agent."

Relief lifted Marcus's spirits. "And this has been accomplished."

"I believe so. However, a good spy never trusts another spy, even a fellow German." Zero's blue gaze penetrated his. "That is why I need you. In Paris, I realized you were an honorable and fair man. You will go and verify the package is what I asked for. Once you confirm, I will set up the time and place of our meeting and the transfer of the Black Book." He hesitated. "If I find the Allies have tricked me, the deal is off."

Marcus's pulse pounded. "Where is this package?"

Zero removed the canvas and turned it around so he could see it.

Instead of his portrait, Marcus stared at the painting of a city, as though seen from a hillside. Rose-colored buildings with red ochre rooftops sprawled among the leafy tops of trees, while in the foreground, a dark green river drifted lazily beneath a vaulted arch bridge. "What place is that?"

"*La Ville Rose*, my friend." Zero smiled at him. "Toulouse."

CHAPTER

9

TOULOUSE, FRANCE

he sunset was a mere shadow on the horizon by the time the train arrived at the Toulouse station. Colin disembarked with "Mrs. Mabry," and after arranging for a porter to gather their luggage, they made their way outside the terminal to the lamplit street.

The porter hailed them a cab, and while their baggage was being stowed in the taxi's boot, Colin and Miss Reyer slipped inside the shadowy confines of the car.

"I think, Lieutenant, we should start calling one another by our Christian names." Miss Reyer spoke in a low voice, tilting her head to peer at him from beneath her brim. "After all, as you said earlier, we must maintain our cover as husband and wife to prevent any accidental slips. Do you agree?"

Colin nodded just before the driver opened the door and slid behind the wheel.

"Hôtel Blanc, s'il vous plaît."

As he gave the order, the cab moved forward, traveling west along Toulouse's dark, quiet streets. The tension in Colin's shoulders eased as he breathed in the cool night air blowing through the open window.

The train trip to Toulouse had been long and exhausting. After their stop in Orléans, they traveled on to Limoges, Montauban, and finally Toulouse, with a few other stops in between. He and Miss Reyer had been confined for hours in small, often cramped spaces and subjected to the stifling body heat and chatter of several other passengers.

Colin returned his attention to the illuminated tree-lined causeway taking them westward from the Toulouse station. Eventually the cab slowed near a square with a small grassy area dotted with more trees, a fountain at its center. He could hear the rush of water and see the shadow of a statue rising above the pool.

"Is that a park?" Miss Reyer's gaze had followed his direction.

"Lafayette Square." The driver glanced toward the fountain. "The statue of Goudouli, our beloved poet, sits inside the waterworks."

The cab continued beyond the square and soon pulled up to a multistoried brick building on rue Léon Gambetta. While the driver gathered up their bags, Colin and Miss Reyer alighted to enter the lushly decorated lobby.

A swarthy, barrel-chested man in suit and tie stood behind the desk, smiling expectantly. "*Bonsoir*, madame, Lieutenant. Welcome to Hôtel Blanc. What is your pleasure?"

Miss Reyer stepped forward. "Monsieur, I believe you have a reservation for Lieutenant and Madame Mabry?"

The hotel clerk reached for his reservation book and used a finger to scan the page. "I see no reservation, madame." He gave her an apologetic look. "When did you request it?"

"The telegram was sent to you early this morning from Mademoiselle Moreau in Paris."

He turned and sifted through a box of papers behind the desk, then swung around, shaking his head. "*Non.* I am sorry, there is no telegram." He smiled. "This is not a problem, however. We do have a room available."

Miss Reyer gripped the handle on her cloth kit bag, her stance rigid. "We require connecting rooms, if you please."

As the clerk glanced between Colin and "Madame Mabry," his accommodating mood dimmed. "I am sorry, madame. I have no connecting rooms available at the moment. I can offer you only a single room."

Miss Reyer set down the kit bag and crossed her arms. "That is simply unacceptable."

Colin almost laughed at the tinge of red igniting her cheeks. So much for maintaining propriety.

She looked to him suddenly, jerking her head slightly toward the clerk as if Colin should help. He shrugged, unable to keep the smile from his lips. He couldn't wait to see how she would extricate herself from the awkward situation.

It didn't take long. Miss Reyer's eyes blazed at him before she returned her attention to the harried clerk. "Monsieur, please. Have pity. My husband, when he sleeps . . . his snoring could awaken the dead." She leaned close to the desk. "A wound he received during the war . . ."

The clerk's frown eased, and he looked to Colin as if for corroboration. Colin gave him a brief nod, admittedly impressed by Miss Reyer's quick wit.

"Let me see what I can do, madame. A moment." The clerk perused the warren of boxes along the back wall, many of which contained keys. He finally selected two. "I can offer you and your husband two single rooms directly across the hall from one another. Is this acceptable?"

Miss Reyer's relief was almost comical. "That will certainly do. Until connecting rooms become available, of course."

"Of course, madame."

The clerk retrieved the hotel register, and once they had both signed their names, Colin surveyed the empty lobby. He turned to the clerk. "We would like to speak with Monsieur George Petit, if he is available. Can you please get a message to him?"

"Petit? Why, he is the hotel porter." The swarthy man behind the desk guffawed before appraising him with dark eyes. "Why are you so interested in a porter?"

Miss Reyer turned to raise a brow at Colin, a mocking smile on her lips.

Touché. Colin plunged ahead. "We met a couple on the train who recommended Petit by name. Said the chap provided them with superior service and was a credit to this hotel." He didn't like having to lie, but it seemed necessary.

Miss Reyer gave him a slight nod, her eyes shining with admiration.

The clerk snorted. "A porter." He rang the silver bell on the desk. "Petit! *Venez ici!*"

A tall, slim, clean-shaven man in dark gray livery soon emerged from across the lobby, pushing a freestanding wheeled trolley.

"Petit, you seem to have a reputation to uphold. Take Madame and Lieutenant Mabry's bags up to rooms 308 and 309."

Petit shot Colin and Miss Reyer a curious glance before loading their luggage onto the trolley. As the three walked toward the elevator, Colin and Miss Reyer exchanged another look. This porter was not the man in the photograph.

The elevator operator, a young boy garbed in the same gray uniform, let them out onto their floor. Petit led the way with the trolley down the empty hall before pausing in front of their rooms. Once Miss Reyer indicated her luggage, he unlocked her door and deposited her things inside, then did the same for Colin.

When he returned to the hall, Colin offered him a few francs.

"*Merci.*" The porter pocketed the money. "Will there be anything else, Lieutenant?"

"You're George Petit, correct?"

The porter's expression turned guarded. "I am, monsieur."

Colin's heart thumped in his chest as he withdrew the photograph of the dark-haired stranger and held it up for Petit's inspection. "We are looking for this man. Do you know him?"

Miss Reyer had reemerged from her room to stand in her doorway. Colin flipped the picture to show Petit the message on the back. "Henri Lacourt said you could help us."

Petit looked up slowly, confusion clouding his dark eyes. He glanced at Miss Reyer, then back at Colin. "*Pardon*, monsieur, madame, but I do not know the man in the photograph. Nor do I know any Monsieur Lacourt." He offered a weak smile. "I am sorry. If there will be nothing else, I hope you both enjoy your stay with us."

Colin's mood plummeted as he gripped the photograph and watched the porter depart with the trolley. Titan's teeth! Had Henri Lacourt sent him on a fool's errand after all?

"Goodness. Now what?"

He glanced at Miss Reyer before checking the time on his watch. Almost nine o'clock. "It's too late to contact Lacourt in Paris tonight."

Colin pocketed the photograph, his hand brushing against Gambette's dispatch. "I must leave now to run a quick errand for my Paris office. I should return within the hour. Will you join me for dinner downstairs? I believe the hotel restaurant is open until eleven."

She leaned against the doorjamb, her features pale. "I'm sorry, but I'm quite done in. All the traveling today has worn me out. I'll call for room service and see you in the morning."

"Of course." Colin watched her retreat behind the door, his spirits dampened. He'd hoped to have her company at dinner to discuss the reasons Henri Lacourt might have sent them on a wild goose chase. Still, he understood her exhaustion. The day's travel had taken its toll on them both, and the prosthetic sleeve made his old wound ache.

He checked his room before returning downstairs and had the swarthy clerk arrange a cab. According to MI6, Monsieur Gambette had a flat on rue Lafayette. It took only minutes to arrive at the lighted street in front of a row of Art Nouveau *appartements*.

Colin looked at the driver. "Wait for me. I won't be long."

Climbing the stone steps to Gambette's front door, he exercised the brass knocker, and a woman in service dress soon answered to inform him her employer was out for the evening. With the promise to return the following day, Colin made his retreat to the waiting cab, his frustration mounting. It seemed his first night in Toulouse was determined to be a failure.

Back at the hotel, he entered the elegant restaurant. A few people were still dining late: a French soldier and his sweetheart sat near the window, holding hands across the table, while in a quiet corner, a well-dressed elderly couple enjoyed their meal.

Three other men, two in uniform and one clad in a business suit, drank their wine and feasted on servings of *cassoulet*, the simple meat and bean dish advertised as the night's special. Colin wondered if food was more plentiful this far south, or if Toulouse adhered to the same rationing laws as Paris. Either way, he felt a sense of guilty pleasure in knowing he'd put more distance between himself and the siege guns.

Once the waiter came and seated him, Colin chose a sandwich and bowl of soup from the menu, both easy enough for him to maneuver. When his water arrived, he stared at the full glass, hesitating the barest moment before raising it to his lips to drink thirstily, blocking his memory of the ghosts in his past.

He gazed at the other patrons eating and wondered if Miss Reyer—Johanna—had ordered room service as she'd planned. Likely she now slept.

Recalling their conversation on the train, especially about Ireland, he couldn't help smiling. The woman was feisty, much like his sister, Grace, when she got her back up.

Johanna was also a bit of a rebel, and though he'd conceded to her argument on the rights of women, Colin couldn't imagine turning his back on king and country and all that he'd fought for. Moira's nature sounded equally rebellious, if not more so. The woman not only defied convention with her daughter's scandalous birth but had been consumed with the women's suffrage movement to the point of calling her own child a "small soldier."

He wondered if Johanna's father ever offered for Moira's hand, or if he'd simply abandoned the woman to return to his daughter Jewel in Havrincourt.

Colin tried to imagine seventeen-year-old Johanna crossing the sea to arrive alone in France after her mother's death. She'd been eking out a living in Paris mending uniforms at the age when he'd been at Harrow School in London, preparing for his examinations and playing rugby.

It was by Providence she'd met the Moreaus, who truly seemed concerned for her welfare. Many young women would not have been so fortunate.

"Here you are, monsieur. *Bon appétit.*"

The waiter set his meal down in front of him, and Colin's stomach rumbled. Hours had passed since he'd last eaten, and he murmured a prayer of thanks before he reached for the sandwich and tucked in with gusto. While he ate, he considered the time he and Johanna had wasted traveling south to this place. Why had Lacourt sent them all the way to Toulouse?

He would call Paris in the morning and get some straight answers—a seemingly difficult achievement with these French. No other recourse was open to him, except to go home, and he'd resolved to stay for Jewel's sake. Of course, not knowing if Kepler was the man in the photograph made his odds of finding her in this place nearly impossible.

The well-dressed couple passed by his table, and when Colin looked up, they smiled. The rest of the room had cleared out.

"You certainly take your time. The restaurant is empty."

His mood lifted at the sight of Johanna. She carried two cups of steaming tea and set one down in front of him before taking the opposite chair. "In fact, you are the last person here."

"No longer true since you've arrived."

She rolled her eyes. "Have you considered the poor cook may wish to go home?"

His response was to raise his teacup in gratitude before sipping at the hot brew. She eyed him from across the table, shaking her head, and Colin watched as a lock of golden-blond hair loosened from her pinned coif to fall against her shoulder.

He almost grinned.

She must have noticed the direction of his gaze; she hastily tucked the loose strand behind a pearl-bobbed ear.

"I thought you would be fast asleep by now."

She shrugged. "I thought to come down and keep you company, at least for a time. After all, we have to keep up the appearance . . ."

"Of a loving husband and wife?"

He did smile then, and her cheeks flushed pink. "Did you accomplish your errand?"

His humor faltered at the reminder of his failure to complete the MI6 assignment. Colin didn't like having to carry the secret information on his person any longer than necessary. "I'm afraid the party I wished to see was not at home."

He was glad she didn't question him further.

She sighed, idly stirring her tea. "We've not had much luck since our arrival, have we?"

"No indeed." Once more he lifted the cup to his lips.

"So you'll telephone Henri tomorrow?"

He nodded. "And he'd better have a good answer. If not, I will contact London."

She leaned forward in the seat, her expression earnest. "Well, I support your decision. I cannot imagine why Henri would send us here for no reason, especially after Isabelle said he was taking a great risk doing us this favor. I do not know him well, but I trust my friend, and she's a very good judge of character." She sat back again. "Truly I don't know what to make of it."

She eyed his empty plate. "How was your meal?"

"Simple fare, but good." The sandwich bread had been coarse, convincing him the rationing laws had spread as far south as Toulouse. "How was yours?"

When she didn't answer, he gave her a pointed look. "Did you eat?"

"I wasn't hungry. Probably too much greasy food on the train."

Colin thought she seemed restless. "Is everything all right?"

"Of course. Please don't worry. If I need to eat, I've got sugar biscuits I pilfered from Isabelle's friend at the *pâtisserie*. I'll be fine until breakfast."

A sudden yawn escaped her, and she slowly rose from her chair. Colin stood as well and could see now that she was completely worn out.

"I fear I shall fall asleep right here at the table if I don't retire." She offered him a wobbly smile. "I'm sure you will get things settled with Agent Lacourt tomorrow, and we will continue our quest. Until then, I bid you good night."

Moving around the table, Colin took her hand and brushed her fingers with a kiss. "For appearances." He winked as he whispered the words, and then released her. "Good night, Johanna."

She stood staring at him a long moment. "Good night . . . Colin."

Her voice was soft, barely above a whisper. She finally turned to leave the empty restaurant, and Colin realized he liked hearing his name on her lips. He was glad they had reached some measure of accord, even if they hadn't spoken of it. He also enjoyed having her company on this trip. There was more to Johanna Reyer than he'd first imagined.

Again he took his seat, having decided the cook would still be cleaning the kitchen for a while. Besides, he wasn't ready for sleep. The three days of shelling in Paris had brought on his nightmares full force.

He continued sipping the Pekoe, savoring the black tea's strong flavor. He wondered if Johanna had packed it along for their trip.

Colin became vaguely aware she hadn't drunk from her cup. He hoped she wasn't feeling ill. If things went according to plan tomorrow, they could resume their search for Jewel and Kepler. Should he speak with Lacourt first . . . or bypass the Frenchman and send a coded telegram to Jack in London? He could get directions to the British attaché in Toulouse. . . .

The room began to shift, and Colin lowered his tea as he reached out with his gloved hand to try to steady himself against the table. His eyelids grew as heavy as rocks, and the faint sound of a rattling dish reached his ears as his cup fell back against the saucer.

Blinking slowly, he stared into the tea, the world around him spinning. He began falling . . .

. . . and slumped unconscious over his empty plate.

Colin awoke the next morning, his head aching like an anvil struck by a hammer. With a groan, he blinked against the bright light as he lay unmoving, taking in his surroundings.

Gold brocade curtains, soft white walls. A secretary desk of dark wood along the opposite wall. His hotel room in Toulouse. Raising his hand to shield his eyes, he noticed he was still in uniform . . . all the way down to his boots.

He lifted his head slightly, issuing another grunt of pain. What was happening? His foggy brain tried to recall the previous night. He remembered the hotel restaurant and Miss Reyer speaking with him. And afterward, the room spinning . . .

Had he been drugged? Colin swallowed at the bitterness in his mouth and, despite the searing pain at his temples, gingerly raised himself to sit on the edge of the bed. Why would someone drug him?

Gambette's document! He plunged his hand inside his tunic pocket and howled in panic. The dispatch was gone!

A further search revealed the photograph and his passport were also missing. Colin's heart raced as he tried to swallow past his parched throat. He glanced toward his portmanteau and saw clear signs of tampering. His room had been searched as well.

Rubbing his temples, Colin tried to ease the incessant throbbing against his brain so he could think. Who had done this?

He remembered staring into the tea. Johanna had brought them each a cup, yet she hadn't touched hers.

His head shot up, and the pain made Colin grit his teeth. Had *she* drugged him?

He rose from the bed, Gambette's document foremost in his mind. Jack's warning of days ago rang in his pounding ears. *"Until you learn more about Miss Reyer's situation, please be on guard. . . ."*

Was the J. *Reyer* on the Allied enemy watch list in fact *Johanna* Reyer? Issuing a growl that was part groan, Colin swayed across the room to his door. He shook his pounding head to clear the cobwebs before he flung the door open and strode across the hall to bang on her door.

No answer. He checked his watch, squinting at the small face. Nearly noon. He'd been out cold for hours!

Colin pounded on her door again, anger in his fist as he recalled that MI6 warned him about "green" soldiers being duped by female spies in Paris. He'd been reduced to a naïve schoolboy. How had he allowed himself to be so completely taken in?

It made sense now why Lacourt had led them astray. The Frenchman must have had his suspicions about Miss Reyer and was using Colin in some kind of scheme to set a trap.

His fist went to the door once more, and suddenly it opened just wide enough for a face to peer out at him. "Colin, it's you!

What's wrong?" Her expression conveyed concern. "Why are you trying to break down my door?"

"Please allow me to enter. I wish to speak with you." His tone rasped with anger and pain. "The jig is up as they say, because I know exactly what you are about."

"You do?" She wet her lips before glancing back into her room. "I'm . . . I'm certain I don't know what you're talking about."

She was definitely hiding something. Leaning close, he hissed, "If you don't let me in now, I shall have to force the door open."

He heard her sharp intake of breath. "I . . . I cannot do that." She raised her chin. "I'm not yet dressed."

She cracked the door a few inches wider. Colin saw her dressing gown wrapped tightly about her. "You seem decent enough to me, *Mrs. Mabry*. Now, shall I force the door, or break it down?"

"No, please!" She glanced behind her. "Give me a moment. I'll let you in."

He flexed his fist, looking around the empty hall as he waited. Once she reopened the door, he strode inside. "I was drugged last night, and my room was searched."

"Oh dear! Are you hurt?" Her worried gaze traveled over him as she closed the door.

"I demand the return of my documents." Ignoring her concern, he blinked against the incessant ache in his head. "I was right, after all. You *are* a spy for the Boche."

"What?" Her pink lips parted slightly, eyes wide. "Have you got a fever, sir? And what documents are you talking about?"

He stood close to her and noted for the first time that she wore her clothing beneath the dressing gown. Was this another of her tricks? "My passport and a . . . dispatch that you took from me after you slipped something into my tea last night so I would pass out."

"You're mad!" Color suffused her face, blue eyes shooting sparks. "Why on earth would I drug you, or search your room? To what purpose? And I didn't take your passport or your . . . your dispatch or whatever it is you think I've stolen."

She waved a hand across the room. "Turn this place upside down if you like, but you'll see that I'm innocent." Abruptly she marched to the bureau and began dumping out the contents of each drawer onto the floor. She opened her luggage and hatboxes and then went to the bed, pulling back the coverlet. Finally she tossed the pillows at him. "Well? Are you going to help, or just stand there as my accuser?"

Her angry expression belied the hurt in her eyes. Colin hesitated, staring at the disarrayed clothing on the floor and at her open luggage. She'd even dumped her reticule's contents onto the bed, now bereft of its cover.

Johanna's argument began to penetrate his pounding skull. Why would she steal his passport and, for that matter, drug him when she needed his help in identifying her sister?

His clear thinking began to return, and he reflected on the effort she'd taken to get him to come to Paris on this elaborate pursuit. Suddenly the involvement of the Moreaus and Lacourt made his whole imagined scheme seem a bit fantastical.

Last night, he'd taken his meal downstairs. Had the *tea* been drugged . . . or the food?

He shifted on his feet as new uncertainty assailed him. If it wasn't Miss Reyer, then who? Colin considered the swarthy hotel clerk. The MI6 desk chief had warned him to watch out for spies on their journey. Was the enemy entrenched in Colin's hotel as well?

Gambette's document. Another groan rose in his throat. He must get back to Paris as quickly as possible and warn them of this breach.

"I need to go. I'm finished here." He turned on his heel to leave.

"Wait!" Miss Reyer called to him. "Surely you are not giving up? We cannot abandon the search, not yet!"

But Colin was already imagining his upcoming court martial as he reached for the door.

"Please, Colin, don't leave me! I promise you, I didn't do any of those things."

He heard the anguish in her tone and swiveled around to face her, wincing at the pressure behind his temples. "I'm only going as far as the British attaché here in Toulouse. By some miracle, I hope to obtain a new passport and contact Paris."

He swung around again, opened the door, and headed down the hall, the pain in his head battling his anxiety at the gravity of his situation. Right at this moment, some enemy spy held secret information on the fake city of Paris. Once the Boche realized what the French were up to, it would mean countless more Parisian deaths!

Colin's thoughts had moved from a court martial to envisioning his firing squad when he glanced up to see Petit's approach from the opposite hall, his trolley full of luggage. When the two men reached the birdcage elevator, the lanky porter let Colin go first before following with the trolley.

Petit whispered to the elevator boy, then handed him a franc. The child dashed out, leaving the porter to close the doors and operate the controls. The elevator began its descent.

"I believe these belong to you, monsieur."

A hand shot out at him from behind the luggage trolley, and Colin staggered at the sight of the photograph, his passport, and the MI6 dispatch for Gambette. Snatching the documents from the man's grasp, he hardly dared breathe as he glanced at the seal on the dispatch.

Still intact. Colin closed his eyes, offering up his silent thanks. To think what might have happened . . .

He stuffed the paperwork inside his tunic pocket and glowered at Petit. "What in blazes are you about, man? First you drug me, then nearly give me heart failure by stealing my papers!"

From behind the trolley, the porter shrugged. "There are enemy spies everywhere, monsieur. I had to make certain you are who

122

you appear to be." His dark eyes held humor. "You notice I did not tamper with your dispatch?"

"That does not excuse you." Colin's scowl deepened. "Tell me who you work for. And let me see *your* passport, George Petit."

This time Petit flashed a grin, and when he spoke, all traces of French disappeared. "Well now, I can't do that, Lieutenant. You'll just have to trust that we're both on the same side."

Colin blinked, his anger diverted. "You are an American?"

Petit nodded. "Texan, born and bred." His amusement fled as he pinned Colin with a sharp look. "The man in that photograph. What's your business with him?"

Colin recovered from his surprise. "It's Kepler, isn't it? I have no business with the captain, only the woman in his company. I'm here to see Jewel Reyer."

A low curse issued from the man behind the luggage trolley. Petit looked angry. "I see Lacourt has been sticking his nose where it doesn't belong."

"That may be, but if she is Jewel, I know the woman. If she is not, Mrs. Mabry and I will be on our way."

The elevator had reached the ground floor. Petit opened the doors before he eyed Colin with an appraising look. "Are you certain you can identify her?"

"I can."

The porter nudged the trolley out first. Colin followed, and as he passed him, Petit spoke in a low voice. "That's good to know, Lieutenant. I'll get back to you tomorrow morning."

Colin watched him push the trolley toward the hotel's exit, his confusion over Petit's last words mingling with a new sense of anticipation. Miss Reyer . . . Johanna was right.

It seemed they were about to continue the quest.

CHAPTER

10

Colin's stomach growled as he strode into the hotel lobby a half hour later, his assignment complete. Grateful to have delivered the sealed document into Monsieur Gambette's hands, he was suddenly ravenous.

He wondered if Miss Rey . . . if Johanna had already eaten, and as he walked toward the elevator, he decided to invite her to join him downstairs for a meal. She could enjoy whatever the menu had to offer while Colin made do with humble pie.

Shame heated his face as he recalled again his outrageous claims against her. He owed her more than an apology after accusing her of drugging him and stealing his documents. Of being an enemy spy.

It would be a miracle if she even answered her door.

Upon reaching their floor, it occurred to him that he'd been in the same clothes since yesterday. Colin ran a hand along his jaw. A shave was in order as well. He spent the next thirty minutes—a record time for him—washing up and changing into a fresh shirt before he walked across the hall to her room.

He was about to knock when he noticed the hotel courtesy card,

Prière de ne pas déranger, hanging from her doorknob. He hesitated. Clearly Johanna did not wish to be disturbed. She could be napping . . . or still fuming over his rude behavior earlier.

He turned away, intending to go back downstairs. Guilt halted his progress, however, and he faced the door, determined to incur her wrath if necessary in order to make his apologies.

Touching his knuckles to the wood, he gave the door a light rap. No answer. He knocked a bit harder. Still no answer. With a sigh, he headed for the elevator. Likely she knew it was him and chose to ignore the summons.

Downstairs, Colin continued to berate himself as he headed toward the restaurant. Nearing the front desk, his spirits rose at the sight of her walking toward the hotel exit.

He glanced toward a few hotel guests seated in the lobby before he hailed her. "Johanna, sweetheart, please wait!"

She paused, turning long enough to glare at him before she swung forward again and kept walking. The abrupt movement caused her large hat to become unmoored and tip to one side.

Once more Colin's gaze darted to the curious faces of the guests. So much for keeping up appearances. He smiled at them, giving a light shrug before he summoned his courage and rushed to catch up with her. "Mrs. Mabry, darling, people are watching—"

"So what if they are?" she hissed at him, her feet still moving forward. "Let them witness you accusing me of more crimes." Hurt laced her voice. "Such as trying to poison you, or . . . or stab you with a dagger—"

"My dear Johanna, please." He reached out and gently clasped her shoulder, and she came to a halt, as though frozen in place. "I have been a complete fool and most humbly beg your forgiveness. My behavior this morning was . . ."

"Unforgivable?" She'd turned her head slightly, allowing him a glimpse of her profile. Colin stared at her soft lips, now pursed, and noted how well their fullness fit with the rest of her delicate features. He swallowed. "You are right, it was most unforgivable. Impossible, in fact."

She swiveled around to face him, her gaze searching his from beneath the skewed hat. At last she spoke, and the anger in her voice ebbed. "As Napoleon would say, 'The word impossible is not in my dictionary.'" She dipped her head, and the hat shifted another inch. "So, I suppose I can forgive you."

"Thank you." He couldn't help smiling, not only because she'd absolved him, but because she had quoted Bonaparte in order to do so. Colin didn't think he'd ever met a more extraordinary woman. Just as he had the previous night, he took her gloved hand and pressed her fingers to his lips. "Would you allow me to show my gratitude over lunch?"

Again she went still for a moment before her smile emerged. "It's a good start."

Passing back by the lobby, Colin met the knowing grins of two older gentlemen seated beside their wives and was relieved to know his exchange with Johanna had been taken as nothing more than a simple lovers' quarrel.

Inside the restaurant, the headwaiter led them to a table near the window. Once they were seated, Johanna began removing her gloves.

"I saw the *Do Not Disturb* sign on your door and thought you might be resting."

She paused with a glove in her hand. "I . . . dislike having strangers in my room when I am not there."

A corner of his mouth lifted. "Like the maid?"

She nodded. "I am particular about my housekeeping."

"I see." Colin winced as he recalled the way she'd torn her room apart earlier that morning, just to prove to him her innocence.

"After learning your room was searched last night, I decided to discourage whoever it might be from trespassing into mine."

He found that bit of logic naïve. Did she really imagine a mere sign would bar an intruder's entry? Colin let the issue ride, choosing instead to enjoy their truce. "Where were you headed before I stopped you?"

She continued removing the other glove. "I thought to visit the Place du Capitole. Since we arrived in the dark last night, I decided today I would take a walking tour of La Ville Rose."

After setting her gloves on the table, she reached up and removed her hat. "Do you know why they call Toulouse the Pink City?"

Colin shook his head absently, observing the way her blond hair glinted in the light from the window. "I'm certain you wish to tell me."

"I have been told it's the brick. The many buildings and churches in the city are made from a terra-cotta stone that gives off a pink hue. And the ochre in the tiled rooftops lends a rosy color as well. Hence, Pink City."

She placed the large hat in the empty chair beside her before turning her attention on him. "So tell me, did you apologize because you finally came to your senses, or have you found the true culprit?"

He admired her directness. "Yes and yes."

One blond brow lifted. "Would you care to elaborate?"

"Why don't we have lunch first. Afterward we can enjoy a stroll outside without risk of being overheard."

"Agreed."

Their waiter soon returned, and they each ordered soup and sandwiches. After finishing their meal, they left the hotel on foot and walked along rue Léon Gambetta for a few blocks until they reached the enormous town square of Place du Capitole.

Colin gazed across to the capitol building, a majestic brick edifice covered in white paint. "Not much of La Ville Rose to see here."

"Yes, what a shame. I thought the terra-cotta color of the buildings we passed along the way quite pretty."

They continued deeper into the cobbled square, noting a few horse-drawn carriages and several trucks and motorcars. On the far side of the arcade, an electric tram ran on a steel track along the perimeter, while at the other end of the square, an open market flourished, flocks of dark umbrellas spread over the stalls to offer shade from the sun.

"So tell me."

"George Petit was the culprit."

"What?" She turned to him, the brim of her hat brushing his shoulder. "The hotel porter drugged you?"

Colin noted her fascination yet hesitated to say more. Could he trust her?

Again he considered the genuine hurt he'd seen in her eyes when he'd wrongly accused her that morning. Plus Johanna had the support of Agent Lacourt of the French Secret Service, as well as French Army Intelligence at the dovecote at Vernon. If she wasn't trustworthy, why was he here? He leaned in. "Petit's a spy after all. And he knows Agent Lacourt." Colin relayed his conversation with Petit in the elevator.

"He's an American?"

Colin nodded. "The Yanks brought over their own secret service last year, along with fresh troops. It seems Petit is one of them."

"When did he say he would get back to you?"

"Tomorrow morning."

They walked on past the arcade and the rose-and-white facades of other government buildings to reach the end of the square. On the next street, a small group of men in faded gray uniforms manned brooms as a pair of *gendarmes* stood by.

Colin grimaced. *Boche prisoners.* So much for leaving the war behind. Yet as he eyed the men, he couldn't help noticing their frayed clothes and subdued expressions as they swept the street.

"They look fairly beaten down, don't they?"

As Johanna gave voice to his thoughts, he turned to her and nodded. "I am grateful to be able to walk the streets without having to go up against these men."

"Indeed." Her smile held understanding. "Shall we head back toward the river?"

They continued on past the prisoners. For a while neither of them spoke, and Colin found he enjoyed their companionable silence. Once they reached the banks of the Garonne, he gazed out at the dark greenish waters, breathing in the musty smells of wet earth. The blue sky overhead held only a smattering of white clouds, and the spring sun felt warm against his shoulders—uncomfortably so in the woolen uniform.

Behind him, the city hummed with the sounds of life—motorcars and trams, even the distant squeal of a train's whistle. "It has been some time since I've not heard gunfire or bombs." He glanced at her, smiling. "I believe I could get used to this."

"What about London?"

"I try to avoid that noisy city as much as possible. Too much like Paris, except not as many bombs."

"If you rarely visit, I suppose you do not frequent Swan's Tea Room?"

"I've been to the establishment once since my return from Ireland. It was the time my father offered me a position. I turned him down."

"Why is that?" Her blue eyes held interest. "Do you have an older brother to inherit the business?"

"No, Grace is my only sibling. My reasons for rejecting the proposal had more to do with the position my father offered. As floor manager, I would be forced to parade among the guests, greeting and seating and enduring their curiosity over my battle scars. And I would have to smile at them through the entire ordeal."

She grinned. "I cannot imagine you holding your temper for two seconds in such a position."

He chuckled. "I admit, the job was too daunting to consider. Fortunately, my brother-to-be, Lord Walenford, offered me a less conspicuous post in the seaside town of Hastings."

"Hastings? Why, the Battle of Hastings was the birthplace of English feudalism. William the Conqueror was a general like Napoleon, and equally driven to command all of Europe."

Colin was amused. "William was crowned King of England. A bit higher up the ladder than a general."

"Ah, but Napoleon became Emperor of France. I think an emperor trumps a king."

He threw his head back and laughed. "You win."

She laughed as well, and it was a wonderful sound. He realized in the four days they had known one another, she hadn't laughed before now.

"So you like Hastings?"

He met her amused countenance. "I found the town somewhat quieter than London, but that was before the siege guns began raining down upon your Paris."

Her smile faded. "You can hear the guns there?"

"Water is a good conductor of sound."

"And yet, you chose to come to Paris to meet me . . . to meet Jewel . . . after receiving my message?"

Seeing her astonishment, Colin's humor faded. "Having to leave Jewel in Havrincourt, and later, believing her dead, has haunted me." His voice softened. "You, Johanna, gave me the chance to redeem myself."

Jo didn't know what to say. When had she ever done something so noble? In truth, Colin's praise made her uncomfortable, knowing she was becoming increasingly drawn to the man who was here for her sister.

She kept thinking about the way he'd called her "sweetheart" and "darling" and pressed a light kiss to her hand. *It's all a ruse, Jo.* She had no business being attracted to him, regardless of Jewel's feelings for Kepler. Jo felt more like a heel than a heroine. "You are a man of honor, Lieutenant Mabry. I am certain my sister will agree once we find her."

His brow creased as he studied her. Likely from surprise over her formal address. Jo longed to change the subject and asked about his life in Hastings. "What kind of work do you do for Lord Walenford?"

"Much like yours, Johanna, though I know little about pigeons. I simply decode the messages they bring over from France."

A thought suddenly struck. "You decoded my message, didn't you?"

An edge of his mouth lifted. "Imagine my surprise."

She reached to fidget with her collar. "Yes . . . well. Do you know why the pigeons return to the dovecote?"

His smile widened. "I know they are trained to do so."

Unnerved by his gaze, Jo began walking the path that ran south along the river. Colin kept in step with her. "It is much the same way as in pigeon racing. The birds have a natural homing ability. Some experts say it has to do with the earth's magnetic force."

"Like a compass with wings?"

"Exactly." She gave him a smile, warming to her subject. "There are other theories too, but no one really knows for certain. Regardless of how they do it, the birds are raised in the loft from hatchlings, fed, and cared for until it is determined they will return to the roost. At that point, they are taken some distance away and tested to see how fast they return."

"How quickly do they fly?"

"Pigeons can average speeds of fifty to seventy miles per hour over long distances. On shorter distances, that can climb to over eighty miles an hour."

He whistled softly. "That fast?"

She nodded. "One of my tasks at the château is to collect the birds into cages and take them on my motorcycle to places like the coast of Brittany or southwest to Orléans. At a prearranged time, I free them, and Sergeant Moreau clocks their return to the loft."

His brows rose. "Fascinating. Do they all come back?"

"Most do, though a few birds have been known to lose their way. Even so, like their cousins the doves, pigeons are monogamous creatures. Once they mate and breed, they will make every effort to return to the loft."

"So, you're saying Little Corporal has a girl waiting back home?"

Jo startled and turned to see his grin. Was Colin merely jesting . . . or had he discovered the secret in her kit bag? "Er . . . yes, he does have a mate at the dovecote in Vernon. In fact, pigeoneers sometimes use a clever trick when racing their birds. To keep the racer motivated to return to the loft, my grandfather would allow his paired birds to spend a brief time together just before a race. He found it often made a considerable difference in flight time."

"Why do I imagine we are speaking of male birds?"

Jo raised her chin. "Females can be just as devoted."

He grinned in response. "So what about the mobile lofts? When I was at the Front, I saw trucks with built-in cages."

"Oh yes, the principle is the same." She smiled at him with enthusiasm. "The birds are raised in the mobile loft and have the ability to return to the same truck, even if it travels a great distance.

"In fact"—Jo scanned the area to make certain they were alone—"our pigeons often go beyond the Front. Sergeant Moreau packs them into tiny baskets attached to small parachutes and the French planes drop them over occupied territory. 'Tis hoped someone French or Belgian will find the basket and answer the interview questions stuffed inside the tiny capsule attached to the bird's leg. Things like location, number of enemy troops, or the area's current situation. Afterward the person releases the bird, and the information makes its way back to the loft."

He emitted another low whistle. "I imagine we British must do something similar with our birds."

Jo was pleased to see him look impressed. "The ploy has been successful for gathering intelligence. Unless, of course, the enemy gets to the basket first. Then they either write in false information before releasing the pigeon home to the Allies, or they substitute one of their own pigeons inside the basket, so an unsuspecting Belgian or French citizen will find it and submit critical information to the enemy, including their name and location."

Gazing at him, her mood sobered. "They are desperate to be saved, you see. But writing in their name usually seals their fate."

"The Boche find the poor sod and then take their revenge."

His dark brows drew together, reminding Jo that he had witnessed war's brutality firsthand. "There are other obstacles to gathering intelligence, of course. At times our birds are hunted down and killed before accomplishing their task. Their natural enemy is the falcon, and the Boche employ flocks of them to kill off as many of our pigeons as possible before they reach home. Once a pigeon is downed, there is the chance the enemy will confiscate any message."

She frowned, thinking about her small white bird and what easy prey he would be for a large falcon. It was her constant fear when he flew. Already her little corporal had paid his dues.

"You seem to know a lot about birds."

Jo heard his admiration, and her mood lifted. "I learned to understand them growing up. I told you on the train, I spent much time with Grandfather's pigeons in Kilcoole."

"Do you ever miss Ireland?"

"In many ways, yes." Jo thought to his earlier description of verdant hills and peaceful vales. "Still, there are parts of my past I do not wish to revisit."

His hazel eyes warmed with compassion. "I think we can all speak to that. I once broke my arm while riding horses with Grace. I was teasing my sister and looked back at her to laugh over my own joke when I rode right into a low-hanging branch. It knocked me right out of the saddle."

A smile tugged at her lips. "It sounds like you got your comeuppance, though it must have been painful. Did she laugh at you?"

"No, she was worried about me, of course. Afterward, though, she was a bit smug. Told me God sees everything." He flashed a rueful smile. "I think He definitely saw me going for the branch, even if I didn't."

Jo nodded. She understood about punishment. "In my small village, I grew up believing God was to be feared. He especially disliked bad children."

Colin stopped and turned to her. "That's not what I meant, Johanna. Grace and I were only jesting. God isn't a tyrant. It was by His grace alone that my arm and not my neck got broken."

She eyed him pensively before glancing at his prosthetic. Jo remembered his talk on the train about the miracle of his rescue from the tunnel and hearing God's voice, only to realize it was Lord Walenford. "What about your hand, Colin? Why didn't God save it?"

Her question seemed to give him pause. "I don't have all the answers, Johanna. What I do know is that the broken arm was due to *my* inattention on the horse. The loss of this"—he raised the stiff, gloved hand—"was due to the enemy's explosives that collapsed the tunnel I was in. Neither was God's doing."

His features softened. "He is like a loving Father, Johanna. God metes out justice and mercy. Even miracles." He paused. "Never anger."

"You speak of miracles." Her words tasted bitter as painful memories of her childhood returned. "I haven't seen any. They were never for children like me."

He reached for her hand, and Jo felt his strength through her glove. "I am sorry you were treated badly. Some people are ignorant, or they get so caught up in their high-and-mighty ways, they become blind to the truth."

His expression turned thoughtful. "You might even say the Lord himself was born under a haze of scandal. His miraculous conception before the wedding would have caused His mother to be stoned to death, if not for the angel who spoke to Joseph in a dream.

"Think of it. God chose the humblest of beginnings. He was born in a lowly stable and lived the life of a carpenter's son. Yet during His time here on earth, He fed thousands, healed the sick, raised the dead, and loved us enough to suffer and die for us." He squeezed her hand. "That means He did it for you too, Johanna. How could God not love you every bit as much?"

Emotion rose in her throat at the sight of the warmth in his eyes. "I wish I could believe what you say, Colin."

"You can, Johanna. It's called faith." His expression was intent. "It's about trusting God and His will, no matter what happens. It can be a struggle at times. . . ." A shadow flitted across his face, and Jo wondered if he was still talking to her or to himself. "But it doesn't change the truth. And if you have that trust, you'll begin to recognize His miracles."

He released her hand. "Anyway, none of us is perfect, even those who consider their own opinion God's law. We all have our faults."

"What are yours?"

Johanna's question gave him pause. For all of his talk of faith, Colin remained shackled by the past. He had told her the note she'd sent him would enable him to redeem himself. But would he ever regain what the war had taken?

His gaze swept across the river. What should he tell her? *I am a man made up of many parts: fear of my nightmares and guilt for leaving a woman I cared about behind with the enemy.*

Cowardice, in being so desperate for thirst that I robbed a soldier of his life. . . . "I have plenty of faults, Johanna." He turned to her. "Perhaps too many to count."

"I can think of one." Her eyes sparkled. "You frown a lot. Particularly at me."

"Do I?" He mustered a smile, determined to shake off his mood. "Well, you can be rather unpredictable. You're never on time, and I hardly understand your logic."

Smiling, she tilted her head up at him. "So, you like predictability?"

Again he noticed how fetching she looked in the hat. "I suppose I do. More so, since returning from the Front. I like knowing what to expect." He raised a brow. "You don't?"

"I admit I'm a terrible judge of time and will forever be trying to improve my failing. But I don't relish having my life so charted that there are no surprises. If I had been more practical, I should never have hopped a boat alone to Paris in the middle of a war, seeking out a father I hardly know. I could have run anywhere else."

"You were running?" Colin eyed her sharply. "Someone was chasing you?"

She quickly looked away. "Just the past."

They had reached the Pont Neuf, and it was Johanna who surveyed the water flowing beneath the arched bridge. Finally she turned to him. "We've walked some distance. I suppose we should start back."

"Would you like me to hail a cab?"

She glanced down at her buttoned shoes. "My poor feet would be most grateful."

Taking her by the arm, Colin led her away from the river and back up toward the street. Soon he found a taxi, and they settled inside for the ride back to the hotel.

"Oh, this is far better than walking!"

As she sighed her obvious relief, Colin grinned. For a moment, he gazed at the woman beside him, considering how little he really knew about Johanna Reyer. And then a sudden, disquieting thought . . .

How much more he still wanted to learn.

J̶ardin des Plantes at noon—Lacourt

Colin found the note with the message lying on the floor of his room the following morning. Because it was near the door, he hoped the messenger had slipped the note beneath the portal and not entered his room uninvited while he slept. Otherwise, the intruder surely would have witnessed his thrashing about during a particularly rough night of dreams.

Tucking the paper into the pocket of his britches, he continued to dress and wondered if seeing the Boche prisoners at Place du Capitole yesterday had triggered his nightmares . . . or maybe it had been his rehashing for Johanna the details of the tunnel explosion. Either way, Colin didn't like the idea of anyone—especially Petit—standing over him when he was in such a vulnerable state.

He pulled on a fresh undershirt and slid the suspenders back into place before heading to the washstand to shave. After pouring water into the basin, he dipped his shaving mug just enough to wet the bar soap, then tucked the vessel into the crook of his left arm and used the brush to whip up a thick white lather.

As he applied the foam to his face, his mind turned to the upcoming meeting with "Lacourt." His mouth curved upward. He'd seen through Petit's ploy—using the Frenchman's name on the missive. If the American thought he was being clever, he was mistaken.

He dropped the brush back into the mug and exchanged them for his safety razor. As he wet the steel and began removing his whiskers, a sense of expectancy filled him. After all the games, he was finally going to get some answers about Jewel and her situation with Kepler.

Colin forced himself to take his time with the razor, impatient to share the news with Johanna at breakfast. She would be overjoyed to know the rendezvous with the American was about to happen.

Warmth filled him as he thought about their walk yesterday along the river. The words he'd spoken to her about faith and unconditional love had given Colin something to reconsider as well: the times he wrestled with his own belief, and the fact he wasn't alone in that struggle.

Johanna's illegitimacy had made her growing-up years difficult, subjected to ignorance and the prejudice of others. It bothered him to think she believed herself beneath God's love and His miracles. Colin had told her how people could be cruel, even unintentionally—something he knew firsthand.

His trips to the rehabilitation center in Dublin had been the worst: the cab driver's gawking stare as he'd dropped Colin off, the fear in a woman's eyes as she scurried along the sidewalk to keep her distance while he entered Richmond Asylum.

As though Colin were a lunatic, and not suffering from what physicians had termed as shell shock.

Scraping away the last of the white lather, he rinsed the razor before gazing into the mirror at the haunted eyes in his clean-shaven face. The doctors told him that being on his uncle's farm and working the land was the best medicine; eventually the nightmares would cease, and he'd be free of their chains.

He prayed the day would come soon.

Once he'd headed downstairs, Colin found Johanna at the concierge's desk. Today she wore a long-sleeved dress of dark blue and a wrap in a blue-and-white-striped design. Her eyes seemed more vivid to him this morning, and he wondered if his words yesterday had made an impression. "Ah, here you are, my darling."

She jerked her head in his direction before glancing at the uniformed concierge behind the desk, who watched their exchange with interest. Johanna held out her hand and smiled at Colin. "You have found me, Husband."

Colin was relieved at her poise and leaned in to brush a light kiss against her cheek. "Well done." Whispering softly against her ear, he caught the faint scent of flowers.

He straightened and held her gloved hand. "Shall we breakfast in the restaurant?"

A soft pink hue colored her cheeks as she eyed him from beneath the large brimmed hat. "I thought we might try something new. The concierge recommends Bistrot Charles, not far from here."

"Lead the way." As she moved ahead toward the exit, Colin followed closely, his hand just grazing the small of her back. Once outside and out of view, he stepped away a few inches and offered her his arm.

"The change in venue is a good idea." He still didn't trust Petit, and any discussion he might have with Johanna about the upcoming meeting needed to happen outside the hotel porter's hearing.

They had turned left, walking along the street in the opposite direction of Place du Capitole. Colin told her about the note as they went, and she caught his arm, halting him. "I should like to go with you to this meeting."

"I think we both know the man I'm to meet is not Henri Lacourt.

And since I have yet to learn Petit's true motives, I want to go alone and see what he has to say."

She eyed him unhappily before she nodded. "All right, you win this time."

He smiled. "Are we having a contest?"

The corners of her mouth lifted. "More like a battle of wills, I'd say. Anyway, you will let me know once you return?"

He agreed just as they arrived in front of the small café with its rustic sign and large frontage window. Pausing outside to read the menu board, Colin realized the rationing was being felt more deeply outside the confines of their luxury hotel. Bread, cheese, and Toulouse sausages were listed as standard fare, while eggs, sugar, and milk were an outrageous price.

Still, they entered the establishment and sat near the back, and within minutes, the proprietor had taken their orders and delivered each a cup of coffee colored with the precious milk.

Sipping her hot drink, Jo gazed at Colin across the table, noting his fresh shave. His spiced scent drifted to her, and she imagined she could still feel the imprint of his kiss on her cheek and his warm breath against her ear as he offered words of praise for her acting ability in front of the hotel concierge.

"What's wrong? Have I missed a spot with the razor?"

"Er . . . no, not at all." She realized she'd been staring and sat up straighter. "So, do you think Petit knows my sister's location?"

Colin reached for his cup and took a sip before he answered. "He was rather cryptic with me yesterday, but I believe he knows quite a bit about Jewel and Captain Kepler. I have to assume they are here in the city. Today I hope to find out where."

Excitement pulsed through her. Jo's dream of meeting Jewel and finding their father now seemed more real than ever before. Again she wondered if her sister would like her. And would she like Jewel? From the words Jo had read in the diary, she thought she would.

Colin had told her what Jewel looked like. If she and her sister were to stand side by side, would Jo be able to recognize their similarities?

Jo also wondered if Jewel knew of her existence even though she hadn't written in her diary about having a sister, nor had she mentioned the fact to Colin. And what about Papa? Would he be glad to see both of his daughters together, or would he be embarrassed about Jo?

Perhaps she would need to win over her sister first. . . .

Sudden nervousness battled her impatience. "I hope she isn't too far away. I wish to meet with her as soon as possible."

"Really, Johanna? I hadn't noticed."

Disarmed by Colin's amused grin, it was a moment before Jo realized she'd stated the obvious. Was it being with him that made her turn into such an idiot?

She tried to redirect the conversation. "No one ever calls me Johanna, you know. My friends call me Jo, and I give you leave to do the same." Leaning forward, she whispered, "Especially since we are posing as man and wife."

He set down his cup and leaned across the table as well, until their faces were close enough that she again noted the green flecks in his hazel eyes. "If you don't mind, Mrs. Mabry, I prefer Johanna. It is a lovely name that carries strength, and it means 'God is gracious.'"

Pushing himself back against the chair, his smile returned. "I think it suits you."

The sudden fire beneath her skin could have ignited a forest, but his words pleased her immensely. Jo tried to steady her rapid pulse. "I don't mind." She glanced down at the napkin in her lap. "And . . . thank you."

He didn't respond, and when she looked up, he was watching

the approaching waiter carry their food. His gaze slid to hers. "Believe me, Johanna, I am as eager as you to finally locate your sister."

"Of course you are." *Jo, once again you are a muttonhead!* She shifted in her seat. Just because Colin thought her name lovely didn't mean he felt the same about *her*. And why should he? They were only *pretending* to be married.

Did she need to be reminded of the reason Colin Mabry had come on this quest in the first place?

Jo was relieved to start tucking into the simple breakfast, and her thoughts soon returned to Colin's upcoming meeting. "Do you know how to get to the Jardin des Plantes?"

He nodded and wiped his mouth with the napkin. "The park is about a mile south of here. I plan to set out in that direction once we return to the hotel."

He set down his napkin and regarded her. "When I read the diary, I also gathered from Jewel's words that Kepler knows how to get to your father." His expression softened. "I imagine you are anxious about that as well."

Her pulse thrummed. "I have waited a long time to find him."

Jo spread butter on the fresh bread. She'd removed her gloves to eat, and the silver dove on her ring gleamed beneath the café's lights.

Abruptly she realized Colin was focused on her hand.

"I remember seeing your ring at the restaurant in Paris." His attention shifted to her. "Did your father give it to you? I only ask because it suddenly occurred to me that Jewel wore a similar band."

"Did she?" Jo paused with the knife in midair, her heart hammering. "I mean . . . yes, Papa gave me the ring when he visited me the one time in Ireland."

She was tantalized by the notion her sister had an identical ring. "If her ring is exactly like mine, then they might be part of a set.

I read somewhere that, centuries ago in medieval Europe, gimmel rings were very popular and used in betrothals. The engaged couple would each wear one of the rings, and when they married, the two bands were fitted together to make the wedding ring. Sometimes a third ring was held by the person who would witness the marriage, and given over during the ceremony."

Jo glanced at the shiny dove. "I hope Jewel still has hers." Her eyes lifted to his. "And I hope she will agree to take me to our father."

"I cannot imagine why not." His smile faded as the dark brows drew together. "Though there is much we must first learn about her situation with Kepler."

"You're right, of course." She handed him a slice of the buttered bread. While Jo knew the danger of getting her hopes up, she still desperately wanted to believe. She looked at him shyly. "I suppose we can hope for a miracle."

Colin paused with the bread in his hand, his hazel eyes warm. "Always, Johanna."

The conviction in his voice raised her spirits, and as she took a bite of her own bread, she determined to try to put his words of yesterday to the test.

If she had faith, perhaps miracles *would* happen.

Colin reached the Jardin des Plantes a few minutes early and stood a moment facing the brick entrance to the park, an old artillery gate likely from Napoleon's day. A smile touched his lips. With Johanna's love for Bonaparte, she would have been captivated by the structure.

He walked past the ironwork gate. Ahead, several statues dotted the woodland grounds, and farther on were scattered park benches and a water fountain. As Colin neared the fountain, he spotted Petit's tall, lean figure clad in the khaki uniform of the American Expeditionary Forces, captain's bars on the epaulettes.

Colin gave a sharp salute when he reached him, and Petit smiled. "At ease, Lieutenant."

"Is that your true rank, or another disguise?"

Petit didn't answer. "Walk with me."

Like two soldiers on furlough, they took to the wide, tree-lined path and strolled through the park, with its sculpted foliage and statues of Greek gods and goddesses. The sweet smell of spring grass and the faint perfume of pink and blue hyacinth clusters bordering the green lawns made him think of Ireland and the time he'd spent with his uncle, a time when war's darkness seemed far away.

The image shattered as he and Petit passed another group of prisoners raking the park clean of the last traces of winter's debris, and Colin remembered why he was there.

They reached the edge of a canal winding leisurely through the park's center. A rustic wickerwork bridge led to a small wilderness area on the other side.

Colin glanced at the number of small dovecotes scattered about the wooded area. "Very scenic, but we're wasting time"—he glanced at Petit—"Monsieur Lacourt."

Petit smiled. "I figured you knew I sent the note. The hotel has a few spies, so using Henri's name seemed best." His features sobered. "I checked on you. Quite the war record." His gaze dropped to Colin's prosthetic. "I imagine the tunnel collapse must have been terrifying."

"You imagine correctly." Colin's tone was curt. "Why did you ask me here, Petit?"

"I'm with the American Corps of Intelligence Police."

Finally some answers. Colin shot him a sardonic smile. "After the drugging incident and the return of my documents, I gathered you were connected with the American Secret Service."

Petit nodded before he squinted up at the clear sky. "The man in your photograph—"

"Kepler?"

"Yes, Kepler. We've had our eyes on him for the past several weeks. Something big in the works that I cannot discuss. He and the woman are to be surveilled only."

"Why are you telling me this?"

Petit turned to him. "Because if you go shootin' off your gun in this herd of longhorns, you'll stir up a stampede."

Colin eyed him with confusion. The American certainly had an odd way with words.

"That means, Lieutenant, this is a highly sensitive assignment, and you and your missus need to leave. Go back to Paris or Britain or wherever you call home. You're not wanted here."

Colin's anger flared, and he leaned toward Petit. "I'm not leaving until I see Jewel."

Petit's features were as hard as stone. "You *are* leaving. G-2 wants you out of Toulouse. Your presence here jeopardizes our mission."

The man's statement gave Colin pause. If the American military intelligence agency was demanding he leave, it was possible MI6 would back up the order, and he would have no choice but to return to Paris.

Colin decided to try reasoning with the American. "Look, Captain, I just want to see her. A year ago, I was in Havrincourt and made a promise to Jewel to return after the war. When I thought she'd died, I gave up hope."

Petit scratched his chin. "So . . . what changed your mind? You said you thought she was dead, and the war's not over."

"Recently, her sister—Mrs. Mabry—contacted me, and I learned Jewel was still alive." He straightened. "It was my duty to come back for her."

Petit's dark gaze bore into him. "Your wife is Jewel Reyer's sister?"

"Johanna is not really my wife; we are just posing as a married couple. Lacourt's idea." Colin explained about the message he'd received from Johanna, his coming to Paris, the diary, and their search for Jewel and the women's father.

"So Mrs. Mabry is Johanna Reyer?" Petit seemed to be trying to keep up. "I imagine it's your reason for separate rooms, then?"

"Well, of course." Colin bit back his exasperation. "Captain, you must see why it's important I get a chance to identify the woman with Kepler. If she's not Jewel, we must take our search elsewhere." He didn't add that he had no idea how to proceed if the latter were the case.

Petit stared at the ground a long moment before he faced Colin. "If I tell you where you can find Kepler and the woman, you need to promise me you won't do anything to arouse their suspicions. Strictly observe, make a confirmation, and report back to me. Are we clear on that?"

"Of course, Captain. I understand discretion."

"Glad to hear it." Petit scanned the immediate area, which was mostly empty. On the other side of the canal, a mother watched her three small children run in the grass, and a young couple stood arm in arm near one of the statues. He turned back to Colin. "Kepler is actually staying at your hotel. In fact, he's been at Hôtel Blanc quite some time. He's posing as a Swiss manufacturer and goes by the alias Monsieur Outis."

So Kepler was a spy. Colin grimaced. "*Outis*. A Greek word meaning 'nobody.'"

"Very good, Lieutenant. So, Mr. Nobody dines each night at eight o'clock at Le Bibent on Place du Capitole."

"I know it." He and Johanna had walked past the restaurant the day before during their visit to the square.

"Frequently, Mrs. Nobody will accompany him."

Jewel? Colin disliked the possibility she was posing as "Mrs. Outis." He knew himself to be honorable in his pretend marriage to Johanna, but Kepler was not to be trusted.

Colin could only pray her virtue remained intact. The possibility she'd been ill used by the bounder . . .

He blocked the thought. "You think they will be together at dinner tonight?"

"It's possible." Petit cocked his head. "I'll warn you, though, seeing her won't be as easy as you think. She dresses in mourning black from head to toe, including a hat and veil. When she's not with Kepler, she keeps to her room."

"So you have not seen her?"

Petit shook his head. "I know she has light-colored hair, because I once saw a blond strand escape the veil. I've also stood beside her on the elevator, and I believe her eyes are a lighter shade, blue or gray. The veil she wears is thick, so it's difficult to know for sure."

Colin found himself growing more aggravated. "Exactly how do I identify a woman shrouded in black when I am not allowed to approach her?"

Petit shrugged, then gave Colin a friendly slap on the back. "Hey, with any luck she'll accompany Kepler to the restaurant tonight, and while she eats, you'll get enough of a glimpse behind the veil to determine if she's Jewel Reyer."

Colin's heart raced at the thought of possibly seeing Jewel this very night. "And if it is her, what then? When can I speak with her?"

"When I say you can." Petit's mouth tightened. "In the meantime, you report back to me. I told you before, there is more going on than you know. Just return to the hotel and give me your answer. We'll work something out from there."

Colin bristled. He knew when he was being pushed around. "I came all the way here from Britain to find her. Are you telling me once I do, I will have to walk away?"

"Yes. I don't know. At least for now." Petit pulled off his cap and ran a hand across his crop of dark hair. "Let's take things one step at a time, shall we? First identify the woman. If she is Jewel Reyer, then we can figure out the rest. And you must give me your word of honor you won't try to contact either of them. It'll be my neck if you do."

Chaotic thoughts crowded Colin's mind as he looked on the serenity of the park. What kind of "something big" did Petit and the Americans believe Jewel was involved in? "Are you telling me she could be an agent . . . for the enemy?"

Petit hesitated. "We don't know for certain."

"Perhaps she had no choice." Jack's words came rushing back, and Colin again considered the woman he'd known a year ago and his recent decision to take her back to Britain as his wife. Before coming to Paris, he'd been confident of her innocence, yet here in Toulouse—knowing Jewel remained with the Boche spy *and* the pair was being surveilled by the Americans—his certainty began to waver.

Colin didn't want to believe her guilty of treason, but if she *was* being coerced . . .

His gut tightened, and he stared at Petit. "Is she in danger?"

"We're watching Kepler pretty close, which provides some measure of protection. Still, it's no guarantee." Petit returned the cap to his head. "I wish I could tell you more, but you understand about orders. I have mine."

Colin nodded. "I'll be at Le Bibent tonight. 2000 hours."

"Will you take Mrs. Mabry with you?"

He studied Petit. "Is that a problem?"

Petit frowned. "Only if she fails to follow my instructions."

"You have my word that Johanna will observe and nothing more."

"Good." Petit's face broke into a wide grin. "By the way, I saw her giving you what for in the lobby yesterday. Hooey, what a firecracker!"

Colin tensed as he stared at the peculiar American.

"Relax, Lieutenant." Petit laid a hand on his shoulder. "A filly who shows a little spirit is the best kind."

Dropping his hand, he turned to start back across the wicker-work bridge. Colin followed.

It seemed their interview was at an end.

As they reached the opposite bank of the canal, Petit halted to watch a pair of swans floating with the gentle current. "I'll leave you to carry on, Lieutenant. Let me know what you find out." He shot a glance over his shoulder. "And good luck."

CHAPTER

12

$\mathcal{C}$olin and Johanna arrived at Le Bibent by cab a few minutes before eight o'clock. The sky had already gone from a dusky orange to a dark indigo, and the lights from inside the restaurant cast a warm glow onto the street from beneath the terrace awning.

He was impressed with Johanna for having readied herself on time, yet he imagined she too was more than a little anxious to see the woman with Kepler.

Before they left the hotel, the desk clerk had given Colin an envelope. Inside was a pair of tickets to a jazz concert later that evening, hosted by the American Red Cross Canteen. A note was included: *My peace offering. Meet you and the missus at 2230.—Lacourt.*

Johanna seemed interested in attending the concert, and Colin was glad Petit felt some remorse for drugging him two nights ago. Though at the moment, their focus was on the restaurant and hopefully finding Jewel seated inside with the man in the photograph.

After paying the driver, Colin stepped from the cab and helped Johanna alight. While he'd brushed out his uniform and put a shine on his brass, she surprised him by wearing a pink dinner dress and

151

matching satin coat, along with silver shoes and a less ostentatious hat in pink and white that sported a black feathery plume.

Altogether she looked quite lovely, the colors enhancing her fair features. She smiled at him, her expression a mix of nervous excitement. "Are you ready?"

Colin's pulse raced. Was he ready? All afternoon, his mind replayed the conversation with Petit. Was Jewel working with Kepler? She'd been with him for months—why hadn't she left? Was there more going on than the Boche spy's promise to take her to her father? Was she being coerced . . . or was it something else?

He exhaled a deep breath and forced a smile, offering Johanna his arm. "Let's go."

The tangy smell of garlic, butter, and sausages wafted from the restaurant as they neared the crowded entrance. Several patrons were seated outside on the terrace, and Colin quickly glanced at their faces but found no one matching the photograph. He looked through the window glass at the full tables and was glad Petit had suggested making a reservation.

Colin released Johanna and was reaching for the door when it suddenly burst open. He took a step back to regain his balance as a tall, stout man in trench coat and hat exited to nearly collide with him.

He caught a glimpse of the gold satin band on the fedora before the man shot him a swift glance. "*Pardon,* monsieur."

Head down again, the man rushed around the corner of the building to the next street.

Colin stared after him, shocked. *Captain Weatherford?*

"Is something wrong?"

Johanna's voice propelled him into action. "Wait here."

Colin brushed past her, racing around the corner to intercept the stranger. Yet when he reached the next street, only shadows greeted him. The man was gone. Had his eyes deceived him?

He returned to Johanna.

"You look like you've seen a ghost."

Colin's memory worked to recall the face he'd seen. "I believe I have."

When he refused to say more, she gave him a curious glance. He pulled the door open and followed her into the restaurant, his thoughts still churning over the strange encounter once they were seated.

"Do you know the man who ran into you out there?"

At Johanna's question, Colin's logic returned, and suddenly the notion that Captain Weatherford was in Toulouse and had just bumped into him seemed preposterous. Surely the captain would have acknowledged him, not tried to make his escape. "I thought he looked familiar, but I was mistaken."

"Well then, 'tis best forgotten. We are here for another reason, after all." She removed her gloves. "Have you spotted them?"

While Colin could hardly forget a stranger had just evaded his pursuit, there was nothing for it now. Johanna was right—they were here for Jewel and Kepler. He saw no sign of the man from the photograph among the restaurant's patrons. "Kepler's not here yet." He checked his watch. "We've a few minutes until eight. Let's hope they are on their way."

She sighed and nodded, then surveyed their surroundings. "This place is quite splendid."

Colin followed her gaze. Beneath rows of lit chandeliers lay a sea of white linen and gleaming silver. Liveried waiters, most of them older men or walking with a distinct limp, carried food trays and crystal pitchers of water and cleared tables after their departing guests.

Le Bibent's elegance was reminiscent of the Belle Epoque. Mirror-paneled walls framed in gold friezes were squeezed among the sculpted cherubs, fleur-de-lis, and gargoyles that rose to a ceiling of painted murals boxed in more gold. A clock hung against one colorful wall, accented on either side by a mythical Greek god.

He breathed in the same mouthwatering aromas he'd detected outside: roasting meats combined with the yeasty smell of bread, and the added perfume of violets arranged in milk-glass vases at the center of each table.

He and Johanna sat at the far end of the room, between two of the mirrored panels, one to his right and the other behind him. While he was pleased with the location—he could see anyone who walked in—Colin found the prospect of observing his own reflection throughout the meal disconcerting. He wondered if others viewed him the way he saw himself: careworn and a bit ragged around the edges, not enough to greatly alter his looks, but not entirely himself.

Below the mirror's edge was the reflection he could not see: his artificial hand lying inert against his lap. The element making him part man, part mechanism. Was that how Jewel would see him tonight?

Did Johanna see him that way?

He gazed across the table to find her engaged in the feminine chore of repinning her hat. Tonight she'd swept her hair into an elaborate coil fastened at her nape. He almost grinned, wondering how long it would take for the neatly tucked hair to come undone.

"What are you smiling at?"

Picking up his menu, he pretended to study it. "We're finally making some headway on this quest. Isn't that reason enough?"

"Yes, after your conversation with . . . Lacourt, I was beginning to wonder if we would have to return to Paris empty-handed."

Colin lowered the menu. Earlier he'd relayed to Johanna all Petit had told him in the park, except for the fact Jewel might need to remain in Toulouse until G-2's plan had reached its conclusion.

Nor had he voiced the possibility she was in league with Kepler. He worried most that both sides could be using Jewel as bait.

"Now you're frowning. Again."

"Sorry." He offered a weak smile. "More woolgathering, I'm afraid."

"I cannot see behind me. Are you still watching the door for Kepler?"

No sooner had she spoken than Colin observed a tall, sturdily built man enter the restaurant. He wore a felt hat and a dark suit with a white carnation in his buttonhole, and he carried an ivory handled cane.

Once the hat came off, Colin's pulse sped up. "It's him."

Johanna started to turn around.

"Careful! You'll draw his attention. Try looking at the mirror behind me to see him once he sits down."

The waiter escorted Kepler to a table along the aisle near them. Angling her menu, Johanna whispered, "Yes, I can see him."

"That's fine, just don't stare."

"Where is my sister?"

Colin glanced toward the empty foyer. "She must have decided to remain at the hotel."

They shared a look of disappointment before returning to perusing their menus. Colin continued his surveillance. Kepler's dark eyes scanned the restaurant and its patrons before he placed his cane on the back of the chair. As the man turned his head, Colin caught sight of the scarred lobe.

Conscious of Petit's warning, he was glad Johanna still seemed engrossed in reading her menu. The Boche spy was clearly on edge, as though he expected to be shadowed.

After taking his seat, Kepler was given a menu. A moment later, the same waiter approached to stand over their table. "*Bonsoir,* monsieur, madame. Have you decided?"

Colin glanced at Johanna.

She held up the menu to the waiter. "I'll have the *confit de canard.*"

Colin had also considered the duck confit but shied away in

favor of the *cassoulet*. He'd noted the patron at the next table eating the dish and using a spoon.

When their orders had been taken, the waiter returned to Kepler and wrote down his selection before disappearing to the kitchen.

The rest of the meal continued leisurely. While Colin thought the food excellent, neither he nor Johanna conversed much due to the circumstances. Occasionally he would glance in Kepler's direction to see the man taking his time enjoying his meal. *Tedium.*

After dinner, the waiter brought them hot tea.

Colin reached for his cup. "It seems this was an unproductive venture."

Johanna smiled, yet he could tell she too was disheartened. "We had to eat in any case, and the meal was delicious."

Her words had a way of cheering him. "I'm glad one of us remains hopeful."

"Didn't you tell me miracles happen to those who believe? Anyway, I don't know what else is to be done at this point, except to try again."

"Indeed." Colin raised the tea, taking a sip while he cast another covert glance at Kepler.

The Boche spy had reached for the small vase of violets at his table. Lifting the vessel, he leaned in as if to smell the flowers while his right hand grazed across the bottom of the vase. A smile formed beneath his dark moustache as though the scent pleased him; then he replaced the vase and plucked a violet from among the bouquet, exchanging it for the carnation in his buttonhole.

Colin set his cup down. Was the flower some kind of signal? Had Kepler sensed he was being watched?

"What is he doing?"

"Wait." He hissed a warning at Johanna. Kepler was rising from the table. He tossed down a few francs and pushed in his chair. "He's leaving."

The Boche spy grabbed up his hat and cane, giving the room a cursory glance. His dark eyes flitted briefly over Colin and Johanna before he turned to make his way toward the exit.

"What was he doing with the violet?"

Johanna's attention was still fixed on the mirror behind him.

"I'm not certain." Colin wondered at the man's odd behavior as well. Had he sought something beneath the vase? And why exchange the flower in his buttonhole?

"Now what do we do?"

He considered her question. "We may have been discovered, or at least Kepler seems to suspect someone is watching him. He could be looking to see who follows. Let's remain here and finish our tea. As it is, we're to meet 'Lacourt' at the Red Cross concert in forty-five minutes."

"A sound plan, considering we have no other option at the moment."

She reached for her tea, and as he raised his own cup, her blue eyes gleamed with amusement. "And I am glad to see you have conquered your fear of poisoned drink."

He shot her a sardonic smile. "I forgot to ask our porter how he got me back to my room the other night, but I imagine he used the luggage trolley. I doubt anyone here wants to haul me all the way back to the hotel."

As if to prove his point, he lifted his cup in a grand gesture. "Anyway, with the exception of my passport, I no longer have anything worth stealing."

I hope my amoureux knows what he is doing, sending me here. This is not part of my job responsibilities.

Clad in her maid's uniform, Odette Tremblay stood at the door of room 309 and adjusted her cap while she scanned the hall for guests. Seeing no one, she removed the service key from her apron pocket and reached for the door.

The *Do Not Disturb* sign hanging on the brass knob brought her up short. Pursing her lips, she considered the telephone call she'd received a few minutes ago. He had assured her the room would be empty.

But what if he was wrong? She decided to rap on the door, just in case. After a minute of silence, Odette inserted the key and turned the handle before slipping inside.

Heart pounding, she surveyed the room and noted the disarray—the bed unmade, clothing strewn across its top, and shoes scattered along opposite ends of the polished floor.

Odette was indeed alone. She took a few deep breaths in an attempt to slow her rapid pulse, then glanced toward the desk, hoping to see what she'd come for and leave quickly.

He had warned her not to remain long. The last thing she wanted was to get caught.

A cloth kit bag rested on the desktop, and beside it were a perfume atomizer, several lace handkerchiefs, and a few cosmetics.

Nothing else.

Again she pressed her lips together. Was it inside the bag?

Odette had already started toward the desk when a soft rustling noise sounded from behind the ornate screen where the washstand cabinet stood. She froze, pulse racing against her throat. Despite the fact she was in uniform, the card on the door forbade anyone trespassing.

She listened for a few moments but heard nothing. Releasing a pent-up breath, she looked back toward the kit bag on the desk. Perhaps it was simply nerves.

A book lay on the padded chair beside the desk.

Elation battled her fear as Odette rushed to retrieve it. Clutching the book to her chest, she shot another glance toward the screen. Hearing nothing, she silently retraced her steps and exited the room.

She glanced along the empty hall before she quickly fanned

through the pages of the diary, searching for the particular place her *amoureux* had suggested she start. Seeing the date, she scanned the first few handwritten lines, and a smile touched her lips. Perfect.

She started to close the book when a short white ribbon escaped the pages to flutter onto the carpeted floor. With a soft gasp, Odette retrieved the narrow satin strip. She eyed the book to try to determine where it had been placed.

The rattle of the elevator drew her attention. Jamming the ribbon back in between the pages, she concealed the diary beneath her apron and strode toward a linen closet at the other end of the hall. It shouldn't take her long to slip inside and read the passage before returning the book to its owner. As for the ribbon . . .

Odette chewed at her lower lip. Her *amoureux* would certainly not be pleased. She could only hope the bookmark's placement hadn't been significant and would go unnoticed.

Either way, she must hurry. No telling when the woman would return.

Jo hugged the thin satin coat tighter around her as she and Colin left Le Bibent and walked arm in arm along the lamplit street toward the Red Cross canteen a few blocks away. She had suggested the fresh air would do them good but now regretted her decision, as the April night had turned out cooler than expected.

She was also conscious of each painful step in the tight silver pumps, although she consoled herself by imagining Isabelle's happiness in knowing she'd dressed up for dinner tonight in her friend's favorite ensemble.

Jo was thankful Colin had slowed his long-legged stride so that she could keep pace without pitching headlong onto the sidewalk.

"Do you believe the flower exchange was meant to signal someone?" She hadn't stopped thinking about Kepler's actions.

"I'm almost certain of it, though I hope it wasn't meant to warn someone about us. Petit told me we were just to observe. I believe Kepler knows he was being watched. If he were to become desperate, it could jeopardize the mission these Americans are involved in."

Desperate was a word beginning to fit Jo's mood. She glanced up at him as they walked. "How shall we ever discover if the woman is Jewel? You are the only one who can confirm her identity, but if she never leaves her room, what are you supposed to do? Storm the door?"

"A disastrous plan, to say the least." His head lowered as he gazed at the sidewalk. "No, I would need a disguise—"

"Exactly!" Jo's heart surged with renewed hope. "She takes her meals in her room, so you could pose as one of the restaurant staff."

He glanced at her, raising his gloved hand. "Not with this, I'm afraid."

"And why not? In case you haven't noticed, there are many here in the city wounded from the war. They must have jobs to support themselves." Jo's need for some kind of plan fueled her determination. "You can do this, Colin. No one would take it amiss to see you working at the hotel. And your French is very good."

He said nothing as they walked on, and Jo finally halted him. They both needed this chance, or the search for Jewel and Papa was over. "Think of it, Colin. You will be able to find out once and for all if the woman is my sister." *And your sweetheart.*

She held his gaze, ignoring the unexpected pang in her chest.

He seemed to consider her words. "I doubt Petit would agree to such a plan, but I'll ask him. Working at the hotel, I'm certain he can make all of the arrangements."

Jo's spirits soared. "Thank you!"

She didn't pause to think before wrapping her arms around his waist in a fierce hug. A moment later, she felt his gloved hand rest against her shoulder.

"Nothing to thank me for yet, but let's hope Petit agrees *and* that I'm able to pull this off. For both our sakes."

His voice was gruff, and Jo's heart raced as he held her. When the weight of his hand lifted, she released him and stepped back, averting her eyes toward the ground.

What was happening to her? And why did she have this constant ache? *Colin is here for Jewel, not you!* "I seem to have become . . . carried away. I apologize."

His fingers were warm against her chin as he lifted her face to his. Amusement filled his expression. "You need not apologize, Mrs. Mabry. After all, it is proper for a wife to show affection toward her husband."

Jo stood breathless, unable to tear her gaze from his. "And the husband? What does he show his wife?"

She didn't know why she'd asked the question, but Colin's smile faded as he let his hand fall to his side and stepped back. "He shows her honor and respect, and he always does what is right by her."

He spoke in a low voice, his words as solemn as if he'd made a promise to heaven itself. Jo's heart beat rapidly. She had a fleeting thought about her sister and Kepler, wondering if Jewel's attraction to the Boche remained the same. If not, Colin still stood a chance with her.

Jo ignored the persistent ache. She hoped her sister would be deserving of such a man.

CHAPTER

13

I t's all set." The following afternoon Petit was again dressed as the hotel's porter as he entered Colin's room. "Monsieur Outis hopped a tram a few minutes ago at the square, and I've got someone keeping an eye on him. He likes to sight-see and seems especially interested in the hydroelectric plant on the Garonne River, so he'll be away for a few hours."

Behind him, Johanna entered, her arms laden with clothing. Petit glanced at the bundle as he closed the door. "One of the waiters downstairs is about your size, but I won't guarantee the fit. I've been a lot of things in my life, but never a tailor."

Despite his fatigue from a grueling night's sleep, Colin's pulse jumped as he eyed the white shirt and jacket, black bow tie, dark pants, and shoes that would transform him into one of the hotel wait staff. "I'll make them work."

"Good." Petit checked his timepiece. "Madame Outis usually calls to order her midday meal shortly after two, so you have an hour to dress for the part. Once the food is ready, I'll telephone your room and let it ring once. That's your signal to meet me at the elevator. I'll have the cart with her tray, and from there you can take the meal upstairs to the next floor."

Colin had talked with Petit before the concert last night and was surprised when the American agreed to their plan. Of course, it didn't hurt when Johanna threatened to return to Paris and fetch the entire Deuxième Bureau if he refused. The man was right—at times, she could be a "firecracker."

"Are you certain you want to do this?" Petit was frowning.

Colin glanced at Johanna, and her encouraging smile helped to galvanize him. "I see no other way of finding out if the elusive 'Madame Outis' is Jewel, do you?"

"That's a question for which I have no answer, Lieutenant. All right, you should get a call from me in about an hour."

Petit departed, and Colin moved to relieve Johanna of her bundle. "Better let me have those."

She handed over his disguise. "Can I assist you in any way?"

"Now you sound like my corporal, Goodfellow." His tone was sharper than he'd intended as he took the clothes and tossed them into a heap on the bed. "I will tell you what I've told him: I can still dress myself."

"I was only trying to help."

Colin turned to see hurt dim her expression, before she masked it with anger. *Blast the nightmares!* He smiled at her and gentled his voice. "I know you are."

Her features softened, and he was glad his irritability hadn't done permanent damage. After shaking off his bad dreams that morning, Colin's thoughts had returned to his time with Johanna last night and the way she looked in her pretty pink dress and silver shoes at dinner . . . and afterward, en route to the concert, the moment she'd wrapped her arms around him. She hadn't flinched when he'd rested his gloved hand against her shoulder.

"Goodfellow sounds like his namesake."

Colin refocused his attention. "Albert is a fine soldier and a good man." His gaze returned to the disguise lying on the bed. "I'd better get started."

"Yes, well, good luck to you. I'll expect a full report post mission, all right?"

He nodded, and she moved toward the door. As she opened it, Johanna turned and gave him another encouraging smile. "You'll be grand, Colin. I know it."

Her confidence in him filled him with warmth. "Thanks."

After she'd gone, he drew a deep breath and began shucking out of his uniform, which thankfully took a lot less time than getting dressed.

The trousers fit a bit loose, but Petit had thoughtfully installed suspenders, so Colin was able to manage. The small buttons on the shirt were soon resolved when he decided to fasten only those visible above the opening of the white staff coat.

His next challenge was the bow tie. Despite being a ready-made tie with an adjustable strap, the trick lay in getting it fastened around his neck.

You can do this, Mabry. Frowning in concentration, he bent forward and laid one end of the strap against the back of his collar, then used his stump to hold it in place. Looping around the other end of the tie with his good hand, he fastened the two ends.

Colin went to the mirror to check his handiwork. "Not too badly done, Lieutenant." He grinned as he inspected the fit. A little loose, but it would certainly work.

Once he fitted the harness and his prosthetic back in place, sweat beaded along his brow. Next he braced himself for the shoes, but he laughed in relief to see they were slip-on ankle boots. Colin didn't even care if the elastic-sided boots fit perfectly, so long as he could avoid tying shoelaces.

Seated on the bed, he stared at his shod feet and admitted a grudging gratitude toward Petit. Colin hadn't forgiven the American for the stunt he'd pulled the first night, but at least the man had made a concession with the clothes.

Colin was reaching for the white staff coat when the telephone rang.

All earlier exhaustion fled, and his heart raced as he waited. Silence followed, and he knew it was Petit's signal.

Colin checked his watch. Madame Outis must have decided to order her lunch earlier than usual.

He was waiting by the elevator when Petit arrived with the cart.

"Take this up to room 403. And don't waste time. Monsieur Outis has the connecting room, and there is no guarantee how long he'll be away. I'll wait for you downstairs in the lobby."

Colin nodded, relieved to learn Kepler had separate quarters, especially if Jewel was the woman with him. His adrenaline surged as he exchanged places with Petit. In a matter of minutes, he would see her. . . .

"Good luck, partner."

The elevator boy closed the doors, and the birdcage began ascending to the next floor. Once Colin exited, he pushed the cart along the hall and paused at the appointed door.

Staring at the brass-plated numbers, he wondered what he would say to her. Would Jewel even recognize him? Colin had been much thinner when they first met, but working his uncle's farm had replenished the weight he'd lost during active duty at the front.

He glanced at his prosthetic. There was that alteration as well.

He rapped on the door before he could change his mind. "*Service d'étage.*"

The moments seemed to drag before the door opened to reveal a slender woman dressed in mourning. Colin judged her to be a few inches taller than Johanna—the right height for Jewel, if his memory was correct.

She also wore the black veil and hat Petit had mentioned.

"Your lunch, madame."

He heard a soft gasp behind the veil as her gloved hand reached for the edge of the door. A moment passed before she stepped back to allow him entrance, waving him toward a dark wood table near the window.

Colin rolled the cart to where she'd indicated, and with a quick movement, he used his left arm to support the tray as he slid the covered dish onto the table.

When he turned, he found her standing beside the closed door. Her gloved hand clutched the doorknob as she watched him, her chest rising and falling rapidly. "Colin?"

Her whispered recognition filled him with relief and a measure of triumph. She did remember him. "Yes, Jewel, it's me."

His heart thumped loudly as he took a step toward her, straining to see her face behind the heavy black gauze. His attention dropped to the silver ring hanging from a chain around her neck. It was the same one he'd seen on her finger a year ago—the dove ring similar to Johanna's. He looked up at her. "I came back."

"You kept your promise." Emotion thickened her voice, and the veil moved with the shake of her head. "I still cannot believe you are here. How . . . how did you find me?"

He smiled. "It's quite a story." Taking another step in her direction, he saw her stiffen. Colin paused, heat flooding his face as he glanced at his prosthetic. He had changed much from the man she once knew. Perhaps too much.

He held his place, ignoring his wounded pride. "Jewel . . . my dear . . . I must tell you how happy and relieved I am to see you. After the battle at Cambrai, I thought you had died, along with most of your village."

"Death might have been better."

He heard her sad whisper, and seeing her slender frame draped in mourning filled him with fresh regret. Despite his own fond memories of their time together, Jewel had been forced to survive alone for months in occupied France. No doubt she had changed as well.

He cleared his throat. "I sorely regret . . . not taking you with me when I had the opportunity, but there was so much danger—"

"The danger was everywhere, Colin."

Of course. He hesitated, then added, "I'm very sorry about your aunt's death."

"I still grieve for her, as you can see." Jewel's agonized whisper floated to him. "She was my only family there, and it was so difficult after she was gone."

"It pains me to know how you must have suffered." Remorse edged his voice. "But, Jewel, you still have family." His heart sped. "You asked me how I found you. It was through your sister, Johanna. She told me you were alive and needed my help."

"Sister . . . ?" Jewel's slender frame teetered near the door, looking ready to topple over.

Colin rushed to take her hand and steady her. "I know it is a shock."

"How can that be?" She turned to him, her voice a hoarse whisper. "I have no sister!"

He led her over to sit on the bed. "After your mother died, your father . . . had another daughter."

"My father . . . did he know about her?" Her voice was faint as she raised her head to him.

"Yes, I understand he went to visit her once, when she was very small."

"He saw her?" Jewel gripped the bedpost and rose to her feet. "He *knew* I had a sister, yet he never told me?" The fury in her voice startled him. "He left me to go and fight, knowing he might *never* come back. And still he kept her from me!"

"I'm sorry." Colin ached for her but didn't know what else to say.

Then, as if the anger had drained her, she suddenly collapsed back onto the bed. "He never even said her name. Nor did my aunt, if she knew." She began to cry softly. "All that t-time I was alone. . . ."

Her shoulders shook as she leaned against the bedpost. Colin knelt down beside her and again tried to offer comfort. "I cannot imagine how difficult this must be for you, my dear. Johanna didn't know about you either until recently."

"Johanna." Jewel sniffled and retrieved a black lace handkerchief from inside her cuff, dabbing it beneath the veil. "Tell me about her. How old is she? How d-do you know her?"

"Your sister is two years younger, and I met her when she wrote to me, asking that I come to Paris and begin searching for you. She knew you needed help."

"How did she find out about me?"

He smiled. "She discovered your diary in the remains of the cellar where you once hid me. We both came here to find you."

"My diary." Her voice held wonder. Abruptly she turned to him. "Both of you? She is here, too?"

He nodded. "In this very hotel."

"Where?" Her breath hitched behind the veil. "I want to meet her!"

Jewel started to rise from the bed before her attention turned toward the connecting door to her room. "*Non*, I . . . I must wait."

Colin's gaze narrowed. "Why?"

"Monsieur Outis will return soon. I should be here."

Colin rose to stand over her. "Why are you still with Monsieur . . . with Kepler?"

Her head jerked up at the question, and she was still for a moment. "He . . . he brought me safely out of Havrincourt, before the battle. He saved my life."

Her words triggered in Colin another stab of guilt. It should have been him. "But why do you remain in his company? The man is an enemy of France."

Her gloved hands knotted together in her lap. "He promised to take me to my father—"

"When, Jewel?" Colin cut her off. "When will he keep his promise? You left Havrincourt months ago. How do you know the man is even telling the truth?"

More tears rose in her voice as she turned from him. "Colin, please don't say that."

"My dear, I do not mean to upset you." He touched her lightly on the shoulder, and she flinched. Withdrawing his hand, he fought back the hurt. "Jewel, come with me now. Let us take you to Paris."

She said nothing, her body hunched over as though defeated.

"I made you a promise, and I intend to keep it." Again he crouched beside her and put his hand over hers. He was glad she didn't pull away. "I feel like I failed you before, but I'm here now. I want to take care of you, Jewel."

She straightened to face him. "It is enough that you have come for me, *mon noble chevalier*."

My noble knight. Wistfulness filled him, recalling the name she'd bestowed on him while tending his wounds at Havrincourt.

"But now, Colin, I release you from your promise. You must forget about me."

Her words rocked him back on his heels. "Forget?" He stared at her. Could she so easily dismiss the love and grief she'd written about in her diary? Her kiss . . .

Again he caught her eyeing the connecting door. An ugly suspicion lurking in the back of his mind rushed forward. "Are you and Kepler . . . a couple?"

Her attention swung back to him. "Yes! Yes, we are in love. Colin, I'm sorry. Now you must go, before he finds you here."

"I don't believe you. You seem frightened of him." His voice gentled as he reached for her veil. "Show me your face, Jewel. I want to see the truth of your feelings."

She drew back from him. "*Non*, please!"

"Why are you hiding from me?" Humiliation finally bullied its way forward, slashing at his tattered confidence as he knelt before her. Was he a wretch, then, that she wanted him completely gone from her life? Another thought struck, and his muscles tensed. "Has he hurt you?"

"Of course not!" Her voice sounded agitated. "You do not understand, Colin, I am trying to save *you*. Monsieur Outis . . . Kepler . . . he could return at any moment!"

"I'm not afraid of him." Determined, Colin reached for the veil once more. He heard her shivering breath as he inched up the black gauze covering her face. His first glimpse was of the smooth olive skin at her throat, then the soft wisps of golden hair he remembered so well. Her delicately rounded jaw came into view next, and he was about to unveil the edge of her mouth when a soft clicking noise sounded behind him. A lock turning . . .

"*Non!*" Jewel thrust his hand away, breaking the chain from around her neck.

"What is going on here?"

Colin turned to face the harsh male voice behind him. Werner Kepler stood on the threshold of the connecting room, arms crossed and feet spread apart. He glared between them. "Why is he on the floor?"

Colin quickly rose to his feet, mind racing. "I brought madame her meal and . . ."

"And he helped me to find this."

Jewel rose too, holding up the silver ring with the chain. "It broke, and I thought I had lost it. You know how important the ring is to me."

Colin ducked his head and returned to the table, laying out the linen napkin and the silver. He removed the dish cover and set it aside before pushing the cart toward the door.

"What else was he doing?"

Kepler glared at Jewel.

"Please do not be angry, *mon coeur*. I was hungry and ordered lunch and this . . . this waiter helped me to find my ring."

Kepler ignored her as he turned his full attention on Colin. Relaxing his arms, he approached, and Colin kept his head lowered, fearing the man would recognize him from Le Bibent.

"I have not seen you at this hotel before. When did you hire on? And why do they employ someone with that kind of injury?"

Colin was mere inches from him. He glanced up to see the man staring at his prosthetic. "Many wounded have returned from the war, monsieur. We must all work to feed ourselves. And I still have the use of this."

He held up his good hand for Kepler to see—so close in fact, Colin was tempted to lunge for the man's throat.

Petit's warning came back in a rush, and he lowered his hand to the cart. "Now, if there will be nothing else, I will go. Enjoy the rest of your day, madame and monsieur, and thank you for staying with us at Hôtel Blanc."

Colin didn't dare look at Jewel again as he left the room. His pulse was still racing as he reached the elevator, anger and shame thrashing at what remained of his dignity.

How could he go up against the likes of Kepler? He glared at his offending appendage. At least his wooden hand might have thrown a good first punch and given the man another scar to damage his looks.

Mon coeur. My heart. Jewel had spoken those words to Kepler. Was it of her own free will . . . or did the Boche spy demand such endearments? She had said she loved the man, but Colin sensed she was lying. He'd heard her fear; for the most part, he imagined Kepler was its source.

But what if Jewel feared *him*? Colin remembered the way she had stiffened when he started to approach her, and then when he touched her shoulder.

Perhaps she just got a good look at you, Mabry, and chose the easiest way out.

Arriving on the ground floor, he tried to shake off the thought as he exited the elevator. Petit was waiting for him in the lobby and nodded to indicate a service door several feet beyond the restaurant entrance. Colin took the lead in pushing the cart, and while the American held the door, both men entered the sizable kitchen.

"In here." Petit opened a second door, a pantry with shelves stacked full of root vegetables and dry grains. He turned on the overhead light and shut the door.

Colin's chest tightened in the small space, and he gripped the cart.

"What happened upstairs?"

"Kepler walked in on us—what do you think? Why weren't you watching him?"

Petit frowned. "Monsieur Outis gave our man the slip. He must have suspected something, because he hightailed it right back here. Are you all right? Did he recognize you?"

"I'm fine and no, I don't think he suspects me from the restaurant. If Kepler had doubts, Jewel took care to alleviate them." Colin's jaw clenched, thinking of the broken necklace. *She saved you in there, Mabry.*

"Jewel?" Petit's gaze narrowed. "So you saw her? You were able to identify her?"

Colin began to nod, then hesitated. "I'm certain it must be her."

Petit's mouth flattened. "Exactly what does that mean, Lieutenant?"

He shifted. "Well, I didn't actually *see* her. Jewel's face, I mean. I was about to lift the veil when Kepler barged in."

Petit sighed. "So you can't be sure."

"It was *her*, I tell you! She knew me, and we spoke about things in the past, things only Jewel would know. Then she told me to leave before Kepler returned, but of course it was too late for that. She won't admit it, but I think she's afraid of him." *Or of me.* The knot of failure tightened his insides.

"Did she mention any injuries?"

Colin shook his head. "I asked if she was hurt, and she said no."

Still, Petit's question gave him pause. Was that the reason she'd been so reluctant to let him see her? Had she lied to him, thinking to save him from Kepler with the broken chain?

He thought of his fist, so close to Kepler's face. His chance to prove to Jewel he could defend her. *And instead you backed down, Lieutenant.*

Petit blew out a breath. "So, it sounds like we're back to square one. Anything else you can tell me?"

Only that Kepler saved her before I did, and she says she loves him. Colin scowled. He wasn't about to share that information with Petit. Aside from incurring more damage to his pride, he didn't want the American condemning Jewel as Kepler's accomplice. "No, nothing else."

Petit seemed to appraise him. "Too bad you didn't get a look at her face. A positive identification would have been invaluable."

"Give me more time with her." Colin's demand sounded more like a plea, but he didn't care. His honor was at stake. He had to know without a doubt that Jewel was being truthful about her relationship with Kepler and not speaking out of fear. Otherwise, he was leaving her in as much danger this time as in Havrincourt. Perhaps more, when he considered the Boche spy's stalling over taking her to see her father.

Colin didn't want to consider the fact Jewel simply didn't want *him.*

"I don't know, Lieutenant." Petit shook his head. "I went out on a limb for you today. Maybe it's best we end this now."

Colin gazed at him, incredulous. "Are you suggesting I walk away and leave her here?"

"I told you before—there's much at stake you know nothing about. Your taking chances like you did today only jeopardizes things for the rest of us."

A sinking feeling settled over him, and he knew Petit was right. Yet every instinct in Colin rebelled at the idea of abandoning Jewel.

True, he hadn't seen her face, but he'd sensed her fear and her hopelessness. She was being made a pawn in a game where Kepler and Petit were the players.

He couldn't walk away. Even if Jewel had rejected him for his appearance, Johanna was counting on him. "I'm staying. Get me another chance to see Jewel."

The American eyed him with a pensive look for a few moments. "I'll need to check with my superiors," he said at last. "Meanwhile, you keep a low profile. Monsieur Outis has seen you now, so you must continue to pose as part of the restaurant staff. Keep the cart with you, and if you're seen coming or going, anyone will think you're delivering room service. Oh, and inform Mrs. Mabry, so she knows what's going on."

Colin nodded. "When will you let me know something?"

"By morning."

As Petit left, Colin decided to go and brief Johanna on his meeting with Jewel. Grabbing an empty tray and cover from the kitchen, he loaded the cart and took the elevator upstairs.

CHAPTER

14

o's head shot up during her pacing as a knock sounded at her door. She glanced to the floor near the chair, where Little Corporal sat in his small cage, pecking at the dried kernels of corn she'd given him. Another knock sounded.

"*Service d'étage*, madame."

Room service? She hadn't ordered food . . . Colin?

"Just a moment." Her alarm was replaced with excitement. Had he spoken with Jewel?

Jo went to her pigeon, speaking softly as she retrieved his cage from the floor and tucked him back inside the washstand cabinet behind an ornate screen. "You'll have to continue your lunch in here, *mon ami*. I won't be long, I promise."

Quickly her eyes swept the room for any telltale evidence of the bird, but she found none. Jo had been so anxious for Colin's return, she'd straightened up her things, putting away all of her clothes and shoes, even making the bed.

She opened the door and was surprised to see Colin still wearing the waiter's uniform. He'd brought along a cart with a covered dish.

"Hurry and let me in."

Jo stepped back as he pushed the cart into the middle of the

175

room. Once she'd closed the door, she noted his strained look. Had something happened? "Did you see her?"

He nodded. "We spoke to one another."

Anticipation fluttered through her. "Come, sit down." She indicated the chair next to her desk while she sat on the edge of the bed. "Is she my sister?"

"I feel certain of it, though I saw only a glimpse of her face behind the veil before Kepler charged in."

"Kepler! Oh my goodness. What happened? Did he recognize you?"

Colin shook his head, and Jo noted his heightened color. "I think my cover is still safe. Needless to say, I got out of there quickly. Before his unexpected return, Jewel and I did have a chance to talk . . . about her aunt and my coming back to keep my promise." He nodded toward her hand. "She also wears the same silver bird ring, though on a chain about her neck."

"It must truly be her!" Jo's hopes soared. "Did you tell her about me?"

He offered a tired smile. "She is eager to meet you."

"Is she?" Nervous energy vaulted Jo to her feet. "Did she say anything about our papa?"

"Kepler still hasn't taken her to see your father."

Jo's elation plummeted as she threw her hands up in the air. "What is he waiting for?"

Colin shook his head. "I asked Jewel the same question, and it seemed to upset her." He met Jo's gaze, and his look turned thoughtful. "Do you remember Kepler's exact words to her before they left Havrincourt? Did the Boche say anything to her about how long it would take, or if your father was being held somewhere?"

Jo tapped a finger to her chin. "I think Kepler simply told her he had located Papa and would take her to him." She went to the desk and retrieved her sister's journal. "Actually, I've been rereading that part of the diary. Let's take a look to be certain we haven't missed anything. I confess I've read Jewel's words so many times now, I should know her story by heart."

Standing near Colin, Jo was still looking at him when she opened the diary to the ribbon bookmark. When she looked down at the page, she frowned. "Now, that's odd."

"What?"

"The bookmark. I was reading the passage near the end, as the battle was coming toward Jewel's village. But the ribbon marks a place months before, right after her aunt's death."

"Are you certain you didn't just put the bookmark in the wrong place?"

"Of course I'm certain."

He rose from the chair, concern etching his features. "When did you last read the diary?"

"Yesterday afternoon." She glanced back at the book. "Before I dressed for dinner."

"So someone could have trespassed while we were at Le Bibent." He quickly scanned the room. "Have you noticed anything else amiss?"

Jo's heart pounded as she too surveyed the room's contents. Had an intruder broken in?

Her gaze faltered at the ornate screen. Since arriving at the hotel, she'd kept Little Corporal hidden in the washstand cabinet whenever she wasn't in the room. Did someone discover her pigeon?

She swallowed and turned to him. "No . . . nothing."

He grimaced. "It could have been Petit. We were at dinner a couple of hours before we left to meet him at the Red Cross canteen. Although he seems to prefer to drug his victim first and then keep the goods he's stolen overnight."

Jo heard the scorn in his voice. "But when I returned last night, the diary was exactly where I'd left it." She pointed to his chair. "There, where you've been sitting."

His frown deepened. "I'm still not ruling out the American. There are other spies at the hotel as well, so either way we remain on our guard."

"Yes, of course." Jo tried to shake her unease as she quickly searched the diary and found the passage Colin had asked about. "It says here, 'Captain Kepler knows where Father is and has promised to take me to him once we leave here. He says it could be dangerous, but I do not care. I am counting the days until I see my dear papa once more.'"

At the last line, Jo's throat constricted with emotion. How many years had she yearned for the same thing as her sister?

She looked to Colin. "I . . . imagine Papa in some prison camp. What if he *is* being held somewhere, and Kepler cannot get my sister there safely?"

"That could be the reason." He was frowning. "But I think there is more going on."

Jo closed the diary. "What do you mean?"

He sighed. "Please, Johanna, take a seat."

For the first time, she noted his haggard expression. She sat on the bed. "Tell me."

Colin returned to the chair across from her. "As I said, Jewel wants to meet you."

"I am excited to meet her as well!" Jo sat forward. "Did she say when?"

"I suspect she will need to find a time when Kepler goes out again."

Jo studied him, concern gnawing at her. "Is Jewel afraid of him? Is he keeping her a prisoner?"

"She worried over Kepler's return, but I'm not entirely certain what to make of it."

Jo waited for him to continue as he leaned forward in the chair, resting his arms on his knees. "When I arrived at the room, Jewel was shocked to see me, then very surprised to learn about you.

Yet she seemed pleased that I had kept my promise." He looked up. "Living alone all those months in occupied France after her aunt died . . . it was very difficult for her."

"My poor sister." Jewel had written about the hardships in her diary, but knowing she'd voiced them to Colin made Jo ache for her even more. "What . . . what else did she say?"

"Jewel released me from my vow." He lifted a sober gaze to her. "She told me to forget about her."

"What?" Jo's pulse raced despite a nagging sense of guilt. "Did she say why?"

"She claims to be in love with Kepler."

Hearing his words, Jo flinched with the full force of her shame. She had dragged Colin all the way from Britain, only for him to learn what she'd already suspected. "I'm sorry."

She meant it.

"I don't know if I believe her."

The desolate pain in her heart returned, but Jo thrust it away. "You think she still loves you?"

His bark of laughter sounded bitter as he glanced at his gloved hand. "I think maybe she had second thoughts about the man she once wanted to marry."

"Nonsense!" Again Jo launched to her feet, this time full of righteous anger. "I cannot believe any woman who truly loves you would change her feelings because of an insignificant issue."

She waved a dismissive hand toward his prosthetic while outrage, guilt, and yearning made a tangle of her emotions. "Listen to me, Colin Mabry. Napoleon said, 'All men are equal before God: wisdom, talents, and virtue are the only difference between them.' Which means you are more of a man than . . . than Kepler, André, Henri Lacourt, and Petit put together! You're a war hero! And even if you weren't, it does not change the person you are inside."

Johanna's words were a balm to his injured pride, and Colin couldn't help smiling. "Your friend Miss Moreau said I was to be Jewel's champion. It seems I have one in you."

Her cheeks flushed a rosy hue, bringing out the blue in her eyes. "I'm just saying, you have value and . . ."

"What was that?" Colin turned at a soft rustling noise coming from behind the washstand screen. A moment later, it sounded again. He rose from his chair. "Did you hear it?"

"Hear what?"

His eyes narrowed. Johanna wore the same look he'd come to know only too well. "I am certain I heard a noise coming from over there." He pointed to the screen. "It sounded like—"

A soft cooing floated into the room, and his eyes widened. "Is that . . . a bird?"

She averted her eyes and nodded. "Little Corporal."

Falling back onto the chair, Colin gaped at her. "How . . . when . . . do you mean to say . . . ?" He stared at the cloth kit bag on the desk, then back at the screen. "Titan's teeth! You've smuggled a carrier pigeon all the way from Paris!" He blinked. "How is that even possible?"

Her chin went up as she faced him. "It wasn't so difficult. I told you how pigeons are stuffed inside tiny baskets with parachutes. They can survive well for some time in a small space. Little Corporal's cage fits perfectly into the bottom of my kit bag."

Again he glanced at the cloth bag. "But on the train . . . how did you keep the bird quiet?"

"Darkness is a natural sedative for pigeons. So as long as I left the bag open to the fresh air, he was fine." Her brow creased. "Though with such a long trip, I did worry he might create a fuss, but being in the noisy coach section and then the compartments full of people, any sound my little bird might have made would not be heard." She smiled. "I also packed a vial of chamomile tea. It calms him."

He shook his head in wonder. "And here at the hotel?" Colin

KATE BRESLIN

remembered the *Do Not Disturb* card on Johanna's door whenever she was out. "No wonder you dislike the maid entering your room to clean."

A new thought struck, and his pulse sped. "Anything unusual with the pigeon when you returned to your room last night?" If Petit or some other spy had discovered the bird . . .

"Little Corporal was fine. Whoever was in my room didn't notice he was here."

"You had better be right." He rose to his feet, anger battling his relief. Did she not realize the danger she'd put them in traveling with the bird? "Because if Petit *does* find out, he'll have us both arrested as spies."

Her face grew pale as she stiffened. "André—Sergeant Moreau—was concerned for our safety, especially around Kepler. I decided to take Little Corporal along in case we met with trouble and needed to send for help."

He glared at her. "We *will* need help if the Americans find out we've got a trained carrier pigeon in our possession!" Taking a deep breath, he struggled for calm. "You have to free the bird, Johanna. Let him return to Vernon."

"No."

Her blue eyes challenged him, and he moved closer until he stood over her. "You *will*, Johanna. The bird puts us at risk."

She searched his face, and her features softened. "Please, Colin, not yet. No one except you knows Little Corporal is here, and we may have need of him. Our quest is not over."

Johanna's words and pleading expression doused the fire of his anger. He realized he hadn't yet told her about his conversation with Petit. "I'm afraid it might be over. Now that Kepler has seen me up close, I must remain in disguise so as to keep my cover. At least until after Petit speaks with his agency. I came here to inform you."

"But . . . we cannot give up! I need to see Jewel and learn more about Papa."

181

Colin's chest tightened at her crestfallen expression, and he took a step back. "I am sorry. I know how badly you wanted to meet her and find your father. I did ask Petit to allow me another chance to speak with Jewel, but it's up to G-2 now. I doubt they will risk the mission by granting me more time with her."

"'The truest wisdom is a resolute determination.'" Once again her chin bobbed up.

A smile touched his lips. "Napoleon?"

She nodded before crossing her arms. "Are you certain the woman with Kepler is my sister?"

"Yes."

"And is Jewel still worth fighting for?"

"Of course." Not only for the sake of his honor, but God had brought him here for a purpose, a future with the woman to whom he owed so much. *If* she still wanted him.

"Then you must try again, Colin. Regardless of what the Americans think." Johanna wore a determined look. "Petit told us Kepler likes to sight-see, so when he goes out tomorrow, you can march right back in there and speak with my sister. Find out her true feelings for you, and tell her she must press Kepler for our father's whereabouts. If he refuses to tell her, we will rescue her and have Henri Lacourt and the French Secret Service arrest him and make him talk."

Colin couldn't help grinning. Johanna Reyer was the most outrageous woman he'd ever met. She carried pigeons in her purse, wore men's clothes, and revered Britain's old nemesis, Bonaparte. Now she planned to tell the American Secret Service how to run their operation.

In their brief time together, he'd developed quite a fondness for her. They were friends as well as partners in their quest. And Johanna seemed to think him competent to do anything. "I'll look for another chance to see Jewel tomorrow."

"Thank you. And Little Corporal?"

He was tempted to repeat his order to set the pigeon free, but her beseeching expression made him hesitate. So far, Johanna had done a good job in concealing the bird, and if he did get another opportunity with Jewel, it was certain Kepler would act rashly if he found them out.

Colin realized almost a year had passed since he was in any kind of danger. From that time on, he'd done all in his power to make his life safe and predictable. Yet since the first moments of his meeting Johanna Reyer, his world had become a series of surprises and risks.

Had he merely come to France to fulfill his promise to Jewel? Or was he here for another reason as well?

He gazed at Johanna, her eyes lit with hope. She believed him fearless. Perhaps he had been safe for too long.

"Keep the bird hidden."

15

Colin stood at the washstand mirror the next morning, refreshed after a rare peaceful night's sleep. Dressed in the same white shirt and dark trousers he'd worn for his meeting with Jewel yesterday, he hoped today's attempt to see her would not be in vain.

He and Johanna had spoken last night, and she'd agreed to go down to breakfast early and keep watch for Kepler's departure. If he left the hotel, she would telephone Colin with a single ring, as Petit had done.

Taking a moment to straighten the bow tie, Colin jerked his head toward the sudden frantic pounding at his door.

"Colin, let me in!"

Johanna? He crossed the room and opened the door.

She wore her gray traveling dress, looking agitated as she moved past him. He closed the door. "Is something wrong?"

She spun around. "Yes, my sister is gone!"

"What happened?"

"Kepler is taking her to Spain."

The words sent a shock wave through him. "How do you know this?"

Johanna twisted her gloved hands together. "I was on my way to breakfast, as we'd arranged, when Petit stopped me before I entered the restaurant. He said Monsieur Outis checked out of the hotel two hours ago and took my sister with him. Petit spoke with the hotel driver who took them to the train station and overheard Monsieur Outis tell the porter to take their bags to the Barcelona platform."

Colin curled his lip. "I wonder if Petit concocted the story just to get rid of us." He still didn't trust the American, especially now that they suspected someone had broken into Johanna's room.

"The thought crossed my mind as well." She nodded. "So I spoke with the driver myself. He corroborates Petit's claim. Kepler and Jewel seem destined for Barcelona."

Colin's mind reeled. *Had* Kepler found him out and decided to flee? But why Barcelona? "Did Petit give a reason why they might be going to Spain?"

"No." She straightened, seemingly forcing her hands to her sides. "I'm going to my room to pack, and I will be back in a few minutes. If we hurry, we can catch the noon train!"

And then she was gone, leaving Colin in the middle of the room, still dumbfounded by the news. Had the Boche spy taken Jewel against her will . . . or were they both on the run?

He gazed at his white jacket and dark slacks. With Jewel gone, he no longer needed to pretend.

Colin began removing the clothes as he walked to the armoire to fetch his uniform. Perhaps he should take the waiter's disguise with him. It might come in handy.

Fifteen minutes later, clad in his khaki britches and boots, Colin struggled to work the buttons on his shirt when another tap sounded at the door. "Are you ready?"

He growled. It seemed she could be on time when it suited her. "I'm still getting dressed. Give me a few more minutes."

"I thought you were dressed."

He ignored her question while he continued fumbling with the buttons.

"Let me in, please."

For some reason, his shirt buttons weren't cooperating. He blew air through his nostrils and stared at the door, then glanced at the shirt cuff dangling beyond the stump of his left arm. The harness and sleeve, along with his wooden hand, still lay on the chair.

"Colin, the next train leaves in thirty minutes. We must *hurry*."

Titan's teeth! His jaw muscle flexed as he marched to the door and flung it open. "As you can see, I am not ready."

She pushed her way inside, wearing her large hat, her purse slung over one arm. With the other, she carried the cloth kit bag. "Why did you change?"

"Because if I must go out in public and travel by train, I'll do it as a British officer and not as a waiter."

"Have you packed yet?"

She set down the kit bag and removed her gloves, scanning the room for his luggage. Colin saw her glance halt at the chair with his apparatus, and heat rose into his face.

Tucking the gloves into the small purse on her arm, she turned and reached for his shirt.

He brushed her hands away. "What are you doing?"

"I'm helping you."

A snarl rose in his throat. "I do not need your help."

Her smile was tight. "If we want to leave before nightfall, you do need my help."

Again she reached for his shirt. He pushed her hands aside once more, and she gave him a hard look. "Allow me this, if you please."

Colin gave up and expelled a breath that stirred a few errant wisps of blond beneath her voluminous brim. *Be calm, man.* He angled his head. "Why do women wear such hats? I imagine you must get migraines from all the weight on your head."

186

She eyed him drolly. "Don't be silly. 'Tis called fashion. Something I suspect you know little about."

"And I suppose you do?" His frustration sought a target. "I didn't realize Kilcoole was the center of *haute couture*."

"In case it slipped your mind, I've lived in Paris two years. And don't forget I attended boarding school in Poole."

"Ah yes, a proper English education. How was that, by the way?"

She looked up at him, pain reflected in her expression. "I found unkindness doesn't have limits, even among the well-bred."

Colin's hostility fled, and he sorely regretted his badgering. "Johanna—"

"You'll have to take care of the rest." She'd stopped buttoning midway down his shirt and stepped away from him. "I'll get your things together."

Colin continued with his buttons, watching her clean out the armoire and pack his clothing into the portmanteau. Again he thought about the harsh way she'd been treated most of her life, due to circumstances she had no control over. It put a new perspective on his own situation.

In the back of his mind, he'd always believed others ridiculed him for being different, yet no one had ever taunted him about his prosthetic or acted maliciously toward him. And while he despised anyone pitying him, Johanna did not seem the least bit disturbed by his injury.

By the time he finished with the shirt, she had all of his clothing packed. He ducked behind the screen to fetch his shaving kit, and when he returned, he found her holding his harness and the sleeve with his prosthetic. "Shall I help with this, or would you rather I take the luggage down?"

Her tone was matter-of-fact. Still, Colin wasn't ready for that kind of intimacy with anyone. "I'll do it. You're certain you can manage our bags?"

"I'll just use your handy cart." She set his portmanteau on top, along with her kit bag. "I'll get the rest from my room and meet you downstairs."

"Thank you."

Her smile broadened. He opened the door and held it while she exited and went across the hall. She turned to him. "Don't be long."

Leaning his head against the closed door, Colin chuckled. Part of their luggage included a contraband pigeon, and they were certainly breaking all of G-2's rules by chasing an alleged German agent into Spain, a country to which Colin had never been before.

He and Johanna could be discovered by either side, especially if the bird got out of hand. If so, they could find themselves behind bars, awaiting trial as enemy spies.

Once more Colin considered the merits of predictability. He'd spent a lifetime following an established set of rules, always acting the sensible twin, balancing out his sister's headstrong antics. And after his time in the war, he had tried to entrench himself deeper into those self-imposed standards, hoping to regain the part of himself he had lost—each time coming up short and feeling the lesser for it.

But now . . .

For the first time in his life, he was feeling just a bit reckless.

Despite their efforts to hurry, Jo and Colin missed the noon train by minutes and now sat in the next one, awaiting its departure.

Seated on the plush bench seat inside an empty compartment, Jo gazed at the opened kit bag near her feet. Considering the hours it would take to reach Barcelona, she was glad Little Corporal had enjoyed a brief change of scenery at Hôtel Blanc before being cooped up again in her bag. "I wish we could get this space to ourselves."

"Will the bird attract attention, do you think?"

Colin sat across from her in his officer's uniform. His brow creased as he glanced from the kit bag to Jo.

She shrugged. "I gave him a dropperful of the chamomile tea before we left, but I would feel much better if we didn't have to worry about him causing a fuss with others about."

He rose from the bench seat. "It's early yet, and most of the other passengers haven't boarded. I've got an idea." He went to open the compartment door.

"Where are you going?"

"I need to speak with the conductor. I'll be right back."

He soon returned with a sheet of white paper tucked under his arm. After closing the compartment door, he withdrew from his pocket a small spool of adhesive tape. "Help me with this, will you?" He handed her the spool. "We need just a small strip."

Jo tore off a short piece of the tape. "Now what?"

He handed her the sheet of paper. As she read the words on the opposite side, laughter bubbled up inside of her. "Brilliant."

She affixed the tape and then rose to post the sign against the compartment door window so that the words *le voyage de noces* could be read by any boarding passengers who thought to enter their sanctuary.

He stood behind her. "That should keep most of them away."

"I believe it shall." She turned to him, still smiling. "You really are a clever fellow, Lieutenant Mabry."

He grinned at her. "I've been known to have an idea or two, Mrs. Mabry."

When Jo returned to her seat, Colin followed and settled close beside her. Heat rose in her cheeks as she leaned away to eye him curiously.

"The sign says *honeymoon*, so if we want to convince people to stay out, we should at least look the part of being newlyweds." His eyes glinted with humor. "Of course you'll need to remove the hat. There isn't enough room on this bench for all three of us."

"Oh yes, of course." Jo's pulse thumped against her throat at his lighthearted banter. She reached to unpin the voluminous hat, and he rose to take it from her, placing it in the upper rack behind them.

As he returned to sit beside her, she considered the anxious, regimented man she'd first met in Paris a week ago. Jo couldn't help marveling at how relaxed he'd become, as though he too was eager for their upcoming adventure.

To find Jewel. Her thoughts cooled as the reality of her relationship with Colin returned. They were friends, nothing more—partners in Jo's search for her family.

Clearly, he was still anxious to pursue her sister, the woman he intended to marry.

Jo ignored the tightness in her chest as she watched passengers begin filing steadily past their compartment. Women in stylish mourning black gave her nostalgic smiles through the glass while a pair of American soldiers on furlough grinned and applauded before moving on.

She smiled at them, relieved for the privacy, but her secret longing for a real husband and a honeymoon made her ache.

When Petit's face appeared at the glass, she and Colin shared an uneasy look. The American carried a French newspaper and now posed as a businessman in his dark linen suit and felt hat. Jo held her breath as he lingered a moment; then he smiled and gave Colin a brief salute before moving on toward the back of the train.

Jo pushed out a deep breath. "That was close. He is the last person we want in here with Little Corporal."

"Agreed." Colin leaned back against the seat. "I'm glad you mentioned wanting privacy."

"I wonder why he didn't catch the earlier train."

"I would imagine he was sent along to keep an eye on us." He turned to her. "Perhaps it's the reason he told you about Kepler and Jewel's departure in the first place. Petit knew we were not going to give up, so better to have us where he can see us."

Jo considered his words. "Or perhaps Petit still hopes you will have another chance to meet with my sister."

"Yes, I thought about that, too. He may not have had a chance to talk with his office, and he does seem keen to confirm she's Jewel Reyer."

"I admit feeling the tiniest bit guilty for keeping him out. Petit has been helpful after all, and we're not certain he's the one who trespassed into my room the other night." She glanced at him. "You did tell him we were not man and wife, so he knows our honeymoon sign is a ruse."

Colin flashed a contented smile, his face so close to hers that Jo's heart leapt. "Petit will get along fine sitting by himself, Johanna. He can read his newspaper."

Marcus Weatherford sat in a corner of the last compartment, the brim of his hat pulled low over his brow as if he slept. The coach seats outside the space had filled up fast, so the sooner Petit arrived, the better. Trains had ears, and Marcus didn't have much time.

As the door opened, he tipped his brim back and stared into the face of the American. Once Petit sat down across from him, Marcus got right to the point. "Has he returned to Paris?"

Petit removed his hat and shook his head. "He's with her, here on the train."

Marcus growled. Two nights ago, he'd been stunned to run into Colin Mabry while leaving Le Bibent. "You had your orders. He was to leave Toulouse days ago. Why didn't you get rid of him?"

Petit stared into his hat. "I suppose I could have shot him, Captain. Would that satisfy you?"

"Hardly the time for jokes, man. This is still G-2's operation, but Mabry is a British officer and happens to be an acquaintance of mine, so you *will* be careful with him."

Petit looked up as if assessing Marcus. Marcus had only known the man a few days, but he recognized a poker face when he saw one.

He didn't like poker faces.

"You know I'd planned to get the lieutenant to leave, but once I found out about Johanna Reyer, the situation changed. I realized the only way to get her to come along willingly is if he's part of the deal. Since they're both determined to rescue Jewel and find the father, I made a decision to string them along." Petit shifted against the seat. "Because of the fix we're in, we need to keep them hot on the trail."

"I know about the fiasco. I was briefed by your local office." Marcus gave him a hard look. "I'm also aware, as acting liaison for this mission, that your people have put me in a tight spot."

"Believe me, Captain, it wasn't planned."

Marcus glanced out the window at the train terminal, his anger simmering. After arriving in Toulouse two days ago, he'd been informed by the Americans that they had failed in the one condition Zero demanded before he would hand over the Black Book.

He turned to Petit. "At this point, we must continue with the mission. Especially now that we have another chance."

Marcus adjusted the brim of his hat and rose from the seat. "When you arrive at the Spanish border, delay the lieutenant. Bring the woman to Barcelona, and we'll talk then. You know the place and the hour."

"I'll meet you there."

At the door, Marcus turned to Petit before opening the compartment. "I've already overstayed my time here, so no more surprises. The stakes—"

"Are high," Petit cut in. "I'm familiar with high stakes, Captain."

"Yes, I imagine you are. I read your file. Among your many occupations, you were once a professional gambler in New Orleans."

He bore his gaze into the American. "But the stakes in this case are worth more than their weight in gold. Take no chances."

"Rest assured, Captain." Petit's dark eyes glinted. "All will go according to plan."

Marcus found himself unable to shake his sense of unease. There were too many variables to this half-baked scheme. Someone—or something—could still go wrong.

And the poker-faced American wasn't giving him any comfort.

CHAPTER 16

The last whistle had sounded, and Jo smiled as the rumble of wheels signaled the train's departure from the Toulouse station.

She was thrilled and relieved to be able to continue their quest. Surely her papa was the reason Kepler had taken Jewel south.

She turned to Colin. "Do you think my father is being held in Barcelona?"

"I doubt it. Spain is neutral and to my knowledge has no facilities for French POWs. Kepler is either taking Jewel there for another reason, or your father is not a prisoner as we'd thought."

He glanced out the window, and Jo followed his gaze. The train terminal had disappeared from view, replaced by the rose-colored brick and ochre rooftops of the city's shops and homes.

Colin turned to her. "I've given it some thought, and it's possible Kepler's leaving has nothing to do with us or your father. He could have received a signal at Le Bibent the other night."

"But what is his purpose?"

He leaned back and sighed. "That is the question, isn't it?"

A light tapping on the compartment window brought them both

around. An elderly conductor smiled apologetically through the glass and held up his stamp.

Jo handed Colin their tickets, and he went to offer them to the old man at the door.

"*Merci.*" The conductor's withered face split into a wide grin as he returned the tickets. "*Félicitations pour votre mariage*, monsieur."

Colin thanked him and closed the door. He turned and chuckled. "You were right about the French. They are romantics."

Returning to his seat beside her, Colin stared out at the passing scenery. Jo remained acutely aware of his closeness to her, his wonderfully spicy scent filling her senses. She appreciated him for pressing on in the search with her, even though he was half convinced Jewel's affection for him had changed.

Her guilt returned, thinking about how she'd blotted from the diary her sister's words of admiration for Captain Kepler. Yet now it seemed Jewel might be feeling more fear than attraction. Had her sister told Colin the truth? Was she in love with Kepler? If she was afraid, surely she would have asked Colin to stay and help her.

Or had Jewel rejected him for the reasons he seemed to believe?

"What has you scowling?"

Jo met Colin's curious look and smiled to cover her brooding thoughts. "I was just hoping our journey on the train isn't too long. I am tired of all this sitting for hours at a time."

He checked his watch. "It's after two o'clock now. According to the train schedule, we should arrive at the Spanish border around five-thirty this afternoon." He looked down at her bag. "How's the bird doing?"

Jo reached down to remove the floral chiffon scarf she used to camouflage the cage. Inside the bag, her pigeon nested quietly in the fresh straw she'd packed along for the trip.

"He seems fine." She re-covered the cage with the scarf. "I think Little Corporal will behave himself for the next few hours."

"Wait. Little Corporal . . ." His gaze narrowed. "It was the nickname given to—"

"Napoleon Bonaparte." She tipped her chin and faced him. "And what better name could I have given to one so small who accomplishes so much for the war effort? Little Corporal braves all kinds of danger, from foul weather to weapons *and* those bloodthirsty falcons. Do you know he nearly died once?"

He looked surprised. "How? The falcons?"

Jo glanced down at the kit bag. "Gunshot. I'd worked at the dovecote only a few weeks when this little white pigeon returned to the loft, bloody and weak. The bullet pierced him just below his right wing, no doubt from a Boche rifle. Still, he carried out his mission and delivered important intelligence. That's when I decided to name him."

"And he lived to fight another day?"

Jo turned to him, fully expecting his mockery. She knew his sentiments about Napoleon. Yet she was surprised to see his lips parted in a smile that made her pulse race.

"Indeed he did." She pursed her lips, appraising him. "Just because he had been wounded didn't mean his life was over."

He studied her a moment before a gleam lit his eyes. "So tell me more about your birds, Mrs. Mabry. You said you helped your grandfather to raise and train racing pigeons. Did any of them ever win?"

"Of course." A wave of pride rippled through her. "Grandfather often took first prize."

Colin seemed impressed. "What about your . . . Moira? Did she enjoy pigeon racing?"

Jo thought about her mother, and the familiar, dull ache pressed in on her. After two years, she still grieved for the woman who gave birth to her and who had loved Jo in her own fashion. "Moira stayed preoccupied with her various crusades. She had little time for such petty enjoyments as pigeons."

She realized her hands were clenched and quickly relaxed them. "She spent much of her time in Dublin, likely to stay away from Grandfather."

"Did your father ever offer marriage?"

Jo's eyes widened, and Colin reached for one of her hands. "Pardon me for asking such a question. I had no right—"

"It's fine, really. And yes, Papa did propose to my mother." She laid her other hand over his in an effort to put him at ease. "I've mentioned to you that they met in Paris when Moira spent a year at art school. She told me Jacob Reyer was handsome, a widower, and a teacher there. Once they had become . . . aware of my presence, he offered to marry her and take her to his home in the north. She refused."

Jo shook her head, her smile bittersweet. "My mother had such a stubborn and independent nature. Like Grandfather, she was unwilling to compromise or to soften to the point of letting down her guard. When I was older, I learned about Papa's marriage proposal. Moira said that even though she held great affection for him, she wouldn't be 'chattel to any man,' so she had declined his offer."

She recalled her mother's lectures about marriage and the perils of subservience. "I think her mother's life married to Grandfather must have been difficult. Moira didn't want that for herself or for me."

"I can understand now why you hold the memory of your father's visit so closely."

Her heart warmed at his look of compassion. "I've always wondered why he never returned to Kilcoole. I thought perhaps Grandfather told him to stay away. My grandfather did hate being at the center of 'Moira's shame,' as he liked to call it. I think about my papa's visit often, and it always comforts me, knowing he loved me without reservation. It didn't seem to matter that I bore the name of Dougherty instead of Reyer."

"But you use his name now."

Realizing her misstep, Jo quickly withdrew her hand from his before resettling against the seat. She decided to offer him a partial truth. "When I first came to France, I thought having my father's name would make the Red Cross more likely to help me find him. Then, once I learned he was reported missing and I was on my own, I decided *Mademoiselle Reyer* stood a better chance of easing into Parisian life and getting on with the French."

Her chin rose in challenge. "He is my father after all, and I have my birth certificate to prove it."

"Of course." His gentle look held no judgment. "I hope you get the chance to see him again, Johanna."

"Thank you." She smiled in relief at his understanding, and at the pleasure she felt being in his company. "I've told you all I know about pigeons, so shall we talk about horses? You said you broke your arm while on a horse. Did you ride often growing up?"

"I loved horses the way you love your birds."

His expression softened, as if recalling a memory. "When Grace and I were in our teens, Father gave us a pair of beautiful bays. We were raised in London, in the district of Knightsbridge, so the horses were stabled on Garret Street, and we rode them at every opportunity."

Jo had never sat on the back of a horse. "Do you and your sister still have them?"

He shook his head. "Both were requisitioned for the war. When I went into the cavalry, I received an American-bred quarter horse, a sorrel gelding named Wyatt." The light in his eyes dimmed. "He was killed by a mortar blast just before I found the farm and your sister."

Wyatt. Jo recalled Jewel's words. "Oh dear! I thought the way Jewel had written about him in her diary . . . I assumed Wyatt was a person. A good friend of yours."

An edge of his mouth lifted. "Jewel knew Wyatt was a horse and said that made him no less faithful a friend." He looked away, but not before she caught the sadness in his expression. "She was right."

Jo ached inside. So much had been taken away from him. "I am sorry."

When he faced her again, she saw obstinacy had replaced his sorrow. "It was the reason I refused a post to train more horses for battle. And before long, God willing, we'll see an end to this war."

"Do you believe that?"

His lips compressed before he nodded. "It seems distant to me at times, but yes, I do have faith it will happen sooner rather than later."

"I hope you are right. If my father is in a prison camp somewhere, he'll be allowed to return home after the war, don't you think? Though there is little left of the farm in Havrincourt."

Again he reached for her hand, and Jo savored the strength of his grip. "You remember I spoke to you about God loving all of us, despite our circumstances . . . and how miracles happen for those who have faith?" He regarded her. "Have you ever prayed, Johanna?"

She searched his gaze. His talks about a benevolent Father in heaven and the ability to recognize miracles both intrigued and unsettled her. "I told you before that Moira did not care for religion. I think she was angry with the church. But Grandfather did teach me the Lord's Prayer when I was young, and he made certain I was baptized."

Jo had been eight years old at the time, and Moira was furious over Grandfather's high-handedness. "When I went off to boarding school in England, all of the girls attended Sunday services." She paused. "Is that how you seek God? By praying?"

He nodded. "You already know about my broken arm, but I also had a stutter for a short time while I was growing up. I was subjected to much teasing. My mother would tell me to pray each night before I went to bed, asking God to give me the strength to overcome my speech problem."

She eyed him in wonder. "You have obviously conquered your impediment."

He chuckled. "I spent a lot of time on my knees asking God's help. After a while, we got to know one another, and I simply began talking to Him, explaining how much I wanted to be like the other boys in school."

Jo had never thought of God as being her friend. "What happened?"

"I was at Harrow School in London. The church vicar needed boys to sing in the choir, as several members had taken ill and the annual Christmas concert was approaching. Despite my trouble speaking, I had a sound voice, but I'd never thought about joining choir.

"My father knew the vicar, who stopped in at Swan's for tea occasionally. One day, I happened to be there at the same time, and the vicar recognized me from school. Once he learned Patrick Mabry was my father, they both pressured me to audition."

She leaned toward him. "How did that go?"

"I sang 'Silent Night,' and when my audition finished, the vicar recruited me for the concert. Later, I was asked to join the house singing, and a few months went by before I realized my speech had improved. If I did stutter, I would sing whatever I was trying to say, and the words would come out. Eventually the problem left me altogether."

He smiled. "I believe God answered my prayer, Johanna. He placed me and the vicar at the tea room at the same time, and He gave me the opportunity I needed to help myself." Colin squeezed her fingers. "You can pray to Him too, for peace and for your father. He will hear you."

Jo's brow creased. She only knew the one prayer. Could she just . . . talk to God? Like a person, a friend?

A rustling sound drew her attention to the kit bag, and she reached in with her free hand to pull away the scarf. Little Corporal was stirring.

"What's wrong?"

"Nothing. He simply wishes to move around. You would too, if you were cooped up for hours in the dark. . . ."

Her words trailed off, and she slowly turned to stare at him. "Oh, how thoughtless of me. Of course you know what it feels like, having been in that tunnel."

Seeing her embarrassment, Colin tried to put her at ease. "It's all right, Johanna. At least I can sympathize with him more than most." Especially now, knowing the pigeon had also been a casualty of war.

She smiled her relief before turning toward the kit bag. "*Tout ira bien*, my little corporal. All will be well."

Johanna's dulcet tone relaxed Colin as well. "You really do love them, don't you?"

She flashed him an impish smile. "Much the same way you love horses."

"*Touché.*" He laughed. "So what started your passion for pigeons? Was it your grandfather's birds in the attic, or that pretty bird ring your father gave you?"

She seemed to consider his question. "Neither. Or perhaps both. I was very young when Papa gave me the ring and quite taken with it. And it's true that when I was older, I was fascinated with Grandfather's dovecote. But I believe my devotion to birds developed through reading."

Colin was intrigued. "What kind of reading? Ornithology?"

"Hardly." Her eyes lit with mischief. "I was just a child at the time, so bird studies were a bit beyond me. No, after my lessons were finished, I would hide upstairs in the attic with the birds and with my book of fairy tales." She clasped her gloved hands neatly in her lap. "Have you ever read 'The Old Woman in the Wood' by the Brothers Grimm?"

Colin had a vague memory of it being among his sister's collection. "Why don't you tell me the story?"

Her face glowed as she settled back against the seat. "Once upon a time, a young woman and her family were set upon by murdering thieves as they traveled through the forest. The young woman was thrown from the carriage, the only survivor, and being lost, she had nowhere to go. She was hungry and tired and heartbroken."

"Now I know why they called them the Brothers Grimm." Colin made a face. "Pretty ghoulish so far."

"True, but it does have a happy ending."

He grinned. "Go on, then."

"A white dove suddenly appeared to the lost girl, holding a golden key in its beak. She took the key, and the dove told her it would unlock a tree where she would find food to sustain her. After she ate, she became tired, and the white dove brought a second golden key that opened a tree where she could shelter for the night. On the third day, the dove provided yet another key, this one to a tree yielding the most beautiful clothes.

"Time passed, and the white dove brought the lost girl a golden key each time she needed help. Then one day, he asked a favor of her: to visit the house of the old woman in the wood. She was to ignore the old woman's greeting and enter the house to search for the room where beautiful rings were kept. There, she was to locate a plain gold band among the bejeweled rings and return it to the white dove."

Johanna's face lit with such enthusiasm, Colin found he enjoyed the sight as much as her storytelling. "Why was the girl not allowed to speak with the old woman?"

She drew back from him, frowning. "Be patient—I am getting to that part." Johanna relaxed her hands to smooth her skirt. "Where was I? Oh yes, the lost girl set off for the old woman's house, and just as the dove instructed, she ignored the woman's greeting and went inside to find the room with the beautiful rings. Enraged, the old woman followed her inside. When she couldn't stop the girl, she grabbed up a birdcage and tried to flee. But the girl rescued the cage, and inside was a bird holding a plain gold band in its beak. She took the ring and returned it to the white dove in the woods, and he became a handsome prince. He told her how the wicked witch had trapped him in her spell—the plain gold band set him free of the enchantment."

When she didn't say more, Colin leaned forward. "Well, what happened then?"

"He took the lost girl to his kingdom, of course, where they married and lived happily ever after."

Colin grunted at the predictable ending. Still, he smiled. "It's no wonder your favorite pigeon is white."

She nodded and laughed. "I admit, the moment I saw Little Corporal, I thought of my handsome prince."

The sound of her laughter captivated him, just as it had before. For a fleeting moment, he wondered if Johanna had ever met a prince she wanted to save. Surely she would go up against the most wicked of witches for the man she loved. . . .

"What are you thinking?"

Colin realized he was frowning. "What am I thinking?" *That I am much more attracted to you than I should be.* He shifted on the seat, putting some space between them. "I'm thinking Petit must have some idea where Kepler is taking Jewel."

He immediately regretted his abruptness when he saw her startled look. But he had no right to think of another when he still sought the truth about Jewel's feelings.

Johanna inched over to add even more space between them. "I imagine the Americans must have men in Spain, watching for Kepler and my sister. If Petit doesn't already know where they're going, he should be able to find out." Her brow creased. "I suppose we must offer him some reason for excluding him from our compartment. What would be appropriate?"

Colin smiled without humor. Likely the American already assumed they were sweethearts, despite knowing of Colin's promise to Jewel. "We'll say nothing unless he asks."

"And if he does ask?"

He gave her a wink. "Then we will continue to pretend we are *amoureux*."

CHAPTER

17

*I*t was six o'clock in the evening when Colin and Johanna finally reached the end of the French line. After leaving the border town of Cerbère, they passed through a lengthy tunnel to arrive in front of the small terminal building at Portbou, Spain.

Johanna secured her kit bag while Colin observed the passengers starting to disembark. He wondered how long before they could continue on to Barcelona.

Suddenly their inner compartment door opened, and Petit stood grinning in the doorway. "You two lovebirds enjoy your honeymoon?"

Ignoring Johanna's blush, Colin frowned at the American. "Most of our trip from Paris was spent stuffed inside a compartment with a dozen other passengers. The sign was our solution to avoid that on this journey."

"And it worked." Petit dipped his head. "We should get moving, though. This is the break-of-gauge station, and we'll have to change trains."

Johanna turned her head and raised a brow. "What is a *break-of-gauge* station?"

"France and Spain each use a different gauge of railroad track," Colin explained. "It means we have to transfer to a Spanish train for the rest of the journey."

"It also means they'll be offloading our luggage now." Petit stepped through the compartment and opened the outer door. "Shall we go?"

Johanna picked up her kit bag, and Colin allowed her to disembark first, making Petit the rear of their party.

On the platform, they approached the staging area, where porters were busy hauling off steamer trunks, leather bags, and boxes. "They should transfer our luggage once it goes through Spanish customs." Petit glanced toward the terminal. "I'll go inside to see when the next train leaves for Barcelona."

Colin and Johanna were watching their bags being piled high onto a wagon along with other cargo when Petit returned. "Bad news, I'm afraid. The last southbound train left fifteen minutes ago. There won't be another until ten o'clock tomorrow morning."

Colin scowled. "Why am I not surprised?"

"Where will we stay?"

Johanna spoke in a tired voice, and he laid his hand on her arm. "I'm sure there must be adequate lodging nearby." He glanced at Petit.

"After we get our luggage and passports inspected, we'll take a taxi into the town of Portbou, a few kilometers down the hill."

"Inspected?" Johanna's face paled. "Will all of our possessions need to be checked?"

Petit nodded. "Is there some problem?"

Colin glanced at her. While their passports had been checked during the trip, no one had taken a look in Johanna's bag. "Mrs. Mabry dislikes having strangers paw through her things." He turned to Petit. "Her bag contains a woman's personal items, you understand."

He almost laughed as the American colored slightly.

"Well now, I could smooth the way, so to speak, with regard to your purse and the bag." Petit dug into his coat pocket, jingling coins. "A few Spanish *duros* should do the trick."

"Bribery?" Colin's amusement vanished. "And if your method doesn't work?"

Petit shrugged, and Colin's gut tightened. He looked toward a two-story building near the terminal and saw the wagon full of luggage. "I suppose that is the customs office?"

"Yes, and as you can see, passengers are already waiting to get inside. If we want to arrive in town before dark, we need to get in line." Petit turned to Johanna. "What would you like to do, Mrs. Mabry?"

Johanna turned to Colin. "What do you think about this bribery business?"

Colin knew that if Petit's attempt backfired and the pigeon was discovered, all three of them risked getting thrown into a Spanish jail.

His mind sifted through possibilities, but aside from bribery, there seemed nothing for it but to release the bird and be done. Colin knew Johanna would be unhappy, and oddly, he'd developed a sort of camaraderie of his own with the pigeon.

A vague plan began to form as he met Johanna's imploring gaze. Colin made a decision and reached for the canvas satchel he wore at his side—the bag containing his prosthetic attachments.

He wasn't certain his idea would work, but the scheme stood a better chance than Petit trying to bribe a Spanish customs agent, especially if he ran up against an honest one. "Give us a moment, will you?" He glanced at the American. "We will catch up."

"Don't be too long."

As Petit left for the customs office, Colin spoke to Johanna. "I want to talk with you privately—"

"I am not setting Little Corporal free."

Fiery determination had replaced the pleading look in her eyes. He sighed. "If my plan works, you won't have to." *And if it fails, we both go to jail.*

"What plan?"

"Open the kit bag, and I'll show you."

She did as he asked, and once he'd made the quick transfer, Colin took the bag and carried it while Johanna walked beside him. "Pray this works."

She bit her lower lip, nodding.

Petit had moved up in the line quickly, and they took their places beside him. Colin noted four tables in the customs office, each manned with an agent.

Petit's brow lifted as he eyed the kit bag in Colin's grasp.

"We've decided I shall take Mrs. Mabry's bag through the inspection to save her any undue embarrassment."

One side of Petit's mouth lifted, but he said nothing as the line moved forward.

Johanna went first when it was their turn, handing the agent her passport and purse for inspection. When she finished, Colin turned to Petit. "You go next."

Of the four agents, Colin had observed one walking with a distinct limp and bearing a scar from nose to ear—the way a bayonet might strike a soldier on the battlefield.

It was a long shot, but he decided to hold back until that agent had finished with his passenger. When the dark-haired man finally gave him the signal to approach, Colin took the kit bag to the inspection table.

The agent's frown eased as he glanced at Colin's uniform. "Welcome to Spain, Lieutenant. You are British Army?"

Colin nodded. "Second Cavalry Division under General Haig."

The Spanish man beamed. "French Foreign Legion. Second-class legionnaire."

Colin smiled and offered the man his passport. The agent

KATE BRESLIN

hardly gave the document a glance before handing it back. "And the bag?"

Colin reached to open it, but his fingers fumbled with the strap. He held up his prosthetic. "Would you mind? I am a bit clumsy with this."

The agent's dark eyes brightened with emotion. "It would be my honor."

The man quickly opened the bag and peered inside. Colin's pulse raced, watching the agent's eyes widen at the array of devices—Colin's steel hooks, eating fork, and the steel pick.

Silently the man closed the bag and refastened the strap. His face contorted with emotion as he stepped back and offered Colin a salute. "Thank you, Lieutenant, for your service with the Allies in France."

Colin's heartbeat began to slow as he returned the salute. "And you, Legionnaire."

He picked up the kit bag and joined Petit and Johanna, who had already reclaimed their luggage. The American raised a brow. "What was all that saluting about?"

"Merely an exchange between comrades-in-arms." Colin glanced at Johanna. "Are we ready to go into town?"

She took the kit bag from him, smiling her relief.

Petit scratched his head and glanced at both of them. "Sure. I'll go outside and hail a cab."

When he'd gone, Johanna linked her arm in his. "That was very brave of you, Colin. And clever, too."

He glanced at her kit bag. "Luckily our mutual friend behaved himself."

Her smile broadened. "I consider you both my champions."

Colin squeezed her arm, basking in her praise.

"We've a cab waiting outside." Petit returned to hoist Johanna's small steamer trunk under his arm before grabbing up his own bag.

Johanna smiled. "Why, thank you, Mr. Petit. You are most kind."

209

Grinning, Petit winked at her. "I've been known to be a little chivalrous myself."

Colin snorted.

Grabbing up the rest of the luggage, the three went outside. While Petit and the cab driver stowed the bags, Colin and Johanna slid into the back seat. "Mr. Petit is being rather helpful on this trip, don't you think?"

"Charming as ever."

Johanna's tranquil expression faded. "Obviously, you don't appreciate his efforts. You must admit, he seems to know his way around this place. And he's got Spanish money."

"I still don't trust him." Colin scowled. "He was ready to bribe the customs agents!"

"And what about you?"

"I may have used my situation as a British officer to my advantage, but there was no bribery involved."

"Only a little duplicity, then." A smile touched her lips. "All things aside, I suspect Mr. Petit likes you, and that is why he goads your temper."

He grinned. "Like someone else I know?"

She gave him an innocent, wide-eyed look. "I cannot imagine who you mean, sir."

He chuckled before a sobering thought intruded. "I wonder if Petit isn't being too hasty about our leaving in the morning. Could our two friends be here in Portbou?"

"I hadn't thought of that. Let's ask him if he can find out."

"We're all set," Petit called through the open window before he opened the cab door and slid into the open seat in front.

When Colin voiced their question, Petit turned to appraise him with a look. "It's possible they are still here. Once we find a hotel, I'll check back with the ticket office to see the passenger lists." Again he jingled the coins in his pocket. "I should be able to find out if they arrived and whether they've gone on to Barcelona."

More bribery. Colin stifled his irritation. It was important to know if Jewel and Kepler were still here. Petit's money could buy the information and perhaps save them more traveling time.

The driver returned to sit behind the wheel, and Petit exchanged a few foreign words with him before glancing at Colin and Johanna in the back seat. "Our man here says there are a number of hotels in Portbou on Passeig de la Sardana, a street near the beach."

Colin raised a brow. "So you're fluent in Spanish as well?"

He nodded. "My second language, growing up in Texas. But these folks speak Catalan, a different language from the rest of Spain."

Despite his annoyance, Colin was impressed with Petit's linguistic skills and his ability to adapt in a new land. Johanna was right. Having him along substantially improved their situation and the chances of finding Kepler and Johanna's sister. "Let's go."

Petit relayed a few more words to the driver, and the cab pulled away from the busy railroad station, traveling past a large cathedral and down a steep hill toward the town.

The setting sun cast a pink glow against the scattered clouds in the sky, reflecting a rosy hue against the Mediterranean Sea. Clusters of red ochre rooftops huddled beside the sandy shore, many of the buildings more modern than those in Toulouse.

The taxi finally pulled up in front of a white two-story brick building, and Colin gazed at the wrought-iron lettering above the door. *Casa a prop del Mar.*

"This is the place, and we're in luck. They have at least one vacancy." Petit pointed to the sign in the front window. "Let's see if we can try for three rooms, shall we?"

A portly man in white shirt and black bow tie greeted them at the front desk. "*Bona nit!*"

Petit returned a few Catalan words, and Colin was relieved when the innkeeper addressed them in French. "I am Senyor Vilar. Welcome to my house near the sea. How may I help you?"

Johanna stepped up. "We will need three rooms, if you please." The innkeeper pulled out a box with keys. "I have just two open upstairs."

Petit spoke up. "You both stay here. I'll find lodging down the street."

"That's decent of you." Colin suppressed his relief. "You're certain?"

"It's no problem. Besides, I still need to get back up the hill and check with the train station."

"And you'll let us know?"

Petit nodded. "If they're still here, I'll telephone your hotel. Otherwise, I'll bring the taxi around in the morning, a half hour before our train leaves. Be packed and ready to go."

Once he departed, Colin and Johanna signed the hotel register, and Senyor Vilar helped to carry their luggage upstairs. He deposited their bags on the polished wood floor between two numbered doors and gave Johanna the keys. "You may choose which you prefer, *senyora*. Both rooms are the same, though they do not connect. The bath accommodation is there." He pointed to a door across the hall. "Will there be anything else?"

Johanna darted a glance at Colin. "Is there a place we can dine, sir?"

"*Sí*, several cafés along this street offer delicious Catalan dishes, including our own dining room." Senyor Vilar puffed out his chest. "My wife, Senyora Vilar, will be serving our guests early *tapas* and drinks downstairs in half an hour if you care to join us."

Johanna smiled. "Thank you."

Nodding, he offered a slight bow. "Please let me know if you need anything."

When he'd gone, Johanna held up the keys marked 201 and 202. "Any preference?"

"Ladies first."

She took 202 and entered the room with her kit bag. Once Colin had helped her with the rest of her luggage, he settled into his own room before they went downstairs.

The dining room was small yet well-appointed. Within minutes, Colin and Johanna were savoring the local fare of *escalivada*—roasted vegetables in olive oil—various other *tapas*, and Senyora Vilar's native Valencian dish *paella*.

Once replete, Colin leaned back in his chair, gazing at the nearly empty plates on the table. "I cannot possibly eat another bite." His mouth curved upward as he rubbed his full stomach. "No wonder Senyor Vilar has such a jolly look about him. His wife certainly knows her way around the kitchen."

"It was delicious." Johanna blew out a sigh and dropped her napkin beside her plate. "Though I think I ate too much. Would you care to take a walk down to the beach?"

He glanced out the dining room window. Darkness had settled, and beyond the terrace, a quarter moon shone white against the sea. Colin could make out the waves crashing along the shore.

"It might be a bit cold." He turned to survey her lightweight traveling costume. "My uniform is warm enough, but do you have a heavier jacket?"

Smiling, she rose from the table. "I'll get my woolen shawl and be right back."

CHAPTER

18

*J*o returned with her shawl to find Colin waiting by the terrace doors. While she was glad for the covering, she would much rather have had her tunic and britches. And the boots were a much better choice for warding off the night's chill air. "I'm ready."

She paused as a thought suddenly struck. "Or should we stay in case Mr. Petit calls?"

"He would have done so by now." Colin checked his watch. "Likely our friends went on to Barcelona."

Jo nodded. "You know, it has been some time since I've been to the seashore when there wasn't a fear of a U-boat or planes dropping bombs out of the sky."

"That makes two of us." He smiled, his brow lifting. "Are you sure you'll be warm enough in that?"

"I'll be fine." Wrapping the woolen shawl tighter around her shoulders, Jo felt a sudden tug at the back of her head. She hadn't worn her hat and realized the pin holding her hair in place had become caught in the shawl's weave.

Colin realized her dilemma. "Here, let me help."

Jo's senses heightened at his touch, his fingers gently working

214

the fabric from her hair before he tucked the shawl snug against her collar. A blush crept into her cheeks. "Thank you."

"My pleasure." His eyes glinted as he opened the terrace door and allowed her to pass.

Jo was glad for the wool shawl once she stepped outside. The air was cool, the breezes off the water making her shiver and clutch the wrap more tightly about her.

"You're certain you wish to walk on the beach?"

She nodded. "It's not likely we'll have another chance. Mr. Petit said he would be here thirty minutes before the ten o'clock train tomorrow morning, and we must be ready to leave."

"All right, then." He extended his left arm to her. "Shall we?"

Jo tucked her gloved hand into the crook of his arm. Strolling beneath the lamp lights along Passeig de la Sardana, she noted two cafés and another small hotel. "I imagine Mr. Petit found himself lodging there."

"Yes, and I admit I'm glad he had to stay elsewhere."

Jo looked up at him. "I know you don't trust him."

"Nor should you. We still don't know whether or not he entered your room at Toulouse." He shot her a sideways glance. "If you recall, he and I did not get off to a good start."

Colin looked ahead as they neared the quay and the steps leading down to the beach. "And of course, we don't want him knowing about Little Corporal. The farther he stays away from the pigeon, the better."

"I know I have created a bit of a problem, having my little bird with me. . . ." Jo caught his sardonic look in the lamplight. "All right, quite a problem. But we don't know what awaits us in Barcelona with Kepler. If he *is* coercing my sister for some reason, then Jewel may benefit from Little Corporal's service." She frowned. "Though I'm not sure how."

"We'll find her, Johanna." He squeezed her hand. "Have faith."

"Believe it or not, I am trying, Colin."

"Good." He smiled. "Now, watch your step."

Jo grabbed the rail as she carefully descended the stone steps leading onto the beach. Reaching the bottom, her ankles wobbled in the button-up shoes as the short heels sank into the sand. "Perhaps this wasn't a good idea." She sighed. "I really miss my boots."

He chuckled. "Well, I'm wearing mine, so give me your arm again, and we'll take things slow. If you do end up falling on your face, I'll return you to the quay."

"Thank you for your kindness." Jo couldn't see his face in the shadows to know his reaction to her teasing. She smiled. Likely he was grinning.

The sand became firmer as they neared the water, though Jo still clung to him. Finally they stopped at the water's edge, and she breathed in the briny smell of the sea, the cold breeze blowing against her face and teasing wisps of hair from her coil.

Ignoring the tendrils fluttering against her cheeks, she gazed at the white quarter moon. "'Tis so beautiful here, and peaceful. I think I could stay forever."

"If it were in any other time, we could just be two people on holiday."

Jo turned to see him looking out at the moon's reflection on the water. "Wouldn't that be lovely? No war, no worry about getting enough to eat. No waiting for missing loved ones to come home."

He turned to her. "I am praying you will get to see your father, Johanna." Moonlight revealed the compassion on his handsome face. "We'll locate Kepler and Jewel, and once I determine the truth of her feelings . . ."

"How could she not care for you, Colin?" Jo struggled with the emotion in her voice. "She hid you from the enemy and fed you from her own meager stores. And did she not tend your wound?"

"Yes, she did all of that. But the old wound eventually healed, while this one . . ."

He glanced at the prosthetic between them, and anger rose in her.

"'Tis nonsense! You have so much to offer the woman you love."
She glanced away. "Sister or not, if Jewel lets you go, she is a fool."

He went still beside her, and it was a moment before she could
look at him.

"Have you ever loved anyone, Johanna?" He paused. "As a
woman loves a man?"

Jo longed to tell him the truth about her feelings, but her conscience prevailed. "My . . . particular circumstances in Kilcoole
didn't offer many opportunities for meeting young men. And in
Paris, well, except for André, the only males that hold a place in
my heart have feathers."

He flashed a grin before his smile faded. "If you were Jewel,
could *you* love someone who was . . . altered?"

"How has it altered you, Colin?" She spoke softly as she ached
for him. "You have an injury resulting from an act of bravery. And
despite what you may think, it does not change who you are."

Pulse pounding, she disengaged her arm from his and reached
for his gloved hand. She placed it over his heart, covering it with
her own. "I would love that man, no matter what his appearance.
You told me God loves us all, remember? He does not judge by our
outward appearance or our station in life, but by what lies within
us. Isn't that true?"

She was not aware of the vehemence in her tone until Colin
reached to tuck a loose strand of her hair behind her ear. His touch
caused a shiver along her spine.

"It is absolutely true." His voice had gentled. "God sees us
with the heart."

She regarded their hands—hers flesh, his not—lying against his
chest. "Then the man I love would be perfectly whole in my eyes.
Because my heart would see his integrity, his humor, his kindness,
and his wit. It would see his honor."

When she lifted her eyes and started to remove her hand, he
reached around with his free arm and pulled her to him. Their faces

were so close she could feel his breath against her skin before the night wind carried it off. His spicy cologne surrounded her as he bent his head toward hers, and she heard the rush of the waves lapping onto the beach before closing her eyes to experience the first, light brush of his lips against her own.

Jo opened her eyes a moment later and met the intensity of his gaze, the tight angles of his face drawn with emotion. He dipped his head again, and this time captured her mouth in a hungry, relentless kiss, as though he deemed words useless to express what was in his heart.

She stopped thinking as she kissed him back, hesitantly at first, then without reservation as she matched his desire with her own. Jo wasn't certain when he drew her into his embrace, but she pressed closer, savoring his solid warmth while he sheltered her against the cold night and eased the incessant longing in her soul.

They stood together for seconds, or perhaps hours; Jo lost all track of time.

It was the water soaking through her shoes that finally roused her from his intoxicating kiss, bringing her back to the present. She pulled away as another foamy wave washed across her feet.

"Come, Johanna."

She heard his voice, felt him tuck her hand back into the crook of his arm as he slowly drew her farther up the beach, away from the water's edge.

Jo looked up at him, caught in the riptide of her own anguish and guilt. What was she doing, enticing this honorable man to break his vow to Jewel when even now her sister might be Kepler's hostage? How could Jo assume her sister's feelings for Colin were any less than her own?

Blinking back tears, she was only half aware Colin still held on to her. "You'll catch your death of cold if you're not careful."

And why shouldn't she?

"Johanna . . ."

She looked at him. "Oh, Colin, what have we done?"

His jaw tightened, his eyes searching hers. "You've done nothing. I am to blame."

She shook her head and pulled away from him, nearly losing her footing in the sand. "It was a mistake. I never should have suggested a walk on the beach together."

Jo cast a desperate glance toward the quay and beyond to the lighted terrace of their hotel. "I . . . I must go back and check on Little Corporal."

"Let me help you—"

"No!" She held up a hand. "No, please . . . I can manage." She turned from him, determined to crawl back to her room through the sand if necessary to hide her shame.

She made slow progress in her heels, hoping he wouldn't follow. As she reached the quay, Jo paused to glance behind her, relieved to see his shadowed frame still standing near the edge of the sea.

Nursing her ache along with her guilt, she turned and fled back up the street toward the hotel.

Colin gazed after her as humiliation, anger, and a deeper emotion he dared not examine consumed him. What had he been about? Johanna had spoken to him so eloquently of honor and integrity, and then he'd gone and ruined it all by taking unfair advantage of her!

No wonder she wanted to be as far from him as possible. He was a bounder to seduce her.

And what about Jewel? Colin had yet to determine her true circumstances and feelings; he still believed she'd spoken to him in Toulouse under duress. Until then, he was bound by duty to the promise that had called him back to France: God's plan for his future with Jewel, offering her a home and happiness, making up for all that she had sacrificed. . . .

You're in love with Johanna. Colin's heart beat dully in his chest while the truth settled over him like a heavy stone. His feelings for her had nothing to do with duty or honor, and everything to do with love. Yet he was still bound by his vow to her sister.

Standing in his misery, he watched as Johanna finally reached the quay. She looked back at him before turning to head up the street, and he quickly followed at a safe distance, making certain she returned to the hotel unharmed.

As she passed through the terrace doors to go inside, he paused, hovering beneath a street lamp, his skin numbed to the bite of the chill wind.

Never would he forget their kiss. He'd tasted her passion, felt the softness of her as he drew her into his arms. Colin thought of the words she'd spoken about love being a matter of the heart, and the way her stirring declaration had made him yearn inside.

How would he face her tomorrow? Colin briefly considered the idea of going upstairs to apologize, but her emotions were likely too agitated, and he was still too on edge to go inside just yet.

He walked the streets instead, and it was late when he returned to the hotel.

Senyor Vilar sat behind the desk, his dark features filled with concern. "I hope your wife is feeling well, Lieutenant?"

"A bit too much of the cold night air." Colin forced a smile. "She'll be right as rain tomorrow."

The sound of voices coming from the dining room drew his attention. "You've got a party going on?"

"No, the guests are having dinner."

Colin nodded. Like the French, the Catalans seemed to enjoy dining late.

"Are you hungry, Lieutenant?"

"No, but I would appreciate tea if you have it."

The innkeeper shrugged and shook his head.

"All right, how about a coffee with cream?"

"*Sí, molt bé.*" This time Senyor Vilar beamed. "Shall I have it brought upstairs?"

"Yes, thank you. Room 201."

Upstairs, Colin neared his door but continued a few more steps to Johanna's room, where he listened for a moment. No sound emerged, and he supposed she had gone to sleep.

Relieved, Colin had worried she might be weeping and knew he wouldn't be able to stand himself if he didn't offer to comfort her.

He entered his room and had just removed his cap and jacket when a knock sounded.

Johanna? Colin rushed to open the door.

His hopes fell as he regarded the plump innkeeper's wife holding a tray with his coffee. "*Bona nit, senyor.*" She beamed. "*Cafè amb llet?*"

He allowed her inside to set the coffee on his nightstand. "*Gràcies, senyora.*"

She offered a gracious bow. "*De res.*"

When she'd left, Colin finished getting ready for bed. Removing the leather chest harness and arm brace holding his prosthetic in place, he sighed with relief, glad to be rid of the constrictive metal. Once he'd donned his nightclothes, he set his alarm for the morning and then reached for his coffee.

He sat on the edge of his bed sipping the warm drink while the image of Johanna's tormented face continued to permeate his conscience.

Colin still didn't know how he would face her in the morning. And what if Jewel, once they found her, admitted she still had feelings for him?

A loud yawn escaped him as a weariness he'd not felt since coming home from the war suddenly descended upon him. In truth, he'd endured an exhausting day.

Returning the cup to its saucer, Colin extinguished the lamp. Perhaps things would look better in the morning.

He didn't see how, but he must have faith.

*J*o returned from breakfast the following morning and decided to finish packing. It was early yet—barely eight-thirty—and while Petit wouldn't arrive to collect them for another hour, she needed to stay busy to fight off the fatigue making her light-headed and causing her eyes to burn.

Dressed in yesterday's gray traveling suit, the only clothes to repack were her nightgown, robe, and of course the shawl. Jo brushed her hand over the heavy wool, her thoughts returning to the previous evening, when she'd clutched the fabric about her, bracing against the cold breezes coming off the shore. The way Colin's kiss had ignited her senses, every raw nerve attuned to his touch and his scent, the warmth of his lips . . .

A stab of longing pierced her, another reminder of her sleepless night. Lying awake in the dark, she'd replayed over and over in her mind their kiss. In the light of day, it was foolish to imagine that either of them had not wanted it to happen, yet guilt continued to plague her, the knowledge that she had betrayed her sister, and in the process, fallen in love with Colin Mabry.

If Jo felt miserable, what must Colin be going through? Last night, he'd taken all of the blame for their actions. He, a man who prided himself on being honorable. Was he feeling remorse?

As far as she knew, he still held the hope that Jewel cared for him, convinced Jo's sister was somehow under Kepler's power.

Again Jo wondered if Jewel was being threatened. She knew the feeling; it was the reason she could never return to Ireland. Not without being hunted down and exposed . . .

She compressed her lips as she folded the shawl, placing it inside the open steamer trunk on her bed. Colin was a man of worth. He would pursue her sister and seek out the truth of her feelings.

While Jo must forget hers.

As if that were even possible. She fought against a growing sense of melancholy. More than ever, she needed her papa, the one person alive in the world who had loved her.

Petit must know where to locate Kepler and her sister in Barcelona. The sooner they found them, the closer Jo would be to discovering her father's whereabouts.

Before closing the trunk, she retrieved her toiletries from behind the screen and gazed fondly at her small white bird in his cage on the floor. "We are about to continue our quest, *mon ami.*"

She had just finished packing the trunk when a knock sounded at the door.

Her glance darted toward the screen before she moved to answer the summons. Jo's pulse pounded as she deliberated over what she might say to Colin.

"Good morning, Mrs. Mabry."

She had inched the door open and was surprised to see Petit in the hall. "Mr. Petit! You're certainly early. Has something happened?"

"I've located Kepler and your sister in Portbou."

"They are here?" Stunned, Jo cracked the door a little wider. "Where exactly?"

"At the train station." Removing his hat, he glanced at the floor.

"Look, I made a mistake about the train schedule yesterday. The next one leaves for Barcelona at nine o'clock. We have only minutes to get there if we want to board the same train and follow them."

"Oh, my goodness!" A quiver of excitement raced through her. "I'm almost packed. I need to go and fetch Colin—"

"There's no time."

Her eyes widened. "What do you mean?"

"We have to catch that train."

Jo opened the door wide and stood with arms crossed. "Colin *is* going with us, Mr. Petit. I am not leaving without him."

He stared at her, then muttered something unintelligible before slamming the hat back onto his head. "Get your luggage together. I'll go and see if he's ready. But we've got to hurry!"

Closing the door, Jo finished securing her trunk and placed it with her hatboxes near the door. She returned to her pigeon behind the screen and carefully fed Little Corporal a dropperful of the chamomile tea, listening for Petit's knock and hoping he wouldn't return before she had finished.

"You are such a brave boy." Jo soothed her little bird as she returned him to his cage.

She was setting out the kit bag with her other luggage when Petit returned. This time, Jo allowed him inside. "Is Colin ready?"

"The lieutenant was still in bed. He's not feeling well. He said we should go on to Barcelona, and he'll catch the afternoon train and meet us there."

Jo's eyes widened in alarm. "What is wrong with him?"

"He didn't say. Maybe it was something he ate at dinner?"

Jo swallowed past the ache in her throat. She doubted it was the food. Colin obviously didn't want to face her so soon after last night. He must feel awful. "I should go to him."

She started for the door. Petit blocked her way. "Mrs. Mabry . . . Johanna . . . if we do not leave this minute, I fear we'll lose your sister altogether."

Frowning with a sudden uneasiness, she searched his face. While Petit had been most helpful during their quest, Colin didn't trust the American. Jo also recalled the mysterious intruder in her hotel room back in Toulouse. Colin hadn't ruled out Petit there, either.

Was he telling her the truth? "I need to see Colin." Determination edged her voice. "It won't take but a minute, Mr. Petit."

He blew out a heavy breath and turned to open the door for her. "Suit yourself, ma'am."

Once they exited to the hall, Jo went to Colin's door and knocked softly. "Colin? Are you all right?"

Silence. She glanced at Petit.

"He probably went back to sleep."

Jo knocked again. "Colin?" Still no answer. She bit her lower lip. Was he so terribly ill? "I'll go and get a key from Senyor Vilar."

"No need." Reaching into his pocket, Petit removed a set of picks, and in less than a minute, he'd quietly opened Colin's door. "After you," he whispered.

Jo peered inside. Colin lay sound asleep in his bed. She debated a moment on whether to wake him or not. But if he was feeling ill . . .

She stepped back out into the hall.

Petit spoke in a low voice. "Look, Mrs. Mabry. I've got a cab waiting. If you'd rather stay here, I understand. But I need to continue following your sister and Kepler. Maybe you and the lieutenant should go home to Paris."

"No! Wait." Jo frowned as she tried to decide what to do. If she remained in Portbou, she would lose her best and last chance to find Jewel and the trail leading to their father.

Still, she didn't want to abandon Colin. "Are you certain he said he would follow this afternoon?"

Petit's expression softened. "I'll fetch him myself from the train station."

"All right." She peeked in at Colin's sleeping form one last time before gently closing the door to return to her own room.

While Petit hauled the bulk of her luggage downstairs, Jo carried her purse and the kit bag. She regretted now not leaving Colin a note and decided to stop at the front desk for pen and paper. The innkeeper was not there.

"Can you get the door?"

Petit stood at the hotel entrance, his arms loaded with her bags. Jo quickly obliged, then cast a glance back at the empty front desk. She knew their taxi waited outside and that Petit would leave her behind if she didn't follow.

"Mrs. Mabry?"

She blew out a frustrated sigh as she moved to enter the back seat of the cab. Irritated at being pressured despite the necessity, Jo spoke to him in a brisk tone. "When Colin arrives in Barcelona this afternoon, Mr. Petit, I'm going with you to meet his train."

"Of course." Petit closed his eyes as he rested his head back against the seat.

His assurance improved her mood somewhat. Regardless of what had transpired last night, Jo wanted Colin by her side.

At the busy station, Petit purchased their tickets while the bags went with a porter. On the platform, Jo's attention turned to seeking out Kepler and her sister. She scanned for any sign of them, knowing Jewel typically wore black. "Have you some idea which car they're in? Can we sit nearby?"

"We shouldn't get too close, or we'll arouse Kepler's suspicions." Petit's expression eased, and he smiled. "Tell you what. When we disembark in Barcelona, we'll watch for them and follow to see where they plan to stay."

"An excellent idea!" Jo's heart thrummed with new anticipation as she and Petit found their seats in coach. Settling the kit bag onto the floor beside her feet, she cracked it open, making certain her filmy scarf lay over the cage.

Jo searched the passengers entering the car and realized this was the closest she'd ever come to actually meeting her sister. With a pang, she realized how much she missed Colin and wished he were here to share the moment with her. Perhaps they could talk. . . .

The train's whistle pulled her back to the present. The wheels beneath them lumbered forward, and again she surveyed the dozens of noisy people now seated in the same car. A number of women wore the black of mourning, but there was no Kepler accompanying them.

She turned and whispered to Petit. "You are certain they are on this train?"

He eyed her with a languid expression. "I saw them enter the second car ahead of ours."

Satisfied, Jo leaned back in her seat and tried to calm her jangled nerves. It was no use, however, and she fidgeted with her gloves, ready to burst with excitement at the thought of meeting Jewel for the very first time. The trip to Barcelona would take almost two and a half hours. Could she sit still that long?

Her gaze darted to the kit bag at her feet.

She hoped Little Corporal at least would be able to contain himself.

CHAPTER

20

This could not be happening twice.

The thought filtered through Colin's pounding skull as he awoke to the bright light shining in through his hotel window. Blinking against the glare, he slowly turned his head to eye the suspect cup of coffee on the nightstand. He glanced at the alarm clock beside it.

The hands had stopped at 0800.

"No . . ." He groaned as he reached for his wristwatch lying beside the clock and squinted at the dial. *0900.*

Titan's teeth! He'd slept through the blasted alarm. *Petit* . . .

Muttering a curse, this time at the American, Colin raised himself to sit on the edge of the bed. He held his head for a full minute until the room stopped spinning, then rose and stumbled toward the washstand.

He met his bleary-eyed reflection in the mirror before splashing his face with cold water. How had Petit managed to drug his coffee?

Just thirty minutes remained before the American was to arrive and take them to the train. *If* the bounder was coming for them at all.

Either way, Colin must hurry. If Petit failed to show, Colin and Johanna would hire their own cab to the station.

Colin abandoned the idea of shaving and went through the rest of his ablutions with lightning speed. He dressed quickly, leaving off with most of the shirt buttons before fitting the harness and shrugging into his uniform tunic.

By the time he fled his room in a somewhat presentable state, it was 0925. He knocked on Johanna's door, dreading his confrontation with her. He was glad at least the ache in his head had dulled enough that he would have his wits about him.

When Johanna still hadn't answered after the second knock, Colin wondered if she was downstairs having breakfast.

Reaching the lobby, he spied the portly innkeeper behind the desk, reviewing his books. "Excuse me, *senyor*, have you seen my . . . Madame Mabry?"

Senyor Vilar looked up and smiled. "*Bon dia*, Lieutenant." His face abruptly registered confusion. "But . . . I thought you were with them?"

Colin frowned. "Who?"

"Senyora Mabry and the tall American you arrived with. I saw them getting into a cab when I returned from the back room about an hour ago. I thought perhaps the three of you wished to enjoy an early meal at one of our cafés."

Johanna had left the hotel . . . with Petit? Colin's heart pounded. "Do you know where they went?"

Vilar shrugged. "The American dined here with us last night and asked for recommendations, but I do not know which café he might have chosen."

Petit was at their hotel last night? Colin scowled. It would explain how the man had managed to get the sleeping draught into the coffee. He and the American were going to have it out one of these days and soon.

But why hadn't they returned? A sense of dread filled him. "Do you have a spare key for 202?"

The innkeeper's dark brows drew together as he reached for the box of keys. "I will accompany you upstairs."

Upon reaching their floor, the portly man unlocked Johanna's room, and Colin rushed inside.

Everything was gone—her steamer trunk, the hatboxes, even her kit bag with Little Corporal. Had she purposely left him behind?

Colin checked the time. 0945. Anger at Petit warred with his self-reproach. Johanna must have decided to duck out early with the American for the train station, wishing to avoid Colin as long as possible. Not that he blamed her. He'd been three kinds of a fool yesterday, making her run away from him.

Teeth clenched, Colin fished a folded wad of francs from his pocket and handed the cash to the innkeeper. "Take what you need for our rooms. I have to pack. If you would also arrange a cab, I've got just minutes to catch the ten o'clock train to Barcelona."

Vilar paused with the money in hand. "There is no ten o'clock train, Lieutenant."

Colin stared at him. "What do you mean?"

"The train for Barcelona . . . it leaves at nine o'clock each morning. The next one does not depart until this afternoon."

So Petit had lied. Colin didn't know why he should be surprised. "Get me the taxi. I'm going to the station anyway."

Ten minutes later, Colin arrived at the terminal to discover the innkeeper was correct—the train left at nine, not at ten as Petit had led him and Johanna to believe. The timetables were clearly posted on the wall next to the ticket office, so the American could hardly claim a mistake.

Colin was also devastated to confirm that a couple fitting Johanna and Petit's description had boarded the early train.

Guilt and despair pummeled him all the way back to the inn.

Johanna had left him. Colin had overstepped the boundaries of gentlemanly behavior, and with Jewel's sister, no less.

But why had Petit tainted his coffee? If the man had been at the hotel last night, had Johanna met up with him when she returned from the beach?

Despite Colin's distrust of Petit, Johanna seemed to think him helpful. *Ha!* But . . . what if she *had* expressed to him her desire to get away from Colin?

He wouldn't put it past the crazy American to drug him in order to ensure their escape.

Colin was in a foul mood by the time he returned to the hotel. Upon reaching the stairs leading to his room, he abandoned the idea and instead headed for the quay and the sandy shores of the Mediterranean.

On the beach, he stared out at the water sparkling beneath the morning sun. Over and over his mind taunted him with the memory of last night's kiss and of holding Johanna in his arms. Then rose an image of her traumatized face when she pushed him away and stumbled off, clearly wishing to be far from his company.

He trekked north along the shore's edge, as though he could distance himself from his thoughts. Vaguely he noted the incoming tide, the rhythmic waves rushing toward him, but only after a splash of seawater doused his boots did he pause and look down.

Last evening those waves had interrupted their kiss.

Again images crowded his mind: the two of them huddled together, their kiss warm and tender, quickly turning into desire. Not thinking, only feeling as Johanna's fervor matched his own . . .

Colin compared the precious memory with her reaction afterward, and his pulse sped. She *had* responded to him, most eagerly in fact. Could her distress have been due more to embarrassment than to anger, as though she had also wrestled with her conscience?

His hope flared. Perhaps it was her guilt and not an aversion to him that prompted her to go with Petit. It made sense; the woman they had both betrayed with that wondrous, forbidden kiss was Johanna's own sister.

But would Johanna simply leave him here without so much as a note?

She wouldn't. Thinking back to her impassioned speech of last night, Colin realized it wasn't the first time Johanna had spoken her mind to him, nor was she a woman to cower off without a word, especially after dragging him all the way here from Britain to help her.

She would have offered him something: a word, a letter. So why hadn't she?

Uneasiness settled over him as he resumed his walk along the beach. Petit had lied about the train, and he'd tainted Colin's drink—twice. He was also a suspect in the incident with the diary back in Toulouse. The man was not to be trusted.

A sudden thought struck Colin, and his pulse accelerated. What if Petit's motives had nothing to do with the current situation between Colin and Johanna?

Perhaps Petit never intended for Colin to accompany them south.

The disturbing thought quickly gave way to another, and his gut tightened. Was Johanna in any kind of trouble? Colin knew next to nothing about the American, other than what the man had told him. Petit hadn't even been willing to show his passport.

Colin's alarm hovered on the edge of fear as he paused near the pier and glanced at his watch. The train for Barcelona wouldn't depart for hours. Even if he traveled south, how would he find either of them in such a metropolis?

He stared unseeing toward the fishing boats offshore, his mind working. There must be something he could do.

Lacourt. He would send the Frenchman a telegram.

With his new call to action, Colin turned to walk back toward the quay. Already he'd traveled some distance. He intended to inform the Frenchman about Johanna, and since Lacourt and Petit were friends, or at least acquaintances, perhaps find out how to contact the American in Barcelona.

Nearing the quay, Colin was still planning his strategy when he spied a man approaching from the opposite direction of the beach. The stranger wore dark clothes and walked with his head down, so Colin could see only his hat—the same one worn by the man who had collided with him at Le Bibent in Toulouse.

Colin narrowed his gaze. Was he being followed?

As if reading his thoughts, the stranger glanced up at him, and then rushed at a half run toward the quay. Colin took up the chase as both men struggled against the loose sand to reach the concrete seafront.

Back on hard ground, the stranger took off at a run. Colin did the same, and as he closed the distance between them, he again sensed the man in front of him was Captain Weatherford. Colin had only met the captain twice in London, but this man's height, the breadth of his shoulders, even his loping gait seemed familiar.

His quarry turned left at the corner of Passeig de la Sardana. Colin followed in time to see the man move past Vilar's hotel toward the next block. The stranger paused, darting another look at him before making a hard right onto Carrer de la Unió.

Colin arrived at the corner and caught sight of the mysterious man disappearing down an alleyway beyond the street. He continued pursuit, grateful for the strength he'd regained during the months working with his uncle on the farm.

Eyes on his target, Colin sprinted through the maze of narrow streets, passing colorful laundry strung from second-story windows and wide-eyed children pausing in their game of hopscotch to watch the two men rush by.

After running past a small café, Colin turned onto another side street and halted in front of a shop where an old woman sat outside mending fishnets. Chest heaving, he scanned the line of storefronts and flats but saw only the woman. He'd lost his quarry. Exhausted, he lowered his head and retraced his steps to the hotel.

He spotted the innkeeper at the desk. "Have you got paper?"

Senyor Vilar produced several sheets from beneath the desk. He also handed Colin his change and a receipt for the rooms. "Are you planning to leave on the afternoon train to Barcelona, Lieutenant?"

"I'm not certain." He hesitated. "I need to send a telegram. It will depend on how quickly I receive a response."

Upstairs, Colin crafted his message to Lacourt using the same encryption as Hastings, knowing the agents at the château in Vernon could decipher the code. Next he wrote to Jack Benningham in London, advising of his delay in returning to Britain. Before ending the telegram, he added the cryptic note, *Believe to have found your best man.*

Colin paused over the words. While he'd sensed the man in the hat was Marcus Weatherford, he still couldn't fathom why the captain would run from him like some criminal. Surely he would have recognized Colin and remembered his injury.

In the end, he left the words intact. There was more that Colin didn't understand about this trip than anything that made sense.

After Senyor Vilar directed him to the local post office, Colin dispatched both messages, then took his lunch at a small café near the establishment. Seated outside on the terrace, he continued to survey the streets for the man in the felt hat.

The afternoon wore on, and Colin's apprehension over Johanna's departure with Petit increased. He hovered near the post office, checking back a few times in the hope of receiving Lacourt's reply.

The train's whistle echoed from atop the hill. Colin glanced at his watch. The Barcelona run was departing. With an agitated sigh, he returned to check the post office once more before leaving instructions to have any response sent to his hotel.

That night as he lay in bed, Colin thought about Jewel and his all-too brief conversation with her before their hasty departure from Toulouse. Then he considered Petit's trickery and Johanna's abrupt leave-taking.

Was this mission truly God's purpose for him . . . or was Colin merely trying to appease his guilt for leaving behind the woman who had once saved him? Jewel didn't seem to want him anymore, and Johanna had left without even a word. Was she safe with Petit and glad to be rid of Colin . . . or was she in danger?

Weary from the day's chase and overcome by his unanswered questions, Colin rolled over and closed his eyes. His last waking thought was to pray that Lacourt would shed some light on his bleak situation.

CHAPTER
21

*J*o sat fuming beside the open window in her room at Barcelona's Coloma Hotel as she waited for Petit's return. She'd told him she wanted to go with him to meet the afternoon train from Portbou, but he'd claimed a meeting with his superiors and insisted he would retrieve Colin afterward and bring him back to the hotel.

She continued scanning the promenade below. The sun's afternoon rays filtered through the green leaves of the plane trees lining either side of La Rambla, the city's busiest boardwalk, while women in dark skirts and bright blouses sold fresh blooms of red carnations, purple heather, and pink lantana from their carts. Jo saw street artists seated with their easels, paints, and charcoal creating scenes of the famous Barcelona landmarks, or sketching the likeness of any tourist willing to sit for a portrait.

On the other side of the street, several black-jacketed waiters dashed back and forth serving the crowded terraces outside their cafés. Jo breathed in the delicious aromas of Catalan cuisine, and her stomach growled. Where was Petit?

Unable to sit any longer, she rose from her seat and walked to the nightstand beside her bed, where a brass clock revealed the time as just minutes after four in the afternoon.

Beside the clock stood a slim candlestick telephone. Jo picked it up and lifted the receiver, waiting a few seconds before a male voice came on the line. "Front desk. How may I assist you?"

Jo was grateful the hotel staff spoke French. "This is Madame Mabry in room 320. Can you tell me if the afternoon train from Portbou is running late?"

There was a pause before the clerk came back on the line. "The train arrived on schedule over an hour ago, madame. May I help with anything else?"

"No . . . thank you." She frowned as she hung up the telephone. Why hadn't Petit returned? Was Colin with him . . . or had he decided to stay in Portbou a while longer?

A worry she'd been nursing all day rushed forward. What if Colin was dangerously ill . . . and she'd left him there?

The guilt and longing that robbed her of sleep had continued to haunt her throughout most of the day. Not only did she feel bad for running off and leaving Colin, but Jo knew he and her sister must arrange for a time to talk.

Jo was still fretting over him when a knock sounded at her door.

Relief washed over her. Finally they had arrived. "A moment, if you please!"

She cast a quick glance toward the en suite bath the luxury hotel afforded, grateful to have a room in which to hide her pigeon. Giving her cheeks a pinch, Jo tucked a lock of her hair behind her ear as she strode for the door.

Pausing, she took a deep breath before she opened it—and was startled to see a woman in black standing on the other side.

"Johanna?"

Jo nodded, unable to find her voice.

The woman's soft French accent floated to her from behind the dark veil. "I am Jewel. May I come in?"

"Jewel." Stunned, Jo's head moved up and down woodenly as she stepped aside and allowed her sister to enter. Graceful, like a beautiful wraith in black, she glided inside to stand in the middle of the room.

When Jo and Petit arrived in the city, they had intended to follow Kepler and her sister from the train station. However, with so many people disembarking and others waiting to get on the trains, they'd lost the pair in the crowd.

Now, as Jo stood staring at the slender woman garbed in mourning, she noted Jewel's height, a little taller than herself. The matching silver ring Colin had mentioned glinted on a chain around her neck.

Mesmerized, she closed the door and finally managed to speak. "I . . . cannot believe you are really here. I've waited so long."

"I have just learned about you, but I am . . . oh, I am feeling beyond joy at this moment!" Emotion filled her voice. "Colin said you knew nothing about me until you found my diary at Havrincourt. Is that so?"

Jo nodded, her gaze once again dropping to the silver ring dangling from the chain. Her chest tightened with emotion. It had been such a long time since she'd had a family. Tears suddenly blurred her eyes, and she cleared her throat. "May I see you?"

"Of course, please forgive me. I think perhaps I have been in mourning too long." She reached with gloved hands to remove the black veil.

Seeing the golden-blond hair so much like her own and the warmth in her sister's powder blue eyes broke the floodgates of Jo's emotion. She crumpled into tears. "Sister."

Jewel started to cry as well, and she reached with outstretched arms as Jo rushed into her embrace.

"I am so happy to meet you at last." Jo's choked whisper came out muffled against her sister's shoulder.

"And you, *ma chère*." Her sister's voice trembled. "When Colin t-told me about you, I was so overcome. . . ."

They held each other a long moment, gently rocking back and forth until Jo pulled away and wiped at her eyes. She observed her sister's tear-streaked face. Her nose was a bit more curved than she'd imagined, and the rounded face, much like Colin had described. Jewel seemed to glow with health. "You are beautiful."

Her sister smiled through her tears. "And so are you, Johanna."

Jo smiled, her excitement and curiosity overriding her emotion. "Please, come and sit down! I want to know everything. How did you find me?"

Jewel's lovely features creased with uncertainty. "I cannot stay long, Johanna. I managed to slip away from Monsieur Outis only long enough to see you."

"Is he holding you against your will?"

"Sometimes it feels that way." Jewel flashed a weary smile before taking a seat on the edge of the bed. "I saw you at the train station with the tall man, that porter from the hotel in Toulouse. When I noticed your pretty golden hair . . . well, I had a feeling you were Johanna."

"You saw me? Mr. Petit and I tried to find *you* but lost you among all those passengers."

"Leave it to chance!" Jewel laughed. "In fact, chance was again in my favor when we checked into the same hotel. I happened to see your signature in the register as *Madame Colin Mabry* and knew my hunch had been correct. You *are* my sister, Johanna." Smiling, her face took on a look of bemusement. "But where is Colin? And why are you here with that hotel porter?"

Jo didn't think she should divulge Petit's real purpose, even to Jewel. "Colin and I followed you after you left Toulouse. We'd intended to continue south together from Portbou this morning, but he felt unwell and told me to go on ahead. Mr. Petit was kind enough to offer me escort. He's en route to Barcelona on holiday."

"Ah, I see. Well, I am glad you made the decision to follow us."

Jo nodded, making an effort to smile. She hated having to tell the small lie to her sister, but a fabrication seemed safer than the truth at the moment. "So . . . where is Monsieur Outis?"

"Right now he is having his lunch across the street on the terrace. It seemed the perfect time to meet you." She paused. "How well did you know our father? Colin said you met him only once?"

"Yes, when I was about three. He came to our village in Ireland, and I thought he had the most incredible eyes." Jo's smile widened. "I remember he smelled of tobacco."

Jewel's eyes gleamed as she nodded. "Father often sat and smoked in the evenings beside the garden behind our farmhouse in Havrincourt. I enjoyed the smell of his pipe, too."

"Please tell me more about him."

Jewel extended a hand. "Why don't you sit down as well?"

Jo pulled the padded chair over from the vanity and sat across from her, and Jewel looked at Jo's folded hands. "I see you wear the same ring." She lifted hers from the chain.

Jo held up her hand. "Papa gave it to me when he visited."

Jewel examined both silver bands. "It looks as if there should be a middle ring that fits between the two, yes?" She flashed an impish smile. "Perhaps we have another secret sister?"

"I have no idea." Jo grinned before her humor faded, and she leaned toward Jewel. "What I do know is that I've waited years to see our papa once more, and I am thrilled to finally meet you." She reached for Jewel's hand. "I also know that Monsieur Outis is really Captain Kepler."

Jewel gave her a guarded look and started to pull away.

"Please, 'tis all right." Jo held her fingers. "I read in your diary that he promised to take you to our father, and . . . I would like very much to go with you."

Jewel relaxed her hand, new warmth filling her expression. "I cannot imagine leaving you behind."

Touched by her sister's words and elated at the prospect of being included, Jo released a ragged sigh. "Colin said Kepler has not yet told you where he is. Is it because of the danger? Is Papa being held in a prison?" She shook her head. "I don't care. When you leave, I'm coming with you."

"*Ma petite soeur.*" Jewel leaned to touch her cheek. "We will go very soon. That is another reason I came to see you. I wanted to tell you to be ready."

"Where will we go?"

"Not a prison." Jewel smiled. "Captain Kepler has promised to take me to our father in a few days."

"And he will let me accompany you?"

"Of course he'll allow it. Kepler will grant whatever I ask." She squeezed Jo's hand. "I want you by my side when we are reunited with our father."

Jo's heart filled with such pleasure and relief that it took a moment to realize the contradiction in her sister's words. If Kepler was as accommodating as Jewel claimed, then why did her sister feel the need to slip away behind his back? "I don't understand. If you and Kepler are in love, then why—"

"Goodness, no!" Jewel flicked her gloved wrist. "He loves *me*, so I know he won't mind my asking you along."

"So why hide our meeting? *Are* you afraid of him?"

"It is difficult to explain our *relation amoureuse.*" Her sister gave a pensive look. "Kepler . . . he can be dangerous when crossed. And while he is very attentive to me, I must take care when I am with him. I would not wish to turn him against me." She eyed Jo, her eyes sad. "Like you, I have waited a long time to see our father."

Jo's compassion for her sister mingled with the uncertainty in her own heart. If Jewel was no longer attracted to Kepler, did she still have feelings for Colin?

The kiss on the beach again flashed in her mind, along with the ache in her heart. Jo needed to know the truth. "Do you hold the same affection for Colin . . . as you did a year ago?"

Jewel lifted a brow, her blue eyes dancing. "After seeing *Madame Mabry* in the register downstairs, I had thought you and Colin were *amoureux*."

"Oh no!" Jo's face flooded with heat. "I mean, we've only been posing as a married couple, much as you and Monsieur Outis have done. 'Tis all been very proper, I assure you. Colin and I are just friends." She knew the last words for the lie they were, but Jo wanted to give her sister every chance. "So, do you still love him?"

Jewel sighed. "I released him from his promise in Toulouse. I no longer feel any romantic attachment to him." She grinned. "In fact, if you wish to pursue his heart, you have my blessing."

Jo's immediate joy and relief were soon extinguished by doubt. "But you wrote pages and pages in your diary about your love for him, your hope to marry and have children. And about your grief when he left you behind."

How could her sister now act so . . . unfeeling toward him? Irritation surged through her. Since Jewel claimed no affection for Kepler, was the situation as Colin had feared? Were her sister's feelings so shallow as to be revolted by his prosthetic hand?

"What has happened to change your mind, Jewel?" Jo challenged her as she raised her left arm toward her sister. "Are you put off by his injury?"

Jewel leaned back, clearly surprised. "Don't be silly, Johanna. I tended his wound a year ago, and it did not bother me then. Why should it do so now?" She paused. "It is exactly because a whole year has passed that my feelings for Colin *have* changed. I no longer hold him in the same regard."

Jo dropped her arm, forcing a pleasant expression. Colin had told her it was a gash in his leg Jewel had tended, not the damage to his hand, which occurred months later.

Hair rose along her nape. Something was wrong. Jo decided

to test her sister further. "Did you ever chance to meet Colin's friend Wyatt?"

Jewel shook her head. "*Non*, and I am sorry for his death. None of the other soldiers were with Colin when he appeared out of the darkness and fell into my arms. I know the man was his good friend."

Jo gazed at her sister as coldness swept through her. "What about the swan that drank tea? I read about it in your diary and wondered—"

"Why are you asking me all of these questions, Johanna?" Jewel rose from the bed with a trill laugh. "I feel as though we're playing charades."

Heart pounding, Jo feigned a contrite expression. "I'm sorry, Sister. I have so many things I've been saving up in my head to ask you. Please forgive me."

Jewel's taut expression eased. "No apology is necessary." She glanced toward the door. "I should go. Kepler will be back soon."

"How will you arrange things with him?"

"Do not worry, *ma chère*. I shall approach him when the time is right." She took Jo's hand. "Once I know exactly when we are to meet our father, I will return and let you know."

Jo watched her replace the veil and then followed her on rubbery legs to the door.

"Until that time, take care of yourself." Jewel reached again to brush a gloved finger across Jo's cheek before she slipped out of the room.

Jo didn't move for several moments, shock numbing her senses. Only belatedly did she realize Jewel had never once asked for the return of her precious diary.

No one but the daughters of Jacob Reyer could appreciate its value; Papa's beautiful artwork was hidden against the leaf-edges of the book. And like Jo, her true sister had treasured it.

There was also the injury that hadn't happened until after

Havrincourt. And Wyatt was not a man, but a horse, which Jewel had known.

Which meant the woman in black was not Jewel. She was a stranger.

Jo's insides ached with humiliation, rage, and confusion. She had called the woman her sister. She'd even cried in her arms!

Yet Colin too had felt certain it was Jewel, though he hadn't actually seen her face behind the veil. *She*, on the other hand, had recognized *him* and spoken to him about her aunt and her difficulties living alone in occupied France. She even wore Jewel's ring on the silver chain around her neck! A ring that connected her to Jo and her papa. *Why is she pretending to be my sister? Where is Jewel?*

Jo hugged herself and returned to the window. How did this woman know enough details from her sister's life to try to dupe both Colin and herself into believing she *was* Jewel Reyer?

The diary, of course. The bookmark.

Was this woman the intruder in Jo's room in Toulouse? If she had managed to read even a part of the diary, it would explain her knowledge of Colin's time with Jewel at Havrincourt and their first meeting. Jewel had also written about the small garden behind the house, but nothing about their father's pipe smoking. Had this stranger simply made up the rest, like some actress on a stage?

And how did she know about the diary in the first place?

Petit. Jo shivered as a chill coursed through her. Petit had drugged Colin that first night in Toulouse, taking his passport and documents, and he'd searched his bag. The American was with them at the jazz concert that night, keeping her and Colin away for several hours. He could have arranged for the diary to be taken from her room.

And if Petit was guilty, that meant Jo was all alone in Barcelona.

She stared out the open window, barely aware of the tram passing below her on the street or the guitars strumming Spanish music along the promenade. Jo wondered now if Petit had told her the truth when he said he'd spoken with Colin. Was her lieutenant still in Portbou wondering why she had abandoned him? She hadn't even left him a note!

Rising from her window seat, Jo began to pace while fear and uncertainty tried to unnerve her. Except for Colin, she had no idea whom to trust, and right now she could only assume he must still be in the north.

For a moment, Jo considered putting through a telephone call to the hotel in Portbou. What she had to say, however, posed too much of a danger if overheard.

Instead, she quickly went to the desk and wrote out a few brief words to André at the dovecote in Vernon. When she had finished, she rolled up the tiny paper and withdrew from her kit bag the small metal capsule that strapped to Little Corporal's leg.

Stuffing the note inside, Jo then retrieved her beloved little bird from his cage. She attached the capsule and took him back to the open window.

"Safe travels, my little one." She spoke softly as she released him, watching his white wings flutter across the sky.

When her pigeon finally disappeared from view, Jo bent her head, and for the first time in her memory, she spoke to God.

You helped Colin to find me once, Lord. Now please let him find me again.

CHAPTER

22

Early the next morning, Jo awakened to the telephone ringing beside her bed.

Petit? Anxious, she rolled over and picked up the instru-
ment. Yesterday, after the strange woman in black had left her
room and Jo released Little Corporal to the skies, she continued
to wait hours for word from the American.

He had sent Jo only a note through the front desk late last night,
informing her Colin wasn't on the train. Petit also promised to
join her for breakfast this morning.

"Mrs. Mabry, good morning! Are you ready to meet me downstairs?"

"Mr. Petit." Jo recognized his affable tone. She glanced at her
nightgown. "I need a bit more time. Would a half hour be acceptable?"

"I'll be waiting here in the lobby."

Jo rang off and flopped back onto the bed, staring at the white-
paneled ceiling. She wondered what she should say to him: *Did
you arrange to have an intruder enter my room in Toulouse and look at
my sister's diary? Are you acquainted with the phony woman in black
posing as Jewel? Can I even trust you anymore, Mr. Petit?*

Releasing a pent-up breath, she raised herself to sit on the edge of the bed. Of one question she was certain: had he really spoken to Colin in Portbou yesterday before their departure?

Sliding her feet to the floor, Jo padded off to the armoire to fetch her clothes. She hadn't brought much in the way of dresses, so she chose the dark blue with matching wrap, and after she'd finished her toilette, she made for the elevator.

Downstairs, Petit waited near the front desk. "You look lovely today, Mrs. Mabry. I trust you got a good night's sleep?"

Jo jerked a nod. "And you, Mr. Petit?"

Despite his smile, she noted the slight crease in his brow. Perhaps sensing her agitation? Jo considered waiting until after they had eaten to broach the subject of Colin. The dining room would be full of guests, after all.

"Slept like a log." His smile broadened as he took her arm and escorted her into the restaurant. The delicious aromas of sausage, bacon, and yeasty bread filled the dining room. The hotel staff seemed surprisingly scarce; only three waiters rushed about the dining room, and it was several minutes before she and Petit were seated. In lieu of a menu, a sideboard with buffet fare had been prepared for the diners.

Jo served herself at the board, selecting *pernil ibèric*, a delicious cured ham, sliced paper thin; crusty baguettes covered in cheese; and *pa amb tomàquet*, the grated tomato on toast that was a breakfast staple of the city.

Pouring a glass of fresh orange juice from the pitcher, she overheard that a cook, a dishwasher, and two busboys were out sick with influenza.

Jo informed Petit of this once she returned to the table. Already he'd filled his plate, including *xuixos*, custard pastries fried and dusted with sugar. In addition, the waiter had brought them each a cup of *cafè amb llet*.

Petit tucked his napkin into his collar. "The desk clerk told me there are a few cases of influenza among the hotel staff. Don't be surprised if you're short on maid service."

Jo had removed her gloves, and as she retrieved her fork, she saw Petit wasted no time tucking into his food. "Considering the scant help, I am grateful for room service, since I was left to my own resources yesterday. Otherwise, I should have starved."

Petit paused, glancing at her. "I'm sorry for my lengthy absence yesterday, Mrs. Mabry. It was necessary to check in with my business associates." He looked about the dining room before returning his attention to her. "A confidential reconnaissance involving our two friends."

While Jo was somewhat appeased by his words, her distrust of Petit and the uncertainty of her situation in Barcelona remained. Was he telling the truth? She decided not to wait with her questions. "Tell me, Mr. Petit. How long have you known the woman with Kepler is not my sister?"

He'd taken a bite of the custard-filled pastry just as she asked the question, and he nearly spit the contents back onto the table as he began to convulse with coughing.

Jo's irritation quickly turned to concern. "Are you all right, sir?"

He nodded, grabbing for his glass of water. He drank half before he recovered enough to speak. "Excuse me, Mrs. Mabry, but what kind of question is that?"

Despite her pounding pulse, Jo eyed him with a level gaze. "A direct one, I hope." Ignoring his surprise, she relayed to him her conversation with the veiled woman. "Did you know she was an imposter? And where is Colin? Did he know about her, too?"

Dropping her fork onto the plate, she pressed her hands against the edge of the table and continued. "Did you in fact speak with him yesterday before we left . . . or was that another lie?"

"Whoa now—slow down, missy." Petit set down his glass. "I did talk to your lieutenant, and you saw for yourself he was in no condition to travel. I fully expected him to arrive on the afternoon train."

Petit pulled the linen napkin from his collar and tossed it on the table. "As for your visitor yesterday, I can't say, but I'll certainly check with my superiors." He leaned in, his expression intent. "Until I get back, I want you to remain upstairs in your room. Do not open your door for anyone except me. Is that understood?"

Jo's eyes widened. "Are you trying to scare me?" Her heart sped even faster as she too lost her appetite and set her napkin beside her plate.

"I'm only thinking of your safety." His dark eyes held hers. "I ask your trust on this, Mrs. Mabry. It's no joke."

He looked so earnest, Jo couldn't help wavering in her suspicions. Perhaps Petit hadn't arranged for the intruder to enter her room. Could it have been Kepler?

She remembered how the Boche spy had looked at her and Colin before leaving Le Bibent that night. Kepler could have broken in and paged through the diary while she and Colin were with Petit at the jazz concert.

Still, Jo had doubts. Without Colin here, she could trust no one. She decided on an uneasy truce instead. "All right, Mr. Petit."

She offered a smile, though it took effort. "I am still worried about Colin, though. With the illness that seems to be spreading, I hope he hasn't contracted this flu. I shall telephone the hotel in Portbou once we finish breakfast."

"I'd be happy to call him for you." Petit's smile faltered as he leaned forward and lowered his voice. "The telephones are not private, Mrs. Mabry, and there are spies all over the city. We must be careful about what is discussed over public lines."

As Jo knew only too well. "It is not necessary, Mr. Petit. I'll be discreet."

He paused, staring at her before he nodded. "Very well. Would you like to finish eating?"

Buoyed by the small victory, she inclined her head. "I do think my appetite has returned."

His eyes glinted with the laughter in his voice. "And mine."

Afterward, he escorted her upstairs to her room. "Remember what I said. Keep the door locked." He paused. "And keep your telephone call short. Will you be all right until I return?"

"I'll be fine. Just don't leave me stranded here again."

When she'd closed and locked her door, Jo heard his receding footsteps. She went to sit on the edge of her bed and telephoned the front desk, requesting a call be put through to the Vilars' hotel in Portbou.

A few minutes later, the desk called back to inform her there was no answer. "Would you like me to try again later, madame?"

Jo's hopes plummeted. "Yes, please. Let me know when you get a response."

Returning to the window seat, she gazed out on the flower sellers and artists still plying their trade. Horse-drawn wagons and a taxi clattered along the street.

Another hour passed before she turned toward the unmade bed. Petit's comment about the lack of maid service amplified her worry over Colin's health. What if he did have the flu?

She rose and made another call to the front desk. "Any luck?"

"No, madame. The operator insists there is much traffic on the lines. We will keep trying."

Jo hung up and began pacing back and forth across the room, anxiety over Colin combining with a new fear at Petit's implied warning. *Was* she in danger?

A thought struck, and she halted. What if Petit thought Kepler would come after her now that Jo knew the truth about the veiled woman?

And where in all of this was Jewel?

Having exhausted her nerves and her energy, Jo returned to lie on the bed. She reached for the diary on the nightstand, wondering anew about the fate of her *real* sister, and whether or not either of them would ever see their father again.

Curling up on her side, she stared out at the room, thinking of Colin. She missed his warm touch and his kind smiles, his steady reasoning. His kiss.

Most of all, she missed his goodness and strength. If only he would come and find her.

Had God heard her prayer yesterday? Or was it as she'd always believed, that miracles didn't happen for people like her? The misbegotten. *Leanbh tabhartha . . .*

Tears blurred her vision before she ruthlessly wiped them away.

"I wish I could believe what you say, Colin."

"You can, Johanna. It's called faith."

Hugging the diary to her chest, Jo finally closed her eyes. For his sake, then, if not her own, she would continue to pray for his safety and the safety of her sister.

CHAPTER

23

*A*h, Lieutenant, *bon dia*. How did you sleep?"
Colin was on his way into breakfast and then to the
post office when Senyor Vilar met him at the base of the
stairs. "Well enough, I suppose."

In truth, it had been a fitful night, though without the usual
nightmares. *And I wasn't drugged.*

"I was just coming up to deliver this."

The innkeeper held up a yellow telegram envelope, and Colin's
heart raced. Finally word from Lacourt! Grabbing for the sealed
missive, he was about to tear it open with his teeth when Vilar
took it and extracted the contents for him, placing the telegram
into Colin's eager hand.

Smiling his thanks, Colin quickly read the brief message:

*One white dove arrives. Need another with golden key. Lost girl on
La Rambla.*

His heart pounded as he reread the note. Colin recalled Johanna's fairy tale from the train. The story of the white dove, a
lost girl, and golden keys.

She was in trouble. His mouth formed a grim line as he shoved

252

the telegram into his pocket. "Have you heard of a place called La Rambla in Barcelona?"

"*Sí!*" The innkeeper bobbed his head. "Everyone in Catalonia knows La Rambla is the busiest street in Barcelona. It's near the city's waterfront."

Colin eased out a breath and checked his watch. Just after 0800. "I need to go pack, *senyor*. I'll catch the nine o'clock train south." He fished for the wad of francs in his pocket. "I owe you for another night's lodging—"

"No money is necessary, Lieutenant." Vilar reached to stay his hand. "Go to La Rambla and find her, and may God be with you."

Colin gazed into the kindly man's face. "*Gràcies, senyor*, and give my thanks to your lovely wife as well."

Back in his room, Colin hurried to pack his belongings. Johanna's words continued to haunt his thoughts. Had Petit done her some kind of harm?

His insides did flip-flops as he imagined various macabre scenarios—Johanna wounded, or held captive in some dark place, or even imprisoned!

He was still fumbling to fasten the straps on his portmanteau when a knock sounded. "Come in, *senyor*." Colin would ask Vilar to call him a taxi.

Another rap sounded, much sharper than the first.

"One moment!" He rushed to fasten the second leather strap when the metal tongue on the buckle broke loose. *Titan's teeth!* Glaring at the door, he abandoned his task to answer the summons. "I am sorry, *senyor*, I must have locked it—"

"Good morning, Lieutenant."

Colin stood gaping at the man in the brown felt hat with its wide gold band. The dark trench coat was the same one he'd seen before. "Captain Weatherford . . . it *is* you."

The captain smiled beneath his dark moustache. "You're looking a bit dazed, Mabry. Are you feeling all right?"

Colin struggled to collect himself. "Yes, sir, I'm fine."

He remembered to salute then, and the captain returned the gesture. "May I come in?"

"Of course." Bemused, he stepped back to let him enter. "It *was* you I saw at Le Bibent in Toulouse. And yesterday on the beach, near the quay." He closed the door. "Why are you here, sir?"

"I could ask you the same question, Lieutenant. Why are *you* here?"

The captain's amiable tone was gone, and Colin shifted. "Well, sir, it's a long story. I left Britain over a week ago, when I received a message from a woman I knew during the war—"

"I know all of that." The captain cut in. "George Petit briefed me. What I want to know is why you haven't taken the train back to Paris. Your being here puts our operation at great risk."

Colin caught up with his statement. "You're working . . . with George Petit?"

The captain nodded, and Colin gazed at him in wonder. Petit never mentioned it. "May I ask, sir, why you've been avoiding me? First in France, and then yesterday?"

"My assignment is secret, Lieutenant. I'd hoped to remain unknown to you, but when you didn't take the train north yesterday, it became necessary to confront you." His expression was stern. "You need to return to Britain and say nothing of our meeting."

Colin straightened. "Sir, if Petit told you my story, then you know the importance of my being here. I owe it to Jewel and to her sister, Johanna, to fulfill my promise. I cannot go home."

He cast another glance at his watch. *0815.* "In fact, I need to be on the train to Barcelona in forty-five minutes."

The captain's tone eased. "I admire your chivalry, Lieutenant. However, there is much you are not aware of, and our success with this mission is crucial. You need to return home."

Colin's chest grew tight. He couldn't leave Johanna. "Let me stay and help you, sir. I've already been cleared by MI6, and I recently completed an important assignment in Toulouse for the Paris office."

A corner of the captain's mouth lifted. Colin's stomach knotted. Was he mocking him?

He withdrew the telegram from his pocket and handed it to him. "Johanna Reyer is in Barcelona, and she's in danger. I must go to her."

The captain scanned the few lines. He handed back the note. "This tells me nothing."

"It's . . . a sort of code that we came up with." Colin wasn't about to tell him about Johanna's fairy tale. "I know she needs me, or she would not have sent Little Corporal back to France."

The captain gave him a guarded look. "Who is this corporal?"

Colin's collar suddenly felt tight. "A carrier pigeon, sir. Johanna brought him along on our trip. She thought we might need the bird if we had a run-in with Kepler."

"For the love of . . ." Captain Weatherford gave him a hard stare. "Johanna Reyer is with George Petit in Barcelona on my orders, Lieutenant."

Again Colin was taken completely by surprise. "Your orders, sir? How . . ."

"Like I said, there is much you do not know." The captain flexed his jaw. "Go home, Lieutenant. Do not force me to give you a direct order."

Despite being intimidated, Colin stood his ground, his shoulders back. "With all due respect, sir, I must go south. Not only for Johanna's sake, but for Jewel. I owe the woman more than I can say."

"She's dead, Lieutenant."

Colin's stance faltered. "What did you say?"

"Jewel Reyer passed away a few months ago." The captain sighed as he removed his hat. "She contracted pneumonia just days before the battle at Cambrai. During the German retreat, an American G-2 agent did manage to get her out of Havrincourt in a Red Cross truck, but her condition had worsened. She succumbed shortly after arriving in Paris." His brown eyes held compassion. "I am sorry, Lieutenant."

Colin reached for the bedpost and sat down, staring at the floor. Jewel *had* died after all. His throat grew tight, remembering the last time he'd seen her beautiful, laughing face and heard her songs that had brought his weary soul such consolation. She had given him so much, even offering her love.

His heart grieved anew, aching for Johanna as well. She'd lost someone else in her life, a sister she had come to know in the written pages of a diary.

Colin lifted his gaze to the captain. "If Jewel is gone, who is the woman with Kepler?"

"A French actress that Petit hired. The woman occasionally does work with the Americans over here."

She had seemed so real, so believable to him. Colin shook his head. "I don't understand. Why does someone need to pretend to be Jewel?"

"That is confidential information, Lieutenant. Suffice it to say that if our ruse with the decoy is discovered, it will prove disastrous to the mission."

Colin thought about the veil and woman dressed all in black. "So she must remain hidden. The mourning clothes?"

"Yes, attire which is sadly seen all too often in these times."

He was still confused. "How did this actress end up with Kepler?"

The captain hesitated. "Jewel had an aunt—"

"Madame Rochette." Colin nodded. "She helped Jewel with my care when I was in Havrincourt. I understand she died late last year."

"And that's why Kepler was sent in. His orders were to infiltrate the enemy and protect the girl. He was to get her out of Havrincourt at the first opportunity." The captain grimaced. "When Jewel died in Paris, G-2 came up with the idea of using a decoy."

"Wait. Kepler . . . works with the Allies?" Colin's thoughts were spinning. "But I thought the French Bureau listed him on the enemy watch list as a spy."

The captain moved to lean against the wall. "The man posing as Werner Kepler is a German-American agent working with G-2 in France. His name is on that list you speak of because it strengthens his cover.

"Unfortunately, when the French Bureau in Toulouse received the inquiry from Paris, Kepler had also been seen in the city. G-2 hadn't yet let the local Bureau in on the details of their assignment, so some clerk gave Lacourt the information and a photograph, which"—the captain scowled—"he turned over to you."

Colin could only stare in wonder. Kepler was engaged in a highly secret operation for the Allies? A thought struck. "At Le Bibent . . . you must have left Kepler some sort of message on the bottom of the vase. Afterward, he exchanged the flower in his buttonhole. Was it to signal his receipt of the message? Is that why he took Jewel—the actress—to Barcelona?"

"You've become quite the detective, Lieutenant." The captain's eyes glinted as he straightened and withdrew a pocket watch from inside the trench coat. "But your part in this is finished." He checked the time. "I need to be on a train, and you need to return home."

Colin launched to his feet. "It's hardly finished, sir. Johanna still needs me."

"I told you, she is safe with Petit in Barcelona."

Seeing his flat expression, Colin had a moment of uncertainty. The captain was right—there was much he hadn't been aware of.

Like Kepler working for the Allies, or the fact that Jewel was gone and a complete stranger had taken her place.

Questions pressed at him. Why was G-2 so interested in Jewel Reyer? Enough to get her out of Havrincourt and, after her death, to create a double, a woman who must be seen . . . but not seen? Was nothing as it appeared?

Except for Johanna. She was real enough, and the only person in this entire farce he could trust. Colin was going after her. "I'm leaving too, Captain."

He stood eye to eye with his superior, the man who was also his future brother-in-law's best friend. "That train for Barcelona leaves in twenty minutes, and I plan to be on it. Johanna is some-where on La Rambla, and I will search out every inch of space until I find her."

The captain's dark eyes glittered. "I could give you that direct order, Lieutenant."

"Respectfully, sir, I would rather you didn't. I intend to see this through, and I was given leave by Jack—Lord Walenford—to come to Paris."

"Then return to Paris!"

Colin refused to be daunted by the captain's wrath. "Sir, I will go to prison if necessary. If that happens, you will need to return to London before next week." He angled his head. "The wed-ding, sir."

"Blast."

Abruptly the captain's anger abated, and he averted his gaze to the window.

Had he forgotten his commitment? "Please, Captain." Colin didn't care if he sounded desperate. He had to see Johanna. "I need to do this."

The captain's eyes slanted back to him with a trace of humor. "I recall once upon a time that Jack made a similar plea." He drew in a deep breath and expelled it. "I suppose if I let you run off on your own, you'll only get yourself killed. If that happens, Jack will never forgive me, because your sister will never forgive Jack."

The captain's features sobered. "You may accompany me on one condition: obey my instructions without question." A slight frown curved beneath the moustache. "Think you can manage that, Mabry?"

Relieved, Colin offered a salute. "Yes, sir!"

"And you can leave off with saluting and using my title. Spain is teeming with spies, so during our time together, you will simply call me Marcus and I'll call you Colin. Have you any other clothes besides the uniform?"

"I have a waiter's livery. White jacket, dark pants."

Marcus looked doubtful. "I suppose it will have to do. Are you already packed?"

Colin responded by grabbing up his portmanteau. At least one of the straps was secure.

"You can change as soon as we reach Barcelona. I'll loan you my trench coat in place of the white jacket."

He donned his hat and headed for the door. Colin followed. "One more thing, sir . . . uh, Marcus."

Marcus turned, looking impatient. "What?"

"I did send word to Jack yesterday, with an update. I suspected something, you see." He paused. "He knows you are here."

"Well, that's jolly news." Marcus scowled. "I guess we'd better hope this mission winds up soon, before the whole of Europe knows what's going on."

The train was crowded once the two men finally boarded. Noting the full compartments, they found two seats together near the back in coach.

Once they settled in, Colin whispered to the captain. "Sir . . . Marcus, I was wondering if Jewel—"

"Not here." Marcus raised a hand to halt him. "Save your questions for Barcelona."

Colin nodded and pressed his head back against the seat, his mind working over theories he wanted to test but couldn't. The trip south would take at least two hours. Perhaps by the end of it, he would have figured out a few things for himself.

The plan the Americans had hatched in liberating Jewel and then using an actress to pose in her place also seemed to involve Johanna. Why? The two women had never met before, and Johanna, at least, had claimed no prior knowledge of her sister before the diary.

She and Jewel were each raised in a different country, with different mothers. In fact, the only commonality between the two was their father, Jacob Reyer.

Colin sat forward. *J. Reyer.* The name Jack read from the watch list before Colin's departure to Paris.

Jack had thought it belonged to Jewel, and Colin had scoffed. Yet later, he'd mistakenly attached it to Johanna.

Could it be *Jacob* Reyer?

He was impatient to confirm his suspicion, but he'd agreed to obey the captain's orders. He tried to quash his impatience, forcing his attention toward the window and the passing landscape of northern Spain.

In the distance, craggy hills of bronzed rock were dotted with pine, hornbeam, and maple. Below the hills and along the valley floor spread verdant farms, fields of purple lavender, and the green of budding vineyards. Occasionally, clusters of stone cottages with ochre rooftops and the prominent rise of a church steeple marked another village along the way.

As they neared their destination, Colin glanced across the aisle to the opposite window and glimpsed the coastline and the glittering blue of the Mediterranean. The white sand beaches triggered a pang of longing, and he thought of Johanna, standing close in the circle of his arms, her flowery scent mingled with the salty air of the sea.

He recalled her words about love and the beauty of the soul, and more than ever, he was determined to find her.

The train arrived at Barcelona's França Station, and by the time he and the captain disembarked, collected their luggage, and hailed a cab, it was close to noon.

Minutes later, they arrived on La Rambla, in front of a mammoth building several stories high and constructed of beige-colored stone. Colin stared up at the white lettering, *Gran Hotel de Oriente*, above an arcade façade, its arches and pillars decorating the lower floors. Each room appeared to have its own wrought-iron balcony. "This is quite the place."

"I've been staying here for weeks. Wait until you see the inside."

Once Marcus paid the driver, the two men entered the hotel. Indeed, the interior was equally elaborate, with polished white-marbled floors and more pillars supporting bright framework ceilings.

At the front desk, Colin was relieved to get a room on the same floor, not far from the captain. The clerk also informed them that, due to the current shortage of staff because of illness, they would need to porter their own bags.

"Perhaps you should seek employment at the hotel while we're here."

Marcus made the comment as the two lumbered up the stairs, and Colin turned to see if he was serious. At the captain's amused expression, he smiled, grateful the man wasn't growling at him anymore. "I'll wager it pays a sight better than what I'm earning at Hastings."

Marcus chuckled. "You're probably right."

They reached their floor and halted at Colin's room first.

Marcus set down his suitcase. "Take this." He removed his

trench coat and draped it across Colin's arm. "I'm in 211. We'll talk when you get there. About an hour?"

Colin nodded. "Thanks."

The captain touched his brim, then grabbed up his bag and continued down the hall.

Colin unlocked the door to his room and noted the elegant furnishings, which differed greatly from the simple fixtures in Portbou. Soft yellow walls complemented the wide brass bed, while a green brocade divan sat in front of the set of floor-length windows that likely led out onto one of the balconies he'd spied from below.

His injured wrist throbbed with pain from wearing the prosthetic, and Colin longed to remove the sleeve. There wasn't much time before his meeting with Marcus, however, so instead he contented himself with washing his face and hand in cool water before stepping outside onto the balcony, praying for a glimpse of Johanna.

He surveyed the majestic line of leafy green trees and the cobbled promenade buzzing with humanity. Farmers sold fresh milk from shiny metal urns, there were booths with baskets of citrus, and a woman was selling balloons in the red and yellow colors of Catalonia.

Colin breathed in the delicious smell of food wafting up from an open terrace café across the street. As he observed the masses strolling back and forth, Colin wondered if Johanna was among them. Was she staying somewhere along this street? Perhaps here in his hotel?

Marcus had sent her here with Petit. Surely he knew Johanna's whereabouts.

Determined to get answers, Colin returned inside to change into the waiter's garb, exchanging the white jacket for the trench coat Marcus had loaned him.

At the appointed hour, he rapped on the door to 211. Once Marcus ushered him inside and closed the door, Colin shared with him his theory from the train. "The name *J. Reyer* from our enemy watch list belongs to Jewel and Johanna's father, Jacob."

"You might have a future as an agent for the Crown, Mabry." Marcus's gaze held approval. "Now, take a seat while I finish unpacking."

Colin sat down on the divan, similar to the one in his room. "After reading Jewel's diary, Johanna and I assumed her father was a French soldier being held in some prison camp, and that Kepler knew which one. If so, then why are we in neutral Spain?"

Marcus shut the doors to the armoire and returned to sit on the edge of the bed. His glance flicked to the closed window before he lowered his voice and faced Colin. "Jacob Reyer is not in a POW camp, nor is he with the French Army." He leaned forward. "The truth is, he is a German spy known to us as Zero. And he wishes to defect."

"Johanna's father . . . an enemy agent?" Colin stared at him, incredulous. "How is that possible?"

"I won't go into detail, but his condition of surrender was the safe return of his daughter. In return for Jewel, he promised to give the Allies a prize worth a king's ransom."

Colin inched forward on the divan. "How will you manage to return Jewel to him? He's going to discover the woman in black is the actress—" Colin suddenly rose to his feet. "Johanna! You found out she was Jacob Reyer's daughter, and now you plan to use her as the bait."

"Take it easy, Colin. Sit down, so I can explain."

Grudgingly, Colin obeyed. Marcus clasped his hands in front of him. "G-2 chose to continue the ruse after Jewel's death because they hoped Zero would keep his end of the bargain and retrieve the prize from its hiding place. The Americans have had agents scouting for him for months, and the plan was to confiscate the prize from him *before* he learned the fate of his daughter.

"So far the plan has failed because Zero has managed to elude them all and still holds the prize. I didn't learn about Jewel's death until I arrived in Toulouse days ago and spoke with G-2. It was then I also learned of Johanna Reyer's existence." He paused. "She became our only chance to salvage the mission."

Marcus stared at the floor. "Zero and I are somewhat acquainted. We met last year when he was posing as a journalist. He called me into this arrangement because he trusts me and wanted me to find out if Kepler had his daughter in Toulouse. Once I confirmed the information, he set up the place and time of the meeting."

"But you lied to him."

"No, I told him a specific truth." His brown eyes held a challenge. "That his daughter was in Toulouse."

Colin frowned. "But you meant Johanna, not Jewel."

"Zero doesn't know that. Anyway, I gave the order to Kepler to come to Spain."

"At Le Bibent."

Marcus smiled. "Believe me, I was just as surprised to see you."

"And you placed his instructions beneath the vase of violets?"

Marcus nodded. "Once he took off with our decoy, Petit was to make certain Johanna followed. He later told me the only way she would go willingly was if you accompanied her. That's why he kept up the pretense that you were following Jewel."

"That bounder drugged me twice!" Colin leaned forward, scowling. "Once in Toulouse, and then two nights ago in Portbou, before he took off with Johanna."

Marcus bent his head. "I apologize. It was my instruction to delay you while they made for Barcelona. I'd hoped you would simply tire of the chase and go home." He glanced up. "I should have known better. You weren't injured in any way?"

"Only my dignity."

He growled the words, and Marcus grinned. "I've been told that the men recruited for the American Corps of Intelligence Police come from all walks of life. Many are considered wild cards—high-stakes gamblers like Petit, or madcaps and stuntmen. Some have previous criminal records."

Colin's jaw dropped. "The Americans employ criminals over here?"

"Of course not. The men go through intensive screening. In the end, those hired are dedicated to flushing out enemy spies in Europe and to winning the war for the Allies. But they are chosen from those backgrounds because G-2 needs the kind of men who will do whatever it takes to get the job done."

"But I am *not* the enemy."

"So consider yourself lucky." Marcus sat back. "Petit could have had you arrested in Portbou as a spy, or tied you up and left you under the pier. I wouldn't put either past him." He offered a smile. "In any case, I stayed behind to make certain you were in one piece. And to demand your return to Paris, for all the good it did me."

Colin's thoughts flashed back to his meeting with Petit at the Toulouse park. Colin was the one who had told the American that Johanna was Jewel's sister, and hours later, Petit had sent them off to spy on Kepler at Le Bibent, knowing the agent would be alone. Knowing he could keep his two bloodhounds on the scent.

He ground his teeth, turning his anger on Marcus. "You allowed us to be played. All this time, Johanna and I have been pawns in some elaborate, secret plan."

"Call it what you will." Marcus's eyes blazed. "You of all people should know we've already lost too many good men in this war. The prize we're after will remove a considerable amount of leverage from the enemy and hopefully hasten their defeat."

With that, the captain's anger fled, and he sighed, rising from his seat on the bed. "The plan may not even work. Everything depends on Zero's reaction to the death of one daughter and his acceptance of the other. We can only hope he will still agree to the bargain we've struck."

"What is this prize?"

"I cannot say, but trust me, it's extremely valuable and needs to be in our possession."

As Colin sifted through Marcus's words, he realized that, whatever the prize, at least two Allied countries were working to get their hands on it. And if it would help to bring about a swift end to the war . . . "When does the meeting with Zero take place?"

"Kepler will take Johanna to meet with her father tomorrow."

"Will it be here in the city? On La Rambla?"

Marcus shook his head. "Zero has chosen the spot. The caves of Sant Sever, near the Salnitre Caves at Collbató and Montserrat. About fifty kilometers north of Barcelona."

Caves. Colin's skin flashed hot and cold as he imagined a series of cramped, dark spaces. Like Passchendaele. He swallowed. "I want to see her first."

"I don't know where she is staying."

Alarmed, Colin rose to stare at Marcus. "But I thought you said Johanna was here?"

"She is here. Petit already knows the time and place of the meeting with Zero. He and G-2 are making all of the arrangements with Kepler for tomorrow."

"I need to know she's all right, Marcus. Johanna sent me the message—"

"I understand." He checked his watch. "I've got to be at the consulate for a meeting in fifteen minutes. Afterward I'll see Petit and find out where she is."

More waiting. Colin forced a smile. "I appreciate it."

Marcus smiled knowingly. "I realize you care about her." The two of them started toward the door. "And believe me, it is in everyone's best interest to ensure Miss Reyer remains safe."

"Yes, I suppose it is." The assurance eased Colin's apprehension, despite his dislike of Petit.

They exited into the hall. "I'll see you later." As Marcus strode off, Colin followed at a slower pace, a plan taking shape in his mind. He wasn't about to sit in his room waiting for word about Johanna. Besides, the captain hadn't given him any specific orders to the contrary.

Determination quickened his steps as he headed back to his room for the other jacket.

Colin was about to take matters into his own hands.

CHAPTER

24

*J*o raised the rifle to the window and flipped off the safety as Moira had shown her.

Smoke from the shop fire stung her eyes as she brought the tall soldier into her sights. Despite bullets flying, he brazenly remained where he stood, his rifle aimed for another shot at her mother.

He must have seen Jo then; he turned his aim slightly, and through the haze, their eyes locked.

A scream tore from her lungs as she squeezed the trigger, and gunfire seemed to explode around her as a barrage of bullets flew in her direction. Mindless with fear, she dropped down against the wall and drew back the bolt to load another shot. As she frantically worked to shove the bolt back into place, she raised herself up enough to glance out the window.

The soldier went down just as a flash of gunfire burst from the open shop door. Moira lay there on her belly, her smoking rifle still poised.

More gunfire erupted, and Jo dropped the rifle, crawling to where Moira was dragging herself inside to lean against the door.

Rage and pain ravaged her mother's sooty face. The front of her uniform was soaked in blood.

"Mama." The cry came out hoarse from the smoke, and Jo struggled *with a fit of coughing as she grabbed for her petticoat, intending to staunch the bleeding.*

A red-smeared hand reached for her. "Never mind that, girl. 'Tis . . . too late."

Jo stared at the hand while memories flooded her mind: her head being cradled as she'd slept, the gentle ruffling of her hair before another of Moira's secret departures to Dublin.

"Go." Moira's breathing had turned erratic. "Find your father . . . in France."

Tears welled in Jo's eyes. "I won't leave you."

"Barrett . . . at the dock in Kilcoole. He has . . . money for you, and Jacob's address. He'll take you across." Moira tried to smile, but her pain made the effort ghoulish. "Contingency plan for my . . . little soldier."

The front of the shop was ablaze. Jo felt heat singeing her exposed skin. She coughed again as she glanced toward the back, where a closed window led outside.

She turned to her mother. "Mama . . . I cannot . . ."

Moira gripped her hand, her gray eyes glazed with pain. "You were my first love and my last, child. My most noble action." Her expression crumpled. "Now . . . run!"

The hand in hers suddenly went slack, and Moira's head leaned oddly to one side. Her eyes open yet lifeless . . .

Jo awakened from the dream, a sob lodged in her throat. Her pulse hammered as she took in her sumptuous surroundings; then she turned her face into the pillow and cried the tears that she'd held inside for so long.

Colin had done this to her. He had opened her heart, made her weak.

When her emotion was spent, Jo rose to sit on the edge of the bed. Loneliness engulfed her as she ached for her mother. For family.

She thought about her friends back in Paris. Isabelle and André, even Henri Lacourt. Yet it was Colin she missed most of all.

Had her beloved pigeon succeeded in making the flight back to Vernon? Or did no one save Petit know she was here?

Rising, she went to the bathroom and washed her face. Jo hadn't heard the telephone ring, which meant the operator still hadn't gotten through to Colin's hotel in Portbou. Her stomach growled, reminding her it was already late afternoon and she hadn't eaten. Where was Petit?

Another rumble against her insides made her walk to the outer room and gaze at the telephone. She remembered Petit's warning about keeping the door locked, but surely he didn't mean for her to starve. She could still have food sent up and make certain it wasn't a trick.

Lifting the telephone, she removed the receiver when a knock sounded at the door, followed by a muffled voice. "Room service."

So Petit hadn't forgotten about her after all. Grateful for food, Jo went to the door, then hesitated. Should she open it? Or have the waiter leave it in the hall?

She leaned close to the wood. "Can you tell me who requested the food?"

"Mr. Mabry, madame."

Jo's heart went still. Colin?

She opened the door wide, her heart ready to burst at the sight of him. Clad in his hotel livery, he quickly pushed the food cart over the threshold, and she closed the door.

"Johanna?" He turned to her with a hesitant smile and then opened his arms.

She nearly knocked him over, rushing into his embrace. "Colin!"

As he held her, she began to cry. "It's all right, sweetheart. You're safe now."

He gently stroked her hair, his deep voice soothing her ragged emotions. She finally looked up at him. "I was so afraid my prayers wouldn't be answered. . . ."

He stole the rest of her words with a kiss so tender she nearly

270

melted into a pool at his feet. Her eyes closed, and she sighed against his lips before surrendering her desire with all of the longing and love in her heart.

His arms tightened around her, his lips tasting of coffee and yearning. Jo was reassured by the familiar scent of him and slid her arms up around his neck. His solid strength was like her own wall of comfort as she lost herself with him, forgetting the world or what might happen next. Just being in his arms and knowing he was safe was enough.

"How I missed you, Mrs. Mabry." His warm whisper fell against her cheek as their kiss ended, and he pressed his forehead to hers. "I prayed all the way here that I would find you safe."

Still languid from his kiss, Jo slowly opened her eyes. "I prayed for you, too. What took you so long?"

He let out a deep chuckle and lifted his head, eyes gleaming. "A fine thing coming from a woman who doesn't know the meaning of *on time*."

She grinned before her features sobered, remembering her uncertainty and guilt of the past two days. "I thought you had stayed behind in Portbou because you were ill, but I can see that is not the case." Her gaze surveyed his obvious good health. "I also imagined that you wished to avoid me." Her cheeks heated. "After our . . . evening together on the beach."

He reached up to touch her cheek, his eyes searching hers. "I feared the same about you at first—that you had fled because of my ungentlemanly behavior."

"Oh no, I thought you were ever the 'gentle man' with me." She leaned into his touch and then sighed, pulling away from him. "But now, here I am, throwing myself at you and betraying my sister all over again."

"Johanna, please, don't punish yourself. You have betrayed no one." A hint of sadness touched his features. "I need to tell you some things, but right now, you need to eat."

He released her toward the covered dish on the cart. "I heard your stomach rumbling."

She gave him a shy smile before removing the covered dish. Taking up the plate of small sandwiches, she sat on the divan. "What do you want to tell me?"

"First, you eat." He pointed to her plate.

"Very well." Despite her growing anxiety, she was hungry. "Why don't you tell me how you found me. Did Little Corporal succeed in his mission?"

"Yes, I received your message about the golden key." A smile touched his lips as he pulled over the padded vanity chair to sit across from her. "Do you remember the man in the hat who bumped into me at Le Bibent? Turns out he was an acquaintance of mine from Britain, Captain Marcus Weatherford."

Jo nibbled at her sandwich, listening as Colin relayed how the same man had shown up in Portbou yesterday, and how Colin had given chase before he had unexpectedly turned up at his hotel door that very morning. "We traveled together to Barcelona.

"Right now, the captain's here at the British Consulate. He told me he would find out where you were from Petit this afternoon, but I didn't want to wait to see you."

She stared at his waiter's garb. "Did you get a job here at the hotel?"

He grinned. "Actually Marcus is the one who gave me the idea. In this disguise, I went to the front desk of hotels on La Rambla and claimed 'Mrs. Mabry' left behind her passport while dining at my table on the café terrace across the street. I inquired at the Oriente first, but the clerk said no one by that name was registered. When I came here, the clerk demanded your passport."

"Well, you don't have my passport, so what did you do?"

"I insisted on delivering the valuable document myself, of course. I told him I expected a reward." He bent his head. "I admit I paid the desk clerk a few *pesetas* to have a look at the hotel register, which is how I managed to get your room number."

She laughed. "A brilliant plan, even though you had to resort to bribery."

His face reddened. "It was important."

"Indeed." She reached to touch his arm. "And I am very glad you did."

Jo picked up another wedge of her sandwich. "How did you manage the room service?"

"It seems the hotels here are desperate for help at the moment due to the flu."

She nodded. "'Tis what we heard at breakfast this morning."

"We?"

"Mr. Petit. You know, I accused him of lying to me about his coming to see you yesterday morning before we left Portbou."

"He did lie." Anger filled his voice. "Petit knew I was sleeping off the drug he'd put in my coffee the night before. I didn't awaken until after you'd both left."

Jo drew in a sharp breath. Petit *had* lied? Her own fury flooded her as she dropped the sandwich back onto her plate. "That . . . that . . ."

"Bounder? Lunatic? Pick either one; they both fit." His mouth twisted. "After I had a chance to think about your hasty departure, I realized that, with Petit's stunt, something else must be going on. I was worried for you, and when I received Lacourt's telegram this morning, I was determined to come to La Rambla and find you."

He tipped his head. "Aside from his lies, has Petit harmed you in any way?" His gaze traveled tenderly over her. "What happened yesterday?"

Jo told him about her visit with the woman in black. "She knew things about Jewel and about you, but she made mistakes, too. After she left, I realized she could not be my sister and had somehow gotten hold of the diary. Remember the misplaced book-mark? I suspected Petit had something to do with it, of course. Then I wondered about Kepler." She frowned. "Now, however, I'll stick with my original theory that Petit orchestrated the intrusion."

He nodded. "I believe your instincts are good, and it would explain how she was able to convince me that she was Jewel the day I brought food to her room."

Colin leaned to remove the plate from Jo's lap, set it aside, and reached for her hand. Again she detected the sorrow in his eyes, and a chill of foreboding ran along her spine. "Something is wrong. What aren't you telling me?"

"Johanna, your sister was . . . taken quite ill in Havrincourt. Kepler got her out, but there were complications." He paused. "She died of pneumonia a few days later, in Paris."

Jo stared at him a long moment while she searched his eyes for the truth. *Jewel . . . is dead?* "I cannot believe it." Her voice was a whisper. "There must be some mistake."

Yet the grief in his expression didn't lie, and her vision blurred as tears welled in her eyes. She was vaguely aware as Colin released her hand and wiped at the wetness along her cheek. He rose from the chair and sat beside her, taking her into his arms.

She leaned into him, clinging to his comforting presence as he held her. Her silent tears continued, though Jo didn't understand why she wept. She and Jewel had never even met one another. But in those written pages . . .

Jo had come to love her sister, a woman who shared with her not only the bond of blood, but an understanding of what it meant to survive alone in the midst of a war.

Colin's arms remained around her as he gently explained about Kepler's mission into Havrincourt to get Jewel, and the woman who subsequently became the decoy for her sister.

When Jo finally drew back to see his face, anger and confusion overshadowed her grief. "So Mr. Petit knows that Kepler works for the Americans. And this woman . . . she was hired to pose as Jewel?"

He nodded. "It's critical for the mission."

"What mission?" She stared at him, bewildered. "What was my sister involved in?"

"She was innocent." His tone was fierce. "Just like you are innocent. Both of you are pawns in a game being played by the Allies."

"Game? Colin, explain to me why Kepler brought this . . . imposter to Spain. And why is she pretending to be my sister?"

"Because your father is here. She was to meet him."

His words sent shock waves through her. "Papa is here . . . in Barcelona?"

"Here, or in the vicinity." He reached up to stroke her cheek. "Kepler never lied to your sister. He had every intention of reuniting father and daughter." He laid his hand on her shoulder. "There's more, Johanna."

Again Jo felt a chill ripple down her back. "'Tis my papa, isn't it?" She gripped his arm. "Has something happened to him?"

"No, he's fine, as far as I know. But you need to be aware of his . . . occupation." His gaze shone with compassion. "Your father has been working with the Germans, Johanna. He's a spy."

The coldness of moments ago transformed into a queasiness roiling her insides. Jo pulled away from him to sit forward on the divan as the room around her suddenly shifted.

This couldn't be happening. Her father, the gentle man of her memory, with his deep blue eyes and strong, capable hands, the lingering scent of tobacco . . . a Boche spy? *I want nothing more in the world than to be your Papa.*

Jo was only half listening as Colin continued to enlighten her on the conditions her father had set in exchange for some prize the Allies needed. She turned to look at him. "A German spy. You are certain?"

He nodded. "I know it must be a shock."

A *shock?* Bitterness rose like bile in her throat, and her nausea worsened until Jo thought she might be ill. She remembered her dream that afternoon, about Moira and her subversion toward Britain. Now it seemed Jo's father was a traitor to the Allied nations.

And what of herself? She'd taken up arms against a British soldier with a rifle, trying to protect her mother.

". . . the Americans tried to outsmart your father, trying to get this 'prize' from him before he learned that the actress wasn't your sister."

She realized Colin was still speaking to her, and she focused on his words. "What prize?"

"I have no idea, but Marcus claims it's crucial in helping to speed up an end to the war. Apparently Zero has it, but so far he's managed to evade detection. Until you arrived in Toulouse, G-2 was losing hope."

"Zero? Is that what they call him?" Her papa was a stranger to her, living some secret life she didn't think Jewel or even Moira had known about.

The rest of Colin's sentence finally penetrated. "What has this to do with me?"

"Once Petit learned you were Jacob Reyer's daughter, G-2 decided to offer you up in your sister's place. They hope Zero will still agree to the bargain and hand over this valuable prize."

"And that's why Mr. Petit brought me to Spain."

He nodded. "They determined my presence was unnecessary to their plans but believed you would not willingly go without me."

"And they were right." She reached to clasp his hand. "I am relieved you are here."

He pulled her back to sit beside him. "And I am as well."

"The actress . . . she told me the meeting would happen soon."

"Yes, it is set for tomorrow, near a place called Montserrat." His eyes searched hers. "I know I've burdened you with a lot of truth,

276

but the decision is yours as to whether you want to go through with this meeting or not. Whatever you choose, I will defend it with Captain Weatherford." His features took on an almost wild look. "Even if it means a court-martial."

"No! You mustn't do that." She laid a hand against the strong line of his jaw as a whirlwind of emotion raged through her: grief over a sister she would never get to meet, excitement in knowing she would see her father. Anxiety, wondering how the memory she'd nurtured for so many years could possibly reconcile with an enemy spy, perhaps even an assassin, living among the shadows. Jo didn't even want to imagine the heinous crimes he must have committed over the course of the war.

Yet regardless of her feelings, it seemed their reunion was destined. Jo didn't know if she should be afraid or thankful.

Colin read her thoughts. "You need to remember, Johanna, it was your father who approached the Americans. He wants to defect, and he's willing to hand over something the enemy values just as highly as the Allies, perhaps even more so. I believe he worried about Jewel after her aunt died, and he wanted her to be safe."

He put his arm around her shoulders. "Jacob Reyer loved her, and I know he will love you, too. I don't think a man like that can be such a monster." He paused. "But I meant what I said. The decision is still yours."

She rested against him, her gaze drifting toward the ceiling. "Well, I won't have you losing your job or standing in front of a firing squad on my account."

"None of it matters. I made a promise to protect you. Your welfare is all I care about."

She turned to him, her emotions still jumbled. "You said this 'prize' my father has is important to helping end the war?"

"According to Captain Weatherford. And he is a man of honor."

"All right."

Rising to her feet, Jo left him seated on the divan as she walked toward the bed, where the diary still lay. "I can only imagine how much Papa must have loved my sister."

She reached for the book and turned to Colin. "I will give him this tomorrow when we meet." Once again tears misted her eyes, and Jo wiped at them before hugging the diary. "A keepsake to remind him of the daughter he has lost. And a peace offering, in the hope he will accept the daughter who is found."

CHAPTER 25

I thought we agreed, no more foul-ups."

Marcus sat on a park bench in Barcelona's busiest public square, looking at the man seated beside him.

"I have no idea what you're talking about, Captain."

Petit lounged against the bench and lifted a lazy brow.

Poker face. Marcus's jaw worked as he removed his hat. The weather was warm, the clouds overhead acting like a blanket to keep in the heat. He could hear the rush of water behind him as a waterworks shot streams of frothy liquid toward the sky, only to have them fall back into the enormous pool with a resounding splash. "I am referring to Johanna Reyer. Why would she send a message through to Paris, addressed to Lieutenant Mabry in Portbou, telling him she was in trouble?"

Petit leaned forward on the bench, muttering a curse. "How did she manage it? I bribed the front desk manager to prevent any outgoing calls from her room."

"Apparently she brought a carrier pigeon with her."

"You're joking."

"Hardly." Marcus was almost pleased he'd managed to shake the man's composure. "Care to tell me what happened?"

279

Petit looked out at the square. Marcus followed his gaze. An enormous flock of pigeons hovered at the feet of an old woman who held a small paper bag of either dried corn kernels or nuts. As she threw out a handful of the feed, the birds rose in a fluttering wall of gray wings, circling before they glided down again beside the food, each pecking madly to get their fill. The old woman tossed another handful into the air, and the dance repeated itself.

"I suppose Johanna could have hidden that bird in the cloth bag she carried on the train." Petit sounded impressed. He removed his hat and turned to Marcus.

"She had a visit yesterday from our actress, Miss Tremblay. I thought if Odette went and introduced herself as Jewel and invited Johanna along to see their father, the woman would be all the more eager to participate."

He bent his head. "Obviously the plan backfired. Odette must have missed something in the diary, because Johanna's now convinced she isn't her sister."

Marcus felt a sudden soft breeze and heard the rustle of the palms that lined one end of the square. It failed to cool his anger. "So now we must take Johanna to the meeting by force, because she no longer has an ally in her sister. Is that correct?"

Petit tilted his head toward Marcus. "That about sums it up."

"And this . . . Miss Tremblay? You said she read the diary."

Petit nodded. "In Toulouse, I managed to keep the lieutenant and Johanna Reyer out late one night while Odette slipped into her room and borrowed the book. She put it back before they returned to the hotel."

"Sounds as if she should have kept it longer."

"True." Petit's smile was grim. "But our actress learned enough to fool the lieutenant the very next day when he insisted on seeing 'Jewel.' After a brief encounter, he left fairly confident it was her, though he never got the chance to see Odette's face. I made sure

Kepler returned to the room before that happened. Odette told me later that she and Kepler made a pretty believable case out of it."

"I had to bring him along, you know."

Petit emitted another curse. "All my efforts for nothing. I don't suppose you could have ordered him to go home?"

Marcus smiled without humor. "He's a man in love, and after the dire note he received from Johanna, he was willing to risk prison in order to come here and see for himself she's all right." He flashed a sideways glance. "She is all right, isn't she, Petit?"

The American eyed him sullenly. "I settled things with her this morning. She still trusts me but not Odette. I ordered Johanna to stay in her room and said I'd speak with my superiors about the phony woman in black."

Marcus again looked out at the square, observing the beautiful architecture surrounding the Plaça de Catalunya—neoclassic, neo-Gothic, Baroque, Art Nouveau. The foot traffic was growing busier, a normal occurrence this time of the afternoon. He noted a group of aproned women collecting jugs of water at the public fountain. "Considering this new snarl, I suppose it's fortunate I brought the lieutenant along. I've briefed him to a certain extent, and he can speak with Johanna about the meeting tomorrow. Where is she?"

"We're at the Coloma Hotel on La Rambla. She's in room 320."

"I'll follow up with the lieutenant." He eyed Petit sharply. "Is everything else ready for tomorrow?"

"We're all set. I went out to the caves after breakfast this morning and put up the sign. I got back an hour ago." He turned to face Marcus. "Why these caves, exactly?"

Marcus shrugged. "Zero is a painter by trade. The Sant Sever Caves have attracted artist types for years, including sculptors and a few prominent architects. And right now, we need to accommodate Zero's wishes as much as possible. He and I will arrive at the caves an hour ahead of the meeting. I want Lieutenant Mabry to accompany Kepler and Johanna; otherwise, I doubt she will go willingly."

Petit frowned. "I suppose you're right, but too many cooks spoil the stew."

"You should have thought of that back in Toulouse." Marcus turned away, eyeing the old woman feeding the birds.

"Does the lieutenant know about the Black Book?"

"No, but he's aware Zero has something we all want." Marcus rose from the bench and resettled the hat onto his head. "So let's hope our master spy accepts his second daughter in lieu of the first, and wants his amnesty badly enough to hand over that book."

CHAPTER

26

*M*adame Mabry? It is me, Madame Outis. May I come in?"
Jo had heard the knock at her door and now stood
beside it clad in her nightgown and robe as she deliberated over whether or not to let the actress inside.

She'd been awakened by Petit's telephone call at seven o'clock
that morning, telling her the woman would arrive shortly with a
package. After all Colin had told Jo yesterday, she was still resent-
ful toward the woman who had pretended to be her poor sister.

"Madame Mabry? Please let me in. I mean you no harm."

Jo let out a resigned breath. She supposed the woman had only
been doing her job for the Americans. And admittedly none of her
actions had been malicious toward either Jo or Colin.

She finally opened the door and saw the same beautiful face
she'd seen days ago, haloed in golden-blond hair and wearing an
anxious look. Instead of the black mourning clothes, Madame
Outis now wore a lovely red skirt and jacket ensemble. She carried
a package in her arms, the brown paper crackling as she hugged
the parcel.

Jo eyed her with reserve as she stepped back and allowed the
woman entrance.

"I would first like to introduce myself and to apologize for misleading you the other day. I did not know your sister, but I am very sorry she is gone."

The soft blue eyes glistened with the same emotion Jo had seen the last time they'd met. The woman certainly was a good actress. Except for the few mistakes she'd made with details, she had been convincing as Jo's sister.

Jo closed the door.

The woman shifted the package to extend a hand encased in gold satin. "I am Mademoiselle Odette Tremblay with the Théâtre du Châtelet in Paris. I sometimes do work with the Allies in France. Monsieur Petit tells me you know about our circumstances, so I hope you are not too angry with me?"

While Jo disliked the fact Petit and Kepler were trying to trick her father, she understood why they were doing it. And in truth, she had no idea what kind of man Jacob Reyer had become. Would he be glad to see her . . . or enraged because she wasn't Jewel?

She twisted the ring on her finger. Either way, it wasn't this woman's fault. Jo took the proffered hand. "I'm not angry with you, Miss Tremblay."

"Please, you must call me Odette."

She smiled, and again Jo was reminded of how much she resembled Colin's description of her sister. "What do you have in the package?"

"These are the mourning clothes I was wearing when we met. You are requested to put them on for the meeting today." Odette offered her the paper bundle. "If you will permit, I would like to stay and act as your lady's maid."

Jo didn't need help with getting dressed, and since she and Odette were about the same size, there was no reason the clothing might not fit.

She was about to object when Odette reached for her hand. "Please, I insist, Johanna. You are a lovely woman and so kind.

I feel very badly that I had to deceive you in such a personal way." She dipped her head and smiled. "This will be my atonement, *oui*?"

Jo found she couldn't refuse the offer; it seemed important to Miss Tremblay. "All right, I would appreciate your help, Odette. Thank you."

Soon they had the package opened on the bed, and Odette began assisting her in slipping the heavy one-piece silk dress over her head.

After thrusting both arms into the narrow black sleeves, Jo settled the double skirts over her hips. "There is certainly a lot of fabric here." She reached to adjust the gauzy, V-shaped neckline of the bodice. "Did you have to wear this same heavy dress all the time?"

"I have a second black gown, similar in style." Odette spoke from behind her. "It was important that I remain hidden from the world as much as possible."

The world being my father. Jo quashed her resentment and held steady as Odette fastened the hooks of the wide black cummerbund at her waist.

Next the actress prepared Jo's hair, then came around front and fitted her with a round black crepe hat and a dark veil reaching just below her chin. The silk chiffon was so thick as to be barely transparent.

Jo raised the veil to stare at her. "How did you ever manage with this? I can hardly see."

Odette gave her a rueful smile. "Believe me, I have had to spend much of my time looking down at the ground in front of me. The veil was another reason I kept to my room so often in Toulouse. Not only to keep from bumping into the first solid object I encountered, but there was the constant temptation to rip it off so that I could see everything around me." A sigh escaped her. "I spent much of the time staring out my window instead."

Jo hadn't considered the monotony of Odette's life behind the veil. "It has not been an easy assignment for you, has it?"

The actress shrugged. "Not so difficult, but certainly the longest. I have been with Captain Kepler almost three months, and honestly, I am very glad to know my part is coming to an end."

"And I am supposed to wear these clothes today so that nothing seems amiss?"

Odette nodded. "I do not know the details of your meeting, except that you are to see your father. I think they wish to break the news of your sister's death to him as gently as possible."

Jo's hand went to her stomach as she tried to still her fluttering nerves. Likely she would be the one to tell her papa that Jewel was dead—after he removed the veil and saw she was a different person entirely.

She picked up the black gloves and went to stand in front of the cheval glass. Except for the bodice being a bit snug, the dress fit her well, and the skirt was long enough to hide the white tops of her button shoes.

The color seemed appropriate as well. An unexpected lump rose in her throat as she stared into the mirror, seeing the memory of Moira lying dead near the open door of a burning grave, and a sister who had slipped from Jo's life as quickly and as quietly as she had entered it. Too many of her family members lost . . .

Her grief returned in a rush, and she quickly dropped the veil so Odette wouldn't see. Jo would never know the young woman who had shared their father's blood, the beloved sister who was a true heroine amid so many difficulties of war.

"And now for the final touch."

Her attention returned to Odette as the woman stood behind her and fastened around her neck the long silver chain with the dove ring.

"For all to see." The actress stepped back. "You are to wear it until you meet with your father."

Jo fingered the ring, noting how the tiny silver dove was identical to her own except for a ruby that winked back at her from the bird's eye instead of her own sapphire.

"I must leave you now. Captain Kepler will arrive for you shortly." Odette tilted her head, surveying her work. "You certainly look the part." She smiled at Jo in the mirror. "I wish you *bonne chance.*"

Once she'd gone, Jo removed the hat and veil. Colin had telephoned her after his visit yesterday, informing her they would be taking the nine o'clock train this morning, which would leave in an hour. She'd asked him where they were going, but he would not speak of it over the telephone and promised to tell her when he arrived.

In his absence, Jo had been allowed the chance to absorb all he'd told her, and she began to wonder what the future held for them. For a few uncertain moments, she'd been tempted to believe Colin's feelings for her were a mere convenience after Jewel's death. But how could she deny the growing attraction she'd sensed in him during their quest, or the tender way he held her in his arms, and the longing in his kiss. His whispering sweet endearments to her . . .

Jo knew down to her bones that Colin hadn't been hedging any bets; his heart had already spoken volumes to her well before he knew her sister was gone.

But what of her own legacy—a child born out of wedlock, daughter to a pair of traitors? She had withheld much from him, and he didn't yet know the extent of Moira's participation in Ireland's fight for freedom, or Jo's part in the Dublin Rising.

Colin was a British officer, and Jo had taken up arms against just such a man. Perhaps he'd even known the soldier. How far would duty outweigh his love, if he did love her as she supposed?

A knock at the door startled Jo from her troubling thoughts. As she went to answer it, anxiety about the future and anticipation at seeing him made her heart race.

"You look like her . . . the actress, I mean."

Colin stood on the threshold, staring at her. Jo glanced down at her black mourning garb. "Miss Odette Tremblay. She brought me the clothes. It seems we are to fool my father to the very last."

It was hard to keep the bitterness from her voice. She allowed Colin to enter the room, and after she'd closed the door, he reached for her and pulled her into his arms. He kissed her deeply, and Jo closed her eyes, meeting his need with her own as she clung to him for strength.

When he leaned back, his expression was tender and full of compassion. "I can only imagine how difficult this meeting will be for you, Johanna, but in the end, I pray both you and your father receive what you want from the encounter."

Jo smiled. She would pray for the same thing.

She finally noticed he'd changed his appearance for the coming rendezvous as well, adding a brown felt hat and a dark double-breasted blazer. Jo stepped back to survey him. With the dark trousers and shoes, Colin could pass for any local businessman—except, perhaps, for the large steel hook he wore in place of the gloved hand.

He caught her glance. "Our meeting is supposed to take place in a set of limestone caves, so I thought this device might be a bit more useful."

She was relieved he felt comfortable enough now to wear a more practical appliance than the useless wooden hand. Then she caught up with his words. "Caves?" Her gaze narrowed. "Mr. Petit's idea?"

"No, your father's choice. Seems the caves appeal to his artistic side."

That surprised her. Perhaps Papa felt safer conducting his dealings there.

Colin dropped his hat on the small table and then led Jo to sit on the divan. As he leaned back against the cushions, his jacket fell open, revealing a pistol holstered at his side.

It dawned on her suddenly how clandestine, and perhaps even dangerous, this upcoming meeting would be. She huddled against his side while her heart thrummed with a sense of excitement—or was it fear?—and her next words tumbled out. "When are we to leave for the station?"

He checked his watch. "Kepler should arrive anytime now."

She looked up at him. "'Tis strange to think of the man in such a different light." Jo was still coming to terms with the fact that Werner Kepler worked for the Americans. "I mean, until yesterday, you and I thought he was a Boche spy. Now it seems we're all on the same side."

"Let's hope so anyway." Colin's smile was tight. "Our meeting today is scheduled for noon. The Sant Sever Caves are near Montserrat, which means 'serrated mountain,' so I imagine we'll have some climbing to do." He glanced down at her black gown. "Hopefully nothing too difficult."

"Goodness, I'm beginning to wonder at my father's eccentricities."

"You and me both."

She noted his hand flexing against his thigh, and concern filled her. "The idea of going into those caves bothers you, doesn't it?"

"A bit too much like the war."

Seeing his forced smile and the way his Adam's apple bobbed above his collar, she was suddenly filled with a burst of love. Colin was going through all of this, facing his worst fears—because of her. He'd promised to stay with her and make certain she was safe.

Jo reached for him, touching the side of his face. "You are the bravest man I know, Colin Mabry."

She leaned up and gave him a light peck on the lips, but he closed his arms around her and held her in place.

Returning the quick kiss, he gazed into her eyes. "I hardly feel brave at the moment."

"That just means you've got more courage than you thought. After all, even the most heroic of men are afraid at one point or another, but they stand their ground nonetheless."

One of his dark brows rose, and a gleam came into his eyes. "I suppose you mean heroic men like Bonaparte?"

"Exactly!" She smiled at him. "You know Napoleon once said, 'Death is nothing, but to live defeated and inglorious is to die daily.'"

Colin's burst of laughter caused a surge of joy in her heart. "The man must have been a veritable wellspring of maxims. With all of the hours he spent quoting himself, I wonder that he had any time for battle."

She raised her chin at him. "He could do both."

Then she laughed, and he pulled her close, kissing her thoroughly before he let her go. "Ah, Mrs. Mabry, you do like to tease a poor fellow."

She smiled at him before another knock sounded at the door. They both turned their heads, and the reality of what lay ahead dampened their humor.

He looked at her. "We should answer that."

The fluttering in her stomach returned. "Colin, what if he . . . doesn't like me?"

Jo hadn't meant to blurt the question, but his smile was tender. "Trust me, Johanna. Your father will like you. Even I like you." His eyes glowed as he reached to tuck a strand of her hair behind her ear. "In fact, I suspect he will adore you."

He spoke in a low voice, barely above a whisper, and his words made her shiver with pleasure. She saw his reluctance as he finally released her and rose from the divan. "I suppose I'd better let in Kepler."

Colin opened the door to find George Petit in the hall. His surprise quickly gave way to annoyance. "What are you doing here?"

"Good morning to you too, Lieutenant. I see you're chipper, as usual."

"Well, no one's been tampering with my coffee lately."

"Ah yes. I guess I owe you an apology. Again." Petit shook his head. "Just following orders."

And enjoying every minute. "I'll ask once more, why are you here?"

"There's been a little change in plans. This influenza seems to be spreading and has found its next victim in Kepler. The man can hardly stand on his feet, so I'll be taking his place."

Colin's mouth twisted. "Are you certain it wasn't something he drank?"

Petit laughed. "With so much at stake? What do you take me for?" His humor faded. "You wound me, Lieutenant."

Colin snorted. "I doubt that much could injure your feelings, Petit."

"Ah, Mrs. Mabry, I swear you could be Odette's twin in that gown." Petit effectively ended their conversation as he walked past Colin toward Johanna.

Colin frowned after him. He still didn't trust the man, G-2 or not.

"Mr. Petit."

At Johanna's stiff greeting, Colin felt satisfaction, knowing he wasn't the only one who resented the man and his tricks.

Smiling broadly, Petit seemed oblivious as he reached for her hand. "I've got a taxi waiting downstairs, and once we arrive at the train station, it will take less than an hour to reach the town of Martorell. The railway stops there, so we'll have to drive the rest of the way." He checked his watch. "We're running behind schedule, so if you'll get your hat and veil, we can be on our way." He turned and winked at Colin. "Just like old times."

Colin didn't bother to smile. Instead he watched Johanna don the small black cap, draping it with the same heavy black veil the actress had worn. She rolled back the dark fabric enough to be able to see, then retrieved the diary and her purse, tucking them both inside the cloth kit bag on the table.

With her bag in hand, she turned to Colin, and he noted her pale face and the taut lines around her mouth.

"Taxi's waiting, folks."

Colin ignored Petit's prodding. "Do you still want to go through with this, Johanna?"

"Now, hold on just a minute—"

Colin held up his hand to silence the American. His attention remained fixed on Johanna.

Her lips parted slightly before she nodded. "Yes, I'm ready."

He offered a reassuring smile. "I'll be with you the whole way."

Petit blew out a breath as he opened the door and Colin and Johanna followed him to the elevator. Downstairs, a taxi waited beside the curb.

It would be a short drive to the station. Heading south toward the port, they passed the towering Monument a Colom, where high atop the stone spire, Columbus pointed toward the sea. Turning east along the harbor, Colin noticed the busy waterfront as workers bustled about driving lorries, and dockside cranes transferred cargo back and forth between the moored ships and port buildings. Breathing in the salt air through his open window, he spotted the quay as they passed the port, and beyond that, a beach community with cafés and flats built near the shore.

They reached the train station, and Petit purchased their tickets before the three went out to the platform to board. Inside, the cars were crowded. Colin took a seat in coach with Johanna on his right, while Petit sat across the aisle from him, perusing the contents of a rucksack he'd brought along before setting it down near his feet.

Colin turned to Johanna when her hand reached for his. Because she was once again shadowed behind the veil, he could barely make out her features, yet her tight grip on him revealed her nervousness. He leaned close and gave her hand a gentle squeeze. "All will be well. Just remember to breathe."

"Easier said than done."

Her words made Colin's gut tighten, thinking about their destination and the struggle with his own demons. Descending into a dark, cramped hole was the most loathsome, terrifying undertaking he could imagine at the moment.

He shot another look over at Petit, who now lay back against his seat with his eyes closed. Colin wondered whether Marcus knew of the sudden change in plan with Kepler.

It would be just like the American to have pulled some surprise stunt, and after being drugged twice, Colin intended to stay on guard.

Looking beyond Petit, through the train's window, Colin caught sight of the passing scenery, a hotchpotch of city architecture, followed by neighborhoods with clusters of colored tenements rising above the streets. Eventually those faded into factories and shops, and finally, as the train veered north, to bare fields.

Colin turned to face forward again, his thoughts returning to the upcoming meeting with Zero. He wondered what kind of man Johanna's father would be. He had been surprised yesterday when Marcus praised rather than censured him for going on his own to find Johanna and gain her cooperation for the task. The captain had even indulged Colin's curiosity, sharing with him a bit of Zero's background and how the German, living secretly among the French all of his life, was ready to get out.

Zero's reputation was one of cunning and danger, yet he'd been willing to go to great lengths to get his daughter safely out of occupied France. From what Johanna recalled of her one and only childhood memory of him, the man had loved her as well. Was he still that same affectionate father?

Colin and Johanna would both know soon enough.

As they approached the station at Martorell, the wide valleys they had passed through during the previous hour gave way to steep green and tan hills that hemmed them in. They disembarked at the station, and while he and Johanna waited inside the terminal, Petit checked on the arrangement for their car.

A few minutes later, the three were on the road, Petit behind the wheel. The route to reach the trailhead ran parallel to the sharp incline of rock that narrowed along either side of the passage as they gained altitude.

"That wide jagged range of rocks is Montserrat." Petit pointed to a mountain with unusual spiked edges, covered in pine. "There's a monastery at the top built into the rock. It's over a thousand years old."

Johanna leaned forward. "Are the caves beneath the monastery?"

"No, we're on this side of the mountain. Once we arrive in the town of Collbató, we'll take a road with a series of switchbacks to reach the trailhead. We'll park the car there."

An hour later, they reached the parking area, high above the city. Colin gazed up at the steep gray rock, wondering how far they must climb before reaching the caves.

Petit wheeled in beside another dark car, then set the brake before killing the engine. "The entrance to the caves is a little less than a mile from here. The path is steep in places, but not too strenuous, I hope." He smiled at Johanna.

"Yes, Colin mentioned it." She stared at her shoes. "So long as my feet survive, I'll be all right. I do miss my boots."

Colin smiled. "We'll take as much time as you need. Won't we, Petit?"

The American nodded. "We still have an hour. That's Captain Weatherford's car. He should already be up at the caves with Mrs. Mabry's father."

Colin glimpsed Johanna beside him, clutching the kit bag to her chest. Again he empathized with her anxiety: in less than a mile, he would again descend into the stuff of his nightmares—a deep, dark, suffocating hole underground.

He opened the car door and helped her alight. Johanna turned to Petit. "Is it necessary that I wear the veil on the path, Mr. Petit? I could go much faster if I'm able to see a few feet in front of me."

He lifted his gaze, scanning the limestone hills above them. "Well, I don't see anyone, but if you can manage it, I'd be grateful if you kept it on. Just in case Zero is using binoculars to watch our progress."

"Very well."

She started forward, and Colin took her arm. "Hold on to me, and I'll walk you up the path."

They followed Petit along a well-marked dirt trail leading upward. The air was cool, but Colin soon became warm with the exertion, and sweat broke out along his brow. He could only imagine Johanna's discomfort in the heavy black dress.

After fifteen minutes, Petit's breathing was labored, and he stopped to remove a water bottle from his rucksack. As he held the jug out to Johanna, Colin stepped forward. "You first."

Squinting against the sun's glare, Petit grinned and uncapped the bottle, taking a long drink. He passed the jug to Colin, who in turn offered the water to Johanna.

"Yes, please." She set down her kit bag and opened the bottle, raising it beneath the veil to quench her thirst.

When she'd finished, she offered the jug to Colin. He stared at it, hesitating.

"Well? Aren't you thirsty?"

He flexed his jaw and took the bottle from her. Closing his eyes, he tipped his head back and slaked his thirst. Denying himself wasn't going to bring a man back from the grave. For whatever reason, Richards had saved his life in that tunnel, and Colin owed it to the man to make peace with his gift.

He recapped the bottle, and the three resumed their trek,

stopping twice more so Petit could catch his breath while Colin and Johanna gazed out at the panoramic view of forested rock, and farther below, the green valley.

They soon reached the cave entrance—a single wooden door embedded in rock—and Colin drew in a sharp breath. A large metal sign hung overhead: *Coves de Sant Sever.*

He wondered how wide the cave was inside, and as they approached the door, he saw a sign posted in both French and Spanish:

DANGER OF FALLING ROCK. CLOSED UNTIL FURTHER NOTICE.

"We are *not* going in there." Colin drew Johanna back as he glared at Petit.

"Relax, Lieutenant." He pointed toward the sign. "My handiwork. I came out yesterday and posted the warning to keep hikers and tourists away during our meeting. I assure you, it's nothing to worry about."

Petit slid the rucksack off his shoulder, reached inside, and withdrew a circular-shaped disk attached to a cord.

"What is that, Mr. Petit?"

"Flashlight." He held it up to Johanna. "The Germans call them dynamos, and they use them in the field. You slip the cord around your neck and wear the disk at chest level, like so." Removing his hat, he slipped the corded device over his head, then demonstrated how to turn the flashlight on and off using a small pull chain below the disk.

Colin had seen the devices before. Petit retrieved two more from the rucksack, handing the first light to Johanna and the last to him. "Makes it hands free, Lieutenant."

Taking the device, he offered Petit a grudging nod of thanks.

"You're welcome." Petit's gaze held amused satisfaction. "G-2 confiscated these from our prisoners of war."

Nerves taut, Colin barely acknowledged the comment, though

he was relieved for the concession. At least now he'd have the use of his hand as well as the hook.

Once they had donned the lights, Petit opened the entrance door to the caves. "Shall we?"

Colin's skin prickled as Johanna picked up her kit bag and turned in his direction. "Colin, are you ready?"

He nodded, not daring to speak. Petit held the door as Johanna went inside first; then he quickly followed her into the blackness.

Colin grabbed for the open door, watching the twin beams of light bounce off the rock before they disappeared from view. His feet seemed stuck and his breathing rapid. Already dampness clung to the back of his shirt.

His heart was banging in his chest as he fought to push down panic, and his mind frantically grasped for the words to the psalm he'd repeated for days in the tunnel: *I love the Lord, for he heard my voice; he heard my cry for mercy. . . .*

"Dear God, please help me," he groaned, forging into the nothingness.

CHAPTER 27

BARCELONA, SPAIN

Odette sat at the vanity in her hotel room, brushing her hair to a fine sheen. It was barely nine o'clock in the morning, but with being so busy helping Johanna Reyer into the mourning clothes and then tending to Kepler in his vulnerable state, she hadn't had time to freshen up.

Giving her hair a few more brush strokes, she considered the young woman about to meet her father. Odette knew Johanna hadn't seen him since childhood, and she hoped for her sake that it would be a wonderful reunion.

After all, it was important for a daughter to have some precious moments with her father. Odette herself enjoyed time with her own papa, a *sous-chef* in Paris. They spent many happy hours together, sharing their love of cooking and playing cards.

She smiled into the mirror, thinking of the many times she and Papa had played piquet until dawn, trying to match wits!

Surely Johanna deserved such memories, too.

After setting down her brush, Odette reached for the tin of loose face powder, and using her puff, she dabbed away the dampness at her brow and smoothed out the color around her nose and chin.

She was faithful about using the cold-cream treatments each night before bed, but she'd been somewhat lax with the powder, since much of the time her face had been shielded behind the veil.

But no more. Again she smiled at her reflection, turning her head from side to side, satisfied with the results. She was glad to finally be free of the shroud she'd been forced to wear over the past three months and felt empathy for those heavily veiled Middle Eastern women she'd seen in magazines.

And to think she once complained about all of her heavy stage makeup! Odette shook her head. She missed her acting terribly and looked forward to returning to the stage, where she would rise to stardom just as her *amoureux* had promised her. He'd told her they could live anywhere she chose—Mexico City, New York, even Buenos Aires, as he'd suggested. Whatever she wanted would be hers, and Odette knew the theater was where she was destined to be.

Closing the powder tin, she reached for her bottle of lilac water. Odette began dabbing a few drops behind her ears when a hard thump against the wall jarred her vanity mirror. She paused, listening, and another bump struck the wall, this time harder.

Odette realized the noise was coming from Kepler's room next door.

He'd been asleep when she checked on him before, and she'd made certain to post the *Do Not Disturb* sign on his door. She hoped he wasn't experiencing any further discomfort.

Another loud thump rattled her mirror, and she rose from the vanity seat. He did seem to be thrashing about, and she couldn't let him hurt himself. . . .

She wore her dressing gown over her clothes and checked both pockets before extracting a key. Moving toward the set of connecting doors, she released the bolt on her side before using his key to unlock the door to his room.

Odette arrived to find him awake on the bed, panting from his exertions. "Miss Tremblay, thank heavens you're here! Help me, will you? I've missed the train!"

She stood with her hands in her pockets, staring at him. He was lying facedown, still wearing his rumpled clothing from the night before. His arms and legs were tied behind him, trussed exactly like one of her papa's roasted capons. "Are you in pain, Captain?"

"What do you think?" He glared at her before his eyes closed, and he groaned. "Criminy, my head feels like it's been struck by a mortar." Then he flailed once more against his bonds, and the headboard hit the wall harder than it had before. "Are you going to just stand there, woman? I need to find the lieutenant and Miss Reyer and get to that meeting!"

Odette heard the pained rasp in his voice. "Please do not struggle, monsieur, or you will hurt yourself. I cannot untie those knots."

"I've got a pocketknife there in the drawer." He nudged his chin toward the nightstand. "You can use it to cut the ropes."

Odette closed the distance and opened the drawer, peering inside.

"Can you hurry it up?" He growled a curse. "This is all Petit's doing, I know it! I checked on him. A gambler from Texas. Hah! I'm sure he learned his rope tricks from rustling cattle."

She turned to him, disappointed by the remark. "You think Monsieur Petit did this to you?"

"Who else?" Again he fought against the knots until he lay gasping. "Odette, please . . . the knife!"

"I really must insist you lie still, monsieur." She closed the drawer and turned to him. "And I will not cut the ropes."

"What?" He craned his neck to stare at her. "Why not?"

"Hmmm, why not." She extracted from her pocket the small .41 derringer, a gift from her *amoureux*. "Because I am the one who went to all of the trouble to tie them."

CHAPTER
28

COLLBATÓ, SPAIN

With only the lone beam from the dynamo to guide him, Colin moved deeper into the caves. He followed closely behind Johanna and reached out to grab her arm when she stumbled forward and nearly fell.

"This dratted veil!" She stopped to peel back the dark cloth. "My father cannot possibly see us here in the dark, and I need to know where I'm going."

Colin wondered if, for himself, wearing a shroud would be more blessing than curse, like a horse's set of blinders. He could avoid looking at the shadowy recesses and cramped, rocky spaces responsible for his charging pulse and shortness of breath.

"How's it going back there?" Petit called to them from a few yards ahead.

Colin stared at Johanna.

She released a breath. "I'm ready."

"On our way." He had to force his lips apart in order to shout an answer. With a clearer view, Johanna increased the pace forward as Colin followed doggedly in her footsteps.

Looking straight ahead, he tried to focus on the path. When he had to turn slightly to move around an uneven section of wall, his light beam bounced off a grouping of stalagmites in the distance, the long, menacing spikes jutting upward from the cave floor.

The sweat that dampened his clothes began chilling his skin in the cavern's subterranean temperatures, and his heart continued hammering out a staccato beat.

Petit had mentioned that Marcus and Zero were already here, and Colin agonized over how deep they still had to venture down into the caves before meeting them.

A few yards ahead, the path began to narrow.

"Stay close to the wall on the right side." Petit's voice floated back in the darkness. "There's an exposed ledge on the left with quite a drop."

As if to prove to himself the American was telling the truth, Colin glanced over the ledge and stared down into the dark abyss. His pulse skyrocketed. "Be careful, Johanna."

"I'm doing my best." She paused and turned to him. "Can you see all right?"

"Fine." He gritted out the word, fighting a surge of panic. "Let's just keep moving."

She hesitated, then turned and continued on, keeping to the right side of the path. Colin did the same. He wiped the perspiration from his face with his sleeve. Only his need to protect Johanna kept him from turning around to beat a hasty retreat.

He ran his fingers along the cold cavern wall while he kept the hook poised at his side, ready to snag the nearest outcropping of rock should he trip or lose his balance and start plunging into the black chasm below. His breath came out in short, rapid bursts. *For you, Lord, have delivered . . . my feet from stumbling. . . .*

They moved deeper into the cave, and a musty smell reached his nostrils—the odor of ancient earth mixed with traces of animal scat and, he imagined, the decay of bones.

He held his watch to the light beam, dismayed to see that

already ten minutes had passed. It seemed they'd barely covered a few hundred feet. He went on, keeping his gaze locked on Johanna while he mentally sought strength in more of the psalmist's verse. *That I may walk before the Lord in the land of the living . . .*

Suddenly a beam of light brighter than their own shone back at them. Petit's voice echoed, calling out some kind of code word.

At the sound of Captain Weatherford's answering response, Colin's relief was palpable.

A few more steps brought them to a wide, elongated rock platform where two men stood in a pool of natural light shining through an opening in the cave's ceiling.

Beyond the plane, three narrow openings led deeper into the caves.

Colin's breath eased as he observed the patch of visible sky above. He moved to take his place beside Johanna, who had already replaced the veil.

Marcus's tall frame was easy enough to recognize, but Colin was curious about the man beside him. Shorter than the captain, he had a wiry frame, and his dark moustache and vivid blue eyes were set into a tanned, leathery face.

This must be Jacob Reyer. *Zero.*

Johanna pressed up beside Colin, and he tucked her gloved hand into the crook of his arm. Despite his own misgivings, he wanted to reassure her.

The man beside Marcus caught his action, and Zero's dark blue eyes scrutinized him.

"Lieutenant."

Marcus acknowledged him before turning a surprised frown on Petit. Colin watched the exchange, a new awareness causing his muscles to tense. Had Petit not informed Marcus of Kepler's illness?

Marcus said nothing, however, as Zero advanced a few steps in Johanna's direction.

Colin gave her fingers a light squeeze. Johanna's moment was finally upon her.

———

"Daughter?"

Jo's heart pounded as she eyed her father greedily from behind the veil. She was glad for the natural light above as her gaze traveled over his compact frame, the dark hair cut very short, his moustache full, and his face, angular like her own.

Her stomach churned as she released her death grip on Colin's arm and then handed him the cloth kit bag. Drawing a shaky breath, she offered up a frantic prayer. *Lord, if you are listening, please let him love me.*

She moved forward, unable to tell if she was floating or walking as she closed the distance between herself and her papa. When she stood in front of him, she saw him study her from head to toe before pausing at the ring on the silver chain.

Jo cleared her throat before finding her voice. "Papa?"

At the word, his expression darkened. He turned to cast a glance at the tall man behind him, presumably Captain Weatherford.

When her father's eyes found her again, he reached for the ring and the necklace, giving both a swift jerk. The chain broke free, and Jo let out a gasp.

"Take off the veil."

Jo quailed at the harshness in his tone, so different from the gentle voice of her memories. She quickly raised her head toward the tall captain behind him.

"Do as he says."

Her gloved hands shook as she slowly drew back the dark silk and revealed her face to her father. His eyes widened, and she lifted her chin, removing the veil and hat altogether, oblivious to the fall of hair that came tumbling down around her shoulders in doing so.

She could see his features clearly now. In the light, he seemed alien to her, his weathered complexion creased with age and likely hardship, wearing into the once smooth face she remembered. Yet his eyes were the same blue as her own.

And right now they were angry.

"You lied to me, Marcus."

He tossed the accusation back at the captain, yet his gaze remained fixed on her. "Why would you act so foolishly when you know the consequence for attempting to trick me?"

Jo glanced at Captain Weatherford, whose dark hair and eyes were set against features made of stone. "I did not lie, Zero. I went to Toulouse as you requested. I verified this woman is your daughter."

Her father barked out a caustic laugh. "Then it would seem the Americans fooled you as well." His mouth curled. "This woman is not my daughter. She is not Jewel."

"No, you're right, she isn't Jewel. She is your other daughter, Jacob. She is Johanna."

"Johanna." For a moment, shock erased the anger from her father's face as he stared at her. Then abruptly his features hardened again, and he turned to the captain. "Can she prove it?"

Jo bent her head, tears brimming at the callousness in his tone. This was not the reunion she had imagined with him during those days she'd clung to Papa's memory, the images she'd invented and reinvented over time to assuage the loneliness of growing up.

Sixteen years had passed since he'd last seen her, and Jo had changed much from the small, terribly shy child in Kilcoole. Still, she had hoped and prayed he would see through the changes and recognize her for the same blue eyes, if nothing else. Just as she knew his.

She raised her head, and the loose strands of her hair brushed against her face. Unconsciously, she removed a glove and started to reach to tuck the wisps behind her ear.

A hand grabbed her wrist in midair. Jo startled before looking up to see her father staring at the silver ring on her finger, the dove's blue sapphire winking in the light.

"Where did you get this?"

His throat worked as he turned his face back to her. He drew her forward, beneath the cavern's opening so that she was in the full light. "Answer me."

Though his words had lost their edge, Jo struggled to calm herself. "You gave it to me. When you k-kissed my palm and said you wanted nothing more in the world than—"

"Than to be your Papa." All at once, the leathery features softened, and his blue eyes shone suspiciously bright. "I remember. Ah, my little bluebird, it *is* you."

She choked on a sob. Her father pulled her to him, enveloping her in a fierce hug. Jo wept silent tears against his shoulder, while he whispered endearments in French, German, and English as he held her.

Savoring the comfort of his embrace, she breathed in the scent of his tobacco and Bay Rum, and a smell that was *her papa*.

It was moments before he relaxed his hold, keeping his hands on her shoulders.

"I don't understand why you are here, Johanna. But I am overjoyed to see you after all of these years." He reached to touch her wet cheek. "You have some of your mother's look about you." He tipped his head, his eyes traveling over her hair and her face. "But how could I not know you were mine?" A smile formed beneath the heavy moustache. "You resemble me more, perhaps, than your sister, Jewel."

He turned to the captain, a slight edge in his voice. "Where is my other daughter, Marcus?"

The captain nodded in Petit's direction. "Our American friend can explain."

Jo hardly dared to breathe as Petit stepped into the light. It was the first time she had ever seen him looking so serious.

"Your other daughter, sir . . ." He shifted on his feet. "I regret to inform you that Jewel died from complications due to pneumonia."

Jo felt her father sag against her, and she leaned to steady him.

"When?" His voice was hoarse.

Petit looked past them to Captain Weatherford, then back at her father. "In December, sir. Our man posing as Captain Kepler got her out of Havrincourt before she would have been taken by the Germans, but there was illness in the village at the time of the Cambrai assault." He stared at the ground. "Kepler brought her to Paris, and we arranged for the best doctors, but . . . she was too weak by then."

Petit's face lifted to Jo and her father. "She is buried at Père Lachaise in Paris."

Jo's throat grew tight as she listened to Petit speak about her sister's death. Poor Jewel had been so close to freedom, yet she hadn't lived to taste it.

She glanced at Colin and saw how Petit's words affected him, too. He'd cared very much for her sister, and Jo understood how it grieved him to know Jewel had met with such a sad fate.

"And this ring?" Her father resumed his stance beside her, thrusting the silver chain he'd ripped from around Jo's neck moments ago toward Petit. "You thought to trick me by having Johanna wear it?"

"Not exactly." Petit glanced at Colin, then at Jo before he wet his lips. "We were desperate to get the Black Book and knew that if we told you about your daughter's . . . passing, you might abandon the exchange."

Jo watched her papa's features harden as Petit explained Odette's purpose in the ruse and how the Americans planned to fool him into an exchange of some Black Book.

"Do you think I am blind?" Snarling, her father took a step

toward Petit. "How did you imagine you would get the book from me with this game of yours?"

Petit explained G-2's plan to grab the book when her papa brought it out of hiding—before revealing the truth about her sister.

"You would still have received your amnesty, of course." Petit grimaced. "But you are one wily raccoon to try to tree."

"So you went searching for my other daughter, hoping to pacify me into an exchange?"

"Actually, she found us." Petit glanced at her. "Seems she was looking for you, so we just helped her along."

Her papa turned to her, his brow creased. "Where is Moira?"

"She died, Papa . . . two years ago." Jo hesitated. "She told me to come to France. To find you."

Regret filled his gaze. "And you have been alone all of this time?"

When she nodded, he laid a gentle hand on her shoulder and turned to Captain Weatherford. "Did you know about this when we first met in Barcelona?"

"Not until I arrived in Toulouse." The captain reached to rub the back of his neck. "I did not lie to you, Zero, but I am guilty of omission."

"I trusted you."

The captain straightened and scowled. "I know you did, and while I am very sorry about your daughter, there is nothing we can do to bring her back, and this book is important. Removing it from the kaiser's grasp could mean saving the lives of countless others on both sides of the war."

He took a step toward her father. "You, my friend, still have a chance to do the right thing, and you have a daughter who loves you and needs you." The captain darted a glance at Petit. "G-2 is still willing to offer you amnesty. Are you willing to turn over the Black Book?"

"Papa?"

Jo eyed him anxiously, knowing only that this book meant freedom for her father. He gazed at her, his features sad as he reached to trail the back of his hand along her cheek. "I wish I could, Marcus." He turned to the captain. "But I don't have the book."

The captain's eyes narrowed. "Now who's playing tricks, Zero?"

"No trick." He sighed. "You see, I wanted my daughter Jewel out of Havrincourt, and before I left for the war, I gave her a book. A diary. I asked her to record her life during the war while I was gone so that she could someday read me her words."

"What does that have to do with the Black Book?" Petit spoke up, his voice impatient.

Her papa ignored Petit and glanced at the captain. "Marcus, do you remember the sign of a good spy?"

"Hiding in plain sight." Dawning struck the captain's features. "You mean to say . . ."

"Jewel had the Black Book all along. I never doubted that when the Americans brought her to me, she would have the diary with her." Fresh grief etched lines in his face. "But now she is gone, and I have no idea where the book could be."

Jo's eyes widened as she stared at her father. "I have it, Papa. I have her diary."

He looked incredulous. "Where . . . did you find it?"

"Havrincourt. I went to your village after the German army retreated. I hoped to find a photograph of you, or your pipe, or some other . . . reminder, besides the ring."

She bent her head. "But with so much destruction, there was nothing salvageable. Then I saw a boy standing inside the burnt-out shell of a barn. He tried to lift a door out of the ground."

"The cellar." Her papa's expression took on a look of wonder.

"I helped him to open the door, and we both went down inside.

He collected food from your stores while I searched around and . . . well, I found Jewel's diary."

She shook her head. "But I don't understand this Black Book you speak about, Papa. I didn't see anything suspicious. It's only her words and songs."

Hope lit his face. "You wouldn't see anything, Johanna, because I used a film process to reduce the intelligence. It is concealed inside the book; your sister had no knowledge it was even there. Is it here with you?"

Jo nodded and turned to Colin, who seemed watchful as he gazed at Petit, then at her father and the captain, and finally back at her. His smile was tight.

She wondered at his look as she held out her hand. "May I?"

He stepped forward then, and Jo reached for the kit bag.

The blow that struck her knocked her sideways, and the bag was snatched from her grasp. Jo heard Colin shout before she stared up at Petit, who clutched the bag in his left hand while his right aimed a revolver at her face. "No one moves, or Zero loses another daughter. Up you go, Miss Reyer."

He waved the gun, indicating she should stand. When Jo scrambled to her feet, he shoved the bag into her grasp, then grabbed her from behind and walked her backward toward the series of three narrow cave openings. "We're taking the one on the right."

He held the revolver to the back of her head. "If any of you follow, I will shoot."

For several heartbeats, Colin and the other two men stood frozen as Petit pulled Johanna with him through the narrow opening, his revolver trained on her.

Once they disappeared from view, Colin withdrew his Colt and started to follow.

"Wait, Lieutenant. What will you do? He said he would kill her."

Zero was staring at him, his weathered features ashen.

"I intend to get her back." Colin met his gaze, fury and fear for Johanna outweighing all else. He'd once told Lacourt he would protect her with his life. He would keep his word.

"I'm going with you."

Colin turned his attention to Marcus, and the rage in the captain's face gave him pause.

"Zero, you remain here, in the event Petit invited friends we don't know about," Marcus said. "We'll get your daughter back and bring her here. No doubt she will need you."

The wiry man nodded, his eyes filled with a strange light as he withdrew a revolver from beneath his coat. "Get her back, Marcus." He glanced at Colin. "Both of you."

Colin switched on his flashlight and took the lead, stepping through the narrow opening Petit and Johanna had taken. Marcus followed behind him with his own light.

Keeping his Colt at the ready, Colin navigated the uneven path deeper into the cavern. The blackness engulfed him as the stifling air once again filled his nostrils with a musty, fecal odor. Adrenaline pumped in his veins, making his heart pound in his chest, and he prayed Petit wouldn't get desperate and hurt Johanna.

A light flickered ahead, bouncing off a cluster of stalactites, the limestone teeth plunging downward like daggers.

"Surrender now, Petit, and save yourself. There's no way out!"

Marcus had shouted the words from behind him, and his voice echoed through the cave.

A cacophony of screeching followed, and suddenly the flapping wings of a thousand bats swooped down from the cavern's ceiling and headed directly at Colin's beam of light.

He dropped down to avoid them, narrowly clearing a bullet whizzing past his head.

A groaned curse sounded directly behind him, and Colin turned. "Captain, are you hurt?"

"He got my leg." In the beam of Colin's light, Marcus leaned against the wall, his features knotted in pain while blood oozed from the middle of his right thigh.

Another shot sounded, and Colin threw himself against the captain, knocking them both to the ground. Where Marcus had been standing, the limestone shattered into tiny shards of rock that rained down on them.

Once the dust settled, Colin rolled off the captain's crumpled form. He tried to help him up, but Marcus grunted in pain. "You have to go after them on your own."

He spoke through bared teeth, his breathing harsh. "I know you care about her, Lieutenant. But the mission . . . comes first. Get that book at all costs."

Colin crouched and freed up his hand to remove his own necktie before handing it to Marcus. "For your leg, sir."

Again he picked up his Colt and rose to continue along the path. More darkness greeted him, and his shoulders brushed against rock as the walls narrowed with each step. Sweat began trickling down his face, but he forged on, fighting the panic already waging war in his chest.

Reaching a large fissure in the rock, he searched with the light for an alternate means to continue. There was nothing but limestone walls and impenetrable stalagmites. He wiped more sweat from his eyes, his breathing harsh. *Johanna . . .*

Gritting his teeth, Colin pressed his body sideways through the opening. Halfway through, he began to hyperventilate and stopped moving.

He was stuck.

Colin's nightmare became real as he began to struggle against the rock. Terror lay at the edges of his mind, and he closed his eyes, trying to focus on the psalm he'd memorized while in the tunnel. *When I was brought low, he saved me. . . .*

His lodged cry bullied its way out as he blindly reached forward with the hook. *Oh, God, please help me.*

The curved steel snagged against a rock on the other side. Using all of his strength, Colin pulled himself through the opening.

Gasping for air, he leaned against the wall and tried to catch his breath. Moments later, he straightened and realized he'd entered another chamber. Wending his way through, he glimpsed a flash of light bouncing off the wall ahead.

A second light illuminated the wall, and relief washed through him. Johanna!

"Petit, let her go—you don't need her anymore!"

"Colin!"

He stilled at the sound of Johanna's cry. Was she hurt? "Leave her out of this, Petit!" Colin shouted again. "Then it's just you and me and the book!"

The lights ahead paused.

"Fair enough." Petit's voice called from some distance away. "Take her to her father!"

As one light beam began moving again, Colin rushed forward, navigating a wider passage that ascended upward inside the mountain. Turning a corner, he saw Johanna's silhouette come into view, and his heart wedged in his throat. "Johanna, over here!"

She half ran and half stumbled down the path toward him. As they reached one another, she threw her arms around his neck. "Oh, Colin, when he fired the gun, I thought you were dead!"

She gasped the words, her head buried against his shoulder. He hugged her to him, reassured by her warm presence. "I'm all right, sweetheart, but Marcus took a bullet in the leg."

He pulled back so that he could see her in the beam of light. "Can you get back to your father, or did you get trapped in that rock fissure?"

"No, I slipped through all right."

Colin stared at her heavy skirts and wondered at his own difficulty. "There are no other outlets, so you shouldn't get lost."

"I will take her."

Both of them turned to find Johanna's father holding a flashlight. "I heard the shots. I wasn't about to stay behind while my daughter was wounded or worse."

"Papa!"

Johanna went to him and he held her. "Are you hurt, child?"

"No, I'm fine, truly."

"You two should go." Colin eyed them both. "I've got to get that book."

"No, you must come with us." Johanna turned, squinting against the light.

"I have to do this, Johanna. You know that."

She gazed at him a moment longer before she returned to his side. "I do know. Godspeed, Colin Mabry." She reached to touch the side of his face, then rose up and kissed him lightly. "Please be safe."

As she and her father headed back, Johanna glanced at Colin one last time before disappearing from view.

He resumed his hunt for Petit. Walking a few yards, he spotted the light up ahead. "You might as well surrender, Petit. There's no escape."

Again the light paused. "I thought I was rid of you, Lieutenant!"

"You cannot get out!"

"There's always a way out, boy."

Colin recalled his agonizing days in the tunnel at Passchendaele. "Sometimes it takes a miracle."

"Who needs a miracle? I told you, I was here yesterday to put up the sign. I also did a little reconnaissance. Growing up around San Antonio, I saw my share of caves."

"This isn't Texas, Petit. Surrender now, while you still have the chance."

"Or what? You'll shoot me?"

"Don't tempt me." Colin growled the words as he followed the moving glow of Petit's light. On the cavern floor ahead, between the stalagmites, he noticed telltale droppings. He aimed his beam upward and gave a shudder at the clusters of tiny, dark shapes hugging the ceiling of the cave. More bats.

His path soon emptied out into another small cave. Broken shards of pottery and a deteriorated straw mat indicated the remains of a hermitage.

A patch of bright blue sky caught his attention. Colin stared in amazement at a hole in the side of the rock to his right, open to the outside air. The space was framed in wood and had frayed leather hinges, suggesting it held a door at one time.

Relieved at the sight, he crouched to pass through the opening, keeping his Colt raised as he reached the other side. Once through, he quickly rose to his full height and scanned for Petit—then teetered backward with a sharp intake of breath.

The narrow ledge he stood on overlooked the valley floor hundreds of feet below.

"I have to say, Lieutenant, you're as tenacious as a tick on a dog."

Colin swung his gaze toward Petit, who stood a few feet away, poised on a game trail leading down the mountain. His right hand aimed the gun at Colin while his other gripped Johanna's bag.

"I also admire your nerve, getting through that cave." One side of Petit's mouth lifted.

"What now, Petit? Are you going to shoot me?"

"If I have to." His fingers flexed on the revolver's grips. "Toss the Colt over the side, nice and slow."

Colin straightened and held his Colt pointed downward. His eyes fixed on the kit bag with the diary. "I can't do that, Petit. I need the book."

Petit cocked the hammer back. "You know, despite what you think, I've come to like you. I really don't want to have to pull the trigger."

"If drugging me is your way of cementing a friendship, then please count me out."

Petit chuckled. "I told you, that was all part of the job." His humor faded. "Now drop it."

Colin's teeth clenched as he tossed his Colt over the side of the mountain.

"See, that wasn't so hard." Petit squinted against the sun. "Where is Captain Weatherford?"

"Lying wounded where you shot him."

"That's too bad." He pointed the gun to the sky. "This is where we part ways, *amigo*."

Petit started to descend the path.

"Wait!" Colin held up his hand. "At least tell me why you're doing this, Petit. You know the Black Book can help to end the war. What happened to your patriotism?"

Petit seemed to consider his question and took a few steps back toward Colin. "Well now, I figure G-2's been planning for months to steal the book from Zero, so what's the difference if I steal it first?" He shrugged. "As for patriotism, that's all well and good, but when we're talking about something worth more than its weight in gold, it gets a man to thinking. With the kind of cash I can bring in from any one of the names in that book, I'll be set up for life with my little French firecracker. Maybe in South America."

"French firecracker . . ." Colin stared at him. "The actress? Odette Tremblay is in on this with you?"

"Right now, she's keeping Kepler pinned down back at the hotel." His smile widened. "She can tie a knot better than most Texans."

"So no flu." Colin's mouth curled with scorn. "More like bad coffee?"

"Enough chatter. If you follow me, as much as I hate the idea, I will shoot you."

Petit pointed the gun at him as he backed away toward the narrow path. The uneven trail hugged the side of the mountain.

Colin remained in front of the hermitage opening, his hand fisted as he watched Petit's retreat. How could he stop him without getting himself killed?

He looked down and suddenly glimpsed a pair of shoes in the small cave opening near his feet. A moment later, a gunshot erupted from inside.

"Get down!" Marcus hissed as he dropped to the cave floor. Colin didn't hesitate as he too dropped down onto the ledge.

Thousands of cave bats exploded through the opening. Screeching and flapping their wings past Colin's head, they veered like a thick black cloud down the side of the mountain.

Assaulted by the flying rodents, Petit cried out as he lost his footing on the path and began sliding over the edge.

Colin scrambled the short distance and made a lunge for him, grabbing the kit bag's leather handle. "Hang on!"

He lay on his belly, his grip on the handle alongside Petit's. The American dropped his revolver and clutched the bag with both hands as he dangled hundreds of feet from the ground.

"Captain!" Colin glanced toward the hermitage opening, praying Marcus was able to come to his aid. He blinked as the sweat stung his eyes, and every muscle in his good arm screamed from the strain of holding Petit's weight.

The American was staring up at him with frightened eyes when one of the handles on the bag snapped. Petit let out a cry, and Colin thrust the hook at him. "Grab my arm!"

He grabbed at Colin's metal hook, first with one hand, then with the other. Colin let out a savage cry as he tossed the kit bag back onto the path before gripping Petit's arm.

Again his muscles convulsed, and the stump beneath his metal terminal ached with the pressure.

Suddenly the harness around his chest went slack, and the hook shifted against his wrist.

It was breaking away! *Lord, please help us. . . .*

Colin sensed someone beside him. "I've got him, Lieutenant."

Marcus lay flat against the ledge and, using both strong hands, helped Colin to pull Petit back onto solid ground.

For several seconds, all three men lay on their backs, panting. Then Marcus finally stretched out his hand and retrieved Johanna's bag from the path.

With his face etched in pain, he handed Colin his revolver. "You take it from here."

CHAPTER 29

I wonder what's taking them so long."

Jo stared anxiously at the narrow cave opening through which she and her father had returned to the main chamber. They encountered Captain Weatherford on the way back and offered to give him assistance, but he insisted on going after Colin, and Jo was relieved.

That was before they heard the gunshot echoing through the cave. Now she fretted, waiting for their return.

"Your young man seems capable of taking care of himself."

Warmth tinged her cheeks. "He's not really my young man, Papa. At least, he . . . he hasn't said anything."

"I saw the way he looks at you." His eyes twinkled. "And I saw that kiss in the cave. It's obvious how you feel about him."

Jo ducked her head, wondering if she should tell her father about Colin's initial reason for coming with her on this journey: to keep his promise of love to Papa's other daughter, Jewel.

Yet even now, Jo realized how much she and Colin had grown in their affection for one another. She yearned to be beside him and wondered if he had ever felt this same kind of yearning for her sister. He'd told her that coming back for Jewel was his chance at redemption, but was it the same thing as love?

319

"Do you love him?"

Startled at the question, she looked up at him, then decided to speak her heart. "Yes, Papa, I do love him. But there are things I need to tell him first." She hesitated. "About my past."

"I understand." He touched her arm. Pain flashed across his features. "I have many secrets of my own, and now I must live with them."

"Will you . . . tell me?"

His smile was kind. "I don't think so, at least no more than what you probably already know. It is time for a fresh start."

"What will you do now? I mean, if the book is recovered and you receive amnesty?"

"I've agreed to offer my services to the Americans. Beyond that, I don't know, child."

She started to ask him another question when a flash of light illuminated the narrow opening. "Look, I think they're here!"

Her father raised his revolver toward the dark space, and Jo hoped it wouldn't be Petit. That would mean something had happened to Colin or the captain.

"Jacob! I need your help."

Colin! Jo's chest grew tight as she watched her father approach the opening.

Petit stumbled across the threshold first, dirty and disheveled, his hands tied in front of him. Colin followed closely behind, appearing equally unkempt as he held a gun at Petit's back while Jo's kit bag dangled from the steel hook at his wrist.

Relief flowed through her at seeing him unharmed. Jo rushed to him. "Are you all right?"

"I'm fine." Colin kept his gaze fixed on Petit and held up the bag. "Take this. I've got to go back for Captain Weatherford."

Her father already had his revolver trained on Petit. "Go and get Marcus, Lieutenant."

Fifteen minutes later, Colin reemerged from the cave opening with Captain Weatherford. The captain looked a terrible sight, more tousled than the others and his pant leg soaked in blood.

"Let's get out of here." Colin's face was grim. "Captain Weatherford needs a doctor."

As her father escorted Petit at gunpoint from the caves and down the hill, Colin and Jo helped to support the captain.

"I can take Marcus down the mountain to a clinic in Collbató," her father offered once they reached the cars in the parking area.

Colin hesitated, eyes on Zero. Finally he nodded and turned to Jo. "Can you manage Petit's car while I keep an eye on him in the back seat?"

"Of course."

Once they got the captain into his car, Colin went to relieve her father of Petit's custody.

Jo withdrew her purse before handing the kit bag over to Captain Weatherford, and despite his pain, he grimaced a smile. Reaching into his pocket, he withdrew a card and gave it to her. "Here is . . . information for the general staff officer at the British Consulate in Barcelona." His tone rasped with pain. "Colin can speak with him . . . they will keep Petit confined."

Jo took the card. "We will see you there when you return."

Leaning back in the seat, he winced with his injury. "Be . . . careful."

Her father came around and shut the captain's car door before embracing her in another fierce hug. "I will see you back in Barcelona, my little bluebird."

His voice was as soft as she'd remembered from childhood. Emotion filled her as she closed her eyes against his shoulder. "I look forward to it, Papa."

Once both cars were down the hill, Jo left her father and the captain in Collbató while she drove south with Colin and his prisoner. The trip to Barcelona took two long hours, and through it all, she gripped the wheel and endured the tense silence while Colin sat in the rear seat with his gun trained on Petit, who slept or pretended to sleep.

Jo was relieved to finally reach the consulate, and after Colin nudged Petit from the car, he gave her a quick glance. "Wait here. I shouldn't be long."

Within a half hour, he was back, cranking over the car's engine before he slid onto the seat beside her. "The general staff officer has Petit locked up until Marcus returns and G-2 can be advised."

"Did Mr. Petit say anything?"

A faint smile touched his lips. "He thanked me for saving his life. And then he told me to go hang myself." He shook his head. "Petit doesn't look happy about his situation at the moment."

He pocketed the cord she'd seen bound around Petit's hands earlier. "Is that the rope?"

He retrieved the cord and held it up for her to see. It wasn't a cord at all.

"Your suspender?"

He shrugged. "I'd already given my necktie to Marcus to bind his leg. I'm still wearing the other brace, so no embarrassing surprises with these baggy trousers."

Jo arched a brow, smiling at him. "A clever improvisation."

He grinned and again pocketed the brace.

"What do you think will happen to him? Petit, I mean."

Colin's humor faded. "He let his greed get the better of him; it could cost him his life in front of a firing squad." He frowned. "And now we've got his accomplice to catch."

"What accomplice?" Jo clutched the wheel and stared at him. "Where?"

"Your hotel. And hurry."

Jo did as he asked, and by the time they arrived at the Coloma Hotel, Colin had told her all that transpired after she'd left him in the cave, including Petit's reasons for taking the book—to sell to the highest bidder, with the intent to use the proceeds to run off to South America with his accomplice.

"I should have known better than to believe that actress!" Her anger flared at learning of Odette's duplicity. "She actually has Kepler tied up in his room?"

"That's what Petit claims. The consulate is sending over a man from criminal investigations. He'll meet us in the hotel lobby."

The lobby was full of guests, and it was a few minutes before a short, stocky man in a dark suit came up and flashed his consulate passport. Using the same document, he parted the crowd, moving toward the front desk to obtain Kepler's room number and an extra key.

"Johanna, wait for the elevator and take it upstairs to your room." Colin eyed her with a stern look. "I'll come for you once this is handled."

Her heart raced. "Please be careful."

He reached to tuck a lock of her hair behind her ear. "I promise."

With the elevator busy, Colin and the consulate officer took the stairs and stood outside Kepler's room. Colin banged on the door. "Captain, are you in there?"

Inside the room, a door slammed, followed by a muffled groan. "Unlock it."

The consulate officer inserted the key, and Colin withdrew Marcus's revolver from his holster.

They found Kepler lying prone on the bed, his limbs hobbled with Miss Tremblay's rope. A handkerchief had been stuffed into his mouth.

Colin scanned the room while the consulate officer approached the bed. Another door slammed nearby, and Kepler made more noises, jerking his chin toward a connecting door.

Gun poised, Colin opened the door and rushed inside. He

quickly searched the space, including the bathroom. Both were empty.

He returned to join the two men. "Miss Tremblay is on the run."

"She's got a gun!" With the gag removed, Kepler gasped the angry words while the officer worked to remove his bonds.

Colin paled. Johanna was on her way to her room, a place the actress had visited before. "I'll be right back." He rushed out the door and down the hall, fear knotting his insides.

A shot rang out as he approached. "Johanna!"

He tried the door. It was locked. He began banging on the wood. "Johanna, are you all right?"

A woman's cry sounded from within. Colin's adrenaline surged, and he put his full weight into ramming against the door. When that failed, he used his hook to tear at the wood, trying to claw his way through.

He almost fell forward when the door abruptly opened. Holding a small derringer, Johanna stood with her hair more askew than usual.

The actress lay in a crumpled heap on the floor behind her. Colin rushed inside, checking the woman for signs of blood.

"She's just fainted."

His attention returned to Johanna, who looked more disheveled than frightened.

"May I borrow your suspender?"

It was a moment before he got over his shock, and a smile touched his lips. He obliged her, and soon they had Odette's hands bound behind her back. Kepler and the officer arrived minutes later, and once they had revived the actress with cold water, the men took her and the weapon and departed.

Colin noticed Johanna trembling. "Come and sit."

He led her over to the divan and took his place beside her, holding her while he tried to still her quaking. "Are you cold?"

"N-no . . . just a painful memory." She looked at him. "I was opening the door to enter my room when Odette must have slipped up behind me. She shoved me inside, and I stumbled to the floor. Then I heard her close the door and throw the deadbolt.

"I still had my purse, so I rose up and turned to swing it at her." Johanna pressed closer to him. "I didn't realize she held a gun."

Coldness swept through him. The actress could have shot Johanna at point-blank range.

"My purse knocked the gun out of her hand, and I made a grab for it. I held it pointed at her, and she charged me, so I fired a round just past her ear, into the wood of the armoire. I only wanted to scare her."

"So she fainted?"

She nodded. "I think she believed I had shot her."

He rubbed her shoulder. "You were very brave."

"Irrational would be a better description."

He smiled. "You were a good shot, too."

"I've had some practice. Moira insisted I learn."

Her words surprised him. "Were the bullies at school that terrible?"

She straightened and met his gaze. "You remember I told you that Moira had many crusades. One of them was Irish freedom. She became . . . involved with the *Cumann na mBan*, those women who aided the Irish Volunteers." She bent her head, looking away. "My mother also took part in the Irish Citizen Army with Countess Markievicz. They carried weapons."

Dread filled him, watching her twist her hands in her lap. "And?"

She looked at him. "After she brought me home from England, I became privy to secret meetings, and crates of German guns . . ."

Dear Lord, no. Colin closed his eyes. "What happened, Johanna?"

His question came out harsh, and he opened his eyes to see her crimped mouth and blond brows drawn over her dark blue eyes. Eyes so much like her father's.

Jo flinched at his hard expression even as she knew she must put her love to the test. "We were in Dublin, at a shop on Sackville Street." Haltingly, she told him about the events of that terrible day amid the burning smoke and destruction. "When I saw the soldier who had shot Moira, I drew my rifle up through the window. He must have seen it, because he turned his rifle on me. That's when I pulled the trigger."

She dared a look at Colin, whose features seemed almost white.

"And you killed him. A British soldier."

His voice sounded wooden, and Jo swallowed. "The rifle . . . it was an old Mauser from some other war. It misfired, and nothing happened. I drew back the bolt to drop in a second shot, but then it jammed. I couldn't do anything. After the soldier fired at me, I . . . I think Moira must have shot him. I fell back with the rifle onto the floor."

She told him how she'd crawled to where her mother lay bleeding by the door, and then Moira's final words to her to flee to her father.

Tears stung her eyes as fresh grief over her mother's death mingled with the knowledge she had just surrendered any hope for a future with Colin. Surely her admission had destroyed what little affection he might have held for her.

"So you didn't shoot anyone?"

Jo shook her head.

"Would you have kept shooting, Johanna . . . if the rifle had worked?"

His expression held a mixture of sadness and anger, and she swallowed before lifting her chin. "Yes, I would have kept shooting. I had to protect her, Colin. Moira was a rebel and a militant and a woman who followed her own set of rules, but she was still my mother. I could not let them kill her."

"And you, just seventeen and fighting British soldiers." He

shook his head before he rose from the divan. "I've got to get back to my hotel. See if Captain Weatherford has returned."

Jo stood quickly, keeping her back straight as she mustered what dignity she had left. Inside, her heart was breaking. "Of course. Thank you for your assistance."

"I wonder that you need anyone, Johanna." Grim lines formed along either side of his mouth as he studied her. "I'll see you later."

She watched him leave, and her broken heart split in two at the sight of the scarred door. Only minutes ago, he'd tried to tear his way through the wood to get to her and save her. Now she was a pariah. Johanna Dougherty Reyer, no better than her mother or her father, traitors all.

Her eyes burned, causing a tightness in her throat. He had said he would see her later, but she knew better. Jo would never see Colin Mabry again.

She was wrong.

Two days later, Jo and her father sat across from Captain Weatherford at his office in the British Consulate in Barcelona. Jewel's diary lay on the desk between them.

Colin stood in uniform near the door. Jo glanced at him, her heart aching anew as she observed his rigid posture and remembered for the thousandth time his reaction to her confession.

Her father seemed to sense her distress and reached over to squeeze her hand.

Captain Weatherford sat at an angle behind the desk, his bandaged leg propped against a padded stool. A wooden crutch rested against the wall behind him. He pushed the book across the desk toward her father. "Show me."

Picking up the book, Papa laid it against his lap. He slowly opened the cover and paused at the first page, running his fingers over the words written in dark ink:

Almost reverently he splayed his hand across the page, and Jo's lower lip quivered at the grief twisting his lined face. Then he set the book on the desk, open-faced. "A letter opener, if you please, Marcus." His voice was rough with emotion.

The captain offered him a pearl-handled blade from the desk set, and Papa began to carefully peel back the lining from the book board. Once he'd removed it, he pulled away a protective transparent sheet.

Jo was startled to see that beneath the sheet were rows upon rows of tiny, keyhole-sized squares of photographic paper.

The captain leaned forward to examine the squares. Jo sensed Colin's presence too as he gazed over her father's shoulder at the tiny dark spots. "The Black Book?" Colin asked.

"The Black Book." Her father turned to him. "Thousands of names. Thousands of scandalous secrets."

Jo shook her head. "How can those small bits of paper be an entire book?"

Her father smiled. "Microphotography can shrink full-size documents down to a tiny size, allowing for the transport of hundreds of pages of messages at a time. It had its start with a man named John Dancer eighty years ago. About the time I was born, during the Franco-Prussian War, Paris was cut off from all communication, and pigeons had to carry information in and out of the capital. Once they arrived at their destination, a special lamp or a microscope was used to read and copy the microphotographed information. It's still read that way now."

He carefully replaced the transparent sheet over the tiny images. A second sheet rested beneath the squares, and he lifted the protective paper sandwich and handed it across the desk to Captain Weatherford.

Her father peeled away the back liner to show there was nothing else. "I would like to keep the diary." He turned to Jo. "If it is all right with you, Daughter."

"Of course." The diary with Jewel's thoughts and songs and dreams would surely be a comfort to him in his grief. She looked across the desk. "Captain Weatherford?"

"I don't see any harm in it."

"Thank you, Marcus." Her father's eyes glistened as he reached for the diary.

"You painted the birds, didn't you?" She pointed to the book. "The fore-edge artwork?"

He spread the leaf edges so that the two birds and their nested egg became visible. "You are my bluebird, Johanna. Jewel was my redbird."

Her throat tightened. "The rings. Our birthstones."

"Exactly right. Two parts of a wedding ring passed down to me by my German ancestors. Jewel's mother wore them until her death. After you were born, I decided to have the stones changed for you and your sister."

"Where is the third part of the ring?" She thought of Odette's comment. "Do I have another sibling?"

He smiled sadly and shook his head. "Jewel was the only one."

When he said no more, Jo realized he hadn't answered her question about the ring. Yet the thought fled as she watched his expression cloud again. He fished from his pocket Jewel's silver dove.

"Now, then." He stared at the ruby-eyed ring a moment before handing it to her. "So you can remember your sister, too."

Jo's hand trembled as she took it from him, clenching the ring in her fist.

Across the desk, a chair creaked as the captain sat forward. "Where is the original Black Book?"

"Gone, Marcus. I burned it to cinders." Her father met his gaze. "I told you before, my father was a collection point for information from other German plants in France, many of whom traveled the continent, obtaining intelligence from others installed by the Fatherland to gather information. It was quite a network.

"My father documented the names, dates, places, and events into a large book and kept it under lock and key until such time as the kaiser, then Wilhelm the First, requested it. When his grandson, Wilhelm the Second, finally ascended to the throne, he directed my father to continue his work.

"After my father passed away, the task fell to me. I continued to add information, the darkest secrets of the most affluent people in Europe. I heard about microphotography and I studied the art, purchasing the necessary equipment. Eventually I became proficient enough to begin making backup copies of the Black Book's pages."

Papa flashed a sardonic smile. "Oddly enough, I worried that some French agent would get his hands on the book, and my initial intent was to protect the kaiser's leverage at all costs. When the war started, I was conscripted to fight, so I took the photographed pages and hid them beneath the lining of the diary's book boards, and gave it to my daughter."

He glanced at Jo. "I painted the fore-edge picture for your sister, hoping she would treasure it, and I told her to keep the book hidden so that the enemy would not find it."

His hand caressed the book's cover. "When I decided to defect and the Americans sent their agent to get Jewel out of the village, I knew that Jewel would bring the book with her when Kepler told her that he planned to reunite us."

Jo realized how incredibly fortunate she'd been to find the book under the barn floor. "She must have been too ill to go after the diary when Kepler took her away."

"It is a miracle that you found it, Johanna."

"I have learned a little about miracles." Smiling at her father, Jo's glance darted to Colin, who had returned to stand by the door.

His head was bent, so she couldn't tell if he'd heard her words, and she ached to have back the intimacy they had lost.

"A miracle, indeed." The captain was frowning. "It's alarming to realize a German agent could have returned to your farm in Havrincourt and stumbled across it." He steepled his fingers against the desk. "So you burned the Black Book before you left for the army?"

Her father shook his head. "The kaiser had requested the book before the start of the war. He had a plan in mind even back then. I was ordered to hand the book over to his special envoy, an attorney from Bern, Switzerland.

"When Kepler posted cryptic advertisements in several European newspapers to signal to me that Jewel was out of Havrincourt, I learned through sources that the original Black Book was locked away in the attorney's office in Bern. The Swiss lawyer was to launch an extortion scheme if the war started to go badly for the German Army. The kaiser could blackmail certain people in power to give Germany whatever it wanted in terms of surrender."

He smiled at the captain. "It was the reason you had to wait three weeks before I met with you, Marcus. I had to crack the safe and remove the book, then take it to a secure place and burn it, page by page."

"So you say." The captain's brown eyes had turned guarded. "What proof do I have the book is gone?"

"There is none, so you will simply have to trust me." He paused. "As I trust you."

When the captain's eyes narrowed, her father scoffed. "Come now, Marcus. You and G-2 hold all that is dear to me. My lovely daughter." He reached for Jo's hand. "And my freedom. Why should I risk that?"

The captain frowned for a long moment before he let out a sigh. "You know the kaiser's agents will be looking for you. They will find out soon enough about your defection."

"Papa?" Jo's breathing quickened. Would they come after her father?

"It's all right, Daughter." He squeezed her hand. "The Americans are taking me to a place even I don't know about, perhaps until the end of the war."

Jo hated the idea of not seeing him again, possibly for years. Yet if it saved his life, she would willingly make the sacrifice. She turned to the captain. "May we spend some time together before he leaves?"

"I'll see what I can do." The captain picked up the transparent sheets containing the microphotography and slid them into a large brown envelope. "Meanwhile, I need to find out what the Allies plan to do with these. Who knows? The French may get the information, which could lessen their enmity toward you, Zero."

"Please, no more Zero. Jacob will do." Her father's look turned cynical. "As to the French accepting my peace offering, I doubt even the Black Book would satisfy their desire for retribution. The French are a fierce lot."

"Are you certain you don't mind?" Marcus gave Colin a hesitant look. "It's a rotten business. The man is my best friend."

"Not at all, sir." Colin had stopped by the captain's hotel room before packing for the long train ride back to Paris. "I told Jack it would be my honor to act as his best man, and I sent off a telegram this morning advising him of my return. With the wedding next week, I don't want him to worry that I won't be there."

Marcus sighed. "I wish I could attend, but my orders are to remain at the consulate and tie up loose ends. There's also this leg to get into working order." He sat on the divan, leaning against his crutch. "It's likely I'll be here another few weeks. I appreciate the favor, Mabry."

"My pleasure, sir."

"What time does your train leave?"

Colin checked his watch. "An hour from now."

"Have you said good-bye to Miss Reyer?"

Colin's skin grew warm as he shook his head. He wasn't certain what to say to her.

"Hmm, I see. Well, she's a brave young woman, coming all this way to find her family. I've no doubt it was a shock to be told of her sister's death and then to learn her father is an enemy spy. I don't know Miss Reyer, but I suspect she's been through a lot in her life already, not just on this trip. She has spirit, much like a particular lady I'm acquainted with back in Britain." His expression softened. "I suppose the Lord made women especially strong so they could face life's challenges."

Colin wondered how Marcus would react to hearing Johanna's "spirited" mother had taken up arms in the Irish Rebellion and involved her daughter. He stared at the floor. "I'm certain you are right, sir."

A silence passed between them before Colin lifted his head and caught the captain's knowing gaze.

"Duty and love, Mabry. Sometimes they do not mix."

The dull ache in his chest intensified. Did the captain think Johanna's father kept them apart? Since Colin's conversation with her, his heart had struggled with her admission that if the rifle hadn't jammed, she would have kept firing on British soldiers. His comrades-in-arms.

Let Marcus think what he would. "No, sir, they do not mix." He sought to change the subject. "When will G-2 arrive to take Zero?"

"In due course. I've arranged for Miss Reyer and her father to spend a few days here in Barcelona before that happens. Zero will remain under the protection of the consulate."

Colin nodded. Yesterday, the spy had answered many questions, including why he was delayed in his rendezvous with Kepler and the actress—a botched sabotage plot for the kaiser had led to Zero's being hospitalized with gas poisoning nearly three months. "What happens once Zero leaves Spain?"

"Likely he'll be debriefed and perhaps given training."

"As a spy . . . for the Americans?"

Marcus shrugged. "It would be a good way to keep an eye on him."

"You don't trust him, sir?" Despite the two men's conflicting views of the war, Colin had sensed a mutual respect between them. "Do you think Zero might become a double agent?"

"Anything is possible." Marcus's brown eyes glinted. "And to quote him, '*A good spy never trusts another spy.*' So long as the war continues, there is plenty to tempt a man."

"As we have proof in George Petit."

Marcus grimaced. "G-2 is smarting over Petit's betrayal. One of their own caught committing treason here in Europe is an embarrassment."

"I still don't know why he did it. I never really liked Petit, but he seemed legitimate, at least in Toulouse."

"Money can be an enticement to make even the most honest of men cross a line." Marcus leaned on the crutch to stand. "Well, I need to get going. I'll grab a bite downstairs before I head to the consulate."

Colin straightened, reaching for his felt hat. "And I should finish packing."

"I wish you safe travels home, Mabry." Marcus extended a hand, and Colin grasped it. "You can brief Jack, but otherwise, I expect you to honor your oath of secrecy in this matter." He smiled. "And please convey to him and your sister my very best wishes."

"I will, sir. Good luck to you as well. I hope to see you in Britain soon."

Colin returned to his room, and as he began to pack, he recalled the captain's words about how love and duty often didn't mix. Like water and oil.

His pulse beat heavily at his throat. Once he left Barcelona, he would never see Johanna again. Likely, she would return to her job at the dovecote outside of Paris after visiting with her father, and pick up the pieces of her life.

His thoughts continued to wrestle with their last conversation together; her honest answers had pierced him, yet he realized she must have known what his reaction would be. And still she had told him, wanting truth between them.

Colin tossed clothes haphazardly into his bag. How could he turn his back on his uniform? On all that he had fought for and endured in the war?

Colin had known Johanna barely two weeks, yet with all they had experienced together in such a short time, it felt like months. Never would he forget the touch of her lips, the passion in her response to his kiss, or the longing he felt each time he took her in his arms.

He shoved the memories aside and closed his luggage. He couldn't change Johanna Reyer's past: she had taken up arms against British soldiers, and her mother and father were both traitors to Britain.

A bitter laugh lodged in his throat. Even her hero, Bonaparte, had been Britain's enemy.

Downstairs, he checked out of the hotel, and after asking the clerk to call for a cab, Colin went outside with his portmanteau and savored the fresh air, waiting near the curb for his ride to the station.

A dark automobile pulled up beside him, and he recognized the British consular flag flying out front. Marcus must have decided to skip his meal and go straight to the office.

Colin was therefore surprised when the driver exited and came around to reach for his bag. "The train station, Lieutenant Mabry?"

Had Marcus made arrangements for his transportation?

Handing the man his luggage, he reached for the back door before he froze.

Johanna sat in the back seat, watching him. She wore the dark blue dress and her voluminous hat. "Hello, Colin."

"Johanna." His heart thumped as he opened the door and slid in beside her. "I thought you were with your father."

"Yes, but I knew you were leaving today and wanted to see you off." She paused. "To say my good-byes."

Pain and awareness shot through him like a lance as he gazed at her beautiful pale features. The driver returned to the car, and they soon headed south on La Rambla toward the railway.

An uncomfortable silence ensued before Johanna finally spoke. "I also wanted to thank you, Colin. I could not have found my father without your help."

He noticed the way she clasped and unclasped her gloved hands against her lap. She must have seen him observing her, because she promptly stopped and averted her eyes.

"Are you enjoying your time with him?"

She turned, relief in her smile. "Yes, Papa and I have years to catch up on, so I'll remain here until he has to leave."

"Has he told you the reason he . . . wasn't able to return to Kilcoole?"

"You mean why he didn't come back for me." Her chin lifted slightly.

Mabry, you are an insensitive clod. "I'm sorry, Johanna. I shouldn't have asked such a question."

"It's all right." She dropped her defensive posture. "I did ask him, you know. He said that after my mother refused to marry him and come to France, he was forced to break all ties"—she glanced toward the driver—"because of his work.

"He said he weakened once, the time he came to visit me when I was small, but he already had an established life in Havrincourt with Jewel and his sister-in-law." Her gaze dropped back to her lap. "My being a part of that would have raised questions he could ill afford."

Colin's brow creased. *"Duty and love. Sometimes they do not mix."*

"He regrets our lost time together and wants to make it up to me if he can. Neither of us knows what his future holds."

Despite his anger and disappointment over Johanna's actions in Ireland, he couldn't help feeling compassion for the lost girl who had grown up without a father, in a home filled with strife and rebellion.

Colin thought about his own father and the uncustomary awkwardness between them since his return from Uncle Brian's farm. Patrick Mabry's desperate attempts to compensate for what his son now lacked had only served to grate on Colin's nerves.

Yet somewhere along the line, Colin had come to realize it was his own feeling of detachment and self-reproach that made the situation intolerable. His father, and his sister too, had merely followed his cue.

He was blessed to have his family. And even though Jacob Reyer was a spy, he was Johanna's father, and it was good that he was back in her life. "After your visit, will you return to working at the château in Vernon?"

"Yes, I look forward to seeing André and Isabelle. And my birds."

Her large hat tipped downward, and Colin noticed a lock of her hair had fallen against her shoulder. He kept his hand fisted at his side. "I am certain they will be glad to have you back, especially Little Corporal."

She glanced up at him then, the sudden sparkle in her eyes piercing his heart. "We've had quite the adventure together, haven't we, Lieutenant?"

Her voice was soft, and Colin fought a sudden constriction in his chest. "Indeed, we have, Johanna."

They had reached the train station. While the driver quickly exited and headed toward the luggage in the car's boot, Colin started to open the door.

He paused when he felt Johanna's touch against his shoulder.

Then he turned and watched as her gloved hand slid down to rest over the top of his prosthetic.

"There is nothing on this earth that you cannot master, Colin." Conviction filled her voice. "You have performed your duty admirably and saved lives on this trip, including countless others through your brave act in retrieving the diary."

She paused and pressed her lips together. "You also kept your promise to my sister. I know if Jewel were here right now, she would be proud."

For a moment, grief marred her lovely features, and Colin's grip tightened on the door handle to keep from reaching for her. "Good-bye, Johanna."

He left the car and grabbed his bag, a host of emotions twisting his insides. Love, anger, disappointment, despair, love . . .

As the driver returned to the car, Colin paused at her open window. Dropping his bag, he reached inside for her hand, his gaze searching hers beneath the hat.

"No matter where they take him, you are never alone, Johanna. God is with you. Know it, and trust in Him." He raised her gloved hand to his lips then and closed his eyes as he pressed on her a last tender kiss.

"Good-bye, Colin."

Her voice was a hoarse whisper and her blue eyes brilliant with unshed tears as she withdrew her hand from his. Colin stepped away from the car, and once it began moving forward, she looked back at him through the small rear window.

She disappeared from view, and still he stood there, his heart pounding with the same conflicting emotions. He'd longed to take her into his arms and forget the world in a fiery kiss, yet his reasoning understood only too well the impossibility of their situation.

What kind of life would he and Johanna have together? She could never return to Ireland, or go to Britain, for that matter, not without Moira's past or her own eventually catching up with her. And what about her father, a known traitor who must hide to stay alive?

"Titan's teeth." He ground out the words as he picked up his luggage and headed toward the train station.

He had a wedding to go to.

CHAPTER

31

ood morning, Lieutenant Mabry, and what a fine day it is!"

Albert Goodfellow beamed from the doorway of Colin's upstairs room, his unruly thatch of red hair slicked back as he carried his peaked cap beneath one arm. His khakis were freshly pressed, every brass button shining, while below his puttees, the hobnailed boots shone with a recent polish.

Colin had answered the summons half dressed in his uniform, and Deaton, the Earl of Stonebrooke's stuffy butler, properly averted his eyes. "Will there be anything else, sir?"

"No thank you, Deaton. You may go."

Once the butler had left, Goodfellow offered him a brisk salute. Colin returned it before stepping back so he could enter. "You're looking quite sharp, Albert."

"Thank you, sir." A wash of color flooded Goodfellow's freckled features. "It is an honor to be invited to the wedding of Lord Walenford and your sister."

"I daresay your reward for a job well done." Colin had returned from Paris a week ago to learn that his protégé had admirably kept up with the workload in Hastings.

"Deaton said you had a personal note to deliver to me?" Colin gave him a backward glance as he went to the chair and grabbed up his pressed shirt, purchased along with his new uniform for the day's special occasion. In less than two hours, he would stand by Jack's side in the Cathedral of St. Ives as his sister, Grace, became Lady Walenford, and at some point in the future, the Countess of Stonebrooke.

"Yes, sir." The corporal fished through his pockets while his gaze went to the harness and prosthetic still lying on the bed. The perusal failed to disturb Colin as it had before; he could see now that Goodfellow's expression held only curiosity, not pity or scorn.

The corporal finally withdrew the folded note, and with a quick snap, he opened the paper before handing it to Colin. "Here you are, sir."

Goodfellow's kind gesture wasn't lost on him. Colin smiled. "Thank you, Albert."

He took the letter, his thoughts flashing back to a conversation he'd had with Johanna in Toulouse, when she had claimed Goodfellow sounded like his namesake.

Johanna. Colin's mouth compressed. The effects of her absence still wore on him: a constant tightness in his chest and the ache in his throat that never left him. Over and over his mind conjured her image, the brilliant blue eyes and smooth, fair skin. Lips as pink as roses. And her golden-blond hair, which she could never seem to keep in order.

Was she still in Barcelona with her father . . . or had she returned to her pigeons at Vernon?

"Bad news, sir?"

Colin startled and glanced up to see consternation in his corporal's expression. He realized he'd been frowning. Quickly, he scanned the contents of the letter:

Lieutenant Mabry,

My deepest gratitude for your recent work, and for the duty you now undertake in my stead. Only ask and it shall be granted. Will discuss further over dinner when I return. Best regards. Your friend,

M.

A flush of pride rose in him as he recognized the sender. Captain Marcus Weatherford, a man Colin greatly admired, had called him friend. "No, Albert, nothing wrong at all."

Abruptly the mantel clock in his room chimed the hour, and Colin glanced at the time. Titan's teeth! He looked back at the harness on the bed, then at the buttons on his shirt. He had less than fifteen minutes before the earl's chauffeur was to take him and Jack to the church.

Glancing over at the tunic, necktie, belt, and boots near the chair, he regretted having turned down Deaton's offer of a footman to help him dress.

"May I be of some assistance, Lieutenant?"

He stared into Goodfellow's knowing expression, recalling with some shame the last time the corporal had offered his help. Colin had bitten his head off.

Yet Johanna's easy acceptance of him made him realize he wasn't so very different, and he'd discovered in the caves that the prosthetic, an aberration he'd once rejected, could also become his strength.

Despite previous assumptions, Colin understood now that Goodfellow acted only out of kindness, a gesture he himself might have extended to someone else and not given a second thought. He eyed the corporal. "If you wouldn't mind playing valet, Albert?"

Goodfellow smiled. "Not at all, sir."

Within a few minutes, Colin stood at the cheval glass scrutinizing his reflection. He straightened the lapel of his tunic, his fingers

343

brushing the ribboned medals the corporal had pinned over his left pocket, then adjusted the straps of the saber at his side.

Colin leaned in to inspect the necktie. "Right proper job on the four-in-hand, Corporal."

"Thank you, sir." Albert stood off to the side. "You do the uniform proud, Lieutenant."

Colin's smile faltered as his thoughts returned to Johanna and the chasm that lay between them. He went to the bed and withdrew the steel hook from his canvas satchel, the same hook that had saved Petit's life. Snapping the device into place at his wrist, he picked up the bag and offered it to Goodfellow. "If you would be kind enough to take charge of this for me, Albert. I will have need of it at the reception." He smiled. "There is a fork in there that I intend to employ at the wedding feast—I'll not settle for just a bowl of soup."

Goodfellow grinned. "Of course, sir."

Downstairs, Colin found his father in the main hall, pacing across the carpeted floors. No doubt growing increasingly nervous as he waited for Grace to finish up with her bridal toilette.

"I'll see you at the church, sir." Goodfellow spoke in a low voice as he glanced toward Colin's father.

"Thank you for your help, Albert."

Smiling, the corporal offered a brief salute before taking his leave. Colin strode to where his father continued his brisk stride back and forth. "I think you may wear a hole in his lordship's Turkish rug, Father."

Patrick Mabry looked up at him, startled. "Colin, my boy! I didn't realize you were standing there." He paused, perusing his son from head to toe. "You look very smart, Son."

"Thank you, sir. As do you."

His father glanced down at his own black tuxedo. "Yes, well, the sooner we start the ball rolling, I say the better." He grimaced, pulling on his cravat. "I appreciate Lady Bassett's attendance on your sister with her personal dressmaker, but this is taking a long time!"

Colin chuckled. "I imagine becoming a future countess does take some preparation. And as your patroness at Swan's, Lady Bassett will insist on knowing what needs to be done."

"Quite right." His father sighed. "Though it is a bit nerve-wracking, this is a dream come true for your sister."

Colin arched a brow. "And for you?"

"For us both." His father smiled. "I want Grace's happiness above all else, and I realized some time ago, she's got her own mind. But I am not displeased that the man she has set her cap on is a member of the British peerage." His eyes glistened. "I only wish your mother could have been here to share this time with her."

Colin laid his hand on his father's shoulder. Upon his return from Paris, Colin had chosen to commute back and forth daily from Hastings to his family home in London, at least until after the wedding. It was a chance to reacquaint himself with his father and his sister.

An opportunity he had neglected since his return from the war.

"You know, Son, you've changed." The older pair of hazel eyes searched his. "You seem more assured, more . . . comfortable with yourself, and with us. How are you sleeping these days?"

The question gave Colin pause. He realized the nightmares had been gradually receding ever since his journey to Paris. In fact, he hadn't experienced one of his suffocating dreams since returning from Spain. "Better than I have in some time, Father."

"Splendid." Patrick Mabry looked relieved. "I do not know what happened to you over there in France, but I am glad of it."

Johanna happened to me. His throat tightened as he gazed at his father. "Thank you, sir."

"Now, there is the picture of a dashing father and son duo."

Both men turned to see Jack Benningham descend the stairs, looking resplendent in a black cutaway and matching trousers, his white wing collar shirt sporting a champagne-colored tuxedo vest and cravat. He wore white gloves and carried a black top hat.

"You're looking rather well turned out yourself, Son." Patrick Mabry smiled.

"I thank you, sir. It's a relief to know I shall not shame your daughter." Jack approached to stand beside them and straightened the red rose *boutonnière* against his lapel. He turned to Colin. "I say, is that a new uniform?"

Colin looked down at his khakis. "I thought Grace's wedding would be a good occasion to make a fresh start."

"Fresh start, indeed." Jack glanced at the steel hook and then gave him an approving smile. "I knew you would come around when you were ready. No doubt you will steal my thunder today, giving those dreamy-eyed maids at the church romantic visions of pirates and adventure and being swept away on the high seas."

Patrick Mabry chuckled while Colin rolled his eyes and grinned. "And I think you must be suffering from prenuptial hallucinations."

"Hardly." Jack smiled. "I'm as steady as a rock."

"What? No last-minute qualms?" Colin's father eyed him with amusement.

Jack shrugged. "I imagine most grooms do, but not me." He bent his head. "Some men wait a lifetime and never find their true love, but I've been blessed to find mine. And in these uncertain times, I've no intention of wasting another moment without Grace by my side."

Moved by his words, Colin allowed himself a moment to imagine a life with Johanna, and a smile touched his lips, thinking of her blue eyes gazing up at him mischievously. *"We've had quite the adventure together, haven't we, Lieutenant?"*

Indeed, his future with her would have been a quest that never ended. He recalled with longing their first meeting, when Johanna had arrived wearing men's trousers and boots, her face all muddy and hair askew . . . and looking lovelier than any woman he had ever seen.

"Excuse me, your lordship. Your car waits outside."

At the sound of Deaton's voice, Colin raised his head and quit his woolgathering.

He found Jack and his father watching him with interest. His face grew warm. "Is it time, then? Shall we go?"

Jack arched a brow and grinned. "If you're ready."

More heat rose above his neck. "I'm not the one getting married."

He started for the door while Jack chuckled behind him. Colin glanced back at his father. "We'll see you and Grace at the church."

The Gothic-style cathedral was filled with beautiful spring flowers. Arrangements of pink and white peonies combined with white lilies and green ivy spilling from gold vases near the altar, while smaller posies of white daisies and ivy adorned the ends of the pews.

The church was already filling up as guests were being led by ushers to their seats.

Colin stood beside Jack in a side alcove, both of them hidden from view. The vicar would arrive at any moment—their signal to approach the altar.

His gaze turned toward the bride's side of the church, and he spied his cousin Dr. Daniel Strom seated beside Great-aunt Florence, who wore a fusty-looking Victorian hat.

Behind them, he recognized Miss Ruthie Simmons, whose older sister Becky was the chief baker at Swan's and one of Grace's bridesmaids. Currently, Miss Simmons had her hands full trying to manage the small child trying to wriggle out of her lap. Young Daisy Danner was the daughter of Grace's best friend and maid of honor, Miss Clare Danner.

Gazing at the squirming child, Colin wondered at the father. He thought about Johanna's growing up alone and ostracized amid taunts and cruel jibes. He hoped the little girl on Ruthie's lap would never have to know that kind of hardship.

Beside the pair sat Mr. and Mrs. George Tillman, whom Colin had met yesterday when Grace told him they were attached to Jack's estate in Kent. The couple had brought with them hothouse roses from Roxwood.

"Have you got the rings?"

Colin turned to see Jack looking almost grim as the vicar approached the altar. He fought back a smirk. *Solid as a rock.* "Still right here in my pocket."

Once the vicar took his stance, Colin followed Jack to the front of the church, both men stopping short of the raised dais. The soft strains of wedding music began as the last guests were seated, and suddenly all eyes were upon them.

Colin stood straight and tall beside the groom, his silver hook resting at his side. He had paid his dues in the war, enduring horrors most of the people in the congregation could never imagine. Yet he was no different from anyone else. He had a right to be here among them, to be judged and accepted for the kind of man he was, and not by his wounds.

He felt a tug at his side and looked down to see little Daisy had grabbed hold of the hook with her small fingers, looking extremely pleased with herself and perfectly at home as she stood in the front alongside the best man and the groom.

Colin grinned at her, and when he looked up, a number of people were smiling or chuckling. Ruthie Simmons, her face as red as Jack's rose *boutonnière*, hurried over and eyed him apologetically before whisking the child back to her seat.

Suddenly the notes of Mendelssohn's "Wedding March" rose from the pipe organ into the lofty heights of the church, and Colin brought himself to attention. A wistful sense of happiness washed over him, knowing his sister and Jack were about to become man and wife.

The wedding reception was held in Stonebrooke's grand hall, and while the food was relatively simple, there was plenty to be had. With the current rationing, the four-tiered champagne wedding cake was the only real evidence of extravagance, and slices were shared with the wounded in the hospital wing that the Earl and Countess of Stonebrooke had generously provided for the war effort.

Seated at a place of honor near the wedding couple, Colin eyed the long row of well-dressed nobility at the table, and the snowy white linen, crystal, and silver gracing each gold-lined porcelain plate. Then he glanced at his sister, who had changed from her white satin wedding gown into a green dinner dress that matched the color of the sizeable new emerald on her finger. Having given the requisite wedding toast before dinner, Colin now saw the love reflected in her expression as she gazed at his blond brother-in-law seated beside her.

Soon the new Lady Walenford and her husband would depart for a brief honeymoon in Scotland, and while Colin knew Grace's life as a viscountess would be exciting and challenging, he had no doubt that the love she and Jack shared would overcome all.

Love is patient, love is kind . . . love never fails . . . He thought of the other verses from 1 Corinthians 13. *And if I have a faith that can move mountains, but do not have love, I am nothing. . . .*

He had claimed to Johanna to have that kind of faith . . . but what about love?

It keeps no record of wrongs. Love does not delight in evil but rejoices with the truth. . . .

Johanna had loved him, Colin understood, and she'd been willing to sacrifice that love for the truth.

And now these three remain: faith, hope, and love. But the greatest of these is love. . . .

Love: all important, making the impossible possible. Why then did he continue to resist the song hammering in his heart for the woman he had loved in Barcelona? *Duty and love . . .*

As if outside himself, Colin stared at his father's proud smile across the table. A happy day for Patrick Mabry: his daughter wed and his son finally returned to him, body *and* spirit.

He and his father had bridged the gap of their previous estrangement, but Colin still had no desire to take his sister's place as floor manager at Swan's, and he was grateful Father respected his decision.

"So who will be driving the motorcar now, I wonder?"

Becky Simmons had made the joking remark, as Colin's sister had been Jack Benningham's chauffeur for a time. The guests chuckled while Grace looked down the table at her friend, green eyes filled with mischief. "I will have charge of the car, of course."

"I think not." The humor in Jack's voice belied his decree as he pulled her to him.

"Well, I would never wish to defy you, Husband." She lowered her gaze, a smile on her lips. "But I believe it only fair that we vote on it. Don't you agree?"

Her words clearly amused him. "Our votes would only end in a tie, my love. How is that a compromise?"

"But don't you see?" She beamed at him. "You just agreed to meet me halfway, and soon I shall sway you completely over to my side."

He gave a shout of laughter and took her into his arms. "Indeed, Wife. I have learned never to doubt your abilities." Leaning in, he kissed her soundly, and the table erupted in merry applause. Colin grinned. Yes, Grace and Johanna would like each other.

Another of the women piped up—Miss Lucy Young, who had once worked with Grace in the Women's Forage Corps at Kent.

"Better that she d-drive, my lord, than sit at home d-doing needlepoint, or she may accidentally sew herself inside the cushion cover."

More hilarity rose from the women at the end of the table, and even Grace laughed. Colin looked toward the mirthful ladies still dressed in their bridesmaid gowns and noted that even Miss Danner smiled, though her gray eyes shone with sad tears.

He thought of his last glimpse of Johanna, and the ache in his chest intensified. She'd told him once that she could love a man like him and that what lay in the heart mattered more than what the world saw on the outside.

". . . need a new business manager in my New York offices before long."

Colin turned at the sound of his father speaking to one of the guests at the table. "I received a congratulatory telegram from my company head in America, Mr. Fowler. The position's been vacant for weeks, and we must find someone organized who can come in to run the office and take charge when Fowler's away on business."

Colin's heart thumped in his chest. New York. America, land of the free . . .

He gazed at his father while a lightness he hadn't felt in days came over him.

Love never fails.

CHAPTER

32

Napoleon once said, 'He who hazards nothing, gains nothing.'"

Jo sighed as she sat inside the dim confines of the dovecote, cuddling a pigeon in her arms. Eleven days had passed since Colin said good-bye to her in Barcelona, yet it seemed more like eleven hundred.

"He was my enchanted prince, you know. Much the way Little Corporal is yours." She stroked the hen's smooth gray head. "For that reason I had to tell Colin the truth about Moira. I couldn't let any more secrets come between us, even though I knew what it might cost."

She talked soothingly to the bird, trying to ignore the dull ache in her chest. "Your mate was a big enough surprise when Colin discovered him hidden in my room." A bittersweet smile touched her lips at the memory. "Though, once he got over the shock, he was glad I'd brought Little Corporal with us."

The pigeon in her arms made a soft cooing sound. "Yes, I know your brave mate is off on another mission right now, but he will be back. He traveled more than five hundred miles from Spain to

352

reach the dovecote when I needed help, so I am certain he'll be all right."

Jo spoke more to reassure herself than the hen, as Little Corporal had left the dovecote before her arrival at work yesterday.

She'd been back in Paris two days after an arduous return trip from Spain. Thanks to Captain Weatherford, she was able to spend a precious week with her father, and already she missed him.

They had talked about much—Jo's life in Kilcoole, both the pain and the happier times spent with her birds; boarding school in England; and finally, about the Easter Rising and her failure to save Moira.

Papa had been saddened by her mother's death, and while he did not divulge much about himself, he talked to her about Jewel, sharing with Jo the missing pieces of her sister's life.

Eventually he had asked about her "young lieutenant," and she explained to him Colin's reaction when she told him the truth about her part in the rebellion. There wasn't much either of them could say after that, knowing the past couldn't be changed.

Jo pursed her lips at the miserable reminder of Colin's taut face, his expression filled with anger and disappointment. He had looked as wretched as she had felt.

The gray pigeon began to fidget, and she released the bird to flutter upward to its nest in one of the *boulins*. Leaning back against the cool stone wall, she closed her eyes and listened to the rustling of the birds overhead, yet the steady pang in her heart persisted.

It was Colin she missed most of all—his rugged features and clear hazel eyes, and the way his lower lip curled whenever he knew she was telling stories. His insistence on calling her Johanna when no one else did, and the rare sound of his laughter, lighting up all the little places in her heart.

On the day of his departure from Barcelona, Jo had deliberated whether or not to accompany him to the station. But she had wanted . . . no, she'd *needed* to see him one last time, not only to thank him for all he had done for her and Papa, but to make peace with him.

Colin had become her friend, her partner, and she respected him. As much as his rejection tore at her, Jo wanted no ill will between them.

His look of gentleness and longing as he'd reached through the open window for her had nearly been her undoing. Colin had told her she would never be alone, that God would always be with her. Jo wanted to believe that, but she also wanted Colin, and for the past days and nights, she'd prayed for his return. But maybe God wasn't listening. . . .

"I thought I would find you here."

André had entered the dovecote, carrying a plate of sugared biscuits. "Isabelle has brought these from her friend at the *pâtisserie* in Paris. A little sweetness to cheer you up, eh?"

Jo tried to muster a smile. "*Merci*, my friend, but I'm not hungry."

"You have been stewing in your sorrows since you returned. It is Saturday, and the sky is clear. You should be out riding your motorcycle. Or have lunch with Isabelle and me."

His mood softened as he set the plate down beside her. "I know you feel bad about your sister and your father, but Isabelle and I, we are still your family, *non*?"

"Of course you are, André." Jo reached to give his hand an affectionate squeeze. She'd been sworn to secrecy, so she could not share with her friends the real account of her quest. Only that the woman with Kepler was not her sister, and she had learned Jewel died of illness months ago.

When André questioned her about Little Corporal's unexpected arrival with her cryptic note about La Rambla and a golden key, she had told him part of the truth: she'd become separated from Colin and wanted the lieutenant to find her. *Just as I do now.*

"You are missing your young man, I think." André read her

thoughts and sat down beside her. "Would you like to talk to me about it?"

Jo gazed into his dark eyes, so full of compassion, and shook her head. What could she tell him without revealing secrets from her past that would potentially get her booted out of France?

She sighed. "There is nothing to say, André. I came to care very much for the lieutenant while we were together, but he did not share my feelings, and that's an end to it." Averting her eyes, she added in a whisper, "Trust me, it is for the best."

"Bah! Who could not love my Jo?" André scowled. "I thought the lieutenant had more sense than that, but I was wrong."

"André, please . . . it's not his fault."

"Whose fault?"

The door had opened again, and Isabelle approached. She studied Jo questioningly.

André spoke up. "Lieutenant Mabry deserted our poor girl."

"Papa, quit upsetting her!" Isabelle flashed her father a severe look before she crouched at Jo's feet, her dark eyes gentle with understanding. "You still love him, *ma chère amie*, and nothing we can say will change that. You just need time." She smiled. "Perhaps a nice lunch at the café in town will make you feel better?"

Jo smiled at them both, so grateful for their friendship. "You two go on, and if you like, you can bring me a sandwich. I will stay here and keep an eye on things. I'm very anxious to see Little Corporal."

"Always, you are worried about that bird." André sighed as he tilted his head up toward the empty traps at the top of the *pigeon-nier*. The small bells on the traps hadn't rung for some time, and when they did, the returning pigeons hadn't been her white one.

"He's been gone a long time." Jo met his gaze. "Where did you say you sent him?"

"Do not fret, *ma petite*." He rose from the bench. "The pilot at Orly said the bird would not be gone more than a couple of days—"

"Orly is the airfield." Her pulse leapt as she too rose to stand. "Has Little Corporal been dropped by parachute over enemy territory?"

"It is likely." André flushed. "I took a parachute with the basket . . ."

Jo wasn't listening as she imagined her bird somewhere inside occupied Belgium or France. The basket could get caught in a tree branch or hidden in some brush. "What if he's trapped and—"

"Rest easy, Jo." Isabelle put an arm around her. "Your pigeon will be fine. Did he not just fly across the whole of France to deliver your message?"

Jo frowned at her friend. "Little Corporal made that trip in less than a day, Isabelle. It's been far longer than that since my return yesterday, and I still have not seen him."

"Do not worry, *mon amie*." Isabelle hugged her. "He is doing exactly what he was trained to do. All will be well."

Once they departed, Jo went to stand by the ladder, staring up at the traps in the dovecote's opening. What if her pigeon did not come back?

A familiar loneliness settled over her, intensified by her yearning for Colin. Once again she thought of his assurances, how God would always be there for her. Yet hadn't she tried to speak with Him since Colin had left? *Trust in Him, Johanna. . . .*

She closed her eyes and let the seconds pass as she recollected the same prayer she'd been saying for days. *Lord, I want to have Colin's faith, and you already know how much I love him and miss him. But I do not want to lose my pigeon, either. 'Tis a very small thing, I know, but I would ask you to please bring him back to me.*

As Jo opened her eyes, the only sound was the cooing of the birds above. Maybe she *was* being foolish, asking for such a trifling favor. Or what if she wasn't saying it the right way, and God hadn't heard her prayers?

She left the ladder and had started back toward the bench when the sound of a bell reached her ears. Turning, she glanced high above and caught sight of the fluttering, snowy white wings. "Little Corporal!" Relief washed through her. He was safe after all.

Still bedazzled by his timely appearance, Jo grabbed up the retrieval basket and slung it across her shoulder before she began to climb the ladder. *Had* God been listening?

Upon reaching the trap, she spied the tiny silver capsule strapped to her pigeon's leg.

"Little Corporal, where have you been?" She scolded him gently as she opened the trap and transferred him into the small basket. "I was so worried."

A flash of gold caught her eye as she closed the wicker lid, and it was another minute before she'd brought the ladder back around and carefully descended the rungs to the ground.

Seated on the bench once more, Jo placed the basket on her lap. Reaching inside for her pigeon, she stared at the glint of gold she'd seen moments before.

The ring, a plain gold band, had been tied with white ribbon to his tail feathers.

Jo's heart thumped wildly as she held the bird in the basket while she loosened the ribbon. Holding up the ring, she realized how much larger it was than her own fingers.

Her breath shook as she eyed the silver capsule attached to Little Corporal's leg, and she removed it before releasing him to fly to his nest.

Normally Jo would have taken the small metal tube inside to the agents on duty, but she opened the tiny canister now and removed the message, hope and fear seizing her heart as she instinctively knew the sender:

> *To my lost girl at La Maison des Oiseaux, Vernon, France*
> *Urgent you remember your promise of love. Meet me Napoleon's tomb, 5 May, 1500 hours. You're my last hope. —C. M.*

Elation surged through her as she read and reread his words, and her sudden burst of laughter caused a cacophony of rustling feathers and cooing. Tears of joy ran down her cheeks, and she closed her eyes, hugging the precious note to her chest as she said a silent prayer of thanks to God. He had listened to her after all, and He'd given her more miracles than she could ever have dreamed.

Tomorrow, at three o'clock, Jo would finally see her prince.

*H*ad Johanna received his message?

Colin rechecked his watch as he stood inside the Dôme des Invalides at the railing surrounding Napoleon's tomb.

Fifteen minutes past the hour. She could simply be running late, which was not unusual. Or perhaps the pigeon had failed in its mission. . . .

He clung to the first possibility rather than reconsider the insanity of his plan. After overhearing his father's conversation during the wedding reception at Stonebrooke, Colin had returned to Hastings the following afternoon and sent a telegram to Lacourt. He'd requested an all-white pigeon from the dovecote at Vernon be taken to the Orly airfield outside of Paris, and he'd had Goodfellow sign off on it, so the French agent wouldn't suspect Colin's involvement and share his intentions with Miss Moreau or her father.

Colin had spent three remarkable days since his sister's wedding, starting with the lengthy return trip by car with his father from Bedfordshire to London, giving them both ample opportunity to talk.

In truth, he had done most of the talking. Though sworn to secrecy about the details involving Zero and the Black Book, Colin shared with his father his reasons for going to Paris, and then meeting Johanna instead of Jewel and their quest to find her family. How, in the course of his two weeks away, he had fallen in love, and his whole world had changed.

Because he'd half expected his practical father to scoff or at least dismiss his feelings, Colin was gratified when, after listening to his son's story, Patrick Mabry confessed to his own whirlwind romance with Colin's mother years before.

Filled with hope and praying his father would agree, Colin had decided to broach the subject of his decision to leave Britain and cross the sea.

Colin turned back toward the entrance, searching for a sign of Johanna. It was Sunday, and the Dôme was crowded, mostly with women garbed in mourning black and traveling in pairs, a few clutching the hands of small children. Several older men also wandered about the place, their threadbare uniforms giving evidence of hard times spent at the Front and perhaps even more difficult times at home.

He reached to loosen his tie before unbuttoning the coat jacket of his brand-new suit. Again he considered the risks he had taken, his own personal leap of faith to offer a future to the woman he loved.

Looking at his watch, he realized another five minutes had passed.

Perhaps she *wasn't* coming.

He stared at Bonaparte's red sarcophagus below while his heart thudded heavily in his chest. Johanna had once encouraged him here in this place after Lacourt had rejected him as her escort to find Jewel. She'd told him he couldn't let the opinions of others stop him in his quest.

Yet in this particular case, his situation *was* impossible, because despite all his plans and romantic gestures, he needed Johanna by his side to make his dream come true.

And she wasn't here. Johanna hadn't forgiven him. . . .

"Napoleon once said, 'Great men seldom fail in their most perilous enterprises.'"

Colin's heart leapt, and he briefly closed his eyes before turning around slowly to see her standing behind him. Johanna was a vision in pink with her silver shoes and her little pink hat with its black feather, looking much the way he remembered her from their night at Le Bibent in Toulouse. A lifetime ago, it seemed.

Seeing the sparkle in her eyes, he smiled. "I do tire of having to wait on you, Miss Reyer."

Then his humor fled, and he stepped toward her. "You look beautiful, Johanna."

Her chin lifted, and a sudden blush added roses to her cheeks. "I received an urgent message. And this." She opened a gloved hand to reveal the gold ring he had sent.

Colin had imagined so many scenarios with her: pleasant bantering about the fairy tale she'd told him, or talking practically about the future and making plans with one another. Explaining to her why he had changed his mind and decided to come back for her.

But as he lost himself in the deep blue of her eyes, he was suddenly that man buried beneath the earth, clawing his way toward the surface, unable to breathe and desperate for a glimpse of the blue sky above, knowing it would fill his lungs and save his life.

A groan rose from deep in his chest as he reached for her, pulling her into his arms. He lowered his head, pressing the side of his face to hers while the knot in his throat loosened and he simply held her.

She trembled in his arms, her quiet sobs muffled against his shoulder. Colin closed his eyes, regretting the pain he had caused her. "Please forgive me, my darling." He whispered the words against her ear. "You saved me once, and I find I am in need of saving again . . . and again and again. A lifetime, if you will have me."

He turned to kiss her soft cheek, tasting the salty wetness of her tears. "Love me always, Johanna, and be my wife."

Her grip on him tightened, and he held her in his embrace, both of them oblivious to the curious stares of passersby.

Finally she leaned back to gaze at him. Colin held his breath, waiting for her answer. Perhaps he should have gotten down on his knee?

Her eyes were puffy and red, her little hat askew. A lock of her blond hair had come loose from its coil to fall against her shoulder.

But her smile was radiant. "Yes, and yes, and yes."

Relief and jubilation filled him as he lifted her off the floor and turned with her. Johanna laughed, and he leaned in to kiss her, gently at first, before surrendering to her all of the love and longing he'd been harboring since the day he'd left her in Barcelona.

She responded to his kiss, wrapping her arms around his neck, and it was a few moments before he again set her back onto her feet and drew her close.

Hearing her happy sigh, Colin hugged her tight, knowing she had broken the enchantment and set him free.

Now he would never let her go.

Epilogue

*T*here she is, Colin, and looking just as lovely as her little sister in Paris."

Standing beside her new husband on the deck of the USS *Huron*, Jo breathed in the briny smell of the sea as she pointed toward the Statue of Liberty in the harbor. They had traveled across the Atlantic for many days with the constant fear of attack by German U-boats, but by God's grace, they had arrived in New York safe and sound.

She turned to him. "Just think, we are finally here . . . in America!"

"And a new adventure for us both, Mrs. Mabry."

He smiled at her, the tenderness in his expression making her heart melt with love. Jo leaned against him, and he slipped his arm around her shoulders as they watched the tugboats, stacks chugging out sulphurous smoke as they worked to help the ship into port.

Thinking back over the past few weeks, it still seemed like a dream. She was married to the man she loved and had come to a place far across the sea, where they could both make a new start.

363

She and Colin had married quietly in a small Paris church, with Isabelle, Henri, and André in attendance. And while Isabelle had sighed over Colin's romantic gesture of using a white pigeon to deliver the gold band, Jo's new husband hadn't known at the time that André had sent Little Corporal for the task.

In the absence of her father, she had asked André to give her away. Jo was delighted when Colin's father flew in to surprise them for their wedding. She and her new father-in-law had immediately warmed to one another, and after spending a few days in his company, Patrick Mabry told her how much she reminded him of his own daughter.

A week later, with the help of the American G-2 office in France, Jo and Colin boarded one of a number of returning troop ships leaving out of Saint-Nazaire for America.

Now, as they drew close to the busy New York waterfront, Jo noticed her husband watching more of the large Navy ships gliding in and out of the harbor, and she wondered again at his decision to leave military service.

"Do you have any regrets?" Her eyes searched his. "Everything has happened so fast. I still worry you've had second thoughts about giving up your service to the Crown."

"None at all, I promise you." He drew her close, the gold band on his right hand gleaming in the light. "I'd considered taking my discharge from the BEF when I returned from the war, but Jack offered me the job at Hastings, so I kept my rank even though I would never see action again."

She gave him an impish smile. "But you did see adventure, didn't you?"

He grinned before leaning to give her a quick kiss. "From the moment I met you, my darling wife."

"Truly, though, will you be satisfied working in an office here?" Jo had asked him the question more than once but still wanted reassurance he was happy with his decision. "I spoke with the

American war correspondent on board, and she told me life here is rather fast-paced. Won't the noise and the crowds bother you?"

He looked toward the mainland, and Jo followed his gaze, noting the brick multistoried buildings and skyscrapers crowding one another across the city. Beyond the structures rose a number of tall church steeples, and she glimpsed the steel arches of a bridge.

Alongside the busy harbor, the streets along the waterfront also swarmed with activity: motorcars and omnibuses traveled back and forth alongside lorries and horse-drawn carts, and while she couldn't hear the noise above the drone of the ship's engines, Jo imagined their horns blaring.

Colin turned to her, a look of determination on his handsome face. "After I learned about the job here in America, I saw our chance for a future together."

His expression softened. "I plan to spend the rest of my life with you, Mrs. Mabry. Will our lives change? Of course, and I have no doubt we'll encounter plenty of challenges along the way." He leaned in to touch his forehead to hers. "But with God's help, we will face them together."

Emotion rose in her throat, and she simply nodded and smiled. God had blessed her with this wonderful, courageous man.

Once the ship had docked, the wounded troops were off-loaded first, followed by cargo. As Jo and Colin waited near the gangway to disembark, a short man in uniform strode in their direction. Jo recognized him as the ship's disbursing officer.

"Good afternoon, Mr. and Mrs. Mabry." The officer smiled as he reached them. He held a clipboard and a small brown parcel. "This package is for you, ma'am. Just need a signature."

"For me?" Jo's eyes widened. "Who sent it?"

"It was brought aboard in France by a customs agent. I was given orders to hold it for you until we docked in New York."

She glanced at Colin before taking the clipboard to sign her name. The officer handed her the package. "Thank you."

"Good luck to you both." He stepped back and offered a curt nod before disappearing into the bowels of the ship.

"What is it?" Colin moved forward as she removed the brown paper.

Inside was a small ring box, and again Jo looked at him. She wondered if he'd planned this surprise, though she already wore his mother's beautiful diamond wedding set beneath her glove.

"It's not from me." He'd read her thoughts. "Open it."

She lifted the lid on the small box and drew in a breath as she stared at the large egg-shaped diamond nested in silver.

Colin whistled softly. "Well, I'll be . . ."

"Yes." Tears filled her eyes as she removed the ring and handed him the box. Pulling off her right glove, she removed the ruby and sapphire-eyed dove rings from her finger and replaced them a moment later with the glittering egg nestled between them.

"There's a note here."

Blinking back tears, she took the box from him and withdrew the folded piece of paper.

My little bluebird,

I send this to you with my blessings for a happy marriage and a family of your own. For now, Daughter, we remain an ocean apart, but my heart is with you always.

Love, Papa

She handed the note to Colin. After he'd read it, he gazed at her, his voice gentle. "Perhaps he'll come to America one day."

Jo drew a deep breath and nodded. Looking back across the harbor from the direction they had come, she imagined she could see far across the shining sea. "You once told me that no matter where my papa was, I would never be alone."

She turned to him, her smile soft. "You said God was always

with me, and I realize now He has been there my whole life, watching over me, teaching me to be strong. Through the sadness of Moira's death, He led me to find the diary, and finally, to find my father." She admired the gimmel rings on her finger, now complete.

"God also led me to you, Colin." She looked up at him with her heart in her eyes. "You are the one who helped me to believe in love and in miracles."

"They are one and the same, my darling." He took her in his arms and pressed a kiss to her lips. "Today, tomorrow, and forever."

Author's Note

*D*ear Friends,

    I hope you've enjoyed reading *Far Side of the Sea*. With Colin Mabry wounded and returning home from the war at the end of *Not By Sight*, I wanted to tell his story, one about a world-weary soldier living in an environment to which he no longer feels connected.

While this is a work of fiction, as I wrote the novel, I tried to imagine in some small way our men and women in today's military returning home after serving overseas. I wanted to show how Johanna's love for Colin and her ability to see the essence of the man beneath his scars helped him to heal and find a way toward self-acceptance, and from there, to reconcile with this new person he had become.

Carrier pigeons were also in my thoughts. During research years ago for another book, I came across an excerpt describing the remarkable service of these birds during WWI. I was fascinated to learn that their legacy as message carriers originated in the days of the Egyptians, and in Europe today, pigeon racing remains a very popular and high-stakes sport.

As described in my novel, the advent of the carrier pigeon's wartime use in Western Europe took root during the Franco-Prussian War of 1870. With Paris besieged by the enemy, these birds were used to carry messages back and forth from the capital to other parts of France. The pigeons' marked success despite losses from enemy gunfire, natural predators, and extreme weather conditions established a new means of military correspondence.

During WWI, British Lt. Col. A. H. Osman, a pigeon breeder and fancier, was charged with overseeing carrier pigeons for war use. He employed the birds to serve not only in naval operations and the Air Ministry but for military espionage as well.

Numerous accounts of heroism have been linked to these little birds, and the most famous of WWI was Cher Ami. In October 1918, this extraordinary carrier pigeon flew with gunshot wounds through his leg and breast to successfully deliver a message for help from the "Lost Battalion" to the American Army at the Front, saving the lives of nearly two hundred American soldiers trapped behind German lines. Other pigeons flew amazing distances in dangerous conditions, delivering messages that rescued ship captains, crews, and downed pilots, and bringing valuable enemy intelligence to the Allies. In the next world war, the carrier pigeon G.I. Joe would receive acclaim for similar acts of heroism, including saving an entire village of people in Italy, as well as the British troops occupying their war-torn community.

Aside from these magnificent birds, I was also inspired to write my story after reading about the American G-2 Secret Service agency that operated in France during WWI. According to Thomas M. Johnson's *Our Secret War*, a Black Book did, in fact, exist and contained the scandalous secrets of the most powerful leaders and famous personages in Europe and America. With the help of a German agent called "Zero," the Americans were able to foil Kaiser Wilhelm II's late summer of 1918 plan to expose those secrets in order to gain favorable terms for Germany's surrender.[1] At the time of Johnson's 1929 book publication, the author claimed the Black Book had disappeared again and its whereabouts were unknown. I love a good mystery!

Colonizing a foreign country with enemy spies was another established practice. German Secret Service head Wilhelm Stieber conceived of the original network when he first set up "fixed posts" in France.[2] The "posts" or plants established themselves in a particular French community as tradesmen, shopkeepers, waiters, bartenders—any occupation that put them in frequent contact with the public or the military. This allowed them to earn trust and glean information to forward on to an assigned contact. I have no doubt that the practice is still being used today by various world powers. The spy game continues.

As one who appreciates learning history through stories, I strive for historical accuracy in my novels whenever possible, but there are times when taking literary license is necessary. Such is the case with the Sant Sever Caves near Collbató, where my meeting between Johanna and Zero takes place. Because of the level of detail in the scene, I chose to make my caves fictional, though I did style them after the real Coves del Salnitre in that same area. And when Johanna sets Little Corporal free to fly back to Vernon and deliver her message of help, it's late afternoon; however, when Colin receives the telegram with her message from Lacourt, it's early the following morning. There is no issue with a trained pigeon crossing a distance of five hundred miles in eight to ten hours, but pigeons by nature do not fly at night, so that would have extended the time it took Little Corporal to reach Vernon. While I took license here, I did find research that explains that WWII wartime pigeons were trained by the military to "perform remarkable feats, sometimes at odds with their natural tendencies. One was flying at night."[3]

I'd love to share more with you about WWI history, but with limited space, I hope you'll continue to explore the era on your own. I will leave you with this last, perhaps surprising, tidbit. The close proximity of Hastings and the rest of the East Sussex area to the fighting "meant that the sound of large artillery guns and explosions regularly drifted and echoed across the channel."[4] The bombing from siege guns that Colin hears coming across the water from France *was* a fact of that First World War.

—KB

Notes

1. Thomas M. Johnson, *Our Secret War: True American Spy Stories, 1917–1919* (Indianapolis: Bobbs-Merrill Company Publishers, 1929).

2. Melville Davisson Post, "The Invisible Army," *Saturday Evening Post*, April 10, 1915, 3–5.

3. Linda Lombardi, "Pigeons: Unsung Heroes of War," *Vetstreet*, May 21, 2013, http://www.vetstreet.com/our-pet-experts/pigeons-unsung-heroes-of-war.

4. Chris Kempshall, "The Sound of Guns," *EastSussexWW1*, http://www.east-sussexww1.org.uk/sound-guns/.

Discussion Questions

1. Lieutenant Colin Mabry's quest begins when he receives an urgent message, reminding him of a promise he made the year before. Initially he is torn over whether or not he can keep his vow to Jewel. Have you ever experienced trepidation over a commitment you made to someone? Were your instincts correct, or did things work themselves out?

2. Upon his arrival in Paris, Colin has a strong reaction to the blasts of the long-range siege guns that the Germans are firing on the French capital. Having been at the Front, he suffers from shell shock, now called post-traumatic stress disorder (PTSD). Today many people outside the military are also diagnosed with PTSD. Do you know someone who has suffered the effects? Were you able to help them or can you offer suggestions on how our community might aid these men and women to recover?

3. At story opening, Colin wishes to disassociate himself from his prosthetic. He refers to it as "the gloved hand" and keeps it hidden from view as much as possible. Perhaps to a lesser

extent, we all have self-image problems we've struggled with. Is there something about yourself that you have always wanted to change or to be different? Have you been able to overcome the issue?

4. Johanna has never met her sister, but through the words of Jewel's diary, she comes to know her. Have you researched your family tree and come across details about an ancestor that helped you to gain insight into their nature and what they experienced?

5. George Petit is a Texan who works with the American Secret Service in France. While he can seem annoying to Colin and Johanna throughout their journey, Petit shows his true colors in the end. According to research, G-2 did recruit "wild cards" for service in the intelligence police. Did you have any misgivings about Petit early on in the story, and did you guess his role?

6. Diaries have been kept for centuries, at first to simply record the events of daily life and then, more recently, to note one's own perceptions about those events. Have you ever kept a diary? Was it helpful to you? In what way?

7. In Toulouse, Colin shares with Johanna his belief in our heavenly Father's loving nature, and how faith will help her to see God's miracles. Have you ever had the opportunity to share your faith with someone else? Was doing so beneficial to you as well?

8. Johanna's illegitimate birth made her the brunt of gossip and small-minded cruelty in the Irish village where she grew up. Bullying continues to be a problem today. Share any thoughts

about how, especially in this digital age, bullying can be mitigated in schools or elsewhere.

9. Jacob Reyer turns out to have a secret neither of his daughters knew about. Do you know an anecdote about a family member, past or present, which surprised you? Can you share the details?

10. If the story were continued, which character(s) would you want to know more about? Why?

Acknowledgments

*C*reating a story that readers will enjoy is by far the most thrilling, gratifying, and challenging experience of my life and one which I could not do alone. Above all, I thank God for His gifts and for inspiring me to sit down each day and write the words. To John, my husband, I treasure your love and support, especially during the long days and wee hours when I'm still at the computer, and for being such a great first reader of my work. You are my real-life story hero!

As always, my deep affection and appreciation go to my critique partners, mentors, and friends: Anjali Banerjee, Carol Caldwell, Darlene Panzera, Debbie Macomber, Elsa Watson, Krysteen Seelen, Lois Dyer, Patty Jough-Haan, Ramona Nelson, Rose Marie Harris, Susan Wiggs, and Sheila Roberts. Your willingness to share your time, wisdom, and inspiration with me has been a blessing.

My special thanks also goes to Núria Nieto and Doriane Bertrand for your invaluable assistance with the Catalan and French in my novel. And to pigeon fanciers Jim Novak, Mike Smith, WWII pigeoneer Ed Schmidt (101 years young as of this writing), and to Karen Clifton with the American Racing Pigeon Union. Sharing your vast knowledge and insight in regard to these truly heroic and beloved birds has made me a fan for life. The information you provided was so helpful, and if any errors exist in the story, they are solely the fault of this author.

To my agent, Linda S. Glaz, and to my editors, Raela Schoenherr, Rochelle Glöege, Elisa Tally, and all those at Bethany House who helped to bring this project to fruition, I cannot express enough my thanks for your guidance, encouragement, and support.

A Florida girl who migrated to the Pacific Northwest, **Kate Breslin** was a bookseller for many years. She is a Carol Award winner and a RITA and Christy Award finalist and lives with her husband in Seattle, Washington. Find her online at www.katebreslin.com.

Sign Up for Kate's Newsletter!

Keep up to date with Kate's latest news on book releases and events by signing up for her email list at katebreslin.com.

More from Kate Breslin!

In 1917, British nurse and war widow Evelyn Marche is trapped in German-occupied Brussels. She works at the hospital by day and as a waitress by night. But she also has a secret: She's a spy for the resistance. When a British plane crashes in the park, Evelyn must act quickly to protect the injured soldier who has top-secret orders and a target on his back.

High as the Heavens

⊗BETHANYHOUSE

Captivating Historical Fiction from Bethany House!

You May Also Like . . .

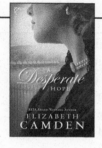

A female accountant in 1908, Eloise Drake thought she'd put her past behind her. Then her new job lands her in the path of the man who broke her heart. Alex Duval, mayor of a doomed town, can't believe his eyes when he sees Eloise as part of the entourage that's come to wipe his town off the map. Can he convince her to help him—and give him another chance?

A Desperate Hope by Elizabeth Camden
elizabethcamden.com

Daphne Blakemoor was happy living in seclusion. But when ownership of the estate where she works passes to William, Marquis of Chemsford, her quiet life is threatened. William also seeks a refuge from his past, but when an undeniable family connection is revealed, can they find the courage to face their deepest wounds and forge a new path for the future?

A Return of Devotion by Kristi Ann Hunter
Haven Manor #2
kristiannhunter.com

A century apart, two women seek their mothers in Pleasant Valley, Wisconsin. In 1908, Thea's search leads her to an insane asylum with dark secrets. In modern-day Wisconsin, Heidi Lane answers the call of a mother battling dementia. Both confront the legendary curse of Misty Wayfair—and are entangled in a web of danger that entwines them across time.

The Curse of Misty Wayfair by Jaime Jo Wright
jaimewrightbooks.com

◆ BETHANYHOUSE

Printed in the United States
By Bookmasters